Winter's
Crimes
21

Winter's Crimes 21

edited by
HILARY HALE

MACMILLAN
LONDON

First published in 1989 by
MACMILLAN LONDON LIMITED
4 Little Essex Street London WC2R 3LF
and Basingstoke

Associated companies in Auckland, Delhi, Dublin,
Gaborone, Hamburg, Harare, Hong Kong, Johannesburg,
Kuala Lumpur, Lagos, Manzini, Melbourne, Mexico City,
Nairobi, New York, Singapore and Tokyo.

ISBN 0–333–51095–X

A CIP catalogue record for this book is available from
the British Library

Typeset by Matrix, 21 Russell Street, London WC2

Printed and bound by Billings and Sons Limited, Worcester

Contents

Editor's Note

The *Winter's Crimes* series was created by George Hardinge in 1969 with one very simple rule: that all the stories it contains should never before have been published. This principle has been faithfully adhered to in the twenty volumes which have followed the publication of *Winter's Crimes 1* and, with profound changes in the newspaper and magazine world in the intervening years, the series has become virtually the last outlet for original crime short stories. That it has survived to come of age – and to celebrate the event with twenty-one stories – is a tribute to its founder, the many talented contributors to the series, and to the perennial support of its readers.

Winter's Crimes 21 continues the established tradition with twenty-one stories from the best contemporary writers. In his introduction to *Winter's Crimes 1* George Hardinge wrote: 'I would like to thank all the very distinguished contributors who wrote stories for this volume, and in so doing set a standard that any future collection of crime short stories will be hard pressed to match.' Twenty years later I am proud to say that challenge has been amply met each year, and this celebratory volume demonstrates the quality, diversity and sheer enjoyment which has become the trademark of the series. So to all the contributors my thanks, not only for their stories which make this collection a very special one, but also for the pleasure they have given me in being its editor.

Hilary Hale

Post Mortem

Robert Barnard

Throughout my father's funeral my mother sternly kept back her emotion. At home afterwards, with the relatives and the top people from the factory, she was controlled, almost gracious, though often I noticed her eyes down-turned, her mouth working. Only when the stragglers had been seen from the door and the last car had driven away did she come back into the lounge, let out a great whoop of triumph, and throw her black hat in the air.

'Hooray! Shot of him at last!'

I looked at her disapprovingly. There were no neighbours to hear, for The Maples is set in extensive grounds, but in the kitchen was Mrs Mottram, who had prepared and served the funeral bakemeats. I pointed meaningfully in that direction.

My mother leaned forward in her chair.

'I don't give a monkey's fart for Mrs Mottram.'

But she said it in a low hiss, which showed that she had taken my point.

Now she started moving restlessly around the room. When our fellow mourners were here she had pressed food on them but had eaten nothing herself. Now she greedily sampled everything, eating voraciously as if she had ordered the lavish spread precisely with this moment in mind.

'I wonder if I should phone the solicitor.'

'Of *course* you shouldn't. How would it look?' Seeing this argument carried no weight with her, I added: 'Anyway you know Mr Blore is away. Otherwise he would have been here at the funeral. He wouldn't want any underling to deal with it. He said he'd be back tomorrow.'

My mother's mouth grimaced into a little moue.

'But how on earth are we going to get through the rest of the day?'

In the end I took her for a long drive, well away from Rotherham, where the McAtee works and the family home are situated. In a small Derbyshire pub she got thoroughly sloshed on her favourite gin slings, and that kept her happy till morning.

It was as much as I could do to stop her ringing Mr Blore immediately after breakfast. 'Solicitors don't get to work at nine o'clock,' I said. As it was she made an awful impression by ringing at twenty past, and finding he was not due in till ten fifteen. She finally spoke to him at twenty past ten, and though she conducted her end of the conversation with the sort of decorum she had shown at the funeral, when she put down the phone she seemed oddly dissatisfied.

'When I said we had a copy of the will here, he said: "Well, we'll discuss all that tomorrow." '

That should have told me.

My mother dressed the part next day. She is inclined to a too bright lipstick for a woman of her age, and to use an inappropriate nail varnish. People say she is vulgar and grasping, but we get on all right. Not because I am vulgar or grasping, but because I like a quiet life. Anyway, her black was irreproachable.

Mr Blore treated us with the utmost respect, as no doubt he always did treat grieving relatives, whether he liked them or not (and in the case of my mother he certainly didn't). He ushered us to seats, offered dry, solicitorial condolences to my mother, enquired of me if the funeral arrangements had been satisfactory. We fed him back with muted platitudes. Then he sat back in his chair and let us have it.

'But that's bloody impossible!' screamed my mother, her mask slipping badly. 'How could there be a later will? He made this one just before he became ill. He had no chance— '

'Nevertheless he made one.'

My mother thought.

'Mrs Mottram. I bet my bottom dollar— '

Mr Blore inclined his head.

'And I believe there were days when you had other cleaning staff in . . . '

'Spick and Span. They gave the house a thorough clean every fortnight. I always went out when they came . . . Witnesses . . . I must have been mad.'

'And your husband had access to a typewriter.'

For those little notices to the workforce – exhortations, pep talks, ironic little comments on slacknesses – which I had dutifully pinned up on the notice-board, and which had aroused more derision than respect since he was no longer on the shop floor to enforce his will.

'Oh God, yes, he had a typewriter,' said my mother impatiently, the social veneer having been cast off long since. 'But this new will— '

'Is by and large the same as the old one. I need not go over the provisions of that. Unfortunately the most substantial clause, the one leaving the works and the bulk of the fortune to you, with reversion to Mr Maurice McAtee' – he nodded in my general direction, and I got the strongest possible sense that he was enjoying himself – 'is changed.'

'Yes. Hurry *up*, man.'

'He expresses the hope that Mr Maurice will be allowed to remain in his present job, as he has been a conscientious works manager, but he doubts he has the drive or flair to head the enterprise. He therefore names Mr Henry McAtee— '

'Harry! But he hated Harry! He cast him off!'

'A change of mind, I fear. Mr Henry is to inherit both the factory and the residual fortune.'

'You're joking! What about me?'

'You, madam, are not named in the will.'

It really broke my mother up. In the car going home she kept sobbing and wailing, 'After all I'd done.' It was notable that she did not add 'for him'. That wasn't what she meant at all. As we neared The Maples she muttered in a vitriolic whisper, 'I'll strangle his bloody pigeons.'

For my father had had a love of racing pigeons, which my mother said was a sentimental relic of his working-class origins. Me, I think he genuinely loved the things. More than he did us. As soon as we got home my mother went out through the kitchen to execute her threat, but she found it a good deal more difficult than she expected. She ended up with her frustration still boiling over, and nothing more to show for her efforts than a few pigeon feathers scattered around the kitchen garden.

My brother Harry arrived home the next day. That in itself showed that he had been forewarned, or forepromised. The solicitor had said he would write on the day he spoke to us. Harry was wearing a sober suit. His usual sort of dress was casual-sexy, in keeping with his image of himself as a trendy pop-star type. He had no doubt bought the suit in preparation for his good fortune. Typical of Harry that he should have spared himself the bother of the funeral.

He was met at the door by Mrs Mottram, who showed him into the lounge. 'Awfully sad occasion,' he kept muttering, as he kissed my mother and shook my hand, his eyes sparkling with pleasure the while. When Mrs Mottram had retired to the kitchen he threw himself into an armchair and let out a great bellow of laughter.

'Oh, what a turn-up for the book. If you two could only see yourselves! You look like dogs who've just had a particularly juicy bone pinched from under their noses.'

My mother could barely refrain from buffeting him

around the head, as she so often had had to do in his delinquent childhood. But that day we observed the decencies, she and I. Mrs Mottram was around all day, with a fair idea of what was going on but an incomplete one. We had no desire – my mother and I had no desire – to feed her raging hunger for gossip material. We ate the meal she cooked us decorously, while Harry fed us a (censored) version of what he had been doing in the seven years since Father had shown him the door of The Maples and told him (erroneously) that that was the last time he would see the inside of it.

The next day Harry once again donned his sober suit and once again assumed his sober manner, and he and I went down to the factory. Changes made in the last few years made it necessary for him to be shown around it, but I had no intention of doing that myself and watching him gloat. I handed him over to the foreman and went on with my own work. Harry was remembered from the old days and thoroughly disliked (he had done the 'boss's son' act to an outrageous degree, and treated everyone from floor-cleaner to foreman with contempt). Now he listened with a display of humility, but as the day wore on I heard him say things like 'That will have to be changed', or 'I'm sure we can devise a better system than that', or – most ominously – 'What seems to be needed is a daring policy of expansion to pull us out of the doldrums.' This last brought visions to my mind of lunatic schemes and spectacular bankruptcy. I had told no one at the factory of Harry's good fortune, but by the end of the day the whole workforce must have guessed.

As he left my brother said to the foreman: 'I'll be in at nine and doing a full day's work tomorrow. Start as you mean to go on – eh?'

Mrs Mottram was off that day. My mother cooked a dinner of all the things my brother particularly disliked. He maintained a flow of unabating geniality through it all, and treated me to a long account of all the changes that he intended to initiate at the McAtee works.

'Father himself saw the need for change,' he concluded, over the spotted dick, which he merely picked at. 'That's why he put me in charge.'

'Then it's odd he never broached the subject to me,' I said sourly.

'Ah, but you're not the boy for change, are you, Morrie? "Do as we've always done," that's your motto. Tried and tested methods. But tried and tested methods don't do in the age of the computer. Industry has to develop and expand or go to the wall. Those were Father's very words.'

'I don't remember them,' I said.

'Well, you wouldn't, would you?' Harry grinned, his habitual self-satisfaction oozing from every pore. 'They were in the letter to me – the one in which he explained the new . . . arrangements. He was very considerate: told me to wait a day or two after the funeral before I came down, to give you two time to get used to the change in your fortunes. Otherwise, of course, my natural instinct would have been to pay my last respects to the old boy.' He crumpled his napkin beside his plate and stood up. 'It was an interesting letter altogether.'

That silenced us. Somehow, though he said it casually, it was as if every word was italicised. The way he looked at us, first Mother and then me, added to the effect. He took a folder of facts and figures from the factory and went up to his bedroom.

My mother was devastated, as well she might be.

'He'll have to go,' she said. 'We'll have to get rid of him.'

'Are you mad? With us the two obvious suspects? You don't even know whether he's made a will or not. He may have a wife, a live-in girl-friend, a child. Then where would you be? I suppose if you *want* to spend the rest of your life doing Open University courses with Myra Hindley . . .'

That silenced her. I think she noticed that I said 'you', not 'we'. It was perhaps cruel of me to rub in my separateness from her by adding: 'If it's not a question of that already.'

The next morning Harry merely snatched a slice of toast on the wing, as it were, and gulped down a cup of tea. Mother and I ate in silence. The reason was that we had both of us heard Harry, while he was in the bathroom, going through the medicine cabinet. He could have found nothing, of course, but it made us uneasy. So did the fact that the reason for his lateness to breakfast was that he was having a long talk with Mrs Mottram in the kitchen. He drove off in his own car to the factory, and I heard little of him during the day, though I registered the fact that he had already put the shop stewards' backs up – unions like change no more than management, and Harry's manner was not an emollient one.

His needling of us began in earnest that night. Mrs Mottram's hours were staggered: sometimes she came in early, cooked lunch and left around tea-time; at others she came late and stayed to cook the dinner. That night she should have been off, but stayed late 'to oblige Mr Harry'.

Harry fetched his own plate from the kitchen, tasted it, and then said, 'Marvellous. Tastes just like steak and kidney pie should.'

That was all, but that was enough. The next evening, when my mother was cooking the dinner again, Harry ostentatiously phoned for a table at Rotherham's best restaurant. It was all show, of course, all a battle of nerves: he had eaten my mother's cooking on the first evening. But it was a battle of nerves that my mother and I did not feel we were winning.

He had been in the saddle at the works for several days – and faces there were getting grimmer, and I was imagining financial disaster staring us in the face – when he took the opportunity of one of Mrs Mottram's dinners to come a little further out into the open.

'Bumped into a chap I used to know today.'

'Oh?'

'Jack Lippincott. Used to be at school with him. He's a dispensing chemist with Boots these days.'

'Oh?' I kept the quaver out of my voice. Why, in any case, should there be one? I didn't know what Mother had got up to. Or perhaps that should read: I didn't *know* what Mother had got up to.

'Useful knowing a chemist. He's doing a little job for me.'

My mother said nothing. This was her new policy: to say nothing beyond conversational banalities to Harry. I didn't see that it could get her anywhere, but then I couldn't think of any policy that would get her anywhere.

There was nothing to do but wait.

Two days later he took up the subject over sherry (actually Harry was drinking beer; he was not a beer man, but he drank cans of it, no doubt to make the point that opened bottles can be tampered with).

'I got the report on that little job I gave Jack Lippincott to do today.'

This time both Mother and I kept silent.

'I took him some bottles of Father's Polifexin.'

'That's nonsense. You couldn't have.'

That was my mother – it was out before she could remember her policy.

'Couldn't have? Because you put them in the garbage bin? Actually Mrs Mottram retrieved them before the dustman came.'

He smiled round at us, like a little boy before he starts torturing a bird. We kept quiet. It never does the bird much good to squawk.

'And he tells me – roughly what I expected – that while two of the eight bottles do indeed contain Polifexin, the other six contain a mixture that he can only guess at: he thinks there's lemon juice, cointreau, a patent cough linctus and maybe other things too. "It doesn't taste the same," my father said in his letter. You tried to make it so it did, but it didn't quite work.'

'This is ridiculous,' said my mother vitriolically. 'If I was trying to poison your father— '

'I'm not suggesting you were doing anything of the

sort. You were withholding the medicine he needed after his first stroke.'

'Either way, why didn't he protest to Mrs Mottram? Ask her to help, send for the police? Come to that, why didn't he say anything to Dr Craigie? He came seldom enough, God knows, considering your father's standing in the community, but he did come.'

'I've thought about that. Mrs Mottram had suspicions of her own, which is why she retrieved the bottles. She tells me that there were a lot of lemons bought that she couldn't account for because no one in the house likes them, or uses them in tea or in gin and tonics. But you're right: Father could have told her of his suspicions, or the doctor. . . . I have a theory about that, anyway.'

'What?' I asked.

'He wanted to die. After all, what sort of existence was it, stuck up in his bedroom there, after the active life he'd led – running the factory, playing cricket, later bowls, walking a lot, seeing to his pigeons and racing them. No, he must have known all those things were of the past. He wanted it over with.'

'He had only to swallow a bottle of aspirin,' said my mother, in that bitter voice she had used when speaking of my father since his death – and before it, come to think of it. 'There was one by his bed. God knows I hoped often enough that he would. That would have saved us all a lot of trouble.'

'I'm not sure he had any desire to save you trouble. Because he must quite soon have got a suspicion of what you were trying to do. Father – remember, Morrie? – always had a wonderful sense of humour.'

That was true enough. Throughout our childhood he was full of conundrums, practical jokes and jolly japes – until, that is, he saw that I always missed the point, Harry hated anything in which he might be made to look a fool, and my mother would remain stony-faced on principle. Being the one with the sense of humour in our family was about as rewarding as being the one with the sense of humour in Mrs Thatcher's cabinet.

'I remember,' I said.

'So he played a game with you. He decided to let Mother go ahead with her little plot, but to arrange an unexpected ending for her.' Harry put down his beer mug and smiled around. 'He was a joker, our Dad.'

The awful thing was the sense of helplessness. We were wounded birds at the mercy of Harry, the cruel cat. Or perhaps it was my father who was the cat? That thought was to my mother the bitterest thought of all. She had fought my father all her life and now to find herself, after his death, unexpectedly his powerless victim – that was hard. But what *was* there we could do against that relishing glint in Harry's eyes?

He waited. Like all cruel cats he played it slow. He ate out a lot, thoroughly enjoyed his new position at the works, and just occasionally made remarks like: 'Remember, if you try anything against me, you'd have to do away with Mrs Mottram as well. Then of course there's my friend Lippincott. Quite a little bloodbath you'd have to undertake. . . . '

These thoughts, I'm sure, had already occurred to my mother. I tried not to discuss anything with her. I preferred not to know. It was bad enough during my father's illness, suspecting.

It was more than a week later, one Saturday at the end of breakfast, that Harry opened fire again.

'I think it's about time you told me your plans.'

'Plans?'

'Yes, plans. I shall be needing this house. My girl-friend will be coming up here in a week or two's time. She'll make a wonderful hostess for the firm – better than it's ever had. She has a touch of class, has Sheila. So you two had better be thinking of moving on.'

'But I've no mon—'

Harry ignored our mother and turned to me.

'You, Morrie, I've decided to keep on as Works Manager. That seems to be what Father intended, and he's right: it's the sort of plodding job you're just about up to. And after all, I don't think you ever *knew*, did you?' I sat there dumbly. 'I don't think Mother would ever have confided in you, not explicitly. . . . You may have had your suspicions, though, eh, Morrie? A little idea that something was going on? But as long as nothing was said, nothing that made you even remotely into an accomplice, then you were in the clear. But anyway I've decided to keep you on in the job. *Provided* it's clear you serve me with the most complete, unquestioning loyalty, and carry out the new policies I'm working on to the letter. Loyalty is always important, but when it's family working together it's quite vital. I'm not going to tolerate an alternative power base in my own firm. Is that quite clear?'

I nodded miserably. He turned suavely to our mother.

'You were saying, Mother?'

'I have no money.'

'I believe there is such a thing as National Assistance, or Income Support, or whatever damned name they use these days. Personally I'm against state charity. It saps initiative. There are plenty of jobs a woman of your age can do – jobs in the service industries, cafeteria jobs, cleaning jobs. Not well paid, of course, or pleasant, but as the saying goes: beggars can't be choosers.'

'I've nowhere to live.'

'Haven't you got yourself on the Council list? They probably have a nice little flat in one of the high-rises. People don't like living in them, but I'm sure you'd find it perfectly pleasant. It's only a penthouse flat under another name, after all. Or perhaps Morrie would let you live with him for a while. If I know Morrie he's got a bit of money saved, so he'll certainly be able to walk into a nice little house or flat. You'll have the rest of your lives to talk things over.'

The post plopped through the door, and Harry went to fetch it while still talking.

'You notice, Mother, I've said nothing about going to the police. . . . Circular from the RSPB. Now *that's* a charity we can cut out. . . . I rather think I ought to. My own father cut off permanently. I'd be fully justified. But I'm a tender-hearted guy. Didn't know that, did you? Well, I am. I don't say I never *will* go to them: "doubts gnawing in my mind" – that's only one of the lines I could take. But for the moment, and depending on your good behaviour, I won't go yet.' He chuckled. 'I don't think that's what Father would have wanted. I'm sure he expected me to dob you in. But what he didn't realise was, I'd have a sort of fellow-feeling with you. Because if I'd still been here, I'd have done exactly the same as you. Maybe we'd have been partners, you and me, Mother. Morrie's a born sitter-out, but I'm a doer. Maybe we'd have sat here and planned it all together. So though I may be going against his wishes . . . '

He talked on, loving it. I was still sitting at the table. Suddenly my eye caught the envelope. I started to say 'But this isn't a circular,' but bit it back. The letter was individually addressed, and to Henry McAtee. A sudden conviction concerning my father's sense of humour washed through me. Feverishly I picked it up and opened it. It was on the notepaper of the Royal Society for the Protection of Birds.

'Dear Mr McAtee,' it read. 'In accordance with your father's instructions in the covering letter, we have waited for a fortnight after his funeral before opening the will he sent us. As you will see from the enclosed copy . . . '

I was glad that at last I had managed to see one of my father's jokes.

The Battered Cherub

Simon Brett

I didn't invite her to the office. When your office is your bedroom you play these things a bit tactfully. Last thing you want to do is frighten a client off and, though I'm not one of them, there are a lot of funny people about. I don't know that there are actually more of them in Brighton than anywhere else, but it often seems that way. Maybe it's an occupational hazard. My line of work means, almost by definition, the only ones I meet are the misfits. The lonely. The sad. And loneliness and sadness can so quickly sour into something nastier.

Or maybe I am drawn to them on the old 'birds of a feather' principle. My former wife certainly said as much towards the end, as our marriage spiralled down into insult and recrimination. She said a lot more, too, in those last sick days when every statement of hers was a loaded grenade from which every response of mine seemed to take out the pin.

Anyway, she's long gone and I'm still in Brighton, still no doubt demonstrating all those negative attributes she catalogued with such relish. Mooching around what the estate agent called a 'studio flat', but what ten years ago would have been called a 'bedsitter', and what I now have the nerve to call an 'office'. When there are no jobs you're qualified for, why not stick a shingle on the door and set up on your own?

Perhaps I disqualified myself from other work. Getting busted for drugs didn't help. I started on that after my wife walked out. Stupid, stupid, I know, but at least I did manage to crack it in the end. Not before the police had found the stuff on me, unfortunately. And prison records aren't exactly assets in these days of mass unemployment.

I sometimes think, having got off the drugs, I could get off the vodka too. I will, one day. But I don't feel quite strong enough yet.

So, anyway, as I say, I had to set up on my own. Can't lose, really. Even if you don't get any business at all, you're no worse off than you were.

Anyway, I do get occasional business. Sad people who think a little information will at least explain their sadness. Frightened people who feel reassured by the illusion of protection. Cowardly or fastidious people who want someone else to perform unpalatable services. Even dying people who think they've still got time to tie up the loose ends.

Some I can help. Some know even when they contact me that they're beyond help. I close my mind to their circumstances and send bills to all of them. They all pay, except for the one or two who don't survive. I disapprove of sending bills to the recently bereaved.

And the trickle of money that comes in helps to keep me in the manner to which I have accustomed myself: 'the office', with its bed, its table, its two chairs, the clothes chest, the vodka bottle cupboard, the shower, the sink, the microwave and – its one good feature – the long window that ignores the terracing of roofs beneath it and looks straight out to the shifting edge of the gunmetal sea.

I don't actually have a shingle on the door. People tend to come to me by word of mouth. I'm not in 'Yellow Pages', either. But I suppose, if I were, my name, B. Cotter, would be listed under 'Detective Agencies'.

*

She edged into the pub, as tentative as a kitten testing a duvet for landmines. My first impression was that she was attractive. She recognised me from the description I'd given her, but with some surprise.

'I didn't really believe it when you said your hair was bleached.' She perched a neat but cautious buttock on the chair opposite me.

'Why not?'

'Well, for a detective . . . I mean, I'd have thought a detective should melt into the background. Bleached hair does kind of stand out.'

'You mean I don't look like your idea of a detective?'

'No. Not at all.'

'Seems to answer your objection. Doesn't matter how much I stand out, so long as no one thinks I look like a detective.'

'I suppose not,' she agreed uncertainly.

The bleached hair was another of the personal attributes my former wife had taken against. That and the black clothes. She saw it as a fashion thing. 'Why do you go round looking like a punk when punks are dead?' She couldn't understand it was more habit, more self, than fashion. After she'd gone I stayed the same out of defiance, some kind of ineffectual revenge maybe.

'Can I get you a drink?'

She asked for a dry white wine. I had a Perrier with ice and lemon in front of me. Didn't say it was Perrier. Sometimes helped to pretend I was on the vodka and tonic. All depended, really. Wary moments, meeting a client for the first time. Always required a bit of ritual circling, rationing out information, assessing the moment to feed out each new fact.

As I walked back to her, my first impression was reinforced. She was more than attractive. Kind of face a randy Florentine painter might have sneaked into the crowd at a Crucifixion, following some carnal deal with the model. A battered cherub. Brown hair, quite stiff and

thick, fringing fanlike over unsettling blue eyes. They were
unsettling partly because everything else in her colouring
predicated brown eyes; partly because they held, together
with innocence, a knowingness which belied that innocence;
and partly because they were beautiful. She had owned the
dark grey leather coat long enough for it to take on her
imprint, its soft curves ghosting her own. For someone like
me, she was trouble.

I gave her the drink and returned to my maybe Perrier.
'Right, what's the problem, Mrs McCullough?'

'Call me Stephanie. I don't like even being reminded
that I've got that bastard's surname.'

I didn't respond to this, but noted the over-reaction.
Premature, I thought. She, like me, should still be at the
circling stage of our encounter, and she was feeding out too
much information too soon. Had to be a reason for that.

'All right. Then you'd better call me Bram.' I got
in before she could say it. 'And I don't think there are
any Dracula jokes I haven't heard. And in fact it is only
short for Abraham. And no, I don't know why my parents
chose it.'

As usual, the speech had the right effect. All she
said was, 'Ah.'

'So . . . what do you want me to do for you, Stephanie?'

She moved closer. Her pupils dilated. When they did that,
the black almost eclipsed the blue, and the eyes' innocence
had the same effect on their knowingness. She looked like
something small and fluffy that'd just fallen out of a nest
and never heard of pussy-cats.

'It's my husband,' she murmured.

'What is he? Unfaithful? Violent? Criminal? Gay? Missing? I may as well tell you now – if it's infidelity, I tend to
think that's just between the two of you.'

'It's not infidelity. Well, I mean, obviously he's unfaithful,' she added dismissively, 'but that's not why I need your
help. . . .'

I let her get there in her own time.

'The fact is . . . Stuart – that's my husband – is . . . well, I think he's involved in something . . . '

Still let her ride it out.

'Something criminal. I mean, he is basically a crook. But this time I think he may have got a bit out of his depth. . . . '

The eyes appealed, but got no help from me.

'Look, all right, normally when Stuart's on a job, I turn a blind eye – I'm not that interested in what he does these days, anyway – but I can always tell there's something up because he's, I don't know, kind of cocky. This time's different. This time he's frightened.'

She petered out. Finally, my cue came.

'What kind of crime is your husband likely to be involved in?'

'Robbery. Always is, he's not bright enough for anything more elaborate. Isolated country houses. Used to all be in Sussex, but the M25 has widened his range a bit.'

'Just breaking and entering or are we talking robbery with violence?'

'He's never looked for violence. Usually tries to do jobs when the owners are away, but, well, occasionally his information isn't all that hot, so there's someone there and . . . ' She shrugged ' . . . someone gets hurt. But the violence is incidental. Means to an end.'

'And you reckon he's just done a job?'

She nodded, her face still disconcertingly close. 'No question. He's flush. Just ordered himself a new BMW. Even bought me something.' She shook a Rolex Oyster out from the shadow of her sleeve. 'Real thing, not a Hong Kong cheapo.'

'But you say he's frightened?'

'Yes. Jumpy when the phone rings. Not sleeping. I find empty bottles of Scotch in the sitting room in the mornings. He's certainly scared of something.'

'Police? Maybe he's got the wink they're on to him?'

She shook her head firmly. 'That wouldn't frighten

Stuart. Always rather relishes a set-to with the cops. Reckons he can run circles round them.'

'And can he?'

'Has done so far.' She looked pensive. When she did that, her top teeth chewed a little on her lower lip. The movement was at least as unsettling as the eyes. I tried not to watch. 'No, he's shit-scared of something.'

'You don't think he's ill? Imagining things?'

She let out a little, bitter laugh. 'No way. Stuart wouldn't know what imagination was if it came up and punched him on the nose.'

'I see.' I sipped the Perrier, deciding that the next drink would definitely be a vodka. 'And you want me to find out what it is that he's scared of?'

'No, it's not that. It's . . . '

'What?'

'Look, I've a feeling I do know what it is that he's scared of.' Once again, she got no prompts and had to flounder on. 'I think the last place he hit, big mansion up at Ditchling . . . well, he got a lot of stuff there, but I think the stuff was already nicked.'

'He cleaned out another villain's place?'

'Yes.'

'What makes you think that?'

'Look, it was a big job, no question, fifty grand's worth at least – I know because of the time he's spent on the phone trying to offload the stuff – but there hasn't been a murmur in the press about it.'

'Ah.'

'Papers, TV, radio – nothing. Suggests to me that whoever was hit had reasons not to make it public.'

'I'll buy that.'

'Doesn't want a public investigation, with the police involved . . . '

'But will probably be organising a private investigation with a lot of muscle involved.'

'Exactly.'

'Which would explain why your husband's worried.'

She nodded and drew back, satisfied that her point had been made. The pupils contracted and cunning returned to her eyes.

'And you don't think he knows who it was he robbed by mistake?'

'No, I'm sure he doesn't, but the size of the house and the size of the haul suggest it could be someone pretty big.'

'Right. And you don't think the . . . aggrieved party has actually fingered your husband yet?'

'I think we'll know pretty quickly when they do identify him.'

'Yes. Which, given the way news travels in that kind of world, is not going to take too long, is it?'

'No.'

I drained the Perrier and grimaced, still maintaining the fiction that it might be vodka. 'What do you want me to do about it then?'

'I want you to find out who it was who got robbed and do a deal with them.'

'To let Stuart off the hook?'

'Right.'

'Is that all?'

'Yes.' She grinned her louche cherubic grin. 'That's all.'

Considering how quickly I obtained the relevant information, Stuart McCullough was living on borrowed time. It cost me two visits to the right pubs, a couple of rounds of drinks, a couple more rounds of 'drinks' in folded form, and I knew the names of the other members of his gang, as well as the identity of the villain they had so incautiously robbed.

If they had been looking for massive contusions and internal bleeding, they could hardly have chosen a quicker route to the supplier. The Ditchling mansion they had so breezily cleaned out belonged to Harry Day, a major London villain, nicknamed 'Flag' Day because of the number of charges the law had tried to pin on him. He was a canny operator, though, who, by employing the right solicitors and bunging the right amounts into the right palms at the Yard, had never actually been inside. But his CV was generally agreed to include robbery with violence, protection rackets with violence, a fairly definite couple of murders with violence and – by way of weekend recreation – violence with violence. Not the kind of big boy a little boy like Stuart McCullough ought to be challenging to a game of conkers.

The only surprise about the situation was that Stephanie's husband wasn't already a mass of multiple fractures. If an outsider like me could get the information that easily, a man with 'Flag' Day's connections should have been on the ball seconds after the kick-off. But apparently he wasn't; or, if he did know the score, he was taking his time to devise appropriately cruel and unnatural punishments for the perpetrator of this professional insult.

I think actually what was keeping Stuart McCullough out of Intensive Care was the absence of his accomplices. He'd done the job with two Brighton small-timers who'd taken their cut the next morning and gone straight off to Tenerife with a couple of tarts. If they'd been around, 'Flag' Day's network would have soon been on to them. Stuart on his own was a marginally better security risk. He had every reason to keep quiet about the set-up, and I felt pretty certain I was the only person in whom Stephanie had confided.

I tried not to think about her. When I did, my thoughts kept spreading like cancer cells into bits of me I didn't want reinfected.

I concentrated on her husband. The thoughts he inspired weren't pretty ones, but they were more the kind I could cope with.

Clearly, if Stuart McCullough was going to evade the attentions of Harry Day in any long-term sense, something had to happen quickly. Day might not be on to him yet, but it was only a matter of time. Brighton suddenly becomes a very small place when a villain starts buying new BMWs and Rolexes.

I had an arrangement with Stephanie that she'd ring me daily for progress reports and that, if I had to phone her home and got through to her, she wouldn't recognise me. I needn't have worried. Stuart snatched up the phone on the first ring as if he were defusing it.

'Mr McCullough?' I always use my own voice on this kind of conversation. For one thing, I'm no good at disguising it and, for another, it's a myth that anyone's going to recognise a person they've never met by the voice heard on a telephone.

'Yes?' I could almost hear the sweat popping on his brow.

'Mr McCullough, I have information that you acquired certain property last Tuesday night . . . '

He didn't deny it.

'Now that property belongs to my employer . . . '

'Oh?'

'And he's far from happy about the situation.' There was a crackle on the line, or it could have been the clearing of a terminally dry throat. 'My employer's name is Harry Day.' This time the crackle was definitely human. 'Now,' I lied, 'Mr Day's not a vindictive man . . . '

'Really?' Stuart McCullough didn't sound convinced by that either.

'No. And he also is not the sort of man to want a fuss made about something like this. . . . I mean, we don't want the police brought in, do we?'

'No.'

'All Mr Day *does* want is the return of his property. . . . '

'Is that really all he wants?' the dry voice croaked. 'He doesn't want any . . . reprisals?'

'Oh, come on, Mr McCullough, everyone makes mistakes, don't they? And it's not as if we aren't all in the same business, is it?'

He sounded encouraged by this. A trickle of saliva lubricated his voice. 'Exactly. Right. Look, I regret it as much as . . . you know, I mean . . . but got to stick together, haven't we?'

'Sure,' I soothed, and bit my lip to stop myself saying, 'Honour among thieves.'

'Good. Good.'

'So . . . Mr McCullough, if we can make some arrangement whereby the property is returned intact, can I assume you would not be averse to that?'

'Certainly. No, you tell Mr Day it was just a silly mistake on my part and . . . '

'Of course,' I purred.

'Look, er, could I ask who I'm talking to? Or where I can give you a bell if— ?'

'I'll contact you,' I said, and put the phone down.

That was the easy bit. I didn't approach the next phone call with quite the same relish.

'Could I speak to Mr Day, please?'

'Mr Day doesn't take calls. If he wants to speak to people, he rings them.'

'Well, could I give him a number and could he call me?' It wouldn't be my own number. I've got various public phones round Brighton I use for that kind of thing. On this part of the job I was going to keep strictly incognito.

'I should think that's very unlikely,' the voice replied, silkily insolent. 'Why should Mr Day want to speak to you?'

'I have some information about some property of his. Property that was stolen from his house last Tuesday.'

'Oh yes?' The tone was still cool, but I could hear an edge of interest.

'Yes, and in fact the person responsible for taking the property does regret what he did very much.'

'You don't surprise me.'

'In fact, all he wants to do is get the property back to its rightful owner.'

'I see.'

'Do you think Mr Day would be agreeable to that kind of deal?'

'Hmm . . . '

'I mean, he does want the property back, doesn't he?'

'Yes.' The voice made a decision. 'Call again in an hour.' The line went dead.

When Stephanie rang in for her daily report, I'd got the meeting set up. 'Crown and Anchor on the seafront. Neutral ground. I've told Stuart. He sounded relieved.'

'Yes. The sooner he can offload that gear, the sooner he can start breathing again.'

'Hm. I know some of the stuff's already been fenced, but Stuart said he could raise cash to cover it, and Day's man's happy with that.'

'I know,' she said ruefully. 'He came and asked for my Rolex back. And he's cancelled the order on the BMW.'

'So, Stephanie, in a couple of days – with a bit of luck – your husband'll be off the hook . . . '

'Mm.'

'And,' I went on, not knowing why I was saying it, 'you can settle back into being a nice cosy little domestic couple again.'

'It's not like that,' she said. 'I thought I made it clear that our marriage is over.'

'Then why're you going to all this trouble to save him?'

'The fact that you've stopped loving someone doesn't mean you want to see him beaten to pulp.'

'No. True.'

'But once this is sorted out, I'm leaving him. There's nothing happening there. I want to get out, find a real man.'

'Ah,' I said, meaning a lot more than 'Ah'. I could

picture the pupils swelling to block out the blue in her eyes. It wasn't a picture I wanted in my mind's private gallery.

But it stayed, damn it.

She phoned me again a couple of hours before the meeting. 'Stuart's just gone out. I need to see you.'

Not for the first time, I knew the words should have been 'Sorry, can't make it' and I heard my voice saying, 'OK. Where?'

'Under the pier. By the rock stall.'

The rock stall was boarded up that time of year. The sea sucked through the shingle like an old man drawing in his breath against the cold. The weather seemed to have frightened off the junkies – or maybe it was too early in the evening for them – but it couldn't freeze the lust of the few couples twined against the encrusted steel pillars, their hands finding inevitable ways through swags of clothing.

They didn't help my concentration. Nor did the fact that, as soon as Stephanie saw me, she rushed straight up and nestled into my arms. She wore leather again, a black thigh-length coat, quilted, but not so quilted that I couldn't feel her outline pressing against mine. She stayed there longer than the strict protocol of a casual greeting demanded. The top of her head fitted neatly into the hollow of my shoulder. I had forgotten the sheer softness of women, and felt a pang when she drew back and trained those huge black pupils on me.

'I had to see you, Bram. This meeting . . . '

'Yes?'

'Stuart had got a gun with him when he left.'

'Stupid idiot! I told him not to.'

'He's not going to meet someone like Day unarmed.'

'He's not meeting Day. Only a sidekick.'

'Doesn't make a lot of difference, so far as the danger's concerned.'

'Look, if he carries a gun, he's only going to— '

Something hard and cold was thrust into my hand. 'Bram, I want you to take this.'

I looked down at it. Watery moonlight pencilled a pale line along the barrel.

'I don't like carrying guns. I can usually deal with anything that— '

'Stuart's got a gun. I'll lay any money Day's man's got one too. You're meant to be refereeing this contest. You've got to be at least as well-armed as they are.'

Maybe she had a point. I shoved the gun into my coat pocket.

'I must go, Bram. I've got things to do.'

But the way she came back into my arms to say goodbye, and the length of time she stayed there, suggested that the 'things' weren't that urgent.

It's remarkable how civilised three people carrying guns can be. The meeting in the Crown and Anchor was conducted with all the decorum of a Buckingham Palace garden party. Day's man was thin, balding, tweed-jacketed, wouldn't have looked out of place behind the counter of a bank; only the deadness in his eyes suggested that his interest rates might be prohibitive. Stuart McCullough was big, fit gone to fat, his features almost babyishly small as the face around them had spread. He wore a leather jacket like a chesterfield, pale grey trousers, poncy little white leather shoes with tassels, heavy gold rings and bracelets – too like a stage villain to be taken seriously as a real one. With my bleached hair and draped black coat, our table must've looked like something from a television series whose casting director was having a nervous breakdown.

But, as I say, the conversation was extremely decorous. Day's man, who incidentally never mentioned Harry Day by name, confirmed that all his boss wanted was the return of his property and cash to make up for any of it that had been irreclaimably sold. Stuart said he was happy with this

arrangement (and I could see from his face just how happy
he was). All that remained was the transfer of the goods.
Day's man said he had a van outside. Sooner it was done,
the better.

The deal had only taken one round of drinks. I should
have had Perrier but had gone straight for the vodka
because I was cold and twitchy. After the easy conclusion
of the agreement, I felt like a second one to celebrate, but
the others wanted to sort out the handover as soon as
possible.

So we left the pub. The sea was dull and flat in
the darkness, no light twinkling on its surface, only the
half-heard growl over pebbles reminding of its presence.
I was to drive with Stuart. Day's man would follow us to
the stash.

We went in my old yellow 2CV. Neither of the others
wanted McCullough's car spotted by the police. Seemed
reasonable enough. He was on their lists for any number of
robberies, proved and suspected; my one lapse had been in
a different area altogether. His car had been parked outside
a lot of places where it shouldn't have been; mine had never
done worse than double yellow lines.

The smell of aftershave in the car suggested that he'd
marinated himself in the stuff overnight.

He was surprisingly incurious as we drove along. I
don't know whether Stephanie had said anything to him
or not, but he didn't ask any questions about my rôle in
the proceedings. Maybe he thought I was just more of
Day's hired help. Or maybe the lack of imagination she
had mentioned was so total that it never occurred to him
to ask anything.

He didn't say much at all, just gave me directions.
The stuff was stowed in a beach-hut at Lancing. Pretty
risky hiding-place, I'd have thought, but he didn't seem
worried. Only temporary, he said, and no one was likely
to break in that time of year. I wasn't sure whether his

confidence demonstrated canniness or incompetence.

He seemed a lot more relaxed now the deal was on. Yes, he'd made a mistake tangling with Day, but now that mistake was being rectified, there would be no reprisals, and in future he'd check his information a bit more carefully. To Stuart McCullough, it seemed, that was all there was to it.

Me, I wasn't so sure. I've said I hate guns, but, driving along, I was reassured by the heaviness on my thigh.

I glanced across at him as a streetlight outlined his pudgy face in sudden gold, and asked myself once again how something as fragile and delicate as Stephanie could end up with this slab of corned beef. Fruitless speculation, of course. Which could only lead to painful follow-up questions.

To get my mind off those, I tried to draw him out on the Ditchling job, but didn't get far. 'How come you didn't know you were doing over "Flag" Day's place?' I asked.

'I was given the wrong info, wasn't I?' he replied grumpily. 'I always get the places checked out. Usually the detail's spot-on. Only do houses when I know they're empty and know they don't belong to anyone who's going to cause aggravation. This is the first time the info's been wonky.'

That didn't tie in with what Stephanie had said, but I let it pass. 'Do you always use the same person to check the houses out for you?'

'No point in changing a winning team, is there?' As he calmed down, I could hear the cockiness his wife had mentioned coming back into his voice.

'Can I ask who you get your information from?'

He was sufficiently relaxed now to chuckle. 'You can ask. You won't get no answer. Some things better just kept in the family.'

'OK. One thing I did want to— '

'Here. Pull over by the kerb. There – between the streetlights.'

I brought the 2CV to a halt. The following van indicated punctiliously and drew in behind us, dousing its lights as soon as it came to a standstill. The beach-huts, regular as crenellations, backed on to the road. Between them came the odd dull flash of the tarnished sea. Once again we could hear it grudging against the pebbles. I looked cautiously up and down the road. A few uninterested cars went past, but there was no sign of any pedestrians.

'Don't worry,' said McCullough. 'Only people you get along here are pensioners with their pooches, and they'll all be safely back in their baskets by now.'

We heard the door of the van behind open. Day's man emerged, pulling on leather gloves, casual as a weekend driver looking for a picnic spot.

'Right, let's get this sorted.' Stuart McCullough got out of the car. I switched off the headlights and, patting the heavy lump against my thigh, followed him.

'Which one is it?' asked Day's man.

McCullough pointed, reaching into his pocket for keys.

We moved down on to the beach, our shoes rasping on the shingle. Day's man brought out a pencil torch, which scanned the hut. It was small, little more than a garden shed, and had been painted a colour that might once have been dark blue. Didn't look a very secure hiding-place for fifty thousand pounds' worth of stolen goods, though maybe, as McCullough had implied, any hiding-place is safe so long as no one's looking there.

'Shall I open it?' he asked.

The balding head shook. 'No. He can.'

'Big one for the Yale, little for the padlock.'

I took the proffered keys. The Yale clicked home easily, but I couldn't get the smaller key into the padlock. 'Could you shine the torch over here, please?'

I heard the crunch of shoes behind me, but no light came. Instead, I was aware of a sudden, shattering impact across the back of my neck, before the plugs were pulled on me and all my circuits went dead.

*

It was the splash of rain that woke me. I felt the cold and damp before I felt the pain. Icy wet pebbles pressing into my face. It was when I tried to raise my head that the pain struck. I think I screamed and lay as still as I could.

But now I was awake, the pain stayed, whether I moved or not. I tried to reassemble my brain into something that could do more than register how much my head hurt.

It was still night, but the note of the sea had changed to a swish of water on sand. The tide had gone out some way. I dared to flex my frozen hands and in one felt the icy outline of a gun.

Slowly, agonisingly, I forced my back to arch and eased myself up on to hands and knees. The pain across the back of my neck winded me, obliterating everything else.

Clutching at my face, I inched my reluctant body upright.

Through the network of my fingers, I saw the outline of Stuart McCullough, lying on the shingle beside me. He was still and silent.

I shambled across to him on hands and knees, then tried to raise myself. My arm gave way under me and I reached forward to save myself from falling. My hand landed on his chest, and slid on the stickiness there.

Seized with a horror greater than the pain, I rose to my feet. The meagre light from distant streetlamps was enough to identify the dark liquid on my hand. I stumbled away and was violently sick.

Then, staggering, scuttering on pebbles, I found my way down to the sea's edge. I was still holding the gun. I dropped it, fell to my knees and grubbed in the sand, scraping off the foul witness from my hands. Then I dug the gun down and rubbed its surfaces with more sand.

I somehow got to my feet and, finding the strength from God knew where, hurled the weapon out into the sea.

Then I managed to get back to the 2CV and drive my trembling way home.

*

The needling of a hot shower was a necessary agony. I tried to crane round and check the damage in the mirror, but my neck hurt too much, so I rigged up a second mirror behind me. I saw an ugly swollen line, red and getting redder by the minute, but the skin wasn't broken. I dressed painfully, pulling on a black roll-neck sweater. Didn't want to advertise my injury. Didn't want to advertise anything that might connect me with the body on the beach.

The vodka bottle was calling out plaintively, but virtue triumphed; I made do with black coffee and a handful of Nurofen. I lay on the bed and tried to piece together my situation.

Didn't do too well. Vital links in my brain's reasoning circuitry hadn't been reconnected yet. All it could cope with was the blindingly obvious.

And it was blindingly obvious that I had been set up. It was also blindingly obvious that, if the rain hadn't woken me and some pensioner taking his pooch for an early morning stroll had found Bram Cotter with a gun in his hand beside McCullough's body, the set-up would have looked very ugly indeed.

That was all the intellectual effort I was capable of. I slipped into a sleep so deep that concussion must have played a part in it.

The buzzing of the entryphone woke me. I staggered across the room and released the door downstairs before the pain had time to hit me. And before I had time to register that the voice crackling in my ear had said, 'Police.'

There were two of them, neat, unassuming men, both in sheepskin jackets. They were hard, efficient and didn't waste compassion on people with records of drug offences. The smaller one did the talking. The bigger one just watched.

'Bram Cotter?'

I made the mistake of nodding, and winced.

'You look pretty bad.'

'A few too many drinks last night,' I mumbled.

'Sure it was just drinks?'

'Yes. I don't do drugs any more.'

'No.' The monosyllable was poised between scepticism and downright disbelief.

'Search the place if you like. You won't find anything. But presumably that's why you've come.'

'It isn't, as it happens. We've come about a murder.'

'Oh?'

'Man called Stuart McCullough has been found shot dead on Lancing Beach.'

Had to be very careful now. Find out how much they knew before I gave them anything. But my brain wasn't in ideal condition for fine-tuned pussyfooting. I kept quiet and let them do the talking.

'Now you may well ask what reason we have for connecting you with what's happened ... '

I didn't ask. I could think of too many reasons. But the one they came up with wasn't on my list.

'Fact is, we had an anonymous call at the station linking you with the killing.'

'Me?'

'Mm. Could be a crank, of course. Someone's idea of revenge. You got a lot of enemies, Mr Cotter?'

I shrugged. Not a good thing to do when you've just been slugged across the back of the neck. 'Some,' I said.

'You knew Stuart McCullough?'

I reckoned a half-truth might be safer than a whole lie. 'Heard of him. Small-time crook, wasn't he?'

The detective nodded. 'He'd been shot near a beach-hut full of stolen property.'

'Oh.'

'Where were you last night, Mr Cotter?'

Time for whole lies now. I didn't know how much they knew. My car might have been spotted in Lancing. *I* might have been spotted in Lancing. But I wasn't going to give in

without a fight. 'As I say, had a few drinks. A few too many
drinks.'

'Where?'

'Round Brighton.'

'With friends?'

'Mostly on my own.'

'Sounds a bit sad, drinking on your own . . . '

I didn't risk another shrug, but I hope my expression
did it for me.

'Would you be able to put us in touch with people
who might have seen you last night?'

'Maybe. I'd have to think about it. All a bit hazy,
I'm afraid.'

'Mm.' He let a silence establish itself. I was aware of the
bigger detective looking round the room. 'We have to take
tip-offs seriously, Mr Cotter,' the smaller one went on.

'Of course.'

The bigger detective picked up the trainers I'd been
wearing the night before, turned them over, and spoke
for the first time. 'Sand on the soles of these. And a bit
of tar.'

'Yes,' I said innocently. 'I go for a walk on the beach
most days.'

The smaller one nodded, assimilating and assessing this
information. 'You said you knew Stuart McCullough . . . ?'

Had that been stupid? 'Knew *of* him,' I qualified.

'Assuming – and as yet we have no reason to assume otherwise – that you had nothing to do with Mr McCullough's
death, can you think of anyone who might have had a reason
to murder him?'

If my brain had been in better nick, I might have
been more cautious. As it was, I said, 'I have heard
that he'd recently fallen foul of someone called Harry
Day.'

The name had an instant effect on both of them.
'I'd be careful what you say about Harry Day, Mr Cotter.'

'Oh?'

'There are laws about slander and defamation in this country, you know.'

'All I said was— '

'Trying to stain the reputation of Mr Day could be a very bad move, Mr Cotter.'

The detectives exchanged glances; some private cue passed between them. When the smaller one next spoke, his words had an air of conclusion about them. 'There are a lot more lines of enquiry we have to follow up, of course. We'll probably need to ask you further questions, Mr Cotter, at a later date.' He handed me a card. 'I'd be grateful if you could ring me on this number if you're likely to be leaving Brighton over the next few days.'

'OK.'

'Thank you for your time, Mr Cotter.'

And they went. Leaving me totally bemused. Why on earth had the whole tone of the interview suddenly changed? It had to be my mention of Harry Day. Up until then they had been looming, aggressive, trying to nail me. But the moment Harry Day's name came up they had folded, given in, surrendered.

My head still hurt like hell, but my brain was repairing itself quickly. I rang through to a contact I had in the West Sussex Constabulary, and he made the situation a bit clearer.

A big operation had been mounted over the last year to nail Harry Day. West Sussex had been working with the Yard on it, following a sequence of robberies in London and tracking the goods through a series of stashes till they were taken to the house in Ditchling. A raid was planned, the raid that was finally going to catch the big operator red-handed, finally pin something on 'Flag' Day.

The raid had happened. A day after Stuart McCullough had cleaned the house out. Nothing was found that wasn't strictly kosher.

The boys in blue were left with egg all over their faces and dripping down on to their uniforms. And Harry Day was mustering his cohorts of expensive lawyers to make the police extremely sorry for the slanderous mistake they had made. In future they were going to be unbelievably cautious and sure of all their facts before they made any further allegations against Mr Harry Day.

I tried phoning Stephanie, but there was no reply. I found out where her house was and went along there. No one answered. The second time I tried, there was a 'For Sale' notice fixed to the gatepost. My battered cherub had vanished as if she'd never existed.

Three days after their visit I had a phone call from the police. The smaller detective apologised for troubling me on the previous occasion, but reiterated that they did have to check everything. Anyway, he could now put my mind at rest, I had been eliminated from their enquiries. He wanted to leave it at that, but I demanded to know if they did have any leads on the murder. He told me that it was thought Stuart McCullough had been killed in a dispute over the division of profits from various robberies he had perpetrated in London. The murderer was probably one of his accomplices. 'A gangland killing', he called it, dismissively, as if the phrase precluded further enquiries.

Clearly Harry Day was still bunging the right amounts to the right people.

I pieced it together as I drove up over the moonless Downs. I wasn't the only one who had been set up. Stuart McCullough, too. He had been very convenient. As soon as 'Flag' Day's information service got wind of the planned police raid, McCullough had been told of an ideal target for his next robbery. That way the London robberies would be attributed to McCullough and Harry Day would remain as Mr Clean. But, of course, for the scheme to work, Stuart McCullough couldn't be around to answer questions when the goods were finally discovered.

He needed to be dead. Killed by some irrelevant small-time crook, someone with a police record. Which was where I came in.

These conclusions raised other questions. Who had tipped McCullough off about the stuff in Day's house? Why hadn't Day taken reprisals straight away? Whose idea had it been to bring me in? Was McCullough's death convenient for other reasons than just keeping him quiet about the robberies?

The answers to all these questions were glaringly obvious, but I tried to evade them, tried to find other explanations. Until I had proof.

I soon had proof. It winded me and made me nauseous like a blow to the stomach. I had crept over the perimeter fence of Day's estate, a dark balaclava masking my bleached hair. I had edged myself through the trees, and dashed across the shadows of the lawn to the house, drawn mothlike to its leaded mock-Gothic windows. Perched on an upturned wheelbarrow, craning like a Bisto kid towards a slit between curtains, I saw them.

Harry Day was as big as Stuart McCullough, white hair, black eyebrows over mean eyes. She sat on his lap. A burgundy leather dress this time, tight, hugging. Champagne glasses in their hands, and on their faces the confidence of their immunity from prosecution. Her vulnerability and innocence had been erased completely. There was nothing cherubic about that hard, hard face. Except its beauty.

I felt the wheelbarrow shift and slid down, clattering on to the patio. I heard a door open, a rough male shout, dogs barking.

I ran.

I had a couple of stiff drinks and fell asleep round one. I woke again before two, feeling, as amputees are supposed to, pain in a part of me that had been cut off. I got out of bed. I hadn't closed the curtains, so didn't have to open them to look out over the blackness of the sea.

The vodka bottle and I sat there, sharing each other's solitude, until dawn first speckled, then linked up the shifting waves in the embroidery of another day's light.

A Case of Mis-identity

Colin Dexter

Long as had been my acquaintance with Sherlock Holmes, I had seldom heard him refer to his early life; and the only knowledge I ever gleaned of his family history sprang from the rare visits of his famous brother, Mycroft. On such occasions, our visitor invariably addressed me with courtesy, but also (let me be honest!) with some little condescension. He was – this much I knew – by some seven years the senior in age to my great friend, and was a founder member of the Diogenes Club, that peculiar institution whose members are ever forbidden to converse with one another. Physically, Mycroft was stouter than his brother (I put the matter in as kindly a manner as possible); but the single most striking feature about him was the piercing intelligence of his eyes – greyish eyes which appeared to see beyond the range of normal mortals. Holmes himself had commented upon this last point: 'My dear Watson, you have recorded – and I am flattered by it – something of my own powers of observation and deduction. Know, however, that Mycroft has a degree of observation somewhat the equal of my own; and as for deduction, he has a brain that is unrivalled – *virtually* unrivalled – in the northern hemisphere. You may be relieved, however, to learn that he is a trifle lazy, and quite decidedly somnolent – and that his executant ability on the violin is immeasurably inferior to my own.'

(Was there, I occasionally wondered, just the hint of competitive envy between those two unprecedented intellects?)

I had just called at 221B Baker Street on a fog-laden November afternoon in 188–, after taking part in some research at St Thomas's Hospital into suppurative tonsilitis (I had earlier acquainted Holmes with the particulars). Mycroft was staying with Holmes for a few days, and as I entered that well-known sitting room I caught the tail-end of the brothers' conversation.

'Possibly, Sherlock – possibly. But it is the *detail*, is it not? Give me all the evidence and it is just possible that I could match your own analyses from my corner armchair. But to be required to rush hither and thither, to find and examine witnesses, to lie along the carpet with a lens held firmly to my failing sight . . . No! It is not my *métier*!'

During this time Holmes himself had been standing before the window, gazing down into the neutral-tinted London street. And looking over his shoulder, I could see that on the pavement opposite there stood an attractive young woman draped in a heavy fur coat. She had clearly just arrived, and every few seconds was looking up to Holmes's window in hesitant fashion, her fingers fidgeting with the buttons of her gloves. On a sudden she crossed the street, and Mrs Hudson was soon ushering in our latest client.

After handing her coat to Holmes, the young lady sat nervously on the edge of the nearest armchair, and announced herself as Miss Charlotte van Allen. Mycroft nodded briefly at the newcomer, before reverting to a monograph on polyphonic plainchant; whilst Holmes himself made observation of the lady in that abstracted yet intense manner which was wholly peculiar to him.

'Do you not find,' began Holmes, 'that with your short sight it is a little difficult to engage in so much type-writing?'

Surprise, apprehension, appreciation, showed by turns

upon her face, succeeded in all by a winsome smile as she appeared to acknowledge Holmes's quite extraordinary powers.

'Perhaps you will also tell me,' continued he, 'why it is that you came from home in such a great hurry?'

For a few seconds, Miss van Allen sat shaking her head with incredulity; then, as Holmes sat staring towards the ceiling, she began her remarkable narrative.

'Yes, I did bang out of the house, because it made me very angry to see the way my father, Mr Wyndham, took the whole business – refusing even to countenance the idea of going to the police, and quite certainly ruling out any recourse to yourself, Mr Holmes! He just kept repeating – and I *do* see his point – that no real harm has been done . . . although he can have no idea of the misery I have had to endure.'

'Your father?' queried Holmes quietly. 'Perhaps you refer to your step-father, since the names are different?'

'Yes,' she confessed, 'my step-father. I don't know why I keep referring to him as "father" – especially since he is but five years older than myself.'

'Your mother – she is still living?'

'Oh, yes! Though I will not pretend I was over-pleased when she remarried so soon after my father's death – and then to a man almost seventeen years younger than herself. Father – my real father, that is – had a plumbing business in the Tottenham Court Road, and Mother carried on the company after he died, until she married Mr Wyndham. I think he considered such things a little beneath his new wife, especially with his being in a rather superior position as a traveller in French wines. Whatever the case, though, he made Mother sell out.'

'Did you yourself derive any income from the sale of your father's business?'

'No. But I do have £100 annual income in my own right; as well as the extra I make from my typing. If I may say so, Mr Holmes, you might be surprised how many of the local

businesses – including *Cook and Marchant* – ask me to work
for them a few hours each week. You see' (she looked at us
with a shy, endearing diffidence) 'I'm quite good at *that* in
life, if nothing else.'

'You must then have some profitable government stock
– ?' began Holmes.

She smiled again: 'New Zealand, at four and a half
per cent.'

'Please forgive me, Miss van Allen, but could not a
single lady get by very nicely these days on – let us say,
fifty pounds per annum?'

'Oh, certainly! And I myself live comfortably on but ten
shillings per week, which is only half of that amount. You
see, I never touch a single penny of my inheritance. Since I
live at home, I cannot bear the thought of being a burden to
my parents, and we have reached an arrangement whereby
Mr Wyndham himself is empowered to draw my interest
each quarter for as long as I remain in that household.'

Holmes nodded. 'Why have you come to see me?'
he asked bluntly.

A flush stole over Miss van Allen's face and she plucked
nervously at a small handkerchief drawn from her bag as
she stated her errand with earnest simplicity. 'I would give
everything I have to know what has become of Mr Horatio
Darvill. There! Now you have it.'

'Please, could you perhaps begin at the beginning?'
encouraged Holmes gently.

'Whilst my father was alive, sir, we always received
tickets for the gas-fitters' ball. And after he died, the
tickets were sent to my mother. But neither Mother nor I
ever thought of going, because it was made plain to us that
Mr Wyndham did not approve. He believed that the class of
folk invited to such gatherings was inferior; and furthermore
he asserted that neither of us – without considerable extra
expenditure – had anything fit to wear. But believe me, Mr
Holmes, I myself had the purple plush that I had never so
much as taken from the drawer!'

It was after a decent interval that Holmes observed quietly: 'But you *did* go to the ball?'

'Yes. In the finish, we both went – Mother and I – when my step-father had been called away to France.'

'And it was there that you met Mr Horatio Darvill?'

'Yes! And – do you know? – he called the very next morning. And several times after that, whilst my step-father was in France, we walked out together.'

'Mr Wyndham must have been annoyed once he learned what had occurred?'

Miss van Allen hung her pretty head. 'Most annoyed, I'm afraid, for it became immediately clear that he did not approve of Mr Darvill.'

'Why do you think that was so?'

'I am fairly sure he thought Mr Darvill was interested only in my inheritance.'

'Did Mr Darvill not attempt to keep seeing you – in spite of these difficulties?'

'Oh yes! I thought, though, it would be wiser for us to stop seeing each other for a while. But he did write – every single day. And always, in the mornings, I used to receive the letters myself so that no one else should know.'

'Were you engaged to this gentleman?'

'Yes! For there was no problem about his supporting me. He was a cashier in a firm in Leadenhall Street— '

'Ah! Which office was that?' I interposed, for that particular area is known to me well, and I hoped that I might perhaps be of some assistance in the current investigation. Yet the look on Holmes's face was one of some annoyance, and I sank further into my chair as the interview progressed.

'I never did know exactly which firm it was,' admitted Miss van Allen.

'But where did he live?' persisted Holmes.

'He told me that he usually slept in a flat on the firm's premises.'

'You must yourself have written to this man, to whom you had agreed to become engaged?'

She nodded. 'To the Leadenhall Street Post Office, where I left my letters *poste restante*. Horatio – Mr Darvill – said that if I wrote to him at his work address, he'd never get to see my envelopes first, and the young clerks there would be sure to tease him about things.'

It was at this point that I was suddenly conscious of certain stertorous noises from Mycroft's corner – a wholly reprehensible lapse into poor manners, as it appeared to me.

'What else can you tell me about Mr Darvill?' asked Holmes quickly.

'He was very shy. He always preferred to walk out with me in the evening than in the daylight. "Retiring", perhaps, is the best word to describe him – even his voice. He'd had the quinsy as a young man, and was still having treatment for it. But the disability had left him with a weak larynx, and a sort of whispering fashion of speaking. His eyesight, too, was rather feeble – just as mine is – and he always wore tinted spectacles to protect his eyes against the glare of any bright light.'

Holmes nodded his understanding; and I began to sense a note of suppressed excitement in his voice.

'What next?'

"He called at the house the very evening on which Mr Wyndham next departed for France, and he proposed that we should marry before my step-father returned. He was convinced that this would be our only chance; and he was so dreadfully in earnest that he made me swear, with my hand upon both Testaments, that whatever happened I would always be true and faithful to him.'

'Your mother was aware of what was taking place?'

'Oh, *yes*! And she approved so much. In a strange way, she was even fonder of my fiancé than I was myself, and she agreed that our only chance was to arrange a secret marriage.'

'The wedding was to be in church?'

'Last Friday, at St Saviour's, near King's Cross; and

we were to go on to a wedding breakfast afterwards at
the St Pancras Hotel. Horatio called a hansom for us, and
put Mother and me into it before stepping himself into a
four-wheeler which happened to be in the street. Mother
and I got to St Saviour's first – it was only a few minutes'
distance away. But when the four-wheeler drove up and we
waited for him to step out – he never did, Mr Holmes! And
when the cabman got down from the box and looked inside
the carriage – *it was empty*.'

'You have neither seen nor heard of Mr Darvill since?'

'Nothing,' she whispered.

'You had planned a honeymoon, I suppose?'

'We had planned,' said Miss van Allen, biting her lip
and scarce managing her reply, 'a fortnight's stay at The
Royal Gleneagles in Inverness, and we were to have caught
the lunch-time express from King's Cross.'

'It seems to me,' said Holmes, with some feeling, 'that
you have been most shamefully treated, dear lady.'

But Miss van Allen would hear nothing against her
loved one, and protested spiritedly: 'Oh, no, sir! He was
far too good and kind to treat me so.'

'Your own opinion, then,' said Holmes, 'is that some
unforeseen accident or catastrophe has occurred?'

She nodded her agreement. 'And I think he must have
had some premonition that very morning of possible danger,
because he begged me then, once again, to remain true to
him – whatever happened.'

'You have no idea what that danger may have been?'

'None.'

'How did your mother take this sudden disappearance?'

'She was naturally awfully worried at first. But then she
became more and more angry; and she made me promise
never to speak to her of the matter again.'

'And your step-father?'

'He seemed – it was strange, really – rather more
sympathetic than Mother. At least he was willing to
discuss it.'

'And what was his opinion?'

'He agreed that some accident must have happened. As he said, Mr Darvill could have no possible interest in bringing me to the very doors of St Saviour's – and then in deserting me there. If he had borrowed money – or if some of my money had already been settled on him – then there might have been some reason behind such a cruel action. But he was absolutely independent about money, and he would never even look at a sixpence of mine if we went on a visit. Oh, Mr Holmes! It is driving me half-mad to think of— ' But the rest of the sentence was lost as the young lady sobbed quietly into her handkerchief.

When she had recovered her composure, Holmes rose from his chair, promising that he would consider the baffling facts she had put before him. 'But if I could offer you one piece of advice,' he added, as he held the lady's coat for her, 'it is that you allow Mr Horatio Darvill to vanish as completely from your memory as he vanished from his wedding-carriage.'

'Then you think that I shall not see him again?'

'I fear not. But please leave things in my hands. Now! I wish you to send me a most accurate physical description of Mr Darvill, as well as any of his letters which you feel you can spare.'

'We can at least expedite things a little in those two respects,' replied she in business-like fashion, 'for I advertised for him in last Monday's *Chronicle*.' And promptly reaching into her handbag, she produced a newspaper cutting which she gave to Holmes, together with some other sheets. 'And here, too, are four of his letters which I happen to have with me. Will they be sufficient?'

Holmes looked quickly at the letters, and nodded. 'You say you never had Mr Darvill's address?'

'Never.'

'Your step-father's place of business, please?'

'He travels for *Cook and Marchant*, the great Burgundy importers, of Fenchurch Street.'

'Thank you.'

After she had left Holmes sat brooding for several minutes, his fingertips still pressed together. 'An interesting case,' he observed finally. 'Did you not find it so, Watson?'

'You appeared to read a good deal which was quite invisible to me,' I confessed.

'Not invisible, Watson. Rather, let us say – unnoticed. And that in spite of my repeated attempts to impress upon you the importance of sleeves, of thumb-nails, of boot-laces, and the rest. Now, tell me, what did you immediately gather from the young woman's appearance? Describe it to me.'

Conscious of Mycroft's presence, I sought to recall my closest impressions of our recent visitor.

'Well, she had, beneath her fur, a dress of rich brown, somewhat darker than the coffee colour, with a little black plush at the neck and at the sleeves – you mentioned sleeves, Holmes? Her gloves were dove-grey in colour, and were worn through at the right forefinger. Her black boots, I was not able, from where I sat, to observe in any detail, yet I would suggest that she takes either the size four and a half or five. She wore small pendant earrings, almost certainly of imitation gold, and the small handkerchief into which the poor lady sobbed so charmingly had a neat darn in the monogrammed corner. In general, she had the air of a reasonably well-to-do young woman who has not quite escaped from the slightly vulgar inheritance of a father who was – let us be honest about it, Holmes! – a plumber.'

A snort from the chair beside which Holmes had so casually thrown Miss van Allen's fur coat served to remind us that the recumbent Mycroft had now reawakened, and that perhaps my own description had, in some respect, occasioned his disapproval. But he made no spoken comment, and soon resumed his former posture.

''Pon my word, Watson,' said Holmes, 'you are coming along splendidly – is he not, Mycroft? It is true, of course, that your description misses almost everything of real importance. But the method! You have hit upon the *method*, Watson. Let us take, for example, the plush you mention on the sleeves. Now, plush is a most wonderfully helpful material for showing traces; and the double line above the wrist, where the type-writist presses against the table, was beautifully defined. As for the short-sightedness, that was mere child's play. The dent-marks of a *pince-nez* at either side of the lady's nostrils – you did not observe it? Elementary, my dear Watson! And then the boots. You really *must* practise the art of being positioned where all the evidence is clearly visible. If you wish to observe nothing at all, like brother Mycroft, then you will seek out the furthest corner of a room where even the vaguest examination of the client will be obscured by the furniture, by a fur coat, by whatever. But reverting to the lady's boots, I observed that although they were very like each other in colour and style, they were in fact *odd* boots; the one on the right foot having a slightly decorated toe-cap, and the one on the left being of a comparatively plain design. Furthermore, the right one was fastened only at the three lower buttons out of the five; the left one only at the first, third, and fifth. Now the deduction we may reasonably draw from such evidence is that the young lady left home in an unconscionable hurry. You agree?'

'Amazing, Holmes!'

'As for the glove worn at the forefinger— '

'You would be better advised,' suddenly interposed the deeper voice of Mycroft, 'to concentrate upon the missing person!'

May it have been a flash of annoyance that showed itself in Holmes's eyes? If so, it was gone immediately. 'You are quite right, Mycroft! Come now, Watson, read to us the paragraph from *The Chronicle*.'

I held the printed slip to the light and began: 'Missing on

the 14th November 188–. A gentleman named Mr Horatio Darvill: about 5′ 8″ in height; fairly firmly built; sallow complexion; black hair, just a little bald in the centre; bushy black side-whiskers and moustache; tinted spectacles; slight infirmity of speech. When last seen, was dressed in— '

'But I think,' interrupted Holmes, 'he may by now have changed his wedding vestments, Watson?'

'Oh, certainly, Holmes.'

There being nothing, it seemed, of further value in the newspaper description, Holmes turned his attention to the letters, passing them to me after studying them himself with minute concentration.

'Well?' he asked.

Apart from the fact that the letters had been typed, I could find in them nothing of interest, and I laid them down on the coffee-table in front of the somnolent Mycroft.

'Well?' persisted Holmes.

'I assume you refer to the fact that the letters are type-written.'

'Already you are neglecting your newly acquired knowledge of the *method*, Watson. Quite apart from the point you mention, there are three further points of immediate interest and importance. First, the letters are very short; second, apart from the vague "Leadenhall Street" superscription, there is no precise address stated at any point; third, it is not only the body of the letter which has been typed, but the signature, too. Observe here, Watson – and here! – that neat little "Horatio Darvill" typed at the bottom of each of our four exhibits. And it will not have escaped you, I think, how conclusive that last point might be?'

'Conclusive, Holmes? In what way?'

'My dear fellow, is it possible for you not to see how strongly it bears upon our present investigations?'

'*Homo circumbendibus* – that's what you are, Sherlock!' (It was Mycroft once more.) 'Do you not appreciate that your client would prefer some positive action to any further proofs of your cerebral superiority?'

It is pleasing to report here that this attempt of Mycroft to provoke the most distinguished criminologist of the century proved largely ineffectual, and Holmes permitted himself a fraternal smile as his brother slowly bestirred his frame.

'You are right, Mycroft,' he rejoined lightly. 'And I shall immediately compose two letters: one to Messrs *Cook and Marchant*; the other to Mr Wyndham, asking that gentleman to meet us here at six o'clock tomorrow evening.'

Already I was aware of the easy and confident demeanour with which Holmes was tackling the singular mystery which confronted us all. But for the moment my attention was diverted by a small but most curious incident.

'It is just as well, Sherlock,' said Mycroft (who appeared now to be almost fully awakened), 'that you do not propose to write three letters.'

Seldom (let me admit it) have I seen my friend so perplexed: 'A *third* letter?'

'Indeed. But such a letter could have no certain destination, since it apparently slipped your memory to ask the young lady her present address, and the letters she entrusted to you appear, as I survey them, to be lacking their outer envelopes.'

Momentarily Holmes looked less than amused by this light-hearted intervention. 'You are more observant today than I thought, Mycroft, for the evidence of eye and ear had led me to entertain the suspicion that you were sleeping soundly during my recent conversation with Miss van Allen. But as regards her address, you are right.' And even as he spoke I noted the twinkle of mischievous intelligence in his eyes. 'Yet it would not be too difficult perhaps to *deduce* the young lady's address, Mycroft? On such a foul day as this it is dangerous and ill-advised for a lady to travel the streets if she has a perfectly acceptable and comfortable alternative such as the Underground; and since it was precisely 3.14 p.m. when Miss van Allen first appeared beneath my window, I would hazard the guess that she had caught the

Metropolitan-line train which passes through Baker Street at 3.12 p.m. on its journey to Hammersmith. We may consider two further clues, also. The lady's boots, ill-assorted as they were, bore little evidence of the mud and mire of our London streets; and we may infer from this that her own home is perhaps as adjacent to an Underground station as is our own. More significant, however, is the fact, as we all observed, that Miss van Allen wore a dress of linen – a fabric which, though it is long-lasting and pleasing to wear, is one which has the disadvantage of creasing most easily. Now the skirt of the dress had been most recently ironed, and the slight creases in it must have resulted from her journey – to see me. And – I put this forward as conjecture, Mycroft – probably no more than three or four stops on the Underground had been involved. If we remember, too, the "few minutes" her wedding-carriage took from her home to St Saviour's, I think, perhaps . . . perhaps . . . ' Holmes drew a street-map towards him, and surveyed his chosen area with his magnification-glass.

'I shall plump,' he said directly, 'for Cowcross Street myself – that shabbily genteel little thoroughfare which links Farringdon Road with St John Street.'

'Very impressive!' said Mycroft, anticipating my own admiration. 'And would you place her on the north, or the south side, of that thoroughfare, Sherlock?'

But before Holmes could reply to this small pleasantry, Mrs Hudson entered with a slip of paper which she handed to Holmes. 'The young lady says she forgot to give you her address, sir, and she's written it down for you.'

Holmes glanced quickly at the address and a glint of pride gleamed in his eyes. 'The answer to your question, Mycroft, is the south side – for it is an even-numbered house, and if I remember correctly the numbering of houses in that part of London invariably begins at the east end of the street with the odd numbers on the right-hand side walking westwards.'

'And the number is perhaps in the middle or late

thirties?' suggested Mycroft. 'Thirty-six, perhaps? Or more likely thirty-eight?'

Holmes himself handed over the paper to us and we read:

Miss Charlotte van Allen
38, Cowcross Street

I was daily accustomed to exhibitions of the most extraordinary deductive logic employed by Sherlock Holmes, but I had begun at this point to suspect, in his brother Mycroft, the existence of some quite paranormal mental processes. It was only some half an hour later, when Holmes himself had strolled out for tobacco, that Mycroft, observing my continued astonishment, spoke quietly in my ear.

'If you keep your lips sealed, Dr Watson, I will tell you a small secret – albeit a very simple one. The good lady's coat was thrown rather carelessly, as you noticed, over the back of a chair; and on the inside of the lining was sewn a tape with her name and address clearly printed on it. Alas, however, my eyes are now not so keen as they were in my youth, and sixes and eights, as you know, are readily susceptible of confusion.'

I have never been accused, I trust, of undue levity, but I could not help laughing heartily at this coup on Mycroft's part, and I assured him that his brother should never hear the truth of it from me.

'Sherlock?' said Mycroft, raising his mighty eyebrows. 'He saw through my little joke immediately.'

It was not until past six o'clock the following evening that I returned to Baker Street after (it is not an irrelevant matter) a day of deep interest at St Thomas's Hospital.

'Well, have you solved the mystery yet?' I asked, as I entered the sitting room.

Holmes I found curled up in his armchair, smoking

his oily clay pipe, and discussing medieval madrigals with
Mycroft.

'Yes, Watson, I believe— '

But hardly were the words from his mouth when we
heard a heavy footfall in the passage and a sharp rap on
the door.

'This will be the girl's step-father,' said Holmes. 'He
has written to say he would be here at a quarter after
six. Come in!'

The man who entered was a sturdy, middle-sized fellow,
about thirty years of age, clean-shaven, sallow-skinned, with
a pair of most penetrating eyes. He placed his shiny top-hat
on the sideboard, and with an insinuating bow sidled down
into the nearest chair.

'I am assuming,' said Holmes, 'that you are Mr James
Wyndham and' (holding up a type-written sheet) 'that this
is the letter you wrote to me?'

'I am that person, sir, and the letter is mine. It was
against my expressed wish, as you may know, that Miss van
Allen contacted you in this matter. But she is an excitable
young lady, and my wife and I will be happy to forgive her
for such an impulsive action. Yet I must ask you to have
nothing more to do with what is, unfortunately, a not un-
common misfortune. It is clear what took place, and I think
it highly unlikely, sir, that even you will find so much as a
single trace of Mr Darvill.'

'On the contrary,' replied Holmes quietly, 'I have reason
to believe that I have already discovered the whereabouts
of that gentleman.'

Mr Wyndham gave a violent start, and dropped his
gloves. 'I am delighted to hear it,' he said in a strained
voice.

'It is a most curious fact,' continued Holmes, 'that a
type-writer has just as much individuality as does handwriting. Even when completely new, no two machines are
exactly alike; and as they get older, some characters wear
on this side and some on that. Now in this letter of yours,

Mr Wyndham, you will note that in every instance there is some slight slurring in the eye of the "e"; and a most easily detectable defect in the tail of the "t".'

'All our office correspondence,' interrupted our visitor, 'is typed on the same machine, and I can fully understand why it has become a little worn.'

'But I have four other letters here,' resumed Holmes, in a slow and menacing tone, 'which purport to come from Mr Horatio Darvill. And in each of these, also, the "e"s are slurred, and the "t"s un-tailed.'

Mr Wyndham was out of his chair instantly and had snatched up his hat: 'I can waste no more of my valuable time with such trivialities, Mr Holmes. If you can catch the man who so shamefully treated Miss van Allen, then catch him! I wish you well – and ask you to let me know the outcome. But I have no interest whatsoever in your fantastical notions.'

Already, however, Holmes had stepped across the room and turned the key in the door. 'Certainly I will tell you how I caught Mr Darvill, if you will but resume your chair.'

'What?' shouted Wyndham, his face white, his small eyes darting about him like those of a rat in a trap. Yet finally he sat down and glared aggressively around, as Holmes continued his analysis.

'It was as selfish and as heartless a trick as ever I encountered. The man married a woman much older than himself, largely for her money. In addition, he enjoyed the interest on the not inconsiderable sum of the step-daughter's money, for as long as that daughter lived with them. The loss of such extra monies would have made a significant difference to the life-style adopted by the newly married pair. Now the daughter herself was an amiable, warm-hearted girl, and was possessed of considerable physical attractions; and with the added advantage of a personal income, it became clear that under normal circumstances she would not remain single for very long. So he – the man of whom I speak – decided to deny her the company and friendship of her contemporaries by keeping her at home. But she – and who shall blame her? – grew restive under such an unnatural regimen, and firmly announced her intention to attend a local ball. So what did her step-father do? With the connivance of his wife, he conceived a cowardly plan. He disguised himself cleverly: he covered those sharp eyes with dully tinted spectacles; he masked that clean-shaven face with bushy side-whiskers; he sank that clear voice of his into the strained whisper of one suffering from the quinsy. And then, feeling himself doubly secure because of the young lady's short sight, he appeared *himself* at the ball, in the guise of one Horatio Darvill, and there he wooed the fair Miss van Allen for his own – thereafter taking further precaution of always arranging his assignations by candlelight.'

(I heard a deep groan which at the time I assumed to have come from our visitor, but which, upon reflection, I am inclined to think originated from Mycroft's corner.)

'Miss van Allen had fallen for her new beau; and no suspicion of deception ever entered her pretty head. She was flattered by the attention she was receiving, and the effect was heightened by the admiration of her mother for the man. An "engagement" was agreed, and the deception perpetuated. But the pretended journeys abroad were becoming more difficult to sustain, and things had to be brought to a head quickly, although in such a *dramatic* way as to leave a permanent impression upon the young girl's mind. Hence the vows of fidelity sworn on the Testaments; hence the dark hints repeated on the very morning of the proposed marriage that something sinister might be afoot. James Wyndham, you see, wished his step-daughter to be so morally bound to her fictitious suitor that for a decade, at least, she would sit and wilt in Cowcross Street, and continue paying her regular interest directly into the account of her guardian: the same blackguard of a guardian who had brought her to the doors of St Saviour's and then, himself, conveniently disappeared by the age-old ruse of stepping in at one side of a four-wheeler – and out at the other.'

Rising to his feet, Wyndham fought hard to control his outrage. 'I wish you to know that it is you, sir, who is violating the law of this land – and not me! As long as you keep that door locked, and thereby hold me in this room against my will, you lay yourself open— '

'The law,' interrupted Holmes, suddenly unlocking and throwing open the door, 'may not for the moment be empowered to touch you. Yet never, surely, was there a man who deserved punishment more. In fact . . . since my hunting-crop is close at hand— ' Holmes took two swift strides across the room; but it was too late. We heard a wild clatter of steps down the stairs as Wyndham departed, and then had the satisfaction of watching him flee pell-mell down Baker Street.

'That cold-blooded scoundrel will end on the gallows, mark my words!' growled Holmes.

'Even now, though, I cannot follow all the steps in your reasoning, Holmes,' I remarked.

'It is this way,' replied Holmes. 'The only person who profited financially from the vanishing-trick – was the step-father. Then, the fact that the two men, Wyndham and Darvill, were never actually seen *together*, was most suggestive. As were the tinted spectacles, the husky voice, the bushy whiskers – all of these latter, Watson, hinting strongly at disguise. Again, the type-written signature betokened one thing only – that the man's handwriting was so familiar to Miss van Allen that she might easily recognise even a small sample of it. Isolated facts? Yes! But all of them leading to the same inevitable conclusion – as even my slumbering sibling might agree?'

But there was no sound from the Mycroft corner.

'You were able to verify your conclusion?' I asked.

Holmes nodded briskly. 'We know the firm for which Wyndham worked, and we had a full description of Darvill. I therefore eliminated from that description everything which could be the result of deliberate disguise— '

'Which means that you have *not* verified your conclusion!' Mycroft's sudden interjection caused us both to turn sharply towards him.

'There will always,' rejoined Holmes, 'be a need and a place for informed conjecture— '

'*Inspired* conjecture, Holmes,' I interposed.

'Phooey!' snorted Mycroft. 'You are talking of nothing but wild *guesswork*, Sherlock. And it is my opinion that in this case your guesswork is grotesquely askew.'

I can only report that never have I seen Holmes so taken aback; and he sat in silence as Mycroft raised his bulk from the chair and now stood beside the fireplace.

'Your deductive logic needs no plaudits from me, Sherlock, and like Dr Watson I admire your desperate hypothesis. But unless there is some firm evidence which you have thus far concealed from us . . . ?'

Holmes did not break his silence.

'Well,' stated Mycroft, 'I will indulge in a little guesswork of my own, and tell you that the gentleman who just stormed out of this room is as innocent as Watson here!'

'He certainly did not *act* like an innocent man,' I protested, looking in vain to Holmes for some support, as Mycroft continued.

'The reasons you adduce for your suspicions are perfectly sound in most respects, and yet – I must speak with honesty, Sherlock! – I found myself sorely disappointed with your reading – or rather complete misreading – of the case. You are, I believe, wholly correct in your central thesis that there is no such person as Horatio Darvill.' (How the blood was tingling in my veins as Mycroft spoke these words!) 'But when the unfortunate Mr Wyndham who has just rushed one way up Baker Street rushes back down it the other with a writ for defamation of character – as I fear he will! – then you will be compelled to think, to analyse, and to act, with a little more care and circumspection.'

Holmes leaned forward, the sensitive nostrils of that aquiline nose a little distended. But still he made no comment.

'For example, Sherlock, two specific pieces of information vouchsafed to us by the attractive Miss van Allen herself have been strongly discounted, if not wholly ignored, in your analysis.' (I noticed Holmes's eyebrows rising quizzically.) 'First, the fact that Mr Wyndham was older than Miss van Allen *only by some five years*. Second, the fact that Miss van Allen is so competent and speedy a performer on the type-writer that she works, on a free-lance basis, for several firms in the vicinity of her home, including Messrs *Cook and Marchant*. Furthermore, you make the astonishing claim that Miss van Allen was totally deceived by the disguise of Mr Darvill. Indeed, you would have her not only blind, but semi-senile into the bargain! Now it is perfectly true that the lady's eyesight is far from perfect – *glaucopia Athenica*, would you not diagnose, Dr Watson? – but it is quite ludicrous to believe that she would fail to recognise the person with whom she was living. And it is wholly dishonest of you to assert that the assignations were always held by candlelight, since on at least two occasions, the morning after the first meeting – the *morning*, Sherlock! – and the morning of the planned wedding ceremony, Miss van Allen had ample opportunity of studying the physical features of Darvill in the broadest of daylight.'

'You seem to me to be taking an unconscionably long time in putting forward your own hypothesis,' snapped Holmes, somewhat testily.

'You are right,' admitted the other. 'Let me beat about the bush no longer! You have never felt emotion akin to love for any woman, Sherlock – not even for the Adler woman – and you are therefore deprived of the advantages of those who like myself are able to understand both the workings of the male and also the female mind. Five years her superior in age – her step-father; *only five years*. Now one of the sadnesses of womankind is their tendency to age more quickly and less gracefully than men; and one of the truths about mankind in general is that if you put one of each sex, of roughly similar age, in reasonable proximity . . . And if

one of them is the fair Miss van Allen – then you are
inviting a packet of trouble. Yet such is what took place in
the Wyndham ménage. Mrs Wyndham was seventeen years
older than her young husband; and perhaps as time went by
some signs and tokens of this disproportionate difference in
their ages began to manifest themselves. At the same time,
it may be assumed that Wyndham himself could not help
being attracted – however much at first he sought to resist
the temptation – by the very winsome and vivacious young
girl who was his step-daughter. It would almost certainly
have been Wyndham himself who introduced Miss van
Allen to the part-time duties she undertook for *Cook and
Marchant* – where the two of them were frequently thrown
together, away from the restraints of wife and home, and
with a result which it is not at all difficult to guess. Certain
it is, in my own view, that Wyndham sought to transfer his
affections from the mother to the daughter; and in due
course it was the daughter who decided that whatever her
own affections might be in the matter she must in all honour
leave her mother and step-father. Hence the great anxiety
to get out to dances and parties and the like – activities
which Wyndham objected to for the obvious reason that
he wished to have Miss van Allen as close by himself for
as long as he possibly could. Now you, Sherlock, assume
that this objection arose as a result of the interest accruing
from the New Zealand securities – and you are *guessing*, are
you not? Is it not just possible that Wyndham has money of
his own – find out, Brother! – and that what he craves for
is not some petty addition to his wealth, but the love of a
young woman with whom he has fallen rather hopelessly in
love? You see, she took *him* in, just as she took *you* in,
Sherlock – for you swallowed everything that calculating
little soul reported.'

'Really, this is outrageous!' I objected – but Holmes
held up his hand, and bid me hear his brother out.

'What is clear, is that at some point when Wyndham was
in France – and why did you not verify those dates spent

abroad? I am sure *Cook and Marchant* would have provided
them just as quickly as it furnished the wretched man's
description – as I was saying, with Wyndham in France,
mother and daughter found themselves in a little *tête-à-tête*
one evening, during the course of which a whole basketful
of dirty linen was laid bare, with the daughter bitterly dis-
illusioned about the behaviour of her step-father, and the
mother hurt and angry about her husband's infidelity. So,
together, the pair of them devised a plan. Now, we both
agree on one thing at least, Sherlock! There appears to
be no evidence whatsoever for the independent existence
of Horatio Darvill except for what we have heard from
Miss van Allen's lips. Rightly, you drew our attention to
the fact that the two men were never seen together. But,
alas, having appreciated the *importance* of that clue, you
completely misconceived its *significance*. *You* decided that
there is no Darvill – because he is Wyndham. *I* have to tell
you that there is no Darvill – *because he is the pure fabrication
of the minds of Mrs Wyndham and her daughter*.'

Holmes was staring with some consternation at a pattern
in the carpet, as Mycroft rounded off his extravagant and
completely baseless conjectures.

'Letters were written – and incidentally I myself would
have been far more cautious about those "e"s and "t"s: twin
faults, as it happens, of my very own machine! But, as I say,
letters were written – *but by Miss van Allen herself*; a wedding
was arranged; a story concocted of a non-existent carriage
into which there climbed a non-existent groom – and that
was the end of the charade. Now, it was you, Sherlock, who
rightly asked the key question: *cui bono*? And you concluded
that the real beneficiary was Wyndham. But exactly the
contrary is the case! It was the mother and daughter who
intended to be the beneficiaries, for they hoped to rid
themselves of the rather wearisome Mr Wyndham – but
not before he had been compelled, by moral and social
pressures, to make some handsome money-settlement upon
the pair of them – especially perhaps upon the young girl

who, as Dr Watson here points out, could well have done with some decent earrings and a new handkerchief. And the *social* pressure I mention, Sherlock, was designed – carefully and cleverly designed – to come from *you*. A cock-and-bull story is told to you by some wide-eyed young thing, a story so bestrewn with clues at almost every point that even Lestrade – given a week or two! – would probably have come up with a diagnosis identical with your own. And why do you think she came to you, and not to Lestrade, say? Because "Mr Sherlock Holmes is the greatest investigator the world has ever known" – and his judgements are second only to the Almighty's in their infallibility. For if you, Sherlock, believed Wyndham to be guilty – then Wyndham *was* guilty in the eyes of the whole world – the whole world except for one, that is.'

'Except for two,' I added quietly.

Mycroft Holmes turned his full attention towards me for the first time, as though I had virtually been excluded from his previous audience. But I allowed him no opportunity of seeking the meaning of my words, as I addressed him forthwith.

'I asked Holmes a question when he presented his own analysis, sir. I will ask you the same: have you in any way verified your hypothesis? And if so, how?'

'The answer, Dr Watson, to the first part of your question is, in large measure, "yes". Mr Wyndham, in fact, has quite enough money to be in no way embarrassed by the withdrawal of Miss van Allen's comparatively minor contribution. As for the second part . . . ' Mycroft hesitated awhile. 'I am not sure what my brother has told you, of the various offices I hold under the British Crown— '

It was Holmes who intervened – and impatiently so. 'Yes, yes, Mycroft! Let us all concede immediately that the, shall we say, "unofficial" sources to which you are privy have completely invalidated my own reconstruction of the case. So be it! Yet I would wish, if you allow, to make one or two observations upon your own rather faithful interpretation of

events? It is, of course, with full justice that you accuse me
of having no first-hand knowledge of what are called "the
matters of the heart". Furthermore, you rightly draw attention to the difficulties Mr Wyndham would have experienced
in deceiving his step-daughter. Yet how you under-rate the
power of disguise! And how, incidentally, you *over*-rate the
intelligence of Lestrade! Even Dr Watson, I would suggest,
has a brain considerably superior— '

For not a second longer could I restrain myself. 'Gentlemen!' I cried, 'you are both – *both* of you! – most tragically
wrong.'

The two brothers stared at me as though I had taken
leave of my senses.

'I think you should seek to explain yourself, Watson,'
said Holmes sharply.

'A man,' I began, 'was proposing to go to Scotland
for a fortnight with his newly married wife, and he had
drawn out one hundred pounds in cash – no less! – from
the Oxford Street branch of the Royal National Bank on
the eve of his wedding. The man, however, was abducted
after entering a four-wheeler on the very morning of his
wedding-day, was brutally assaulted, and then robbed of all
his money and personal effects – thereafter being dumped,
virtually for dead, in a deserted alley in Stepney. Quite
by chance he was discovered later that same evening, and
taken to the Whitechapel Hospital. But it was only after
several days that the man slowly began to recover his
senses, and some patches of his memory – and also, gentlemen, his *voice*. For, you see, it was partly because the man
was suffering so badly from what we medical men term
suppurative tonsilitis – the quinsy, as it is commonly known
– that he was transferred to St Thomas's where, as you know,
Holmes, I am at present engaged in some research on that
very subject, and where my own professional opinion was
sought only this morning. Whilst reading through the man's
hospital notes, I could see that the only clue to his identity was a tag on an item of his underclothing carrying

the initials "H.D." You can imagine my excitement— '

'Humphry Davy, perhaps,' muttered Mycroft flippantly.

'Oh no!' I replied, with a smile. 'I persisted patiently with the poor man, and finally he was able to communicate to me the name of his bank. After that, if I may say so, Holmes, it was almost child's play to verify *my* hypothesis. I visited the bank, where I learned about the withdrawal of money for the honeymoon, and the manager himself accompanied me back to St Thomas's where he was able to view the patient and to provide quite unequivocal proof as to his identity. I have to inform you, therefore, that not only does Mr Horatio Darvill exist, gentlemen; he is at this precise moment lying in a private ward on the second floor of St Thomas's Hospital!'

For some little while a silence fell upon the room. Then I saw Holmes, who these last few minutes had been standing by the window, give a little start: 'Oh, no!' he groaned. And looking over his shoulder I saw, dimly beneath the fog-beshrouded lamplight, an animated Mr Wyndham talking to a legal-looking gentleman who stood beside him.

Snatching up his cape, Holmes made hurriedly for the door. 'Please tell Mr Wyndham, if you will, Watson, that I have already written a letter to him containing a complete recantation of my earlier charges, and offering him my profound apologies. For the present, I am leaving – by the back door.'

He was gone. And when, a minute later, Mrs Hudson announced that two angry-looking gentlemen had called asking to see Mr Holmes, I noticed Mycroft seemingly asleep once more in his corner armchair, a monograph on polyphonic plainchant open on his knee, and a smile of vague amusement on his large, intelligent face.

'Show the gentlemen in, please, Mrs Hudson!' I said – in such peremptory fashion that for a moment or two that good lady stared at me, almost as if she had mistaken my voice for that of Sherlock Holmes himself.

Tumbril Thighs

David Fletcher

They were filling in the 'drowning' pond. My sense of
relief on seeing this was so great that I began to shake.
I nearly caused an accident, hitting the brake pedal too
hard, without warning. The pond lies hard by the A605,
just where the new bypass begins. The driver behind me
accelerated, overtook me, blaring his horn and raising two
angry fingers. I was shaking all over, but I realised that I
did not want to stop and look. It was enough that they were
filling it in. I felt that it would be inviting bad luck to stop,
to permit myself a smile of relief. I drove very carefully into
town.

My mother's Bradstone-clad retirement home seemed
more unwelcoming than ever. There were unthinkable
weeds in the narrow flower borders. Inside, though, nothing
was changed and there was no film of dust or musty smell.
The nice woman I had met at the funeral, Mrs Elphick,
had been in to dust and air the place. Her note included
details of how to use the microwave. There was food in the
freezer.

I wandered around, unable to face any of the tasks
I had come to perform. Especially, I did not want to
touch her clothes. The estate agent was not coming until
ten the next morning. I had not fixed a definite time with

the auctioneer and valuer, had said that I would call in some time during the day, when convenient. There would be time. On impulse, I went out again and drove to the other end of town. The big, always empty supermarket there is run by Pakistanis now – a fact deplored by Mother – which means that the shop is apparently always open. I bought a bottle of Scotch and went back to the house to drink it and to face the reality that it was all over, at last.

We used to live, my parents and I, in a little hamlet about three-quarters of a mile as the crow flies from the pond. For many years I did not understand why we lived there. It was a dismal place, 'off the beaten track', as my mother put it. A scattering of five houses loosely grouped around the dead end of a cul-de-sac. Across the fields which began at the end of this lane, lay the pond, the road and, two miles further on, the town.

We had very little money. This was my father's fault. He worked as a clerk with the local water board. My mother's money, a mysterious, precious, fiercely protected sum emanating from some family trust, the true nature of which was not revealed even by her will, was set aside for my schooling and her 'little runabout'. As a result of this, we were that rare phenomenon of the time, a two-car family. Everyone else in the hamlet, except the farmer who worked the fields roundabout, travelled on bicycles or caught the twice weekly bus.

I came to believe, years later, that we lived there so that my mother could preserve an illusion of superiority. Funds were such that had we lived in town or even in one of the larger villages nearby, our threadbare life-style would have fooled no one. In almost complete privacy, in a community of farm labourers, our two cars and lined curtains, my father's white-collar job and my vaunted public school education set my mother apart, enabled her to indulge her austere snobbery behind a façade of being well-off. Indeed, in comparison to our neighbours, we *were*. They probably imagined that we dined off silver salvers and drank fine wines. Certainly the only one I ever got to know, Elise, used to say to me: 'You're rich. I knows. You're dead posh, you are. I wish I was rich and could be posh like what you are.'

At the age of thirteen, I became a boarder at a minor, a very minor, public school in Buckinghamshire. It was the best, I was assured, that my mother's money could buy. This, too, was my father's fault. It meant that I had to work harder to obtain my birthright. I was left in no doubt that nothing less than an Exhibition to Oxford would satisfy my mother. When I returned, miserable and even more lonely, for the Christmas holidays, Elise said, clapping her hand dramatically to her heart, 'My God, what a scare you give me. I thought you was dead.'

The shocking pink, fuzzy wool of her homemade sweater, squashed by her clutching hand, made me aware of her breasts for the first time. Shivering in my old school sweater, a size too small for me, my knees blue with the cold beneath my shorts, I tried to explain about boarding school. I didn't get very far. Mother called from the front room window and I ran inside, grateful and sad, the memory of that strange, magical pulp beneath Elise's sweater wobbling in my head. I was told, of course, that I must not talk to her.

'They only want to know our business,' Mother insisted. 'They are not our kind of people.'

Who were our people? I knew that they were 'cultured, moneyed' people, for that was drummed into me from a very early age, but for me their dominant quality was their elusiveness. I simply never met any. At my 'kindergarten', Mother was always on hand to use the fact that we lived 'so far out' or 'at the back of beyond' to excuse me from Timothy's birthday party or some other children's celebration. One had to reciprocate hospitality and that meant affording people an opportunity to pry into our business. This was, perhaps, my mother's abiding fear.

When I went away to school, I became, in a sense,

beyond Mother's control, except that one of the many dicta dinned into me was that I was never, ever, under any circumstances to accept an invitation to visit another boy's home. I was, under pain of death, never to issue even the most casual and indefinite invitation of my own.

Consequently, I never wove that thread which connects one's school social life to one's home. I was lonely before I went away to school but that did not seem to matter so much. There were always ways round that. Sufficient boys lived within walking or bicycling distance for us to meet on neutral ground and wile away the empty hours of the school holidays. At my boarding school, the situation became much worse. Such friends as I made went off to distant worlds and, thanks to my mother's prohibitions, friendships inevitably flagged each summer, every Christmas. And by then I had lost any real contact with my former friends.

I was deeply unhappy at school and yet I preferred it to home. Even bullying and almost constant embarrassment is better in a way than constant boredom and the dangerous, silent tension between my parents. Perhaps it was to escape this misery that I got involved with Francis at all.

Francis. It seemed, even then, a curiously soft and inappropriate name for a boy who would, today, have been termed 'macho'. Francis Williams had been on the periphery of my life forever. We never spoke. We never played together, but he was there.

The Williamses were one of my mother's favourite topics of conversation. They represented the lowest form of human life. They lived, the whole teeming horde of them, in a ramshackle cottage in a spinney about half a mile away. You had to pass close by it to get to the pond and the A605. The unfenced yard, hacked from the spinney, source of winter fuel, was littered with old farm machinery, engine parts, rusty vans, the whole festively buntinged by a full line of washing. A fire usually glowed and smoked in some corner of the yard.

Savage-looking dogs prowled on the ends of frayed ropes.

According to Mother, Mrs Williams was a diddicoy and Mr Williams little better. He was a poacher and a thief, a dealer in dubious goods. She went potato-picking and took in washing. They had an astonishing number of children, though Francis was the only one who ever impinged on me.

He was always tall, raggedly dressed, with very dark hair and eyes which followed me from a distance without modesty or embarrassment. Whereas I stole furtive glances, Francis stared, looked, reacted and seemed to smirk to himself. He wore hobnail boots – a sure sign of poverty, lack of culture and 'commonness' in my mother's book – of which I was irrationally but mortally afraid. ·

The school holidays always began, after my mother's inquisition on my report and my doings, with the inevitable catalogue of the Williamses' latest misdeeds. So it must have been that summer of my fourteenth year. She announced that Francis had come to work for the farmer at the end of our hamlet, adding, 'We'll soon see how long *that* lasts.'

This 'news' had no significance for me. At the time, I barely took it in. But I do remember how I met Francis, so to speak, for the first time and because of that I can recall Mother's announcement of his job.

My mother had gone into town. It must have been in recognition of my new maturity, advertised by a sudden increase in height and the relief of long trousers the year round, that she had not made me go with her. I had gone down to the gate, perhaps to look out for her, perhaps because I was made anxious by her unaccustomed absence, and Elise came by, toiling up the dusty lane in high-heeled shoes. She wore a skirt stiff with petticoats and a sweater which clung even tighter to her ever-growing breasts. Her tow-blonde hair had been home-permed and was held back from her pale, pudgy face by two gaudy, unmatching hair slides. She grinned at me. She said it was hot. She put down the battered black plastic 'bucket' bag she was carrying and removed a stone from her scuffed shoe. She wore no stockings.

'You're home again then, eh?'

'Yes.'

'You still at that school away, then?'

'Yes.'

'I'm working now. I've got a job.'

'That's nice.'

'I wouldn't mind weeks and weeks of holiday like you.'

I had nothing to say to this, would have traded them with her willingly.

'I works at the mushroom factory,' she confided. 'Packing.'

I knew the mushroom factory, a collection of old, prefabricated huts about a mile from the pond. It had always been there. According to my mother, all the girls and women who worked there were loose. They were noted for it. I looked at Elise with renewed interest.

'Well,' she said, 'I'd best be off. Mam'll have me tea on.'

''Bye,' I said with some relief.

'See you around.'

She walked slowly on up the road. I watched her, marvelling at her unequal struggle with those impossible heels. At some point I heard the plodding sound of a horse's hooves but I thought nothing of it. Elise disappeared from view. The clopping sound ceased, then started up again, came closer. Francis appeared around the screen of the high hedge which protected our six stunted apple trees, leading a piebald plough horse. It was too late for me to duck out of sight. I remained at the gate, staring fixedly at the horse's fringed feet.

'How do.' The horse stopped. I had to raise my eyes. Francis was taller than ever, his hair black, his skin tanned, exaggerating his supposed gypsy blood. 'I'm going to turn him out,' he volunteered as though I had asked what he was doing with the horse. 'Want to come?'

This surprised me so much that I blinked and blurted out, 'Where?'

'Just down the lane. The field with the big chestnut in it.'

The field he meant was no more than a couple of hundred yards from where I stood. I could think of no reason why I should not go with him. I could go because my mother was not at home. I opened the gate.

'All right.'

I walked along beside Francis, the smell of the tired horse strong in my nostrils. Too late, I realised I should have asked why he wanted me to accompany him. I had, after all, inherited some of my mother's suspicion of others' motives.

'You're Simon,' he said. Unlike him, I was well named. 'Simple' Simon he sometimes called me.

'And you're Francis.'

'That's it.'

We walked to the field gate in silence. I stood aside, hands in my pockets and watched him open the gate. What if my mother should come beetling along in her car and see me? Suddenly, I didn't care. I moved forward and grabbed the gate, held it closed while Francis, murmuring softly to the horse, slipped its halter and slapped it on the rump. It whinnied and trotted off, delighting in its sudden freedom and rest. Francis laughed, turning towards me with all his white teeth showing.

'Look at him go,' he said, for now the horse had broken into a canter. 'That's the life, ennit, boy?' he called to the animal. I pushed the gate to let him through, watched as he fastened it with a loop of old binder twine.

'She fancies you. You could do all right there.' He spoke softly, conspiratorially, his head down, watching the movements of his hands.

'Pardon?'

'You heard.' He grinned at me. 'Elise. She fancies you.'

Blushing, I asked, 'How do you know?'

'Because she told me, stupid. Not that she needed to. It's clear as day to them as has eyes.'

I could think of nothing to say to this. I believed him. It made a kind of sense. Elise had always, even when I was little, created opportunities to speak to me, to smile and wave. I had, though, only the vaguest idea of what 'fancying' someone meant. Thinking this, I blushed deeper.

'You want to meet up with us later?'

I glanced at Francis in surprise. We were walking back up the lane. He swung the halter lightly, rhythmically in his left hand.

'Who?' I asked, bewildered.

'You. And me. I goes home for me tea at six. I usually goes for a bit of a stroll after. About seven. Down by the pond. You want to come?'

How could I say 'no'? How could I possibly say 'yes'? I did not go out after supper, not out of the garden anyway. I remembered Francis's boots and how I had been afraid of them. I remembered a précis of all the tales I had ever heard about the wicked, shiftless Williamses. This time I managed to voice my suspicions.

'What for?'

'*For* nothing,' he said. 'Nothing else to do is there? We could have a chat and a laugh.'

Now I wanted to ask, 'Why me?', but I heard a car behind us, turning into the lane. I looked at Francis and shook my head.

'I won't eat you,' he said. 'Cut my throat and hope to die.' He drew his dirty fingernail across his throat and I saw for the first time the length of leather thong about his neck, like a licorice bootlace, and something odd and slightly unpleasant hanging from it, resting against his chest in the V of his open-necked shirt.

'All right,' I said, a sudden thrill of excitement making the words sound breathless, my voice girlish. I blushed again. Francis nodded once and strode off, swinging the halter. I wanted to shout after him, 'If I can . . . ' But the car was close now and I recognised the familiar chug of its elderly engine.

'You weren't talking to that awful Williams boy, were you, Simon?'

'No, Mother.'

I helped her unload the car.

My father played some part in what followed. Usually he hovered on the very edge of my life, despised by my mother for his 'lowly' position and inadequate earning power, overlooked by me because he made little impression, did not stand up to my mother. After supper that evening, though, when I announced, as casually as I knew how, with every pore actually oozing guilt, that I thought I would go for a walk, my father spoke up on my behalf.

'Whatever for?' Mother snapped, suspicion dancing like a radiance around her head.

'Let the boy stretch his legs, dear,' Father said, passively from the depths of his chair. 'It's a fine evening.'

I think her surprise may have been as great as my own. Her sharp eyes swivelled to him and I felt myself, for a moment, blessedly forgotten. I took advantage of this to slip out into the garden and then onto the dusty road. In minutes I had reached the fields and then I dared to break into a run. I had done it! What's more, there was a purpose in it. For the first time in my life I was going to meet someone of my own volition. I had received and accepted an invitation and Mother knew nothing about it. Therein lay the true excitement, of course.

Later, puffed, nursing a stitch, it seemed less wonderful. Why should Francis Williams bother with me? What did we have in common? As I passed his house at a distance, I began to suspect some trap. I was walking into an ambush, would be beaten, humiliated. In my fevered imagination, Francis became the leader of some terrible gang. I began to feel certain that I was to be the sport of the evening.

I could, I should have turned back but before this idea
had properly formulated in my mind, I had seen Francis
and what is far more important, he had seen me. He was
near the pond, well screened from the road by some scrubby
summer trees. Having seen me, he turned away, stared at the
pond, hands in his pockets. I went up to him, reassured
at least that there was no gang. Whatever I was to suffer
would be at his hands alone.

'Hello,' I said breathlessly, though I had long ago
regained my breath.

'All right?'

'Yes, thank you.'

He grinned at this automatic politeness.

'Fancy a bit of a stroll then?'

'Don't mind,' I said, stuffing my hands in my pockets
to emulate his off-hand, confident manner.

We strolled across the field and climbed a stile. Francis
led the way. Our backs were towards the road. The field
sloped a little. In one corner stood the remains of an old
cow byre. It provided privacy of a kind. Several greying,
mouldering bales of hay served as seats. A stained tarpaulin
lay on the ground in the corner formed by the two remaining walls, protected by a scrap of roof which leaned down
towards us, as though about to crash to the ground at any
minute. Francis offered me a cigarette and looked, or so I
flattered myself, impressed when I took one and smoked
it without coughing. Smoking was one of the few vices I
knew. Emboldened by this success, I asked, 'What's that
thing around your neck?'

He looked down at his chest, picked the pendant up
and examined it.

'This?'

'Yes.'

He leaned towards me, holding it against the flat of
his palm.

'Crocodile's tooth.'

I was impressed. It was an ugly, yellowed thing. I think,

probably, it was from a dog rather than a crocodile, but I had no wish to challenge Francis's statement.

'Touch it,' he said. I did so. 'It's a lucky charm,' he said. 'Wards off evil spirits and brings good luck.'

For once, he sounded like a child and a gypsy. I shuddered in spite of the warmth of the evening.

'Where did you . . . ?' I began, but Francis interrupted me.

'Looks like it works for you, anyway,' he said, grinning. 'Here comes your luck now.'

I turned round. Elise was making her unsteady way towards us, arms flapping to aid her balance.

I don't remember what was said. My habitual embarrassment was increased a hundredfold by what Francis had told me earlier. She sat, she smoked a cigarette. I suppose she and Francis chatted. Whenever I looked at her, she dimpled at me in a way I found both disturbing and oddly exciting. At some point she stood up and moved to the corner of the building. Francis dug me hard in the ribs.

'Go on,' he said, jerking his head towards the open field. 'Make yourself scarce for a bit.'

'What?'

'Won't be long,' he said, standing. 'Here, take these.' He handed me his cigarettes and matches. 'Won't be long,' he repeated.

I knew and did not know what they were doing behind that flimsy wooden wall. I could have spied on them. There were enough gaps in the warped planks, but I lacked the courage. I knew that they were doing something sexual. I had no precise idea what that something was. Nor, oddly, did I speculate much about it. I was too concerned with a problem of politeness. Should I leave them, make my way home? But then Francis had given me his cigarettes and matches and would expect me to return them. I began to be aware of passing time, imagined my mother's wrath. If she found out I had been with Francis . . . If she were ever to learn about him and Elise . . . I paced up and down beside the hedge, not knowing what to do.

Francis appeared around the building, cinching his belt. I almost ran to him with relief. He grinned at me, cat-like in his satisfaction and amusement.

'Go on, then,' he said. 'Your turn.' I stared at him, my mouth slack. I had been going to say that it was late, I must return home. He took his cigarettes from my hand, lit one. 'Go on,' he repeated and gave me a little shove.

My feet moved by instinct. I crept around the corner of the building. Elise lay on the tarpaulin, in the corner, partially screened from my immediate view by the bales. She smiled at me in that soppy, moist way of hers.

'Come on,' she said. 'Come here. I wants you to.'

I did not know until that moment that girls had pubic hair. It was a shocking discovery. What I remember most, though, were her thighs. Great, white rolls of unexpected flesh. The white of dead fish. The word 'tumbril' came into my head. I've never known why. I don't think, at the time, I even knew the meaning of the word, but it lodged there in my head. I chanted it over and over as, at her behest, I knelt between those very thighs while she twitched and fiddled with my clothing, pulled me down on top of her.

It was, inevitably, a matter of moments. Afterwards, she stroked my hair and said, 'I really likes you. You're gentle, you are, Simon.'

I think I grunted something about having to go home. As I was fastening my trousers, I became aware of Francis leaning against the wall, smiling.

'I've got to go now.'

'All right.'

''Bye,' said Elise.

I think I answered her. Francis walked me back across the field.

'All right?' he asked.

'Yes.'

'Want a fag?'

'No, thanks.'

'Enjoy it, did you?'

'Yes. Thanks.'

'That's all right then. I'll see you around.'

'Yes.'

Once over the stile, I began to run.

It continued more or less like that all summer. I developed a taste for it, Francis said.

I credited my father with the fact that my mother seldom opposed my evening and Sunday walks, or asked too many questions about them. Out of gratitude, I tried to be as she wanted during the day, helping her about the house, listening to her endless diatribes and complaints. My heart stopped when she informed me, 'That awful Jennings girl has turned into a real little trollop.' She meant Elise, of course. 'To no one's surprise, I'm sure,' she added with a toss of the head. 'You steer clear of girls like that.' I promised.

I tried to think of Elise as a trollop but when I was with her my mother's comments and warnings seemed hollow and remote, frozen in another, irrelevant time. We met two, often three times a week, Francis, Elise and I. Francis no longer sent me away when he coupled with Elise. He, in his turn, sat smiling to watch us. Elise made no secret of her preference for me and Francis, apparently, never took offence. But then, Elise never denied him 'his turn', either. I assumed that that was all that mattered to him.

One night, Elise failed to appear. It was then that Francis announced, 'You've got a taste for it, boy. I knew you would.'

I asked anxiously where Elise was.

'She won't be coming tonight. She's got the curse.'

Francis explained this enigma to me, reassured me that it was not our fault. In those evenings without Elise my practical sexual education was fleshed out with theory. I returned to school with a new confidence, with an amazing secret hugged to me like a magic charm, my crocodile's tooth. And I left home with a pang of regret. A totally selfish one, I admit, but that did not prick my conscience.

I enjoyed that term. I was knowledgeable. I hinted at sexual prowess. I instructed the ignorant and loftily corrected the inaccurate. I developed a sense of self, a certain reputation. I was no longer bullied. Work suddenly came easily to me. My report that term was excellent. Mother beamed and bought fancy new lights for the Christmas tree. It was by their glow, through the uncurtained window, that I saw Elise again, peering over our hedge. When she saw me, that strange, soppy smile appeared on her face again. Under the pretence of emptying a waste-paper basket, I snatched a few words with her. Our disappointment was great and mutual, but there was no way my mother would countenance anyone going for walks in the dark.

It was the Sunday before Christmas that I next met Elise, beside the pond. I blush to recall that my first words were, 'Where's Francis?'

'In bed with the flu. Come on.' She tugged my hand. 'Oh I have missed you.'

In the cold and damp we did it standing up, Elise braced against the wall of the byre. I warmed my hands on her breasts, beneath her thick sweater. She held my cold buttocks, pulling me against her tumbril thighs. Afterwards, she told me she loved me.

'I don't like that old Francis no more,' she confided, hooking her arm through mine. 'He's not like you. You're ever so clean,' she said, in a rush of enthusiasm. 'And your skin's that soft . . . '

As I recall this now, I realise that my greatest crime was that I never once considered Elise as a human being, a fellow creature. It seems obvious now, of course, that if I had . . . She was a moist, sloppy grin, a speaker of embarrassing, gushing, sentimental words. She was the source of utterly selfish sexual pleasure, the owner of 'tumbril thighs'.

Forgive me, Elise, wherever you are.

The new year had begun when Francis emerged from his sick bed with a hacking cough and dark, bruise-like marks under his eyes. We met, as usual, by the pond and he seemed genuinely pleased to see me, insisted on shaking my hand and clapping me on the back. I felt a rush of real pleasure at this, more intense than anything, except for the act itself, I ever felt with Elise.

We walked against the cold and talked of her. I assumed she had the curse again. Emboldened by my new confidence, I told Francis that she had gone off him. He laughed.

'You don't want to take no notice of her,' he said. 'She's just trying to get you.' According to Francis, my absence had been marked by no cooling in their relationship, no diminution in sexual activity. Instead of feeling a pang of jealousy or disappointment as, presumably, Elise would have wished, I was relieved. I was pleased for Francis, pleased for myself because without him the relationship seemed incomplete.

On the Sunday before I returned to school we all three met up again. Nothing had changed except that, afterwards, Elise wept and clung to me, begged me to write to her, insisted that she loved me and would be lost without me. I was almost ill with embarrassment. I felt humiliated in front of Francis. I stared miserably at him, my cheeks burning.

'You'd best get along,' he said, jerking his head towards my home. 'I'll see to her.'

My relief and gratitude were enormous. I lingered long enough to see him put a comforting arm around her, to see her head rest against his chest. He spoke to her, low, soothing words I could not hear. He jerked his head again, telling me to make myself scarce.

If Elise was going to behave like that, I thought, as I ran

home, my breath puffing in the air like winter dandelion clocks, I'd rather stay away from her. Perhaps I had already outgrown this tripartite yet singular relationship. Whatever, I had no regrets.

That term I received a letter from my father. It was the first of six short notes that made up our entire correspondence. It was wrapped around another, smaller manilla envelope with my name printed boldly on it. It read:

> Dear Simon,
>
> A boy gave me this for you. I thought it best to send it on at once, without consulting your mother. I don't think you need mention it at all, to either of us.
> Mother and I are well and trust you are having a good term.
>
> Your loving Father.

The other envelope contained a letter from Francis. I was staggered by my father's courage and duplicity. I wrote him a careful reply. I wanted to tell him how grateful I was, how much I appreciated the enormity of what he had done, but I could say nothing. I hope he understood some of what I could not express, but he never mentioned either letter. My mother did, in a long, angry, pained letter demanding to know why I wrote to my father and not her. I was an ingrate, a viper in her bosom . . . That letter upset me, but it was as nothing compared to Francis's terse message.

> Bad news. Elise is expecting. She says it's yours. She is going to make trouble if something isn't done. Can you come home early? When you come we must talk. Your friend, F.W.

I did not know his address and he had not written it at the top of the letter. What could I have replied anyway? I tried to think of a way of getting sent home early, but nothing practical came to me. I tore both letters into tiny pieces and flushed them down the lavatory. The term dragged and yet, in no time at all, I was home. My mother still had not forgiven me for my lack, as she saw it, of love and loyalty. My father said nothing.

It was a cold spring and the nights were still long. I saw Francis on my first morning home and stole a few minutes with him in the lane. We met again that night, as soon as he had finished work, while Mother was preoccupied with the making of supper. Time was short. We sheltered from the rain at the back of the barn which marked the end of the hamlet. Our view was down across the fields to the pond, the byre, scene of all our troubles.

Elise was frantic, he told me, mad. He had persuaded her not to come marching up to my front door, but I had to see her soon.

'You'll have to get out,' he said. 'Tomorrow for sure.'

'All right,' I said. 'But what can I do?'

'I don't know.' He squeezed my shoulder. 'We'll think of something. We'll bloody have to.' Then, with a strange tenderness, he added, 'Don't you fret. It'll be all right.'

'But why me?' I asked. I wanted to add, 'I'm only a kid . . . ' but something in his face prevented me.

'Because she thinks you lot are rich. She fancies you. I always told you that. Now she's got herself knocked up she's trying to make the best of a bad job.'

'I'm only sixteen,' I wailed.

'Yes,' he said, and grinned. 'And you can get married at sixteen.'

That was the worst night of my life so far. Many worse were to follow, but I did not know it then. Such little sleep as I got was haunted by nightmares of Elise, her weeping, smiling face, her solid, white thighs. I saw myself manacled to her, drowning in her, crushed in the vise of those tumbril thighs.

Twice I resolved to throw myself on the mercy of my

parents, by which I meant my mother. Coldly, but with
deep dread, I recognised that my mother had no mercy.
My father then? I doubted that he had sufficient reserves
of power to stand against my mother's inevitable anger.
Besides, he would be as angry and as pained as she. I could
blame it all on Francis, of course, swear that I had never
touched Elise. At this thought I felt a real and numbing
shame. I could not let Francis take the blame. I knew he
was not to blame. By dawn I had realised that he was the
only friend and ally I had. I prayed, my fingers locked and
clenched together so hard that bone bruised against bone,
that Francis should be inspired to think of something.

The tumbril thighs reappeared in my dawn dreams,
filling me with a shrivelling disgust. I woke late, with
a sort of cold fever chilling my bones. I felt myself a
condemned man. Unless Francis could save me.

The row with my mother that evening seems totally
unimportant now. At the time, it sent me trembling out
into the rain. I think I just walked out, leaving her to turn
her wrath on my father.

I have not said much about the pond, I realise, have
I suppose been avoiding it even now. It wasn't much of
a pond, served no purpose. The sloping fields around
drained into it, presumably were its source. Spindly trees
grew up around it. The hedge which separated it from the
road had grown with neglect into a sort of sparse thicket.
It was weed-infested in summer, dank-smelling, uninviting.
After twenty-four hours of steady rain, it had become deeper
and blacker than I had ever seen it. Arriving early, I sought
what shelter I could beneath the trees and watched the rain
pit its surface. I chain-smoked soggy cigarettes.

I felt numb when I saw Elise coming hesitantly across the
field, her wellington boots slipping in the mud. Francis was
with her, supporting her and I felt this as a terrible betrayal.
I almost ran for it. Let them do their worst, I thought.

She had a wet headscarf tied over her hair. It made

her face look larger, naked and blank. I did not consider whether it was rain or tears that made her face wet. What I remember most is her sullen stubbornness. Francis, though, had done his best for me.

'I see as how you can't marry me,' she said, sniffing, 'but you'll have to give me some money.'

Francis stood aside and a little behind her, chewing at his thumb, his black hair plastered to his head. He would not meet my eyes.

'He says,' Elise went on, indicating Francis, 'as I should have it done away with but I won't. That's wrong. But I shall have to have money to keep it. My Dad can't help me. We haven't got two ha'pennies to rub together as it is. You'll have to get it for me. A lump sum or weekly, I don't mind.'

She grew angry when I pointed out that she was working, tore her coat open to show me the accusing swelling.

'How can I work like this? I'm sick every morning. I feels dreadful. How can I work?'

In vain, I pleaded that we were not rich. In desperation I confessed that my mother would rather kill me than pay for this child.

'How do you know it's me?' I concluded, looking at Francis who seemed to have deserted me.

'Because I do. Girls know. They always knows. And you can call me a liar and anything you likes,' she screeched, advancing on me and jabbing her finger at my chest, 'but you won't wriggle out of it. Now answer me straight. Are you going to get the money?'

'No. I can't.'

'Right then. I shall go and see your mother now. She'll give it me sure enough, to shut me up and save her precious Simon from scandal.'

She turned on her heel, pulling her flapping coat around her.

'No,' I said and stumbled after her, grabbing her shoulder. My touch sent her slightly off-balance. With a shriek she slipped, one booted foot entering the water.

'Now look what you've done,' she said. Some mud from the pond's edge had splashed her coat. Hitching the skirt up she rubbed at the marks. I was aware of Francis then, beside me, facing her. 'Help us up,' she said, holding out her hand, one foot braced on the comparatively secure ground of the bank, the other slipping deeper into the pond. Francis thrust out his hands like a blind man and pushed her. She shrieked again, pathetically, her arms rotating like windmills, and then she toppled backwards into the pond.

All the violence I had sensed in Francis as a boy exploded. He jumped in after her, bent down, I thought at first to lift her beneath the arms. I remembered his hobnailed boots and the wide berth I had instinctively given them. I remembered how afraid I had been of him.

He did lift her. Somehow he got his hands into her armpits and raised her, but not to rescue her. Despite her screams and her flailings, he managed to drag her, with a staggering, stiff-legged gait, deeper into the water. And deeper. Suddenly she was silent. The thrashing in the water blended with the sound of the rain. Francis was up to his thighs. The water gave off a foetid stink of old, disturbed mud, of rotted vegetation. I saw his face, twisted white towards me.

'Help me. Don't just stand there. Bloody help me.'

I obeyed him without thinking. I ran into the water, lost my footing and fell, fell across her thighs. Her legs stopped thrashing. I could hear it then, those gurgling, bubbling sounds of breath expelled beneath water, of drowning. She became still. Unbidden, I struggled to a kneeling position, watery mud sliding down my front. Francis grunted, dragging her deeper and deeper. I got up and waded back towards the bank, slipped and fell down again. I did not watch the rest of it. I crawled out of the pond and pulled myself up by the trunk of the nearest tree against which I leaned. I was crying.

I don't know how long it took. I don't know where he finally left her. I was trembling with the cold, almost sick with the smell of that mud. Francis was a shadow beside me.

'You're not crying, are you?'

'No.' I shook my head and wiped my face, leaving streaks of mud across it. I looked up at him, at his white, glazed face. His eyes burned into mine.

'You best get off home,' he said. I nodded, looked down at my ruined clothes. 'You understand, don't you? We mustn't ever meet again, you and me?' His voice was harsh.

I didn't understand. I looked at him but do not know how I looked to him.

'It's the only way,' he said gently. 'We won't ever meet again. Understand?' He reached out and shook me by the shoulders.

'Yes.'

'That's it then.' He let his hands fall. I couldn't leave. He blocked my way, staring at me, searching my face for something he seemed to need desperately. I swallowed, opened my mouth.

'What . . . ?'

He bent down and kissed me, full on the open mouth. I pushed him away as hard as I could and began to run. I can still taste his tongue.

The morning after I discovered they were filling in the pond, I put Mother's clothes into plastic bags with a mounting distaste at touching things that had been so close to her skin. I did not allow myself to think about it except to reflect that my actions made a sorry counterpart to her agonised, planned disposal of my father's wardrobe when he died.

I saw the estate agent and made satisfactory arrangements. A young woman accompanied me back to the house and agreed to take all the furniture and fittings, except for a little cake-stand that Mrs Elphick chose, blushing and biting back tears. They all commiserated with me and said they understood. I wanted to say, 'But I'm free at last. They're filling in the pond.'

I ran a very hot bath and soaked in it, dozed when they had gone, much as I had done that night. I had locked the door and jammed a chair under the handle as an extra precaution. Mother wept and shouted, pleaded and hectored outside. Father tried to calm her, reason with her. In the bath, I concocted a story about slipping, about falling into the pond, to explain my ruined clothing. I did not even consider that this would tie me to the scene of the crime when Elise's body was found.

When my story was more or less ready, I climbed out and dumped all my filthy clothing into the water, wrapped a towel around myself and opened the door. I told my tale and went to bed, shivering. Apparently, Mother was up half the night, trying to salvage my clothes. The next day the doctor came. I had a cold, a fever. I remained in bed for the rest of the holidays, making a sudden, miraculous recovery two days before I was due back at school. Mother was barely able to speak to me, but she could not resist her monologues, addressed now to a point above my head, or to my father at supper-time.

'Oh there's no doubt about it. I heard it from that dreadful gossip of a postmistress. I wonder the post office employ such people. It's my belief she steams open the letters. Anyway, swears that Williams boy, the one that used to work at the farm, has run off with the Jennings girl. Apparently the mother knew she was in the family way. They've run off together. Of course, they'll be back. Where could they go? How can they survive? They can barely read and write. Animals, both of them. Mind you, with their upbringing, what can you expect? I just hope it will be a lesson to some people who've been brought up to respect themselves and others, given the benefits of a first-class education. . . . '

When I had finished my bath in my mother's empty house, I drank the remaining whisky and slept like a man who had not rested properly for many years.

*

It would, in fact, have been more convenient to take the bypass out of town at the start of my journey home, but I chose not to. I wanted to see the drowning pond again, to see it filled in and levelled over, finished. There were a number of vehicles parked beside the road, most of them painted the distinctive yellow and blue of the County Council. From some distance I could see the raw stumps of newly felled trees and the upraised, toothed scoop of a mechanical digger, orange against the bright sky. It took a moment, several, for the truth to sink in, the meaning of the digger to become apparent. I parked, without realising it, next to a police car and got out, walked back towards the pond. They were not filling it in. They were making it deeper.

'Excuse me, sir . . . '

The policeman was tall as all policemen are, but middle-aged and kindly. I mumbled that no, I had no business here, had just wondered what was going on. He seemed tolerant of gawpers and bystanders, even happy to give information. Other policemen were busy putting up tape, traffic cones. The top brass, he informed me, rocking as policemen are supposed to do on the balls of his feet, were due any minute.

'What's going on?' I asked.

'Found a skellington,' he said, conversationally, but enjoying the drama of this statement, his own lack of shock. He pointed to a tarpaulined heap at the side of the pond, between the beige stumps of two trees. The knob of a white bone stuck out from it. 'Female, apparently, though bless me how they can tell. Been there for years,' he said, shaking his head.

'I thought they were filling it in,' I said.

'No. Farmer chappy decided to tidy it up at last, clean it out. Eyesore, it was. Environment boys been on to him, I shouldn't wonder. And the Council.' He had to shout this last information over the roar of the digger which bucked and dipped, grovelled its snout in the mud at the bottom of the pond. 'Smells a bit and all,' the policeman remarked.

The digger made a terrible sucking noise, lurched, backed, belching diesel fumes. The scoop came up, mud and white bones sliding from it. Shouts. The policeman ran forward to join his comrades who were gesticulating, yelling at the driver of the digger. The scoop froze some six feet above the ravaged pond. The engine roar settled to a pervasive putter.

'Hold it there,' someone shouted. The man in the cab of the digger called some reply and then, in exasperation, climbed down, demanding to know, 'What now?'

A bone – I thought it was probably an arm bone – slid from the ooze in the scoop and plopped loudly into the water. I went to the tape, grasped it in both hands as though it could give me support, twisting it between my sweating fingers. More ooze slid, black and sickly, from the scoop, revealing a perfect, skeletal head. The policemen fell back. One laughed nervously. The driver, rounding the edge of the pond, saw the cause of this delay. He stopped in his tracks, blinking. The digger, its powerful engine still running, was vibrating and this loosened its deadly load. More mud slid from it, plopping back into the pond. The skeletal head slipped forward, poised, the shoulder bones slightly exposed. I stared in fascination, but not at the empty eye-sockets which seemed to be directed straight at me. What held my gaze and made me feel an emotion I cannot describe or name, was a dangling, half-rotted length of leather thong, like a bootlace. It must have been caught somehow in the vertebrae at the back of the skeleton's neck. At the end of it, swinging in the breeze, was a large, yellow tooth. A crocodile's tooth.

Suddenly, the whole load pitched forward, taking the thong and the tooth with it, back into the pond. I heard the wail of an approaching police siren and turned back to my own car.

I was weeping.

The Moon Was To Blame

Antonia Fraser

Isabel said afterwards that we were really getting too old for that sort of thing: which remains perhaps the best verdict on the whole sad affair. Unless you take the line – as my wife did – that the moon was to blame.

They've never found out who did it: just some ugly little incident among a lot of drunken campers. Since clearly none of us was involved, they let us go and back we all came to England. Not immediately: that would have looked odd since we'd rented an expensive villa, but a little sooner than planned. You could hardly blame us for cutting short our holiday by a few days. A death on the beach below, police crawling all over the place, *Greek* police what's more: not that we put it like that to the charming young woman in the villa rental office, given that she *was* a Greek. In any case she was most understanding. Especially as we showed no signs of asking for a reduction in the rent.

Obviously none of us four was involved: how could we be involved, up in that great big villa on the rock? How could a smart villa party of well-off married people from London be involved with some little scrubber camping down below? Different worlds. Utterly different worlds. Quite soon, the police took that line too.

The world of the campers below was not only a different

world, but a pretty horrible one to boot. Crowds – there must have been nearly fifty of them down there – and squalor naturally, since there was no sanitation beyond the natural shade of the olive trees, those graceful trees whose leaves had flickered so exquisitely in the sunlight on the day we arrived, when the beach was still empty.

'Do you realise that apart from anything else, apart from the noise, ye gods, the noise, we hardly slept a wink last night, did we, Isabel? – Do you realise that it's *illegal?*' That was Nick. Isabel nodded vigorously; she always agreed strongly with everything that Nick said in public. (In private, since the villa walls were not entirely soundproof, we were aware that matters were somewhat different.) But my wife, Dinah, did murmur to me afterwards in that light voice of hers – the one she uses for her really snaky remarks – that it was wonderful to have Nick standing up for the law here on the tiny island of Bexi, it really must be the effect of the sun, since back on the great big island of Britain, Nick sometimes took rather a different line about the law. . . .

But I had better begin at the beginning. No, not at the very beginning, not from our very first business enterprise; suffice it to say that the four of us, Dinah and myself, Nick and Isabel, had become close enough over the years to take villas together in sunny foreign parts over a considerable span of time. The Algarve, Italy, Greece (Corfu followed by Paxos), all these have produced comfortable villas, more or less, and happy holidays, of which the same could probably be said. And frankly a holiday which is more or less happy is way above most holidays you take: which is, I think, why we all persevered with the arrangement.

Did I mention that something else unites us? Beyond the same line of work and living nowadays in the same part of London. We're all childless, or effectively childless. Nick did have a son by his first marriage, I believe, but either the mother kept him to herself or Isabel dumped him – the story varies – at all events he never figures in our lives. As for ourselves, we've certainly never wanted children. We're enough for each other, always have been. I look after Dinah, she looks after me, as we're fond of saying. So that at the age when our contemporaries are spending all their time worrying over their ungrateful twenty-year-olds – and a good deal of their money rescuing them from this, that and the other, also without getting much thanks – we four have the luxury of our time to ourselves. And our money, too, come to think of it.

Douceur de vivre: that's our motto (and yes, it does sound much better in French, but then we four are, I fancy, rather more enlightened in our enjoyment of luxury than the average couples who toast 'the sweet life').

This year we decided to experiment with a lesser island and go to Bexi. An island paradise, said the brochure. And so I suppose it was – in a way. Much less spoilt than Corfu and much nearer to a decent airport than Paxos. Villa Aglaia was pretty near paradise too. At first. Even my wife, who generally finds something to say about the washing arrangements or lack of them, approved the separate showers for each double bedroom, to say nothing of a water supply which actually did not run out. (Remembering that time outside Portofino!) Then the view was so extraordinary, right there on the cliffs; we would look towards Albania at night, and watch the moon rise. A thin crescent the night we arrived – amusing to be drinking retsina again, once the duty free champagne ran out – but rapidly growing.

The moon: yes. Perhaps after all Dinah was right and the moon was to blame. In so far as anyone else was to blame. Certainly the moon appears to have been to blame for what started to happen on the beach. When the first campers appeared – one large grey tent under the olives and one girl who slept under an old boat – we even thought them quite picturesque; the girl anyway. 'The local Samantha Fox' my wife dubbed her on one occasion, since she certainly had the most fantastic figure, the sort you could photograph for Page Three, as we could not help noticing since she seldom wore anything but a bikini bottom.

But 'Samantha Fox' wasn't quite right since Brigitte – that was actually her name – happened to be brown all over, having an amazing tan apart from having an amazing figure. As a matter of fact, I chatted to her quite a bit, in early mornings when no-one else was around, and she was really very polite and friendly. Just a kid working her way around Europe as a waitress, taking a holiday on this beach in between. German probably – or was she Swedish? She had this special feeling about St Peter's, Rome, I remember, the square at St Peter's; she was absolutely determined to see the square. We had quite long talks about it.

Not when the others were around, however. Then, I have to say, the conversation was on a very different level. Well, we were on holiday. There was one famous occasion when Brigitte, topless, wobbled so perilously near Nick, sun-bathing on the stones, on her way to the sea, that my wife and I both involuntarily looked towards Isabel.

The fact is that Isabel, who does sometimes bathe topless (but always discreetly up at the villa), does have the most lovely slim figure, everyone agrees about that. But if Isabel has a fault, it's the fact that, good-looking woman as she is, Isabel is absolutely totally flat-chested. Perhaps that explains why I've never really fancied her, and perhaps that explains again why we've all holidayed so happily together. Be that as it may, on this occasion Isabel merely smiled in her most tranquil manner and murmured something like: 'That she should be so lucky.' Later, in their bedroom, however, I can tell you that it was rather a less tranquil story. What a tigress! That serene, smiling woman. Still the end of it sounded rather satisfactory; at least from Nick's point of view, and I assume Isabel's as well.

All the time, the moon was getting stronger at night; I should say bigger, but was it the increasing strength of the moonlight, rather than the size of the moon itself which was so unsettling? Could you believe moonlight could be so

white? Even when the moon was only half full. That strange
cold ancient light illuminating the sea which washed the
rocks beneath us, the sea stretching out to the Albanian
coast in a vast series of black and silver eddies with that
broad flare path in their centre. We took to sitting later and
later on the terrace with our wine – a light Greek wine, for
after dinner.

'So light, it's like drinking water,' said Nick jovially
on our second night. But of course it wasn't quite like
drinking water, particularly not in the quantities in which
we consumed it. Perhaps it was all that wine late at night
which made us so unsettled. They were odd, quirky, even
slightly sinister, those sessions we had on the terrace. (Yet
hadn't we drunk wine in the Algarve? And Italy? And Paxos
only the year before? The result being mere pleasure,
relaxation . . .) Most unsettling of all, after we finally left
the terrace, my wife and I had to lie, silent and sleepless,
in our bedroom hot behind the shutters and listen to Isabel,
the tigress of the night, who was growing more and more
ferocious in the room alongside ours. Was *that* the wine?
The wine coupled with the moonlight (I noticed they did
not close their shutters). Or was it the noises coming from
the beach?

For the waxing moon brought campers, more and
more campers. And given its provocative light, bathing the
beach in its brightness like a too well-lit stage where there
had been nothing but discreet blackness before, we could
hardly ignore their presence. There was – I can see it now,
and my wife can see it too – a feeling of working towards
some kind of climax, long before we heard the news about
the party.

Besides, one or two fires began to flicker down below:
those fires so dangerous to a wooded island depending on
its olive groves, which was in fact the official reason for
the banning of campers on Bexi. When we went down to
swim in the early morning, we would find the black shells
of night fires among the stones. There would also be cans

of coke, beer and bottles abandoned. And other even more distasteful signs of what had taken place on the beach the night before. Signs of 'safe sex' perhaps, but as my wife observed, wrinkling her nose (I hastily removed one of these signs from her favourite path into the water, burying it under a big cairn of pebbles), 'Safe sex is all very well, but what about a beautiful beach?'

Oddly enough, Brigitte very much kept herself apart from it all. She was friendly enough with the campers – she was a friendly girl, as I've said – but she never joined in with them at their various unpleasant goings on. I know that, because I used to watch her sometimes from the look-out up above, watch her gazing out to sea, smoking the odd cigarette. What was she thinking about? St Peter's Square, Rome, perhaps. Something like that. But I kept all that to myself, just as I never mentioned our morning conversations before the campers came.

At least the Villa Aglaia remained airy and remote from the squalor: in the daytime, when the campers were asleep or away in the little town of Bexi, so long as you did not go down to the beach or visit the look-out, you could cut yourself off from the squalor altogether. My wife cut branches of myrtle from the bushes which lined the steep (but short) path from the villa to the beach and put them everywhere in vases in the big rooms. But as the noise grew in proportion to the number of campers, I asked my wife not to cut back any more of the myrtle: for the bushes did at least conceal the path to the villa. What if the campers, drunk – or drugged, I put nothing past them – all decided to surge up the path in the small hours?

'Then you, darling, will have to be a big he-man and protect me,' said my wife in her snaky voice. 'I somehow don't think Nick and Isabel would notice.'

It was Nick who brought back the news of the party which was going to be held on the beach on the night of the full moon. He had been into the little port in the Land-Rover just before dinner – Isabel was washing her hair – to cash some travellers' cheques. He came back looking white, or as near white as anyone as perfectly cared for and turned out (which means tanned) as Nick can ever look.

'A bloody great notice!' he exploded. 'In English, what's more. Full Moon Party. On Aglaia Beach – our beach. Everyone invited. Bonfires. Dancing. Naked bathing. Come by boat! Come by moped! On the night of the full moon. All this on a notice fixed to a tree just outside the town.' He repeated: 'And in English too.'

'If it hadn't been in English, Nick,' my wife pointed out reasonably enough, 'you wouldn't have understood it.' But Isabel, short, carefully streaked hair in a shining halo, was busy giving Nick a rewarding pat.

'Well done, Nick. At least you've warned us.'

'Warned us! I damn well have. Look, I'm going to have a whisky. Have we got any left? It's a disgrace. Tomorrow I'm going to tell that little Greek girl in the office that I want it stopped, stopped without question.'

'But tomorrow will be too late, Nick,' my wife continued in that same reasonable voice. 'Tonight is the night of the full moon. Didn't you notice last night? Very, very nearly full. Only one tiny sliver missing.'

I must say that I was surprised at the time that my wife had that kind of information at her fingertips; but then I read in one of the magazines you only read in aeroplanes that retaining the capacity to surprise your spouse is the secret of a happy marriage. I dare say that it's Dinah's remarkable sense of order which made her interested in something equally regulated like the phases of the moon.

So we come to the party. I have to admit a certain reluctance in thinking about it all, even now, back in London W11, in our beautiful house, the house which some people laughingly suggest is too big for us – 'too luxurious even for you two' – but is actually a wonderful monument to my wife's exquisite, cool and above all fastidious taste. A showcase for a sense of order, somebody else said.

If that's true about our house, and it probably is, then

you can just about imagine how my poor wife suffered
during that nightmare build-up to the Full Moon Party on
Aglaia Beach. The utter chaos, the noise of course, and the
noise was indescribable, and let me not leave out the fear.
The four of us, four sophisticated people, crouching there
– I'm afraid after a while we were definitely crouching – as
the car lights came towards the beach along the edge of the
cliff, an army advancing on us, and the full moonlight lit
up what went on below. In a way it reminded me of some
medieval picture of Hell – all the couples writhing as though
in torment, their paired limbs gyrating. In fact they were of
course dancing. Dancing and copulating. You would feel
like using that word if you had seen what we saw.

'Supposing they decide to come up here?' Nick said
that, I know he did. 'Just supposing?' Nick is a big man,
very heavily built in spite of all the exercise he takes. We're
both of us big men, come to that, two big men with two
fragile wives, that was another thing we had in common.
Dinah, like Isabel, is wonderfully slender, well preserved
or whatever you call it; naturally she takes marvellous care
of herself. But even Nick sounded frightened. And I was
frightened too.

It was some time after that, that it happened.

'Supposing you went down there? Just supposing.' Who
said that? Who spoke those words? It must have been my
wife, for who else was present when those words were
spoken? Nick and Isabel had gone off to bed at last, their
shutters open to the noises of the hot inflaming night, and
the light of the coldly lustful moon. We could hear that
the tigress was already devouring her huge submissive prey
when those words were spoken.

The excitement comes back to me now, the secret
thrilling fear of it all, and the whispered words which
went on: 'Take her, you want her. She's down there. Find
her and ttake her. You want her, don't you? Take her, you
want her. Take her, you want her.' Take her, you want her,
wanton and naked, wanton and naked, the words became

like a rhythm beating in my brain. Wanton and naked: but
no, these last words were never spoken, even by my wife,
but they too became like a rhythm in my brain.

Those were the words which continued to turn and tumble
in my mind as I went down alone, down the myrtle path
to the Aglaia Beach. It wasn't difficult to find her –
Brigitte, the brown goddess of the beach. She wasn't even
dancing with the others round the fire; she was sitting
by the upturned boat, alone in the dark shadow cast by
the boat; she was smoking one of her cigarettes and looking out to sea. Perhaps she was thinking about Rome and
St Peter's. I rather hope so. I really rather hope she was
thinking about something nice. Even by the boat, the noise
of all the others was incredible, confusing, and they had
transistors now, belting out their dance music across the
moonlit sea, desecrating the moonlight, desecrating the
whole Aglaia Beach.

I took her quite easily. I grabbed her, grabbed that
round brown wobbly body. She was quite little really in
my arms, in spite of her fullness. Much smaller than I
thought she would be. So I took her and held her tight.
She couldn't shout either – not that it would have mattered
much if she had, the noise was so loud, the other people so
busy round the bonfire – all the same I put my hand across
her mouth.

'Now show me you're a man after all, a real man.
Take her.' But she didn't say 'take' this time, she used
something far rougher, cruder. That was my wife's voice
again, she must have followed me down the myrtle path,
but it was a voice so avid, so ferocious, that for a moment
it even might have been the tigress Isabel. And besides
I'd never heard my wife use a word like that in all our
married life.

And I did take her. Didn't I? I would have taken
her. If only she'd co-operated just a little, practised a
little of that love and friendship she talked about to me
on the beach. Instead she struggled: struggled rather a lot.

I mean, why flaunt yourself like that, half naked, sometimes wholly naked, if you're not prepared to co-operate just a little. . . .

As to what happened after that, there's really no point in recounting it all. Sad and rather squalid really, but a complete accident. Even a misunderstanding you could say. If it hadn't happened with me, it would have happened sooner or later with any of the other men she led on and didn't satisfy, I can tell you that.

Afterwards I hardly remembered the details of it all, isn't that odd? Just coming back so carefully and silently up the myrtle path, my wife's eyes gleaming like a cat's as we felt our way. Afterwards holding her in bed, and my wife, usually so fastidious, holding me too. Nick and Isabel were silent by then. That night, very late, it was my wife who was the tigress at the Villa Aglaia.

There's not much more to tell. As I said, the police didn't really bother us much, just a great many questions and all that, naturally; but mostly the obvious questions about the party and the noise and then the tragedy – had we heard anything, seen anything, that sort of thing, it all went on for hours.

Heard anything! Nick really snorted at that one, I can tell you. For a moment I thought he was going to start up all over again about the noise and the camping being illegal and why didn't the police stop it? Which under the circumstances wouldn't have been quite appropriate. But as a matter of fact, Nick's pretty good with the police, officials generally, knows the value of politeness and all that. He also cut quite an impressive figure, all washed and shaved and tidy.

We all were – washed and shaved and tidy. And the villa looked immaculate. As any place with my cool collected wife at the helm invariably does.

As to Nick being so good with the police and officials generally, my wife did murmur afterwards: 'Well, he's had a certain amount of practice, hasn't he?' But then as I already mentioned my wife has always been a little acid – one can't say more than that – about Nick's sharp business practices. As usual, there's a good deal to be said for her point of view. The conversation with Nick and Isabel after the police left really rather proved her point.

First of all Isabel said, yawning slightly, 'Listen, folks, we've been thinking it over; we're really getting a little old for this sort of thing, holidays *à quatre*, I mean. It's been great of course. No need to say that. But it's a hotel for us next year. Villas on the sea can be so noisy. You can hear everything. That's a fact. The most peculiar things. The later at night, the more peculiar. So a luxury hotel *à deux*, in future.'

Isabel didn't seem to expect an answer to what she had just announced and I suppose there wasn't much we could say. She didn't look at either of us as she spoke. I do remember that.

Then Nick chimed in. He'd been thinking overnight as well, it seemed. And what Nick had been thinking about was the next big deal – the one where there'd been a bit of an argument, seeing as I had done all the work from start to finish and couldn't see that he should have more than a very small cut. Well, on this particular deal, he simply stated that the split would be fifty: fifty. With no argument. He didn't seem to expect an answer to that one either.

As a matter of fact, I don't miss our joint holidays with Nick and Isabel. She was right, we really had grown out of all that. It's that fifty per cent which still rankles. But whenever I say so to my wife – I groan and ask: why did I agree? – she replies in her snaky voice (which generally speaking she uses a great deal less nowadays).

'You lost your head in Bexi, that's why.' Then she adds more softly: 'It was the moon that was to blame.' There is even a voluptuous note in my wife's voice when she asks in her turn: 'Wasn't it all worth it?'

The Cobras of Bloomsbury Square

Jonathan Gash

'That's exactly it,' Dean MacDonald countered, eyes atwinkle. 'We dons merely pretend there is a due process! The University of London is an administrative shambles. You're the natural choice, Dr Gaye.'

Elena wasn't taken in by his affability. She did not trust him. Already the threats were less veiled. An ex-St Andrews man, home of ruthless administrators. The John Knoxes of this world take no prisoners.

'This is my very first day, Dean,' she reminded him. 'I don't yet know the ropes of my own appointment, for heaven's sake!'

'That word "very" was superfluous, my dear.' He smiled, precisionist and ruthless. 'And, since you are London's first appointee in Theory of Medicine, who does? Once you have learnt the folk pathways of Senate House, you'll be lost to reason. So now's the time. Advise Grant, please. Bite the bullet.'

Military analogy rules medicine, Elena thought. Good for a research paper, that idea. 'Ignorance is bliss, Dean?' She was surrendering, and could have strangled him.

'Only to the witless observer, my dear. So! Congratulations on joining the staff of the Hunter Postgraduate

Medical College – and tell us which of those two youngsters to promote. Shall we say a week?'

She had never been one to postpone, and caught the pathologist in the microbiology laboratory. He was under a black hood, grumbling loudly and alone. Doing his lissamine rhodamines, doubtless, on his mycobacteria.

'Still moaning, then,' she greeted him, sitting on a lab stool, but not close.

'Hang on, oh world,' he said, muffled. 'Lucky I recognise your voice. Two hours in this bloody thing I can't see. Dr Gaye, isn't it?'

The teaching laboratory was otherwise empty. His mercury-vapour set-up was on a window bench, making its whiny humming. When the bulb went it imploded like a firework. She had seen it once. She glanced about, wary.

'In one, Wat. You've a lovely view.' The lab overlooked Bloomsbury Square.

'I've no such thing. See that frigging Pharmacological Institute? It's creeping nearer daily. See they've taken over History? It's a dump, but we could have used the space.' He emerged, casting off the cloth hood, a stocky, middle-aged man blinking at the light. He switched off the microscope lamp's irritating whine. 'You've got to admire their greed, though. Didn't let those benzylpenicillin hyphenates slip through their sticky little fingers.'

'Monetarist clover,' Elena said, smiling at him. It had been quite a long time.

'Spreading like poisonous bloody cobras.'

'Can't the Hunter's biological engineers make us some cobras of our own?'

He grinned. 'We've got academics. Good to see you again, El. From pit to pinnacle, eh?'

'Pit's about right,' she said coolly, and got a laugh. She had once been his houseman, years since. He had led her a dog's life, partly to her eventual benefit.

'You're the Dean's hatchet man, I take it. Sent to

decide which of our two whiz-kids gets taken on permanent staff?'

'Tell me which you want, Wat, and I'll report accordingly.'

'Nope,' he said unexpectedly. 'I'm ineligible. University Board of Studies, Medicine-stroke-Medicine, no less; they ruled me out. I'm to judge their research applications.'

'Oh, dear.' This really was bad news, that the deputy director was to remain on the sidelines. 'So whichever I pick I get the blame for life.'

Grant rose and stretched. 'Welcome to academic life, Doctor. How's it feel, being a new don – or is it donna?'

'Come for coffee, Wat, and give me a word picture of them, at least.'

'Nope,' he said again. 'University dons are unbiased at all times. Coffee's on, though. Here, El. Did you see those pharmacology bastards aren't subject to the moratorium on hiring new research technicians? Swine.'

She followed, smiling. He hadn't changed, to the untutored eye. He would advise her, one way or another.

They queued at the coffee counter in a hubbub of postgraduate students and technicians.

'The canteen seats one-fifty bums,' Grant said. 'I'll pay, to celebrate your joining this nest of . . . ' He shrugged at the throng. 'We harbour eighty-three nationalities, which is one point eight oh seven chairs for every two racially distinct bottoms.'

Elena made some remark to encourage his harmless prattle, but wasn't taken in.

'You should take on a PhD student, explore the discriminatory implications, Wat,' she finished saying.

'Implications of discrimination,' Grant corrected mildly and made a sign to someone in the crowded middle distance. Elena thought, God, is it always like this? Casual chit-chat corrected for syntax in the coffee thrash? 'And don't put on that surly face with me, El. Expect critiques at all times. Academic life's a higher form of killing. That's

why we've survived longer than any other species. Just thank
your lucky stars you're not in Humanities.'

'They're worse, then?' The queue moved at last, as the
thrombus round the till gave way. She said quietly, 'And
don't call me El. Not any more.'

'Worse? We medics can't hold a candle to the Arts
and Humanities people. And it's little wonder. Honest to
God. Our grammar's crap, logic non-existent, punctuation
random.'

He grabbed the coffees, slung coins, and pressed through
to a non-smoker table where two sat. These dithered about
rising, finally opted for equality and remained seated while
Grant plonked himself down and smiled Elena into the
remaining chair.

'Lads, smile at the pretty lady. El for Elena Gaye. Her MD
fell off the back of a lorry. The subject's Theory of Medicine
– as if there was such a thing. Her appointment here is no
myth, in spite of all my efforts to get her evicted. She's
to recommend one of you two for permanency – whoever
loses joins us here for life. The Hunter Postgrad Medicine
shabeen awaits the result breathlessly.'

'Elena Gaye,' she said pleasantly, taking a coffee before
Wat could start indiscriminate spooning. He was death with
a sugar bowl.

'Reading left to right, El, meet Ben Crupp, PhD,
Leeds – wherever that is. Intense, successful. Buggers
about transforming DNA, dipole moments, all that. Deep
dark theories based on physical chemistry of receptor sites
lurk in that brain.'

Elena said hello to the lank-haired twenty-sixish man. He
was somewhat incongruously dressed in a woollen jumper
buttoned at the neck and a red tie. Trying for trendiness
where linen shirts and suits ruled?

'I hope you'll be happy here, Dr Gaye.'

'I'm sure I shall.' Thank goodness, no pun on her name.
Brown eyes, a ring on the medial finger, left hand.

'Moving on nomenclature-wise,' Grant said – he had

a thing about Americanese spelling and fudge words – 'see David Gervaise Ennis, whose MD is a DM, being from Oxford, where they do everything backwards.'

'Pay no attention,' said the ringless, blue-eyed, pale, smiling, query twenty-eightish man sitting alongside Ben Crupp. Elena thought, surely not more affability, for heaven's sake? 'I'm hooked on behaviourisms, theories of pathogens, up to but excluding all mycology.'

'Hello, David.'

'See, lads?' Wat Grant said proudly. 'Once a lady, always a lady.' He leaned confidentially towards her. 'They're both driven by women – one each, I hasten to add.'

David Ennis seemed to enjoy the older doctor's banter. 'Dr Grant's only jealous of our youth, education, brains, and charm. True, Ben?'

Ben Crupp smiled a tight smile, barely managing it. Charm versus tension, Elena summarised. Easy affability versus the energy of repression.

'And medicine versus science, El,' Wat Grant capped for her in his unnerving way. He always could do that. It infuriated her.

Silly of her to imagine that, just because six years had elapsed, he would have lost that rather terrible skill of knowing what she was about to think.

'Of course,' she said. One more *El* and she'd scream. What on earth was wrong with a name, that people had to clip it to a single expletive? His pet name for her anyway was all in the past. She had to make sure of that right now.

'Sorry, lads,' Grant was saying. 'She has these reveries. She thinks in superfluous superlatives. Women do. I tried to educate it out of her years ago – failed lamentably.'

The canteen was now filled by an inrush of Infectious Disease postgrads calling instructions to friends already in the queue. Elena had to shout to make herself heard.

'Could I have your CVs soonest, please? Include your published papers, excluding those in press.'

'Excluding?' David Ennis was surprised. Ben Crupp was frowning, already probably adding up how many more research papers he had published than his rival.

Grant was smiling. That exclusion was his trick. 'Do as you're told,' he ordered. 'Ungrateful bastards.' Ennis laughed aloud, shaking his head at the impossible conversation while Ben tried on his tightest smile. Grant wagged a spoon at them. 'El. Notice how they treat older academics like you and me?' He was only goading, being well over a quarter of a century her senior. Once, it had not mattered. Here at the Hunter Postgrad, it would. 'They'll question every instruction you give them, when you're giving them the chance of the most honourable title in the world. Don: shared only by us dissolute drunkards, *mafia capi*, and hidalgos of a defunct empire.'

'Get on with you, Wat,' Elena chided, which made Grant suddenly remember something in the lab and leave hurriedly. He had detected her genuine annoyance and was escaping.

No harm had been done, not really. Some of that casual chat had stung, of course, especially after the way they had been once. But one good thing had come out of it. She now knew exactly which one of these two eager young researchers Grant wanted her to recommend. That remark 'Driven by women' had intrigued her, but that had been Wat's way to warn her; leave private considerations out of it.

It was a tragedy of course to lose either one. Young would-be academics were driving vans all over university towns, on account of the government's cutbacks. Qualified doctors were doing their houseman years, only to trudge endless rounds of hospital interviews. As for scientists, PhDs were now ten a penny, drifting into poorly paid technician posts. For the two opposite her it was practically life or death. The old balloon game, but no game.

'Look,' she said, to cut through the hesitations. 'I have to make up my mind by Friday. Today's Monday.

Have your CVs in by this afternoon. I'd like to meet you separately later, quite informally. Somewhere other than this maelstrom.'

They solemnly concurred.

Elena had managed to buy a minute flat above the Phoenix Theatre, Charing Cross Road. The students at the arts school opposite were reputed to club together in fours, taking out a single mortgage in the name of one, so saving on accommodation money. There wasn't room to swing a cat. Even two would be a crush. There was one room eleven by eleven, an impossibly thin bathroom, a thinner kitchen, and an entrance corridor the length of a surfboard. It cost a fortune because it was opposite Foyle's. Hang out of the window and you could see the theatre crowds in Cambridge Circus heading for 'The World's Greatest Ever Musical'.

The problem was suitcase living, inevitable for the transition from hospital-doctor flats to this noisy but private hutch. Home, her parents', still served as a repository. She had brought her two skirted suits, one almost past it so desperate action was needed there soon. Blouses were no problem, thanks to last Christmas and birthdays. The staider the better for the Faculty of Medicine.

Cooking facilities were most primitive. She had been dismayed at first, but become used to the idea. Without a microwave it was nearly hopeless but she had a new one coming within the week. For the past few days she had lived on local restaurants and bought-in meals from Marks and Sparks in Oxford Street and local shops. It would hardly do for any new man in her life too, but cross that bridge.

This worrisome evening, when she had to ponder the two applicants' documents, it was a rather gruesome flan and mixed veg, custard tart to follow. Cream would have been welcome, but lone living excluded certain foods; cream came in froth squirters or those big cartons, in either case enough for a regiment. You finished up throwing away nine-tenths or it went bad.

She dined in regal splendour on her fold-away trestle while darkness fell and Charing Cross Road's traffic churned below. Tonight's read-as-you-dine book was *Mehalah*, because she was incurably addicted to Victorian gothic glums. Reaching the end of her meal and that chapter where they died by drowning was relief squared. She conquered guilt quite easily tonight by simply not looking at the clutter of dishes, and shutting the kitchen door.

The documents were in two folders on her divan sleeper. Nothing for it. Tomorrow would be Tuesday, leaving three clear days. She took up Ben Crupp's folder and began to read, but thinking of David Gervaise Ennis and where she would meet them for that discussion.

'What do you reckon, Ben?'

David Ennis had suggested the Three Greyhounds in Soho because the University Tavern and the Fitzroy were impossible after six o'clock. The old Sun was out of the question since it changed its name and caught rock-and-roll music. It was dedicated now to an ancient rock star.

'Her? Nice. She's written a prolific number of method analyses.'

David eyed his colleague, who had obviously excavated every detail.

'An arid field, it seems to me,' he risked, knowing Good Old Pal Ben would see to it that Dr Gaye heard of his criticisms. 'I mean, Popper's barmy opinions on inductive reasoning and you've said it all.'

'Oh, I don't know about that, David. We don't consider medical theory enough, I always think.'

A good political answer. Ennis shook his head when Ben offered another round.

'What'll you do if you don't get it, Ben?' Ennis shrugged apologetically at Ben's stricken look. 'No good mucking about, Ben, is it? That's why we're here, to talk about it.'

Ben reluctantly entered the discussion. 'Dunno. It's

harder for a scientist, David. You doctors have it made. You've a million other options.'

'What about you scientists? Industry, commerce— '

'Betty's really determined. She's desperate for me to get appointed.'

The once David had met Betty Crupp he had thought her pushy and toxic. In two sentences she had extracted all the details necessary for a competitor to know. Sexless? Hardly; he was convinced there was no such thing. But Ben was hitched to her plough. Clearly, she saw Ben's colleagues simply as rivals to her man. For Ben to open up this way was a sign of Betty's pressure on him, poor sod.

'Maggie and I'll get married if this comes off,' he invented. Tit for tat.

'I guessed that,' Ben said knowingly, his head going like some large toy's.

'That obvious, eh?' David grinned, self-deprecatingly. Maggie would be thunderstruck at this.

They had lived together two years 'on and off' as Maggie often said, needling. Well, he thought defensively, it was an impermanent world. She was as uncertain about her future as he about his. An actress, she was all the more unsure of her career prospects. 'I've done all the right things,' she lectured him when the pain of it struck. 'RADA, three interminable years of posing and speechifying. Now it's one drossy audition after another.' Her acting life was incomprehensible to David. Hours at a time he sat prompting her through her bit in *Electra* or frantically trying to say something meaningful about the audition pieces she kept choosing. 'Sorry, Maggie,' he had to reply. 'It's you suddenly turning into somebody else that I can't grasp. It's beyond me.' She'd fly off the handle, they'd row, and make passionate reconciliations. It was all exhilarating, of course, but both knew that, once either of them got the big break – Maggie's words – that would be it. A film chance, a West End part, and she would be off. The same if he got a don's permanency.

'I suspected it. Betty did, too,' Ben was saying.

David had once introduced Ben to Maggie. She'd thought Dr Crupp a pillock, and told David so later. Ben said he thought Maggie glamorous, which of course she was.

'It's a pity they haven't got funds to take us both,' David said. 'I mean, me a medic, you the scientist. Complementary.'

'That's what I said to Dean MacDonald,' Ben agreed, leaning forward earnestly so far that his chin almost touched the table's beer puddles. 'Otherwise it's survival of the fittest.'

'That's right. Academic life shouldn't be like that. It's all about higher learning.'

Maggie didn't even know he was up for a tenured post. He usually said nothing about work, and only replied in the vaguest generalities when she asked. Was that the trick for compatible living? Except that occasionally she would sense the distance between them, and have an hour's fury. But it was simply the way they were. Certainly, Ben and Elizabeth S. Crupp were as close as any couple could be, it seemed. Maybe their formula was the right one? Ben often cited Betty's strong opinions on departmental matters and University policy. Maggie hardly knew anything about what he himself did all day.

'That's true!' the unbelievable Ben agreed fervently. 'They forget that.'

'I mean, your science and my medicine are the two foundations of medical research.' David was fuelling the fire.

He and Ben had never really got on. He was thinking, surely to God the famous Hunter would never prefer this prat over himself? His crude attempt to sound Ben out a moment ago had not deserved success. Was it worth a walk up the street to suss out the Wellcome Foundation's History of Medicine blokes about Dr Gaye's preferences? No, he decided. Too risky. These theorists might be an entire new clone, their interchangeable minds connecting on the

phone night and day. And canvassing always disqualified
an academic candidate, ho ho ho.

'You're right, David,' Ben answered. The beer was
taking effect, Ennis saw with interest. 'We're both vital.
What criterion will they use?'

'Insuperable, Ben.' David Ennis extended his hand to
his colleague. 'May the best man win.' They shook hands,
even raised glasses in a toast.

'May the best man win, David.'

Walking out of Soho, David pictured Maggie's incredulity had she witnessed the boozy meeting, and laughed at
the image. She would have called him a smarmy sod. He
would have shot back, 'And you think *you* can act? You're
talking to the all-time champ here!'

He sometimes regretted that that sort of conversation
never took place. It never would, either. Not with Maggie
anyhow.

Tuesday passed, and Wednesday.

Thursday morning, Ben Crupp approached Grant dif-
fidently and asked is Dr Gaye about to announce how
she would make her choice. Grant bluntly said to ask
her himself, and went about grumbling all day that these
bloody juniors would soon have him fetching their bloody
pots and pans.

That same afternoon, Elena found Grant in his study,
second floor on the Gower Street side.

'Glad to catch you,' she irritated sweetly. She knew
he hated being caught like this. 'Free for a second?'

He was up to his elbows in data, index cards and
tractor sheets everywhere. He roused from the mess.

'One day I'll do for you, El. You've even begun to sound
like a postgrad, now that I've fiddled your appointment
here. I swear you're starting to look like one.'

'Stop it, Wat.' She was so good-natured. 'I've solved
the problem.'

He gazed at her, trying to clear his mind. She recognised

him at his most dangerous, and sat silent before his stare. 'What kind of brucellosis outbreaks give an ogive graph?' he demanded of the world at large. 'I swear we're making epidemics we've never even heard of.' She was relieved when his opaque look cleared. 'Solved what?'

'Not the pharmacology problem, Wat. Sorry.'

His hope dwindled. He pointed, arm outflung, very *Boyhood of Raleigh*. 'They've had the flaming nerve to propose we amalgamate. Ever hear such gunge?'

'Outrageous,' she said in her most bored voice.

He grinned sheepishly, made as if to kick her foot in annoyance. 'Sorry.'

'I mean Ben Crupp and Dave.'

Oho, Grant thought, for Ben was always Ben, but David Gervaise Ennis was never, ever Dave.

'Don't tell me.' He did a Rodin ponder, his eyes searching the untidy room. 'A competition?' he said finally.

'Oh, dear. Am I that transparent?' She was honestly dismayed.

'No,' he said with gallantry. 'Only sometimes. You naturally have to prove to everyone you used a criterion outside your own judgement alone. The only way, except for our usual oneiromancy.'

She smiled. 'They give their laboratory safety lecture tomorrow. Twenty minutes each.'

'Friday,' he reminded to annoy and get his own back.

'When I report,' she said patiently, 'yes. I'll be in good time. There's that new postgraduate course intake, twenty-five students.'

'So?' He was pleased. A neat solution, worthy of the El he had once known.

'So I sit in on the lecture, score them solely on effectivity.'

'Excellent.' He was looking at her properly for the first time since her arrival. 'You know something, El? You're the only bird I've ever met who makes me wish I was twenty-five years younger.'

'Teenage talk, Wat.' She rose, pleased in every way she could think of. 'And don't get up, please. Just keep your distance.'

They were both smiling. 'Here, El,' Grant asked. 'Want to be an editor for that new microbiology journal?'

'No. Want to edit my new *J. Theory Med. Path.*?'

'Give me a break, El.'

He was miles away among his data before she had even reached the door. She said it anyway, for old time's sake.

'Not El, please.'

Each postgraduate course started as a wholesale mess. Intakes never arrived as one. They drifted in, from the Gambia, Egypt, South-East Asia, from friends' flats in Ealing. It was almost obligatory to drift aimlessly along corridors, in and out of labs, blunder through the library to the wrong departmental offices. Then they would always slowly aggregate and come to rest in a laboratory of their choice. Registration was for ever in its four months of lag phase, in spite of showy attempts at efficiency with desks set up in the main entrance hall.

This course was typical. Elena sat at the rear while the course assembled. About fifty:fifty, doctors to scientists. Average age mid-twenties, one-third women with several in exotic dress. The usual, Wat Grant had described them. She had stopped by on the way to ask in which order Ben and Dave should speak.

'Alphabetical,' he'd said cursorily, not looking up. 'Then you've not influenced the outcome.'

'Right, Wat.' She had withdrawn, annoyed with herself for so obvious a ploy, and entered the lab. She told Ben Crupp and his colleague of the order and said she would just sit in and was that all right.

Dean MacDonald arrived to give his short speech of welcome. He had three anecdotes, tales from his early student days in anatomy. He delivered them with great expertise, the assorted postgrads staring at him uncomprehendingly as he did his laugh and twinkle. He then summarised the Hunter's grand history, assured them of undying help and attention. The staff was always here, so use your tutors. They applauded politely as he left, his six-and-a-half minutes of endeavour in their interest donated.

Ben Crupp went to the rostrum and arranged the slide projector controls and his notes. He had decided to make his own personal intro, which Elena thought a good idea. Doubtless the socially graceful Dave Ennis was somewhere within earshot, but not close enough to distract his colleague. She thought, as Ben started, that she could hear Dave enter the lab behind her, walking with that smooth glide all lab people learned sooner or later, but she devoted her attention to Dr Ben Crupp, PhD.

'My remit is to present a survey of the physical and chemical hazards you are exposed to in any research laboratory,' he began. 'My colleague Dr Ennis will follow, and cover the biological risks. OK?'

The class paid wary attention. Notebooks were out on the benches. But all were awake so far, Elena noted, and seemed likely to stay so.

'Everything in a lab is a risk. Repeat, everything.' Ben clicked the slide onto the drape screen, a list of fatalities by cause and type of lab. Elena saw he had omitted the data source, and scored him one fault.

'One point five volts can kill a seventy-kilogramme standard male,' he went on. 'Imagine how many ways you can electrocute someone: electrophoresis apparatus with the electrodes a little cruddy; your average polyacrylamide gel on a tilt and you borrowing current from a neighbour on the next bench because you're in a hurry to get to coffee. It's all too easy.'

Yes, isn't it, Elena said inwardly. Get on, Ben. Time's ticking away.

'Protein fractionation's another similar risk . . . '

Then why list it, dear Henry, dear Henry? Now she really did turn round, and there was Dave in his white coat carrying a lab tray, slipping silently in and not looking her way. She returned her attention to Ben who was clicking his slides through almost hypnotically.

' . . . explosions caused by thoughtlessness.' He gave a half-embarrassed smile. Elena thought with panic, Oh, Christ, not a joke puh-lease, not after the master of the anecdote had strutted his stuff? But sure enough Ben plodded in. 'It's not all faulty wiring of car ignitions if you want to get rid of a colleague!'

Thud. No response from the class.

' . . . Now for nitrogen tri-iodide, as an example of another class of lab dangers. You all remember that student game in chemistry, driving a cockroach between matchsticks towards a small pile of that unstable explosive halogen compound. Well, if you intend to make explosives, make them in tiny amounts, hey?' Thud. 'These are all self-explanatory. Which brings me to radioactivity.'

How? wondered Elena.

'The life expectancy of *Homo sapiens* exposed to the radio-cobalt unit at Harwell is seconds, hence its efficacy in sterilisation of surgical instruments. Easy to forget some radio-cobalt dust, leak it into food. You don't have to coat an arrow with *Atropa belladonna* extract, or physostigmine, eserines and whatnot!'

Elena did a despairing silent groan. Ben was contributing his own chuckles now, but contentedly, like a comedian she had once seen whose act died the death while he cheerily coursed on disbelieving all signs of audience boredom. That old reference to A. E. W. Mason's novels was in every old edition of pharmacology 'Notes'.

' . . . will remember the Bulgarians' assassination of that political refugee on the streets of London using a stab of a pointed poisonous umbrella . . . '

The class members were yawning, subject to fidgets. Ben saw Elena's glance at the time. He accelerated.

One minute more, Ben, Elena was warning.

' . . . ridiculous crime stories about botulinum toxins,

all spurious. *Clostridium botulinum* exotoxins, for all their speed and potency, oxidise and degrade so swiftly that they would not last long enough to poison a reservoir – or even survive very long in the packet!' Chuckle, chuckle.

She looked at the clock. Ten seconds.

'Now for gases. Well, they are always detectable, but easily created – think of cyanogen bromide, the old niacin colorimetric method, and the buckets of alkali you needed to neutralise it. Simple poisons? Well, you pay for your own funerals here at the Hunter if you mouth-pipette cyanides.'

She coughed, tapped her watch. This was unfair to Dave.

'No, ladies and gentlemen,' Ben wound up. 'Everything is lethal in a research laboratory, but if it came to a competition the physico-chemical killing agents are the ones you must avoid at all costs. That way, I'll be in the clear!'

He stepped down, chuckling, sweating slightly. Elena nodded congratulation and gave a cue glance at Dave Ennis, who took the dais.

'Hello, all.' He stood motionless a second. 'I'm David G. Ennis, a medic. Not a proper scientist. Beast of a different colour.'

The tray he placed carefully on the demonstration bench. He stood looking down at the two petri dishes it held. A couple of the postgrads rose to peer at his wares. He held the pose a fraction too long for Elena's liking, but quickly came to.

'Is there much left for me to say?' he asked the class. 'My colleague has covered all the methods of lab death, the hazards, apart from outright assault. And you've seen it all anyway. You're trained professionals. The MDs among you have encountered the products of death – corpses, tumours, pathogenic changes in tissues. The scientists among you know physics and chemistry only too well.'

Elena watched, curious, as he took a step to gaze at his two shallow dishes. He looked up, capturing attention.

'A volunteer?' he asked casually. Nobody moved. One

or two of the class were smiling, exchanging glances.

'Please?' he asked mildly. The class broke into laughter. Heads were shaken. And it *was* amusing, Elena realised.

'You, Doctor?' Ennis requested, pointing. A postgrad reluctantly came forward, to laughter.

'I have here two petri dishes. One holds simple sugar. OK?' Dave held it up, a stage magician's gesture, and replaced it on the tray. The postgrad, a tall Ugandan in a superb suit, was uneasy but going along.

'The other petri dish is, folks, sealed and covered to protect its contents from light. It is a simple fluid which I sometimes play about with experimentally.' He uncovered it, smiled at the postgrad.

'Ready? I promise I'll do exactly what you do, so we'll at least go together.'

The class laughed. Most were standing now, their interest aroused.

'First, folks, I take my finger, and dip it into the colourless, odourless fluid. Like . . . so!'

He nodded, and the Ugandan copied. The class was crowded close now.

'Now, I touch my wetted finger to the sugar.' He smiled encouragement to the student, who did the same. 'Now, tell what happened, please.'

The postgrad's face brightened. 'Hey!'

'Well?' Ennis asked.

'I can taste the sugar! In my mouth!' He stared at his finger.

'Thank you,' Ennis said briskly. 'End of experiment. Wash please.'

'Sir?' A class member asked. 'How could he *taste* it, when he only touched the sugar with a finger?'

'The fluid is a modified sulphonate,' Ennis explained. 'Which disperses anything assimilable instantaneously throughout the body, from any part of the skin. Toxins, venoms, poisons, even . . . sugar!'

He covered the tray. 'It's a common compound, but not

very well known. Well documented, though. Garlic-scented breath is its only trace. It is rapidly excreted. As far as I know, it has never been implicated in any murder, real or fictional – though if you feel the inclination to publish, I shall expect ten per cent of the royalties!'

He crossed to the wash-basins. Some of the class were lifting the cloth, having a closer look, one or two even trying the experiment.

'Murder?' someone asked.

Ennis returned, wiping his hands, smiling at the success of his demonstration. 'Think a moment. Wasn't it fortunate for us two experimental animals that the test substance was only sugar? What if it was, say, a rare snake venom? A lethal toxin? We'd be dead, the poison distributed throughout our every cell within an instant. And the means would be untraceable, in the right circumstances.'

The tray recovered, he faced the class. 'And before you start asking I'd probably choose the Yellow Scorpion venom, *Leiurus quinquestriatus*. And I'd slap my poor chosen victim on the back in hearty greeting – with a carefully gloved hand, spread with a mixture of sulphonate and venom. The victim would die, and I'd be away scot free.'

A few of the class clapped, and Ennis took a stage bow, grinning.

'Get the point? The academic laboratory is the only place which can provide the perfect means of death,' he told them. 'Accidental or intentional, and even untraceable!' He made his smiling finish. 'OK, everyone. Welcome to the Hunter Postgrad. And "have a nice day!" '

The class dispersed amid laughter. The Ugandan's company was in high favour.

By the time he had cleared up, Dr Gaye had left, but Ben was still there, preparing his fluorescent microscopy.

'Can I have a word, Ben?' David said. 'I've been thinking. I've some news. I'm withdrawing my application. The job's yours. I'm going to leave after my month's notice.'

Ben stared. 'But why? After that performance, David?'

'Oh, a number of things, Ben. For a start, this . . . well, rivalry's been making me think of all sorts of things. Really terrible, horrible things.' He smiled wanly. 'And don't praise my show just now. I could always pull a stunt. But it's not proper teaching, is it?'

'Is that it, then?' Ben looked around the lab, back again.

'Mmmh. And I separated from Maggie yesterday. She's been on about some other woman. Finally we . . . you can guess.'

'Well, David. I'm really sorry.'

The pillock didn't even have the grace to suppress his delight. 'Here,' David said, pulling a small case from his pocket. 'A present. On your promotion to don.'

Ben looked, but did not touch. David finally shrugged and placed it on the bench. A gold fountain pen, expensively labelled.

'David. I don't know what to say.'

'Sorry about the wrapping. Or lack of it. Go on, open it.'

Ben made to do so, hesitated, looked at his gloved hands a moment, and slipped it into his pocket. 'Another time, David. Thanks, though. I've the cohort studies to do.'

'Anyway, congrats, Ben.' David slapped his colleague on the back heartily. Ben winced. 'You deserve it. Good luck.'

A month to the day Grant returned from Lowestoft to find umpteen messages from Dean MacDonald waiting. He was given the appalling news first, and eventually reached the ground-floor office at four o'clock. The Dean was standing morosely looking out across Bloomsbury Square.

'There seems more of them than ever,' he said without turning. 'Notice they all smoke pipes?'

'Afternoon, George,' Grant said as he sank into a chair. 'Been to the coast, two infectious cases dropped from a Rotterdam freighter.'

'AIDS, I suppose?'

'As usual. I should be paid by the bloody mile.'

'You've heard, I take it?' MacDonald sighed, came round to his desk. 'Does suicide go into the national lab accident statistics?'

'No.'

'Thank God for that.' The Dean swung his chair. 'Of course, if you look at it one way, it's no big deal if an academic wastes out by his own hand, is it? I mean, us dons do it three point something above the national average, right?'

'We're in the first division right enough. The technicians found him?'

'Mmmh. They'd know better than anyone not to touch anything. They called young Ennis. Rum way for Crupp to do it, though, eh?'

'Not as rum as all that. Apparently Ennis had mentioned sulphonates, DMSO and variants, in a safety lecture a month ago, to an intake. But, they'd covered all other means of fatality also— '

'I've heard the tape, yes.' The Dean noted Grant's surprise. It was genuine, needless to say. 'Dr Gaye recorded them at the lecture, a means to selection. We reached her by phone. She'll be in presently.'

'Clever girl.' Grant meant it. 'Yes. A mixture of sulphonate and mixed snake venoms from the animal house, fifth floor. He'd smeared it onto a pen, gift from Ennis, actually.'

'Is that really so?'

'Seems so, George. Ben set it all up, apparently, then just touched his hand to it. The stuff was all there, laid out on the bench around him.'

'Was it us did the tests?'

Grant saw the Dean's brow clear for jubilation, and said cruelly, 'No. Our liquid chromatography's always on the blink. That Horton's a cretin. It had to be done at University College.'

'Pity. It would have looked better for us.' The Dean cast about for exoneration. 'Crupp had been a bit odd since his appointment, though?'

'I heard so. Become reclusive. Ritual handwashing, ate only homemade sandwiches, and in the mosquito insectaries at that, clear signs of phobic fixation. Even took to washing the slide projector before he'd touch it. And he was getting worse. Stopped opening his own letters. The students were complaining.'

'Then it's as well he did what he did.' The Dean shot Grant a glance from his politician's brows. 'Nothing in it, was there . . . ?'

'Doubt it. Ennis was leaving, anyway.'

'I'd forgotten that. And you're sure it wasn't an attempt by Crupp to accuse Ennis of anything?'

'Murder?' Grant smiled. 'Don't be daft, George. David Ennis was on leave all last week. And where's the motive, with his application withdrawn a month ago?'

A knock sounded, and Elena entered, white-faced. She came to sit by Grant.

'Ah, Dr Gaye. How did it go?'

'The conference, Dean? Very well, thank you.'

'And my dear old Glasgie Toon?'

'Lovely. Friendly, wonderfully entertaining.'

I'll bet, Grant thought, eyeing Elena. He had almost forgotten; she had attended the BMA conference there last week. He was not a little piqued. She might have sounded a mite less enthusiastic, in the circumstances.

'Did you find the tape they phoned about, Dean? In my cabinet?'

'Thank you, yes. My secretary did the rummaging. Most helpful.' The Dean moved, paced ponderously. Grant recognised a political decision in the making, one which wouldn't matter either way.

'Dr Gaye. From your first appraisal, what would young Ennis say if we offered him the appointment now?'

'Well, I can't really say,' Grant heard. He thought her very sensible to sound so unsure.

'Fair enough. Could I get you to try to persuade him? There's such a hell of a hole left in the course teaching after Crupp.' He made Crupp sound so unfeeling.

'I could try,' Elena offered.

'Excellent.'

Which was how they left it. Grant and Elena went together, up the stairs and passing the Manson Theatre towards the library on the first floor.

'Welcome to academic life, El.' Grant said his first words as they reached the library landing.

'Is it always this hectic?' Which was not a bad attempt, though Grant thought she could have done better, having had all the time journeying south to think up a sentence for him. 'I mean, right from the start?'

'Yes or no,' replied the logician in him. 'But don't feel guilty. Ben Crupp would never have lasted. Dons who make a terrific impact at the beginning nearly always vanish in their first terrific splash. He'd have crumpled anyway before Michaelmas Term. You've got to be silent and unnoticed to survive.'

She ignored that. It was his sort of joke. 'Like Dave, you mean?'

'I was going to say reptilian. Now you've mentioned him I'd better not, eh? And you know better than me, El.'

She said nothing. He stopped at the library door. Postgrads were emerging, grabbing bags, dashing to lectures.

'That's Ben Crupp dealt with. And Dave.' She looked at him directly. 'What about my start as a university don, Wat? Splashy and doomed, or silent and reptilian?'

Grant smiled. She had achieved the ultimate in selection techniques. He would have to watch out, whatever they had been to each other in the past.

'Your entrance, El? Humdrum. Plain simple humdrum.'

And entered the library, fumbling as ever for the scraps of notes in his pocket, shedding his white coat to lie among the rest outside the door, in accordance with the tradition of the place.

Killer

Paula Gosling

He hated her. He did.

Every morning when he left, she was there, staring out the window, waiting for him, watching him. And when he came home at night she was there again, black beady eyes following his every move. As if he would do anything to her.

As if he could.

They'd guess, wouldn't they?

Or would they?

Everybody thought he was so quiet, so polite. Hah!

Neighbours – what do they *really* know about one another? After all, they hadn't lived here long, he was still a mystery, he was sure of that.

Nobody knew his business. He kept to his routine, was always well-mannered when he met one of them on the street. Some might know his name – the postman knew his name, of course – but not much else. He kept himself to himself and so did his woman. Dol knew her place.

She kept the house tidy, did the shopping, made sure he got his meals on time, made sure his life was comfortable, that was all he required of her. So she wasn't very pretty, and lacked imagination, so what? Dol suited him just fine. If home was dull, if the food was always the same on the

same days, and the evenings decidedly lacking in novelty,
what did it matter? It was a place to sleep.

And a place to hide, if necessary.

He had enough excitement outside home to satisfy him.
More than enough.

He was the Expert. He had a reputation downtown –
where a reputation counted. He was the one They turned
to when some little rat fink had squealed once too often,
or maybe caused Somebody Important some damage. They
didn't like damage, downtown. They didn't like trouble. But
they liked him. He worked fast. Neat and quiet, that was his
style. In and out, nothing flashy – and he never talked. Not
once. They liked that, too. He had plenty of work, one way
and another. He kept in shape. He was in control.

Dol knew the consequences if she stepped out of line –
he'd walked out before and he was quite prepared to do it
again if she said anything he didn't like.

Or worse. He could do worse.

Doing worse was his business, after all.

And it *was* his business – nobody else's.

Especially not that nosy old hen next door.

He didn't know much about her, it was true, but she
seemed to want to know all about him, the way she watched,
the way she stared, the way she clocked his comings and
goings.

It wasn't so bad, at first.

At first he'd even felt a little sorry for her.

After all, she was a shut-in, that was clear. Always
in the same window during the day, keeping an eye on
the street, probably making up stories about everyone,
probably putting two and two together in her twisted little
mind, maybe even coming to conclusions.

She might come to a conclusion about him.

That was the worry.

But who could she tell, shut up like that?

Her companion, he supposed.

Would she be believed? Dol said she was a gossipy,

nervy thing. Drove her companion and just about everybody else on the street crazy. Always chattering in that cracked, cranky little voice that went through you like a rusty knife. Always complaining about something. Shut-ins got like that, he knew, went a little funny, got excited over nothing, made things up to liven their dull lives. Most of what she said was pure nonsense, of course. Probably nobody would believe her.

But they might.

Putting two and two together, she might hit on the truth. Stories got around, after all.

He tried varying his hours, changing his routine, but it didn't seem to make any difference, she was always there, watching, watching, watching.

And it played hell with his concentration. In a profession as specialised as his, you had to keep in touch with all the customers all the time, keep the territory covered. They wanted to know they could count on him, or they might turn to another Firm.

The Business might die on him.

Some joke.

But by the time they'd been in the new house a few months, he knew he was going to have to do something about Mrs Murgatroyd. That was her name. He didn't know her first name – probably nobody did, except that poor, haggard woman who looked after her. He'd heard her companion speaking to her one day, when the window was open a crack and he was passing.

Just passing.

Mrs Murgatroyd had been eyeing him suspiciously from under her wrinkled eyelids when her companion had startled her by asking if she wanted something to drink. Well, the fuss that started! Talk about screeching, you'd think the poor woman had asked her if she wanted to be skinned alive!

And all the time she was complaining and crabbing, Mrs Murgatroyd was watching him out of the corner of her eye, watching to see if he reacted to her little performance.

Well, maybe she was a mind-reader.

Because the thought of breaking the bones in that scrawny little neck was beginning to haunt him. The thought of scaring the wits out of her, or even crushing the life right out of her body, kept him awake nights. He did it to others, in a professional way. Why not to her?

But it was only a thought.

Until she began to chatter at him through the glass, telling him off and screeching straight at him. That did it. That was the last straw. Staring was one thing, but jabbering at him another. It made him cringe every time he passed by.

What the hell would people think?

What was she saying?

What did she know?

He couldn't stand it. He knew he'd have to put a stop to it before it went on much longer. She was driving him crazy, and soon it might get back to Dol. He didn't want Dol upset.

Not again.

They'd had to move house twice before when neighbours got suspicious about him, began to point the finger or whisper behind their hands. They seemed to think he was bringing his work home, one way or another. As if he would. Dol had denied everything, of course, she was loyal through and through. She loved him. And he loved her, too, in his way.

But, in the end, they'd had to move.

Well, he was through moving. He liked it here, it was quiet and there were fields to walk in nearby, and he'd really taken to it.

Except for Mrs Murgatroyd, of course.

The thing was, he'd have to wait his chance, move on impulse, trust his instinct. It wasn't professional, it was personal. Which meant no set-up, no back-up, no inside information. Not kill-to-order, and nothing to swell the kitty, afterwards. Not with this one. There had to be no connection with him, that was the thing. No way anyone could guess that he had anything to do with it.

Not easy.

Waiting never is, no matter how much of it you do.

But then, one morning, the moment arrived. All unexpected, the way these things do. He had slept a little late, and left the house just in time to see Mrs Murgatroyd's companion set out on a shopping expedition. She was running to catch the bus.

Which meant she'd left the house in a hurry.

On an impulse, he slipped up the path and went around the side of the house. Oh, Mrs Murgatroyd saw him, of course. Propped in the window, as usual, her little black eyes missing nothing that went on in the neighbourhood. She was agitated, she bobbed about frantically, she even called out for help – but there was no one to hear her, now.

No one to tell, now.

He'd been right. The companion had left the back door ajar. Just a bit. Just enough. He was in like a shadow – he was good at that – and savoured the moment.

Mrs Murgatroyd, you've poked your nosy little beak into a neighbour's business just once too often, he thought to himself. Now you'll find out just what I do, and how I do it.

Slowly, quietly, he moved across the kitchen and pushed open the door into the hall. The house smelled very different from his own. All houses had a characteristic smell, he was a connoisseur of smells, assigned personalities to houses on the basis of smells, knew what to expect the minute he was through a door. Some smelled richly of buttery meals and cream teas, some smelled rankly of cabbage and disinfectant. All of them smelled of death, after he'd dropped by.

This one would, too.

Moving stealthily, he slipped down the hall, his footsteps hardly making a whisper on the thick pile of the carpet.

There – the sitting room door was open, and he could hear Mrs Murgatroyd muttering to herself, alone in the room. She was talking about him. Words like 'murderer' and 'monster' rose above her inane jabbering.

He went in and she stopped her talk.

Gaped at him.

Moved back, as far back as she could.

She knew what he had come for, all right.

For all the good it would do her.

He thought it would be easy, but it wasn't. She *could* move, after all. She fled him, darting around the room, then making a frantic, scrabbling dash for the hall, screeching and flailing and jabbering.

But he got her.

And it was good, so good. She twisted and turned and struggled but he got her, he finished her, and she would stare no more, jabber no more. Nasty, vicious, nosy little bag of bones.

Goodbye, Mrs Murgatroyd.

Now all he had to do was get out.

But luck wasn't with him.

Not this time.

The back door slammed – the companion was back! Too soon, too soon! Now she was in the doorway! Standing, staring, pointing at the scatter of green and blue on the carpet, and screaming!

Why did they all scream? Why were they so shocked?

What did they expect?

No other self-respecting cat would have put up with that damned budgie staring and screeching at him for another single day. Why should he?

He sighed and crawled under an armchair.

There'd be no pink salmon tonight.

The Siren

Nigel Gray

It was only when Adam picked up one of her swimming trophies that she decided to kill him. He had never hit her before with anything other than his hands, but now she realised that his disturbance was on the verge of changing up into another gear. Shaking with rage he made as if to hurl the heavy statuette at her head, but controlled himself. He slammed it down among the others in the bookcase making the shelf bounce, and various of the trophies fall and clatter. What followed was the usual. He took hold of a handful of her hair and marched her up to the bedroom. Once the tension had drained out of him, he became again his usual pleasant self, remorseful and concerned, as eager to please as a faithful mongrel.

She'd lived with this Jekyll and Hyde figure for seven years. For the most part he was kind, gentle, caring, considerate. Only in bed did he want to dominate, to master her. And on occasions when he was angry with her he would punish her with rough sex. At first she'd found these sexual games exciting. It was this dangerous, untamed side of him that had made him so attractive to her (despite her feelings of shame and guilt – a sort of betrayal of her 'sisters' – that this should be so). But as time had passed, his need for power had become greater. It seemed like a drug to him; it seemed that as he became addicted he needed to increase the dose to get his fix. And the times he felt anger towards her had increased too. He was more aggressive, more violent, more often. For some time in their early days together she'd experienced the delicious excitement of being scared, like a child whose father was playing monsters, but this had changed to the insidious bad taste of real fear. It had got to the stage where she began to be apprehensive as bedtime approached, where she began to tread warily each day lest she gave him some excuse to feign anger towards her.

He had warned her often during these rough games that if she ever left him, or was unfaithful in that old-fashioned sexual sense, he would kill her. And he always said this with such intensity that she believed him. In the early days she had enjoyed the awareness of his strength, of her vulnerability. But now, she had come to feel totally powerless, at his mercy, and she had grown to hate him for it.

Too scared to leave him, she felt she needed to find another way of freeing herself from his tyranny, and when he threatened her with her trophy the decision was made. From that moment, whenever she suffered under his oppression, she began to plan. To be sent to prison would be too great a price to pay. It would have to be a perfect murder. And there was the problem of his superior strength. Although she'd been a swimming champion in her teens, she had always been petite. She was beautiful in the water, as graceful as a dolphin, but she had never been well muscled, and not having swum or indeed exercised in any way for all the years of her marriage, she had lost much of the muscle she had once had.

It was a Saturday morning – the first really pleasant day of spring. Adam was a probation officer, and a good one, committed and involved, though he wasn't sure for how long he'd be able to continue. He found it impossible to keep a professional distance from the unfortunates he had to deal with. His concern tangled him up in the web of

their pain and their impossible problems. Often he would
have liked to have brought one of them home to offer real
support and friendship, and indeed on one disastrous occasion had done so. Much of his anger stemmed from his rage
or frustration on their behalf against the injustices of their
lives. On Saturday mornings he used to go unpaid into the
office to try hopelessly to catch up with the paperwork of
his caseload.

'Will you stay home today?' she asked him.

He shook his head sorrowfully. 'I'm so far behind. The
week's taken up with people. Saturday's the only time I get
for paper. You know how it is.'

'Please,' she begged.

He smiled, warmed by being wanted by her, and relented.
'If you really want me to,' he said.

'We could go to the French Pâtisserie and sit outside
and have croissants and hot chocolate.'

'Good idea,' he said. Away from the bedroom there was
nothing he would not give her or do for her. Sometimes,
after he'd been especially rough with her, he would apologise and say, 'It's a small price to pay – isn't it?'

Perhaps, she sometimes thought, it was.

Breakfast was romantic. The croissants fresh. The chocolate hot and sweet. The spring sunshine warm. He smiled at
her, his eyes brimming with love, and leaned forward to kiss
her. She cleaned up the flakes of dark pastry from around
his mouth, nibbling gently with her soft lips like a horse
eating from a loved one's hand. 'It's like being on holiday,'
he said.

'Let's go,' she said. 'Let's have a holiday now.'

'Chance'd be a fine thing,' he said. 'I've got Albert up
in court again next week. And Linton. And I've got to try
and do something about Craigie. And Jonjo's hitting the
bottle again. And I think Kofi's probably back into dealing,
although he won't admit it. And Charlene's walked out on
him again. And who can blame her.'

'But Adam, you've been working so hard. You look

absolutely wiped out. You need a break from it. I just
want to have you to myself for a little while.'

'Really?' he said. His smile broadened and he shook his
head slightly. 'It's a long time since you said anything like
that.'

She put a hand under the table onto his thigh. 'Please,'
she said. 'I want to take you to that place in Spain where I
went with Jill and Angela just after we met, remember? It
was so beautiful there, and I missed you so much. I always
promised myself I'd take you there one day.'

'Well, I couldn't make it during the next three weeks
at least.'

'All right. In four weeks. I'll go to the travel agent on
Monday and try to book up. It should be easy enough this
early in the year.'

The ocean on the west coast of Spain is cold all year round,
and in spring of course more so than in autumn. But May in
Spain is wonderful. There is still the freshness that follows
winter, but already the sun blazes down day after day from
strong blue skies. It is still the invigorating, youthful sun of
romance, rather than the elderly, slightly seedy, over-ripe
sun of retirement. The cold winds that often blow off the
Atlantic are quickening and full of promise; and exciting
and alarming breakers batter ceaselessly against the shore.

She brought Adam to a fishing village that boasted a
single hotel, but she chose instead that they would stay
in a self-catering villa a hundred metres up a dusty track
at the south end of the bay. The days were idyllic. When
they rose at last from the bed of their dalliance and went
out onto their balcony with its view of the bay, the sun would
already be high. They would shower together and go out for
breakfast to one of the little cafés in the town. Late mornings
they strolled in the surrounding countryside, stopping to
chat whenever possible in their broken Spanish to people
they met. Sometimes an old one would insist on taking
them home, and they would be given green olives and a glass

of red wine. They would swim briefly from the town beach, take a light lunch, retire for a steamy siesta. In the afternoons they would drive in their hired jeep along the coast, discovering deserted bays or rocky headlands where they would wander hand in hand, explore the myriad of nooks and crannies, swim, sunbathe, read, make small talk, and cuddle and fool around like unseasoned lovers. On their return they would shower and change and go out to dinner, lingering over a bottle of punchy local wine and endless cups of bitter black coffee till late into the evening.

Ironically, Adam, released from the pressures of work and routine, was as loving and attentive as any woman's dream honeymoon husband. And the romance of the place acted on her like an aphrodisiac, which kept him as satisfied and relaxed as a pampered cat. Mornings before they rose, during afternoon siestas, and sometimes where lonely headlands of stone thrust into the apparent softness of the sea, they played and pleasured and loved. And it was better than it had ever been. And she began to doubt. Her purpose wavered. Her man, she realised, was one in a million. She was perhaps as fortunate as her friends thought her to be. And she knew she could not kill him.

There was one moment of the day when Adam showed signs of agitation. As they walked along the beach from the town to take their late morning swim on their way back to the villa, they passed close to the fishermen who would be mending their nets after the previous evening's work. And there was one among them, a big, bold and striking man, who would watch her with undisguised desire. He was a mature man, in the mould of the working-class hero, mahogany-skinned, and hard-muscled, and handsome in a coarse and angular way. The leers of boys and young men would annoy her like persistent flies, but his gaze thrilled her with a current that buzzed from her throat to her womb. Adam was merely irritated at first by the stares, but, being intuitive, was soon aware of her response, and it angered him. But the hot flush of his jealousy could be soon cooled by her loving words, and their frolics in the cold ocean where Adam would labour along like a land creature that had fallen into the water while she shimmied all around him like a porpoise – or shark.

The ten days of their stay were coming to an end. It was late, at an hour when every previous evening they had been inside the restaurant because of the chill sea wind. But now a dry desert breeze was sweeping across Spain from North Africa, leaving a fine layer of sand in its wake. They had eaten at a table outside. Adam had gone to the toilet leaving her briefly alone with her thoughts. She realised that her plan was fanciful and ridiculous. She was an ordinary, well-raised English woman. Everyone had their fantasies of course, but they were never acted out. She and Adam would return home and fall back into their old habits both good and bad. She sighed a huge sigh of both defeat and relief.

A man's shadow fell across her. It was Pepe. She had learned his name from the calls of his comrades on the beach. Was she enjoying her holiday, he asked in Spanish. How long would she be staying. Only two more nights, she told him. He looked crestfallen. She should stay longer, he said. Wasn't their village beautiful. Yes, she said, it was. The sun, he said, the sea. The fruits, the fish. Why would she want to return to the cold and rain and grey skies and fog. Stay longer, he urged, staring into her face with an intense and unwavering directness. She blushed like a schoolgirl and continually lowered her eyes, but each time she glanced up, his look still devoured her. And his eyes, she realised with surprise, were a startling grey, not the dark brown she would have expected. Why wasn't he out on his boat, she tried to ask. And he shrugged and opened his hands in resignation and gave an explanation she couldn't understand, her Spanish being only fluent in the superficialities of weather and introductions. Adam returned to witness her blushing confusion. You are a lucky man, Pepe told him. The lady is lovely. Good night. And with the arrogance of his manhood, he sauntered away.

'Let's go,' Adam said without sitting down, and she could hear the trembling hoarseness in his voice.

Afterwards, as usual, he was full of remorse. It was just, he said, that he was frightened of losing her. He couldn't live without her, and so on. The following morning he was loving and undemanding. They enjoyed a pleasant walk, a good lunch. At siesta time she told him she didn't want sex, and for once he didn't override her. 'Later,' she said. And they slept for an hour in each other's arms.

'Let's not take the jeep,' she said, as they prepared to go out. 'If we climb over the rocks out the back here we can get down to a tiny horseshoe bay that's completely secluded. It takes about an hour. We found it last time I was here. You can't get to it by road, so there's never anybody there.'

'So why haven't we been before?' he asked.

'I've been saving it,' she said. 'It's just beautiful. It's completely private. And the rocks come right round and over the beach like the mouth of a great cave, and there's no wind, and the afternoon sun shines right in to warm you after you've swum.'

'OK,' he shouted with shining eyes, as gleeful as an excited child. 'You've made a sale. What are we waiting for?'

'No one ever goes near,' she said coquettishly. 'You can do what you like with me there.'

A broad smile of delight lit up his handsome, sensitive face. 'It sounds too good to be true,' he said.

They spread their towels in the shade of a great boulder at one end of the little beach. There she gave him as much pleasure as she was able, using all the skills their seven years together had taught her. In response he was loving, gentle, considerate. He tried to bring her to orgasm, but something was dead in her. And all the time she could hear the ocean hurling itself apparently self-destructively against the hardness of the rock, but she knew that in fact it was the rock that would be worn down, shaped and ultimately broken by the sea. And finally, weary after the exertions of the scramble over difficult terrain, tired by the long session of love-making in the little corner of paradise they had come to, they wandered down to the water's edge where the coldness brought shocked gasps and laughter to their lips.

'Let's skinny dip,' he said.

'No,' she said.

'Don't be silly,' he said, taking off the bathers he'd only just put on, and throwing them back up the beach. 'Nobody can see us here.'

'*You* can,' she said. 'I don't want to.'

'Come on,' he insisted. 'That's not like you.'

'I don't want to.'

'Why?'

'I just don't.'

He grabbed her. She struggled to no avail, her anger mounting. He threw the two pieces of her bikini after his own costume. 'Please,' she pleaded. 'Don't make me.'

'What's the matter with you?' he said, becoming angry himself. 'Don't be stupid.'

She tried to pull back, but he swung her up in his arms and carried her, still protesting, into the awesome, breaking waves. The beach sloped steeply, and soon the water lifted them both, and they were swimming; they had entered *her* element. 'There,' he said, 'doesn't that feel good?'

'Yes,' she admitted. She made a great effort to compose herself, to put honey back into her voice. 'Come,' she said. 'I want to show you something marvellous.'

They rose and fell on the swell as she swam slowly ahead of him, urging him on. Away to the south they could see the ragged coastline, raw in its natural, unspoiled beauty. In front of them the sun was lowering itself down its majestic

blue backdrop towards an ocean that stretched away to the
end of the world. To the north was the long spur of rocky
headland, a crescent with its back to them, that formed one
of the arms that enclosed and protected the little town.

'Where are we going?' he asked.

'You'll see.'

'There's nothing out there.'

'You'll see,' she repeated.

Adam had not been able to swim when they had met. It
was some time before his pride had allowed her to teach
him. A mistimed breath filled his mouth every so often
with choking sea water. She cajoled him, luring him on.
He heard her song but had no mast to lash himself to.

'I'm getting tired,' he told her.

'A bit further,' she said.

He looked back towards land. 'Shit!' he said. 'How did
we get so far out?'

'It looks further than it is,' she assured him.

'I'll never make it back.'

'I'm here,' she said. 'Trust me.'

'I'm cold,' he said. His teeth chattered when he tried to
speak. 'I'm so cold.'

'OK,' she said. 'Let's go back.'

It was dark when she crawled like a turtle exhausted and
shaking up the beach. The fishing fleet was already out. It
was Pepe, still working on the damage to his boat, who saw
the movement on the sand. He turned her onto her back and
looked down at her helplessness. Her breasts rose and
fell and shuddered with her efforts to breathe. He took off
his torn and sweat-smelling shirt and covered her with it.
'My husband,' she repeated over and over. 'My husband.'
He lifted her in his strong arms and carried her along the
beach, staying close to the water, well away from the lights
of the town. 'My husband,' she kept saying. 'Si, si,' he said.

At the villa he laid her, still wet and patterned with
sand, on the bed. He took off his torn shorts and underpants

and mounted her. She struggled weakly, but she was like
a fish in his hands. He emptied himself into her, then lay
with the weight of his body crushing her so that she could
hardly draw breath. Then he began again. Less urgently
this time, talking all the time in language she could not
comprehend. And despite herself, her body was aroused.
She put her arms around his large frame, her hands like
butterflies on his back and neck. She looked at his face, but
saw Adam's eyes staring back at her, wide with terror. She
could feel the strong pull of the current still dragging them
away from the shore despite their efforts to swim against
it. She swam naked on her back and felt her clitoris swell,
tumescent, hard. Adam's face became disfigured with panic.
'I can't make it,' he said.

'Yes,' she called out. 'Yes.'

His cry was submerged by salt water. He was coughing,
spluttering, retching. 'Cramp!' he moaned.

She could see nothing but the frothing water, and then
there was Adam's face again distorted with panic and pain.
'Help me!' he pleaded. 'Help me!'

And then she knew she could not see it through. The
sea lifted her and threw her down and pounded on top of
her. Her tears filled the hollows of her face and she tasted
again the salt in her mouth. 'I'm coming!' she cried. And all
the tension of her body accumulated in her genitalia, and
she felt she must burst with the strength of her sensations.
'I'm coming! I'm coming!'

But it was too late.

Pepe had finished. He pulled out of her and dressed himself. And she was left alone in an icy and tumultuous sea
of guilt.

The police arrived later. And a doctor. Eventually an
interpreter. The consul was notified; and Adam's parents,
who would fly out and make the arrangements to have the
body taken back if it was found.

She was sitting up in the hospital bed. 'We just swam

out too far,' she told them. Maria, the interpreter, relayed this to the civil guards. Maria's breath smelt strongly of garlic. This woman, to whom the civil guards paid scant attention (occupied as they were with ogling *her*), must have been beautiful, she thought, when she was young. She was aware of her own tousled, mousy hair, compared with the shining blackness of Maria's. And realising that Maria was possibly not much more than ten years older than her, a spasm of panic seized her. She was suddenly and for the first time afraid of growing old. And more, afraid of growing old alone. She added, 'It was foolish.'

One of the guards said something. Maria asked her, 'How were you saved?'

'I'm a much stronger swimmer than he was. We couldn't get back against the current. Eventually . . . when he . . . I stopped trying to swim against it. I let the current carry me. It took me out and round the headland. Then I was able to swim into the town beach.' Maria relayed all this. There was some discussion among the guards.

'They say there was a similar incident about seven years ago,' Maria told her.

She could scarcely contain herself from blurting out, *I know, I heard about it. I was here.* Instead she said, 'You'll find our clothes at the little bay.'

'They are collected,' Maria informed her. 'You may be charged.'

'Charged?' she said. Her mouth was suddenly dry and her heartbeat thumped against her chest. The civil guards leered.

'Your swimming costumes were collected too. It is against the law in our country to swim without clothes.'

She began to laugh. The laughter came bubbling out. It would not stop. The three Spaniards looked surprised, then alarmed. And the laughter and the crying mingled, and went on, and on, and on.

Putting The Boot In

James Hamilton-Paterson

Here's an extraordinary thing: a mud-stained, spiral-bound A4 notebook containing scribbled entries which amount to evidence that I'm an accessory to a serious crime. Yet I can't bring myself to destroy it. The years go by and one begins to feel safe. Indeed, one has become a different person almost to the extent of relishing hearing the grossest accusations against one's former self. Almost. But not quite, as recent events have nastily reminded me.

It is now over ten years since I left university with a degree in fine arts and a very reasonable disinclination to do anything strenuous by way of earning a living. University had been pleasant – fairly wild, even – and I was unwilling to swap a diet of lotuses for the bread and butter of career-building. I won't bore you with the familial circumstances which ultimately forced me to look for work; suffice it to say they were acrimonious and demeaning. I reluctantly applied for, and was offered, a post with an audio-visual company as a scriptwriter, production assistant and general dogsbody.

I was supposed to be learning the trade. After a month or so they gave me an assignment which made me feel positively faint, so raw and odious did it sound.

There was apparently a huge construction company who
wanted us to produce a glossy brochure for them with a
section covering one of their projects in detail. This was a
motorway flyover – can you imagine? – and I was supposed to
go down to the wilds of Essex or somewhere once a week and
spend a day on-site making notes and taking photographs. If
six months previously on one of our louche Veuve Clicquot
Club evenings it had been announced that Jeremy de
Rothko would shortly be standing in the Essex marshes
wearing a plastic helmet and carrying a clipboard while
trying to make his *aperçus* heard above the roar of JCBs
there would have been shrieks of incredulity and dismay
– mine loudest of all. And yet there I soon was, complete
with green wellingtons, trying to think of things to say to
men in donkey jackets messing about with theodolites and
tripods.

Well, I mustn't make a meal of it and give the wrong
impression just for effect. It turned out to be quite an
experience. For a start, the construction company was a
little more up-market than I'd imagined. It was called
Heavy ArtWorks and had a most enlightened attitude for
those early post-Modern days in that it specialised in rather
well-designed public works. I admit I was impressed when
I first saw the architect's drawings for Redenham flyover. I
know now that he's a friend of Prince Charles's but in those
days his design seemed courageously un-Brutalist. The concrete supports were fluted and to be faced with local stone.
Instead of crash barrier-style railings for the motorway
overhead there was a sculpted parapet supported by a row
of corbels, light and lacy. And above each span were to be
cobweb-fine steel and perspex canopies projecting like the
peak of a cap over the traffic – no doubt the forerunners of
today's ubiquitous atria.

I was astonished. All this for a humble flyover in the
middle of countryside best hurried through with closed
eyes. Surely it would be fearfully expensive? This was the
dreary part and I'm afraid I took a lot of notes on my

clipboard without understanding half of what was said. But they'd gone into the economics pretty thoroughly; and what with a new technique for pouring something or other and a pioneering method of 'slab grouting' (whatever that is – I never did find out) it could be done for much the same price as the usual hideous concrete bridge. In addition, the use of local stone for the facings would bring employment to the locality and I believe did much to clinch the deal in HAW's favour.

Until then I'd never been on a construction site in my life, thank you very much. However, it wasn't quite what I expected. I had certainly assumed the mud and the cold and the rain and the fumes of diesel engines and in due time found I had not erred, except to underestimate them. But right from the ground-breaking ceremony a strange atmosphere hung over the project. It was eight o'clock on a September morning: a clear sky with some wood-pigeons and smoke from the site huts drifting across six lanes of empty concrete highway. The huts had been set up across the entire width of the motorway and although traffic had been diverted a fortnight earlier it still made me uneasy to stand in the middle of the fast lane wearing a jacket with 'HAW' printed across the shoulders and a rather fetching hard hat in yellow. I took some photographs as Terry and Don on the west side and Patrick and The Blob on the east started up their earth-movers and began, well, moving earth.

That was what struck me from the first: this was a team of men who habitually worked together. It was another of HAW's radical policies that it seldom engaged casual local labour but moved its men in gangs about the country. The theory was that on big civil engineering projects levels of skill and discipline had to be guaranteed and men who always worked with one another did so faster and better than a lot of anonymous yobboes recruited from surrounding towns and villages. Faster and better: that was the company's unofficial slogan (as I put it for them in their brochure some months later). *Faster* was certainly the key

to the entire thing. Superior constructions of this sort could
only be made economically feasible if they could be built
in less time than their conventional rivals. The men were
paid over the odds on the understanding that there was to
be no silly nonsense about strikes and go-slows. On the
other hand the company was most particular about not cutting corners since they realised that substandard work
would lead in every sense to disaster. The enterprise rested
on teamwork and organisation (you see how easily one
slips into BrochureSpeak?), for in the case of Redenham
practically the entire flyover was to be precast in sections
and delivered to the site according to a minutely planned
timetable.

To get what my own company called 'the feel of
the job' I was to spend the whole of the first week at
Redenham and thereafter one day a week, leaving me
time to go and interview HAW's chairman and selected
executives in London. That first stint was a revelation. I
had never before seen so many men who knew each other
all working together as one. They must have looked pretty
askance at me: an outsider with, let us be honest about it,
a cultured accent, asking ignorant questions about their
work and taking pictures like some spy sent down from
head office. But Frank, the site foreman, had clearly put in
some good words on my behalf over cups of oversweet tea
in his hut and I never had the feeling of being ostracised.
Indeed I soon became quite friendly with some of the men,
especially with The Blob who sat perched heroically atop
thousands of quivering horsepower, delicately dumping
twenty tons of earth precisely *there* or scooping out a vast
trench exactly *here*. I learned that he always wore one of six
identical T-shirts depicting a lurid comic-strip monster in
dayglo colours which were an affront to the senses. Of the
big, tanned, blond creature inside the T-shirts I can only
say that he gladdened the eye amid that desolate scenery
and I admit that I spent a disproportionate number of hours

hovering around taking down his most trivial asides with earnest interest. Even the people who processed our films remarked that bulldozers seemed to be the flavour of the month.

In any case by the end of that first week it was Blobbo and Paddy and Terry and Don-boy, while I was Jerry. Half of me could hardly believe it – I mean to say, *Jerry* – but the other half was enchanted to be treated as one of the lads and wanted only for it to go on for ever. It was also just like being abroad and having to learn a completely new vocabulary. Sandwiches were 'sarnies' and poured concrete was 'mud' or 'muddo'. The whole thing was quite exhilarating in an obscure way.

When I first returned to the site after a full week's absence I was amazed at the speed of their progress. I'd expected to see no more than the footings for each of the main piers but instead found three huge concrete trunks already sprouting from the Essex countryside, each with its crowning tuft of reinforcing steel rods.

'We missed you,' said The Blob, cheering me no end. 'I've never had a bloke following me about with a camera before, like I was some telly actor.'

'It's your star quality,' I told him.

'Ah, get lost.' But he gave a pleased smile and revved up his diesel. He'd relinquished the caterpillar earth-mover since that part was over. Now he was driving one of those yellow things which had a bucket in front with long tines sticking out of its lower lip.

'I'll be back in a moment for your story,' I called up at him, brandishing the natty little tape recorder they'd given me. 'I'd better go down to Frank's hut and catch up on progress.'

'Huh, you'll be lucky if you're allowed to speak to him. We've got this visitor, hadn't you heard? His name's Vandyce and he's the Chairman's nephew and he's a right little prat. No more than about twenty-five and he's all over the bloody site shouting and criticising something rotten. He gets to me, and that's a fact.'

'Well, it'll only be for the day, I expect.'

'Too wrong, Jerry. He's here till the job's finished. And if he gets a taste for it he'll probably be at the next one too. And don't worry about forgetting to call him sir. He'll soon enough remind you.' Blobbo let in the clutch and roared off, lozenges of packed earth tumbling from his balloon tyres.

As soon as I reached the foreman's hut it was apparent the atmosphere had changed. In place of the joshing camaraderie I'd left, and which I'd strangely missed, a sullen rancour was pressing up against the steamy windows. Frank was propped on the corner of his table staring glumly at a mug of tea while three of his welders were standing shoulder to shoulder being addressed by a young man who could only have been a chairman's nephew. He was wearing a buffed steel hard hat, a tweed suit and the most extraordinary boots I'd ever seen. If you can imagine a pair of what the Americans so graphically call 'shitkickers' styled by an Italian and with highly polished steel reinforcements on the outside of the toecap rather than inside you'll have an idea.

'Who the hell are you?' he asked me as I came in. I explained. 'Well, you can just come back another day. Can't have you poncing around with your cameras and notes holding up the work. This job's already behind as it is.'

'And not getting any less so while you talk, I'd imagine,' I couldn't help saying. Frank shot me an imploring glance over his mug while Vandyce lost colour.

'That attempt at humour has just cost you your job,' he said. 'You may as well take yourself off. You've no further business with this company. Go on, out! And as for you,' he turned back to the welders, 'any more of that playing the fool and you'll be getting your cards too.'

I left the hut with the three men who said nothing but

stared mutinously at the ground. Neither could I think of
anything much to say. It was, after all, my first proper job
and I wasn't yet sure enough of myself to match this kind
of aggressiveness with ready wit first thing in the morning.
In a moment Vandyce himself emerged, banged the door
behind him and strode off across the motorway to the
east-side plinth. I went back in.

'What am I supposed to do?' I asked Frank.

'What are *you* supposed to do, lad? What am *I* supposed
to do? By my reckoning he's already put us two days behind
and he's close to costing me one of my steelmen. He slagged
off some of Leroy's work yesterday. Best tensioner I've ever
had and that little sod walks up and starts in. He doesn't
know how close he was to getting himself massacred. Leroy
was fit to fill him in and none of us would have blamed him.'

I marvelled at Vandyce's temerity. This Leroy was
a huge West Indian famous for having recently won a
thousand-pound bet in a Scotch egg eating contest. A man
who can eat thirty-one Scotch eggs in the lunch hour and
come back on site to do an afternoon's work has to have a
certain force of character about him.

'What's he doing it for?'

'Vandyce? Oh, trying to prove himself. Youngest son.
The Man Who Gets Things Moving. Wants to take over the
company, I expect. Politics. Christ knows. What I do know
is that head office can't or won't remove him. If things go
on like this he's going to screw up this project. And the
Minister's supposed to be opening the thing on December
the eighth. That's the sort of pressure we're under. I'd go
home if I were you, lad. It's not your fight. You've done
your best.'

I wandered off, thinking I'd certainly carry on until
noon and then ring my own company and tell them
what was up. One has one's pride and it would have
been too humiliating to have meekly allowed oneself to
be chivvied home like some truant. I became absorbed
in photographing a rather aesthetic pile of steel beams

blotched with orange rust when that voice came at me from behind.

'Hey, you! Yes, you! What the hell are you still doing here? I thought I told you to pack up and get off this site an hour ago.'

I looked round. We were alone. The early sun winked off his absurd toecaps, flashed off his hat.

'Oh, do bugger off,' I told him, 'there's a good boy. I'm working even if you're not.'

He stood there breathing heavily for a moment. 'Right,' he said at length, 'I'm glad you said that. That's cooked your goose.'

'And do stop these silly rhetorical gestures.' My tone was really quite severe. 'I'm not your employee, you know. My company was asked by your Chairman to cover this job for the new brochure. That's what I'm doing and that's what I'll continue to do until he personally tells me to stop. Trot off and polish your hat.'

To my amazement he turned and walked away without another word. I won't pretend I wasn't relieved. He looked the type who could easily resort to physical violence and frankly I don't expect I'd be much good at that. I sometimes wish I could stop my mouth saying some of the things it comes out with. In any case I spent the rest of the morning avoiding him and at lunch rang my producer who advised me to take the rest of the day off, let things cool and come back the following morning when maybe Mr Vandyce wouldn't be there. Meanwhile he'd call HAW and see what he could do.

So next day I clocked in again at Redenham bright and early. Vandyce, it appeared, had not yet arrived but already anticipation was souring the comradely mood. The men still worked quickly and efficiently, well aware that the first batch of trusses was due in a matter of days. But there was a tension in their movements; they kept breaking off and glancing up. At ten o'clock a mutter went round: Vandyce had been sighted arriving on foot, looking murderous. I can hardly explain the apprehension which jabbed through me. Why did a young ass scarcely older than I and with no jurisdiction over my job cause me such unease? Yet he did. I think it was the tweed as much as anything. I lurked a bit behind a huge dump of gravel until he had left Frank's hut and was safely on his malevolent rounds. I was going to tell the foreman what my company had said but he gave me no chance.

'Christ,' he said, 'you still here? Please go away, lad. We've trouble enough as it is. You thought he was bad yesterday? He was a pussy-cat. Today his car's broken down three miles away. You should have heard him on the phone to the garage just now. They're to bring it here by four o'clock at the latest and heaven help them if it's not on song—'

Just then the door flew open and Leroy barged in so that the hut creaked and shook.

'Been an accident, Frank. Better come. It's him.'

I know that neither the foreman nor I had any doubt about whom he meant.

'Who's he killed? Oh, I'll have that bas—'

'He's the one who's dead.'

It was a scene of the grandest guignol. There was Blobbo's digger with its bucket half lowered like the head of a bull frozen in mid-charge. Suspended on its long steel horns and jammed up against the concrete wall of no.1 plinth hung Vandyce. His tweed jacket was transfixed and within its unbuttoned gape was the gleam of shiny pink coils. His face was hidden; from that angle all we could see was the polished crown of his hat. Up in the driver's seat poor Blobbo sat looking oddly childlike with his silly T-shirt and white face. 'It got away with me,' he kept saying.

'Let him down, Blob,' Frank called gently. 'Let him down.'

'It just got away with me. He kept on shouting at me, didn't he? Effing this and effing that and I was all confused

by it. Said he was going to get me sacked for knocking over
some bricks back there. My foot slipped, I was that wound
up. Got away with me.'

'Let him down, lad.'

Blobbo reached out a hand. There was a hiss of
hydraulics and the bucket dropped suddenly with an
unpleasantly cushioned thud. The steel hat fell off and all
our eyes met the late Mr Vandyce's. They were wide open;
and I'm sure it was their familiar pettish expression which
counteracted all pity and disgust. Bit by bit Blobbo backed
his machine away until the body could be eased from the
tines. At the end he switched off and there we were, all
forty of us, many still panting from the run to the scene
of the accident.

Or scene of the crime? For this was the crux.

'Who else saw it?' asked Frank as he drew a sheet of
blue polythene over the Chairman's nephew. I was unable
to take my eyes off one of the digger's prongs which was
not only streaked with blood but still carried spitted on it
an unidentifiable mauvish kebab.

'I did,' said Paddy. 'It was just like Blobbo says. It
was an accident, wasn't it, Tel?'

'An accident,' agreed Terry.

'Definitely,' said Don.

And now comes the most curious part of the story.
For long afterwards I tried to think of an apt simile
to describe how a gang of forty men could in a single
instant reach a unanimous decision – and don't forget
we're talking about forty Britons standing around a body
in the middle of Essex. A football crowd suddenly rioting?
No; much too hysterical. This scene was perfectly calm
and, in some way, utterly sane. Then I had it. It was
exactly like a flock of birds in the sky all changing
direction at the same moment, a cloud of birds swerving
as if to avoid an obstacle only they can see, veering
smoothly in a co-ordinated mass before turning back on
course.

'Maybe we should be sending for an ambulance,' said a voice.

'No hurry,' said somebody else.

'There'll be an inquest. An inquiry. Witnesses called.'

'Paddy here. Terry. Don. And Blobbo, of course. They'll throw the book at Blobbo after he drove over that council-man's car in Leicester. They'll say he's not fit to drive.'

'That's his licence down the tube.'

'Hold up the job for weeks.'

'Goodbye, bonus.'

'Doing well not to lose our own jobs.'

'And all because of that little . . . ' A nod towards the cooling lump beneath the polythene.

'Now just hold on a minute,' said Frank. 'Just hold on, you fellas.' There was a short silence. 'Mind you, nobody *knows* he's here. His car broke down, didn't it? He called the garage to get it fixed and bring it here, but as far as they're concerned he could have phoned from anywhere.'

'I don't remember seeing him today. Yesterday, fair enough. But today . . . '

'No, nor me.'

'Never came, did he?'

A sort of communal sigh ran round the men, the sound of a mutually agreed decision being reached.

'So there's only one thing, really,' said Frank. 'Him.'

Forty pairs of eyes turned my way. I can tell you that nothing in my past – not even the inquiry into the goings-on at the Veuve Clicquot Club – prepared me for this moment. I heard myself say: 'I was with Frank here at the time of the accident and *I* certainly never saw the man today. I remember he said yesterday he wasn't coming in.' And there it was, almost without hesitation. The clear intent to commit perjury, to be an accessory after the fact, and witnessed by forty men. All I can say is we did all feel drawn together in the most curious fashion.

There was a long moment during which some of us glanced up and down the barricaded motorway as if to glimpse the distant flashers of the first police cars. But there was nothing. The stained concrete lay empty beneath the bald Essex sky. Vehicles were always arriving to deliver materials but at this particular moment there was nothing. For a limited time the site was an island with its own mores and its own law.

'Right, fellas,' said Frank briskly. 'We've a quick job to do. Let's pour some concrete. You, young Blobbo, get down here and someone'll brew you a cup of something in the shed. Take him, Jerry, would you?'

So I put a willing arm about the poor Blob's shoulders and escorted him to the hut for tea and empathy. About the last I saw of Vandyce was a leaking blue sausage being borne away at a trot. There came the roar of engines starting. Someone darted back with a sheet of newspaper for the kebab before another hand turned a hose on the digger.

Punctually at four that afternoon a mechanic drove up in Vandyce's car and was put out not to find him.

'He said he'd be here.' The man was aggrieved. 'I worked my arse off to get it ready.'

'Well, he isn't,' Frank told him. 'Hasn't been here all day. Never showed up this morning. Where did he phone you from?'

'He didn't say. I assumed it was here.'

'No, like I said, he's not been in. So why not leave the car since he told you?'

'Serve him right if I do. Rude sod, I thought he sounded.'

'He's that, all right. Don't worry, one of us'll give you a lift back.'

From the next morning work on Redenham flyover was heading back to being on schedule again. I spent a day or two elsewhere in a state of considerable unreality. I knew what I'd seen, I remembered what I was a party to. And yet it never quite got through to me. One moment you're a reluctant recruit to the brochure-writing business and the next you're party to a probable murder and a definite conspiracy to conceal a corpse. I could not in honesty grieve for the odious Mr Vandyce. The tweed suit had been beyond forgiveness, his manner even worse. However, I must make it clear that I was not terrorised by those forty workmen to join their plot. I've really no idea what would have happened had I refused to play my part. Probably they would simply have called for an ambulance and let the law run its course. Another unfortunate building-site accident . . . But the truth is at that instant I *wanted* to be one of them: wanted to be trusted by them, wished for them to be my partners in crime. In short, I was proud to be The Blob's accomplice.

I went back a few days later to take pictures of their progress. It was still early and I got a beautiful shot of the three plinths outlined against the sky – all pastel shades with a flock of lapwings in the background. They had just removed the last of the shuttering from no.1 plinth and yellow hard hats dotted the embankment like buttercups. I walked up, winding on film, and found a knot of men looking at something which stuck out of the concrete fifteen feet or so up the plinth. It was the brightly polished steel toecap of a boot.

'Jesus Christ,' said Don. 'That'll have to come off. We've the trusses arriving any minute.'

I would have dithered. Don simply fetched a chainsaw and with a quick snarling noise sheared the boot flush with the wall. A handful of 'mud' inside the pulpy cavity and the job was done.

'I'll just lose this down one of the hollow members,' he said, carefully holding the toecap like an eggcup to avoid spilling its contents. 'He was a right pain in the arse to the end, wasn't he? Give the saw a wipe down, Paddy.'

Not many days afterwards the stone facings went on and young Mr Vandyce retreated a further eight inches from the world which was getting on so nicely without him. It took them a week to discover he was missing rather than just somewhere else. Of tearful relatives waiting in vain and hoping against hope for his return I neither knew nor

cared. Some police made enquiries at the site, listened to
the account of how his car came to be there, drove it away
and that was that. Right on time the Redenham flyover was
finished and opened and received widespread praise for its
graceful lines and detail. Somebody even wrote to *The Times*.
'What a pleasant change,' they said.

As for me, in due course I delivered the brochure
which was expensively printed and well received. I still
have a copy I treasure, not for its embarrassingly fulsome
text (only what was required, after all) but for two of my
photographs they used. One was of the site before the flyover was built – a particularly dim stretch of Essex crying
out for a piece of decent architecture. The other was that
early morning shot of the flyover's supports. If one looks
very carefully (as I myself only discovered when I saw the
finished brochure) one can see a tiny sparkle as of a piece
of mirror set in the concrete high up no.1 plinth. It gives
me enormous pleasure that someone in HAW's publicity
department thought fit to caption the first photograph
'Mother Nature' and the second 'The Hand of Man'. I
love to think of all those tens of thousands of shareholders
– not to mention the Chairman himself – glancing at the
pictures over their breakfast toast unaware that mixed up
with all that hyperbole about looking to the future is clear
evidence of a major crime.

At the beginning of this account I alluded to certain
recent events which had given me a nasty moment or two.
These are the sequel to a story which, after all, took place
ten years ago and which I've scarcely thought about except
when moved to fetch from my wall safe the muddy notebook
in which it is recorded. Nowadays, I'm thankful to say, I no
longer have any connection with the promotional industry.
Certain university friends more fortunate than I took pity
on me and I now have, shall we put it, a status of sorts
in the world of the fine arts – serving on commissions and
that kind of thing. Like increasing numbers of ordinary

people I'm deeply concerned about the vital matter of aesthetics in public works, but unlike them I'm in a position to do something about it. No longer must we permit barbarians and vandals to mutilate our cities and countryside. The fight is on.

Thus you can imagine how exercised I was six months ago when I read in my paper about a planned expansion of the motorway network in Essex which would necessitate, among other things, the demolition and enlargement of Redenham flyover. The word 'demolition' brought all sorts of awkward possibilities to mind and that very morning I began lobbying as soon as people arrived in their offices. The upshot of the matter is that today Redenham flyover was granted Listed status as a building of outstanding architectural interest. For the moment, therefore, one can go back to feeling safe.

And of course the more time goes by the more inconceivable it all becomes. Often as I drive along Britain's motorways I look up at the various bridges as they whiz overhead and imagine them turning suddenly to glass. There, clearly visible and embedded like raisins in a cake, all sorts of victims appear trapped in their different postures. Some are trussed head down, some are spreadeagled flat; still others are in fragments. One is missing half a boot. His blue plastic cerement is pressed against the contours of his body by the cold tonnage which holds him. He is one of the many. Beneath their pre-stressed tombs the roaring world races unheedingly past. They mostly have no historian; they are anonymous flies in amber for future archaeologists. How far in the future remains, you may be sure, not the least of my concerns.

The Obituarists' Outing

Tim Heald

Bognor had first met Ivor Bradley-Smallrat on one of those ineffable weekend courses to which the professional man becomes prone if he wishes to get on in his chosen career. Bognor was not greatly bothered about getting on in his chosen career but his boss, Parkinson, had been told that there was one vacancy on the course – 'Whitehall and the Media' – and he would be required to fill it from his staff at the Special Investigations Department of the Board of Trade. That meant Bognor.

The course had naturally been a waste of time except that Bradley-Smallrat had been lecturing in his capacity as Deputy Foreign Editor of the *Morning Post* and he and Bognor, recognising kindred spirits, had escaped to the village pub for bitter and chatter. Six months later Bradley-Smallrat had been 'moved sideways' (his phrase) to be Editor of the obituaries column. He and Bognor, firm acquaintances for life, had come to an informal arrangement whereby Bognor was Obituaries Consultant for the Civil Service. Whenever a Whitehall mandarin toppled off the perch Bradley-Smallrat or his assistant Dorothy Tomkiss would be on the line asking either for a brand new five hundred words or for some corroborating facts, anecdotes or opinions to bolster the valedictory notice already on

file. In the case of very senior civil servants indeed Bognor
wrote longer obituaries while they were still alive. These
were delivered to the *Post*, buffed up by Bradley-Smallrat
or Miss Tomkiss and then fed to the *Post*'s computer to be
disgorged at the appropriate moment.

Bognor enjoyed writing the obits. Under the new régime
a note of sardonic realism had crept into the column so
that he was able to use the pieces, anonymous of course,
to pay off the occasional lingering score. He had particularly enjoyed writing his boss's obituary and peppering it
with such phrases as 'notoriously short fuse', 'essentially
parochial vision' and 'he had few outside interests'. Obituary writing also involved the occasional lavish lunch and
surprisingly good money to top up his modest Board of
Trade salary.

Not to mention the Annual Obituarists' Outing.

Every year the obituary staff, and one or two sympathetic
Post employees from letters, 'defence' or the diary, would
accompany assorted freelance obituarists on a jolly day out.
One year they had gone to Boulogne for lunch; on another
occasion they had taken a box at Lord's cricket ground;
they had picnicked at Glyndebourne; raced at Chepstow;
and played a cricket match against the Combined British
Undertakers. This year Bradley-Smallrat had arranged a
trip by special steam train to Edgbaster, home of the great
Edgbaster and Bradbury locomotive factory, now a steam
museum.

Simon and Monica, Mrs Bognor, arrived early at
Marylebone and found Ivor Bradley-Smallrat parking his
bicycle. He was wearing white flannels, a vivid pink and
green striped blazer and a similarly ribboned panama hat.

'Ah, Monica,' he exclaimed, somehow contriving to undo
his bicycle clips and embrace Mrs Bognor in the one single
swooping gesture, 'jolly good to see you. Jolly good to see
you too, Simon. Jolly good of you both to come. Should be
a jolly good day.' He rubbed his big pink hands together

and grinned wolfishly. 'I could do with a real British Rail breakfast don't you think.'

The Bognors nodded agreement and Ivor led the way into the station where Miss Tomkiss was already doling out tickets and programmes to a huddle of bleary-looking obituarists, most of whom were already known to each other and to the Bognors, if only from previous outings. There was Brigadier Popjoy, the retired Military Correspondent who specialised in soldiers but could turn his hand to sailors and airmen when asked; Sir Norman Flute, the Art Historian; Peregrine Twentyman, the retired silk who looked after judges, barristers and Real Tennis players; Stewart Porringer of sport, an area jealously guarded by Bradley-Smallrat so that Porringer was only let loose on very minor figures unless they played Association Football, a game the Obituaries Editor despised. Gavin Chu, the poet, essayist, novelist and man of letters, was there in his habitual deerstalker and so was Daphne St John Smart who wrote, naturally, about 'Society'. A young man named Crabbe, previously unknown to Bognor, had been newly recruited to write about the world of pop music, drugs and sex – an area previously neglected by *Post* obituaries. Bognor was particularly pleased to see Cyril Haslinghurst, the one-time Liberal MP, bon viveur, raconteur, luncher, lecher and all round bad hat. He particularly enjoyed Haslinghurst because he was so very obviously up to no good. Other obituarists and *Post* staffers brought the total number of the party to twenty-seven but these were the people best known to Bognor and, on the whole, most liked.

'Bland not here?' he asked. Hugo Bland did minor royalty, minor canonry and minor public schools. He had been at school with Bognor though in a different house.

'Indisposed,' said Bradley-Smallrat. 'Not at all well as a matter of fact. But he has sent his obit.'

'You're not serious about the obits?'

'Naturally.' The party began to move towards the barrier

and the chocolate and cream Pullman coaches beyond, rich with the promise of kippers and mixed grill.

'I haven't done mine.' Bognor lengthened his stride to match Ivor's.

'No problem. You can knock it off over brekker. Bland's is jolly good actually. Did you know that he was related to the Lincolnshire Blands?'

Bognor didn't.

It was a good breakfast. The Bognors sat at a four with Haslinghurst and Brigadier Popjoy.

'First rate scoff,' said the Brigadier, buttering toast as they passed Denham Golf Club. All along the track train-spotters with tripods and long lenses snapped them as they passed by.

'Strange way to amuse oneself.' Haslinghurst had persuaded their waiter to fix Buck's Fizz. 'Not a recreation you often find in *Who's Who*.' He sipped his drink. 'Had you heard that the *News* are trying to poach the delectable Miss Tomkiss?'

'Becoming a damned competitive business, obits,' said the Brigadier. 'That Massingberd fellow at the *Telegraph*'s had a lot to do with it.'

They passed through Gerrards Cross.

'I hope she's not leaving.' Monica was fond of Dottie Tomkiss.

Haslinghurst leered. 'No way Ivor would let that happen,' he said. 'Tomkiss is far too valuable in any number of different ways. Mind you,' he lowered his voice and leaned across the table, pulling at his familiar black eye patch, 'I have heard it said that certain other parties have been making a fairly concerted pitch for Bradley-Smallrat himself.'

The Bognors tried to look knowing but the sudden advent of Miss Tomkiss herself put an end to this line of talk.

'You people all know the drill?' she said. She was

looking more than usually desirable, thought Bognor, in that figure-hugging black polo neck which so prettily set off the remains of her summer holiday tan.

'All present and correct.' Brigadier Popjoy delved into the recesses of his Harris tweed jacket and produced a brown envelope with OHMS in one corner. 'Four hundred and ninety-seven words,' he said, 'give or take a hyphen or two.'

'You are a sweetie, Brigadier.' Dorothy Tomkiss kissed his forehead and he went an even pucer shade of pink. 'Mr Haslinghurst,' she said, 'obituary please.'

'Of course, dear girl.' Haslinghurst's work had been composed in real ink on the back of a number of envelopes. They were not quite cross-hatched but spidered and blotched in a passable imitation of a literary manuscript of, say, later Dylan Thomas.

'I'm afraid I haven't done mine,' said Bognor, 'I didn't think you were serious.'

'Never more so,' said Miss Tomkiss. 'In fact you're very lucky to have been allowed on the train without it. If you haven't done it by the time we leave Edgbaster we'll leave you behind.'

'You wouldn't.' Bognor wiped marmalade nervously from his shirt front.

'We would. If there's going to be a grand reading during dinner then everyone must be included. Frightfully invidious otherwise.'

'It's all right.' Monica snapped open her handbag and pulled out a neatly typed brace of double-spaced pages. 'I did it for him.'

'You never.' Bognor snatched at the papers but only saw enough to read 'Simon Bognor who d y'day was one of the Board of Trade's . . . ' As Miss Tomkiss firmly removed the second page he also read the last sentence which was, 'He is survived by his wife, Monica.'

'That's a bit ripe.' Bognor was genuinely piqued. 'What makes you think you'll survive me?'

'I don't smoke cheroots; I'm not two stone overweight; I
work out; and I'm not under constant stress for no reason
whatever.' She eyed his thick-buttered toast. 'I've given up
butter too.'

'Come on, chaps,' said Brigadier Popjoy, as Miss Tomkiss
passed back down the carriage, bumping gently against
the sides of the seats, 'less of the old marital discord.
I want to catch up on the goss. For a start, why no
Bland?'

'Indisposed,' said Bognor. 'Not at all well, according
to Bradley-Smallrat.'

'Indisposed, my eye,' said Haslinghurst, stubbing a
cigarette into the remains of a grilled tomato. 'That's a load
of tosh. I saw Bland only yesterday. In the London Library
immersed in piles of old Bradshaws and histories of obscure
private railway systems. He was actually reading something
called *The Missing Special*. I assumed he was boning up for
today.'

'Did you speak?' Bognor, of whom it had once been
said – in public too – that 'he had an unerring instinct
for untimely death', experienced a sudden and inexplicable
tingling of the spine.

'Certainly not!' Haslinghurst lit another Gauloise. 'Bland
by name but not by nature in my view. In any case I was
late for lunch and he was engrossed.'

'And did he look ill?' Monica seemed to share her
husband's intuitive unease.

'No more than usual.' Haslinghurst laughed and then
started to choke, took a frantic glass of water and allowed
himself to be hit quite hard between the shoulder-blades
with the flat of the Brigadier's hand.

When this emphysematic convulsion had passed, the
Brigadier leaned forward and said, 'Is it right that Bland's
bonking Miss Tomkiss?'

'I understood he was walking out with Daphne St
John Smart,' said Monica.

Haslinghurst imbibed fizz. 'Left-handed little bugger,'

he said, 'I always assumed he was having a ding-dong
with the Chu person.'

'I,' Bognor spoke with the authority of an adult lifetime of
acquaintance, 'always assumed he was one of life's eunuchs.
Not interested in carnal knowledge animal, vegetable or
mineral.'

'Oh, Simon, darling,' Mrs Bognor patted her husband's
podgy hand, 'you can be so *naïve*. In any case you can't have
carnal knowledge of a vegetable.'

'Now who's being naïve?' asked Bognor.

'I heard,' said Popjoy, seeking to pour oil on these
troubled marital waters, 'that *The Times* were trying to
poach Norman Flute. As a matter of fact I was told they
offered him fifteen hundred quid to do David Hockney.
Payable in claret.'

'Where did you hear that?' Haslinghurst wanted to know.

'At my club as a matter of fact.'

Haslinghurst laughed again, cautiously this time. 'Not the
sort of gossip one normally expects at the Rag. I heard that
some Canadian millionaire's starting up a weekly magazine
devoted entirely to obits.'

'I heard it at my other club, actually.' The Brigadier
was miffed.

'Dead topical,' said Bognor. 'Why is it that death
has suddenly become so fashionable?'

No-one could answer this. Instead all four peered out
morosely at the pockets of photographers and spotters still
lining their route. A few minutes later they were saved by
the drinks trolley.

They were all merry by the time they arrived at Edgbaster
St Tristram's with its mock marble, its hanging baskets
and its typical Basque crêperie – a jewel in British Rail's
crown.

'OK chaps,' said Bradley-Smallrat, 'the Brigadier's leading a party to the site of the Battle of Edgbaster; Sir Norman
is guiding another round St Penda's Abbey; Porringer's

leading an assault on the terraces at Edgbaster Thursday's home game against Clapham Athletic; and I'm making a bee-line for the historic Duck and Compasses. Then we all meet up at the headmaster's study between four and half past for cucumber sandwiches and a guided tour of good old Edgbaster Coll which is, I undeeeerstand, the alma mater of Gavin Chu.'

Gavin winced and gave a hitch to his PEN Club, Lugano Conference shoulder bag.

'Anyone who becomes hopelessly entombed in the Duck and Compasses or similar,' he continued, 'must be back at the station by five minutes to six which is when the train departs Eustonwards. As you know British Rail waits for no man. And there's nothing after that till the milk train which arrives in the small hours and doesn't even have a buffet.'

The massed obituarists grinned.

'OK gang,' said Bradley-Smallrat, 'dismiss!'

And so, in Edgbaster, the obituarists went their separate ways. It was a crisp, sunny, un-English day and the Bognors trawled through the town on their own. A beer and a sandwich in a back street pub – not the Duck; a browse through a couple of goodish second-hand bookshops where Simon almost bought a battered copy of *John Gilpin's Ride* with Ronald Searle illustrations for 50p; a peep into St Penda's where they overheard enough of Sir Norman Flute's echt-aesthetic lecture to make them leave sharpish and have a coffee in a Tea Shoppe overlooking the river; finally a wander through the market where Monica bought a pair of tights and Simon a jug which said 'A Present from Edgbaster' on the side.

'Funny if we did all drop dead,' said Bognor, panting. Edgbaster College, which bore a startling resemblance to St Pancras station, was at the top of the hill.

'Not my idea of a joke.' Monica had brought sensible shoes and was making the pace.

'Tempting fate though.' Bognor paused and tried to catch breath under the obviously false pretence of enjoying the view. 'Tempting fate to make us all write our obits like that. Even if just one of us keeled over it would seem a touch macabre.'

'Is that your way of asking me not to walk so fast?'

'Not at all. It would be awfully neat for the *Post*, being able to collect all the obits fresh from the corpses.'

'Don't be disgusting. Anyway it would have to be Dorothy Tomkiss's corpse. She's collected them all up. Now do hurry, we're late for the head beak's tea party.'

This was true. As they cleared the brow of St Penda's Mount they could see the hands of the clock on the Great Tower nearing four thirty. At the foot of the Great Tower, just in front of Great Gate, a small person lurked.

'Oh look,' said Monica, 'Gavin Chu's late too.'

'You're late for tea, Gavin,' said Bognor as soon as they were within hailing distance.

'Thank heavens I found you,' said Gavin, 'I must have a quick word. In private.' He glanced at Monica.

'No secrets *entre nous*,' said Bognor. A white lie but not a whopping one.

Gavin didn't seem to like this but time obviously pressed.

'This mustn't go any further,' he said, 'but Hugo Bland has asked me to sound you out about writing for his new magazine.'

'What new magazine?'

'*Valete.*'

'*Valete.* Pretty grabby title.' Bognor sniffed.

'It's Latin,' said Chu, patronising him.

'I know it's bloody Latin,' said Bognor irritably, 'I *was* educated. Why should I want to write for Bland's new magazine and what is it?'

'It's a weekly devoted entirely to dead people.'

'Terriff,' said Monica.

If looks could have killed, Chu would have consigned her to the opening number of the new magazine.

'The pay is very good,' he said. 'Hugo's backer is amazingly big in the death business in the States and he's moving into Britain in an equally big way.'

'I'm sorry,' Bognor was aware that he sounded priggish but he had never been afraid to seem prim, 'but my first loyalty is to Ivor.'

'Hugo will pay double.'

'No,' said Bognor.

'Several of the others are moving over.'

'That's their problem.'

'Are you absolutely certain? Hugo needs to know tonight.'

'I thought he was supposed to be ill. Obviously not. Anyway if that's all you've got to say, Gavin, I suggest we make speedy steps for the headmaster's study. I'm dying for a cucumber sandwich.'

'Many a true word,' muttered Gavin Chu in a melodramatic corner of the mouth conversation-stopper, adding, 'but you're making a big mistake.'

If nothing else they were exceedingly good cucumber sandwiches. None of your mimsy crustless garden party/Palm Court nonsense, these were good tuck shop doorsteps, heavily peppered. The headmaster was a similar mixture – a blustering exterior concealing the cool within. Bark *and* bite. Bognor found him alarming and took refuge in trying to compose his obituary.

Once inside the headmaster's study there was an atmosphere among the obituarists. Mingled as they were with a similar number of well-scrubbed Edgbaster sixth-formers their corporate sense of unease was dissipated. But it was still almost tangible.

Only Bradley-Smallrat seemed immune.

'Detained in the Duck, I suppose,' he said, spraying crumbs and cucumber down his I Zingari tie.

'No actually. We've been remarkably active. Seen all sorts of things. Taken lots of exercise.' Bognor wondered whether to say anything about Gavin Chu's unpleasant overture on behalf of Bland. He decided not. Discretion was an integral part of the Bognor armoury. He was not a boat rocker and he saw no point in disturbing Bradley-Smallrat's poise and equanimity. *Valete* would almost certainly be stillborn. Why upset Ivor with news of a birth that was as likely as not to be aborted.

'I gather the Brigadier's battlefield tour was extremely gory,' Bradley-Smallrat grinned. 'The Brigadier revealed a positively Stephen King-like relish for a certain sort of detail. Incidentally, one or two people have decided to stay overnight so they can catch some choral evensong at St Penda's. It's up to you if you want to join them but I've made it plain that they'll have to pay their own hotel and the journey home tomorrow.'

Bognor's hand checked momentarily in its passage from sandwich plate to mouth. He glanced at Monica. She glanced back.

'Not some idea of Gavin Chu's,' he said. A suspicion was crystallising in Bognor's subconscious. It was not wholly identifiable yet but it was emerging.

Bradley-Smallrat seemed surprised.

'Not at all. Gavin's effectively tone deaf. And also passionate about choo-choos. He wouldn't miss travelling home by steam.'

'I see.' Bognor did not see. Not yet.

They were indeed a depleted band by the time they entered the station buffet at Edgbaster St Tristram's. Flute, of course, was absent. So was young Crabbe. And there was no sign of Daphne St John Smart. On the other hand, those that survived did represent a definite *corps d'élite*. Brigadier Popjoy was of the party. Ditto Porringer who had seen Edgbaster Thursday come from behind to win 3-2; also Haslinghurst and Dorothy Tomkiss. And Chu.

Chu's presence confused Bognor. His suspicion was, sort of and up to a point, that the decision to attend evensong was part of the plot to launch *Valete*. Obviously the defectors had all decided to stay on in Edgbaster while the loyalists went back on the train as originally planned. But if so, why? And why was Chu on the train? Chu was Bland's stooge and recruiting agent. If Bognor was right and the defectors were all still in Edgbaster why wasn't Chu among them? It didn't make sense.

In the Pullman they took up the same positions as they had occupied on the outward journey. The obituarists had the entire coach to themselves. In the morning this had made for a convivial gathering with a certain amount of spare space but enough bums on seats to make it seem like a party. Now there was no disguising the fact that they were a rump. Too many empty seats. They rattled around like a pod short of half its peas.

'I say,' Haslinghurst removed his cigarette holder and leaned across the table almost knocking over the half bottle of Veuve Clicquot he had picked up in an Edgbaster off-licence, 'I was propositioned by little Chu on the battle-field. What about you?'

The Brigadier frowned. 'He came up to me with some bizarre proposal about doubling my money if I went over to the other side. Impertinent little foreign person. I've nothing against the heathen Chinee but I do have to draw the line at that hat.'

'Me too,' said Bognor. 'A new magazine about dead people.'

'That's the one,' said the Brigadier.

'Can't see the appeal of a comic devoted entirely to stiffs myself,' said Haslinghurst, 'but little Chu said there was a lot of heavy money in it. Some of which has already attached itself to Hugo Bland if we're to believe what he said.'

The train jolted over points and past rows of dimly lit terraced cottages, windows curtained against the in-quisitive gaze of passing travellers like the obituarists. Dinner was to be served shortly and the attendant passed among them taking orders for the *filet de boeuf Brunel* or the *maigret de canard Peter Parker*. Little smuts from the engine snuck in through window gaps and flecked the antimacassars with smudgy black. In subdued voices the Bognors and the Brigadier and Cyril Haslinghurst talked of death. Aperitifs mingled with apprehension as the 6.30 Special from Edgbaster steamed south.

It happened in a tunnel.

First the lights failed.

The Bognors had been expecting something and so, though they might not have realised it, had most of Bradley-Smallrat's party. There was a crash, then a scream, then the abrupt braking of the train and a clatter of falling cutlery and china. A hissing, a high-pitched human moaning. Moments later a buzz of speculative chatter. Bognor, standing up, saw that the moaning came from Gavin Chu who was clutching his chest with one hand while the other clung to the communication cord. There was something – a knife, a crossbow bolt? – sticking out of Gavin Chu's chest. And blood everywhere. Hot steam hissed from the engine, protesting at this unexpected halt.

Things now happened with a speed which even Bognor, with his wide experience of criminal violence, found quite bewildering. First of all the lights came on again. Then two uniformed policemen appeared as if by magic and ordered calm and silence. There was a sudden flashing light and siren, then two white-coated stretcher-bearers hurried in, laid Chu out and removed him to what, one could only assume, was a waiting ambulance. Outside Bognor could hear sounds which even to his untutored ear seemed to suggest uncoupling. Theirs was, he realised, the last coach on the train. Then seconds later there was another crunch from behind.

Now a third policeman, some sort of inspector in a flat cap, entered. He carried a swagger stick, gloves and a field telephone which crackled.

'Ladies and gentlemen,' he said, 'I regret to have to tell you that every person in this coach is under suspicion of murder. The ambulance attendants have made every effort to revive the unfortunate gentleman but I have to tell you that their efforts have been in vain.

'In view of this situation I have arranged for the remainder of the train to proceed on its way to London while this single coach will return to Edgbaster where the murder inquiry will be headquartered. Until we arrive back in Edgbaster I must ask you to stay in your places and to remain absolutely silent.'

Outside, the steam engine could be heard beginning to move the bulk of the train away towards London. At the other end there was a more mundane clanking and humming. It sounded to Bognor like a small diesel. Some sort of freight engine. All three policemen executed stiff salutes. The senior said, 'One of my men will be riding in the cab. The rest of us will proceed immediately to Edgbaster to await your return.' And then he was gone, almost as swiftly and mysteriously as he had arrived.

Very slowly their coach began to gather speed. They passed through the tunnel where the lights did not fail again, and out into the open where presently the rows of terraced houses with their muffled lights came into view once more.

The whole incident had taken little more than the twinkling of an eye.

'Curious,' said Monica.

'Shhh,' said her husband, law abiding.

'Don't be ridiculous,' she said, 'they've gone.'

'They got here very fast,' said the Brigadier.

'Left in a hell of a hurry too,' said Haslinghurst.

Bradley-Smallrat walked up, pale and shaken.

'Rum do,' he said. 'And Dotty's not in her seat. Do you imagine she's in the loo?'

'I hope so. She's got all our obits.' Bognor glanced out of the window at the lights. They were retreating now. The world beyond the Pullman seemed impenetrably black and fraught with menace. They passed a signal box and Bognor momentarily glimpsed a signalman pulling at levers. There was something about the man which seemed oddly familiar but he couldn't quite place it.

'You know something,' Bradley-Smallrat peered out into the dark, 'we seem to be going back by a different route. We didn't pass that dirty great crane. Ruined by the look of it.'

The track was very poor quality stuff. The train was juddering and shaking. Every obituarist had to hold on to his glass with a tight clasp. Bradley-Smallrat sat down on the Brigadier's lap.

Suddenly Bognor leapt to his feet. 'Watson!' he exclaimed as he fixed Haslinghurst with a frenzied stare. 'Did you say Bland was reading *The Missing Special* in the London Library?'

Haslinghurst fingered his eye-patch. 'The thing about only having one eye,' he said, 'is that it tends to compensate for the loss of the other. I'm proud to say that I can see twice as well with one as most men with two. And, yes, he was reading something called *The Missing Special*. Whatever that may be.'

'Illiterate!' squawked Mrs Bognor. She too stood and in a remarkable display of marital togetherness both leapt at the communication cord. For the second time in less than half an hour there was a clatter of crockery, a scream of steel, the acrid smell of burned brake lining, the massed swearing of disturbed writers.

At the end of it, however, the train stopped. Bognor, with an alacrity that belied his wind and girth, ran to the door, jumped out and sprinted – well, jogged – to the front of the truncated train. As he had surmised, their historic engine was now superseded by a superannuated small tank engine of only marginally post-Thomas vintage.

The cab was empty and the track decrepit. In the lights of the engine the Bognors could see some twenty or thirty yards ahead. Only half that distance was tracked. After ten or fifteen yards the line just vanished. Shaking

rather, the Bognors, now followed at a discreet distance
by the remaining obituarists, walked to the point where
the line vanished and found themselves staring out at a
vast disused quarry. Beneath them the cliff face fell away
into a deep, black, fatal nothing.

'Hmmm,' said Bognor, 'the nearest run thing you ever
saw in your life. As the Duke said to the actress. Or
someone.'

It called, eventually, for champagne: champagne consumed
in the *Post*'s obituary office the morning on which Hugo
Bland's obituary appeared. In a spirit of rare magnanimity
Bradley-Smallrat had carried Bland's obit unchanged and
exactly as he had handed it in.

'Of course,' he said waving his silver tankard towards
Canary Wharf, 'it's a pack of thundering untruths but what
the hell. And it was a sad end.'

This was true. Bland had pulled the old carbon monoxide
trick with the rubber tubing attached to the exhaust pipe
of his Morris Minor in the garage of his three-bedroomed
semi somewhere unexotic south of the river. A lengthy
confession, full of lachrymose remorse, had been posted
to Bradley-Smallrat on the morning of the death. Bradley-
Smallrat had passed it among the loyal obituarists but not
to the police. There seemed no point. It was an incredible
quantity of gambling debts which had prompted the defec-
tion to *Valete*, the attempted massacre and the subsequent
suicide.

'God knows how he got himself into such a muddle,'
said Bognor, 'but I believe anything of a man who lives
alone with a cat.'

His wife told him not to be such an oaf.

Dottie Tomkiss poured more champagne. There was
a question mark over Dottie who was not in the loo as
supposed but who was found wandering by the abandoned
signal box from which Bland had switched the points. She
claimed that she had jumped from the train. Or been

pushed. She seemed unclear but pleaded concussion and amnesia which was consistent with slight facial contusions. On the other hand it seemed at least possible that she was party to the plot but had been abandoned by Bland – blamed possibly – when things had gone wrong and the Bognors jumped to conclusions and the communication cord.

As told in Bland's confessional the whole thing had been absurdly simple. The defectors were, naturally, to be spared. The death of the loyalists would have, on the one hand, wiped out the new magazine's most serious opposition and on the other provided *Valete* with a tremendous scoop for its launch issue. (This was where suspicion focused on Dotty, for *Valete* would have wanted the self-written obituaries and only Dotty had them. But Ivor Bradley-Smallrat did not want to suspect Dotty any more than she wanted to be suspected.)

Gavin Chu, who was not to be charged since nothing could be proved without the confession, had staged the knifing himself with the help of fake blood from some theatrical agency. The 'policemen' and 'ambulancemen' had been laid on by the mysterious millionaire backer of *Valete*. They had lain in wait at the mouth of the tunnel and moved into action so quickly that everyone else was too stunned to suspect them. All matters pertaining to the railway had been the product of bribery, ingenuity, Bland's intimate knowledge – hence the disused track to the lethal quarry – and an assiduous reading of that classic railway murder story *The Missing Special*, which both Bognor and wife recalled in the nick of time.

'As an old school friend, or at least contemporary,' said Bognor, 'I thought I might pen one of those addenda which, in my opinion, add such a distinctive flavour to a good obituary page. You know the sort of thing. Perhaps you'd allow me to read it out loud.'

Bradley-Smallrat said yes and Bognor cleared his throat and read:

' "S.V.T.B. writes . . . " ' He coughed and screwed up

his eyes at his dreadful handwriting. He really ought to
see an optician.

'Oh do get on with it,' said Monica.

There were times when he didn't think he liked his
wife very much.

' "In your notice about Hugo Bland, the obituarist, you
failed to mention the almost pathological tardiness which
dogged him from his earliest years. Even at school it was
universally acknowledged that Bland Mi would be late for
everything from corps to chapel. Unfortunately what was a
joke at school became a liability in adulthood. It could even
be argued that his untimely demise was partly due to failing
to turn up in time for a crucial train departure. Sadly, he
was all too aware of this failing and indeed admitted, shortly
before his death, that 'Sometimes I fear I've missed the boat
of life.' " '

There was a longish silence.

'Did he really say that?' asked the Brigadier.

'Well,' Bognor fidgeted, 'not in so many words.'

'My biographical husband has added a new terror to
death,' said Monica, 'to paraphrase Sir Charles Wetherell.'

Bradley-Smallrat looked bleak and uncomprehending.

'I think,' he said, 'that readers of the *Morning Post*
have probably had enough of Hugo Bland. In fact, as
Obit Editor I declare that this obituary is now closed.'

And they all drank to that.

Heavenly Rewards

Timothy Holme

It looked as though the theft – or removal as they preferred to consider it – was going to be easier than they had expected. The building was derelict and unfrequented in the unfashionable outskirts of the city, far from the library with its 700,000 priceless scrolls, the school of medicine and the great amphitheatre. A guard was mounted on it, but more as a matter of routine than out of any real sense of urgency.

The two men had arrived in Alexandria a week before and had immediately set about their customary bargaining for space. They looked like, and indeed were, two merchants from the Serenissima Republic of Venice, and they did all the things such merchants usually did. They bargained hard and carefully supervised the loading of the spices onto a ship in the harbour; they experimented with the local food and wines; they went into the red light quarter where ancient Egyptian and Greek lore had brought heady perfection to the art of love. And, of course, as men of culture they visited the monuments of this city which, founded more than a thousand years before, was one of the greatest centres of the ancient world.

Nobody knew that these two merchants had been specially and rigorously trained for a mission which, if they managed to achieve it, would be one of the greatest single political coups of all time.

Nor did anybody notice that the cultural sight-seeing of the two merchants took them on various occasions near the derelict building with its single guard, so that they were able to observe it and the surrounding land and learn how often the guard was changed.

'You'd think they didn't realise the value of it,' said one of them, a dark, extremely good-looking young man who, in spite of the prolonged hardship of his training, still persisted in viewing the mission as a glorious adventure.

'They don't,' said the other whose name was Buono Tribuno. He was an older man whose features all seemed drawn with grim lines of determination. From the start he had had no romantic fancies about the undertaking they were engaged on; for him it was a means of attaining ennoblement, for himself first and then for his family.

'But how can they fail to see its importance?'

'It's not that they fail to see it exactly,' said Buono, 'it's that fundamentally it means nothing to them. And so with the passing of time, even though they realise its importance theoretically – they wouldn't put a guard on it at all if they didn't do that – they've lost the sense in practice of its real value.'

Their ship was due to sail at dawn next morning and so they had planned the removal for three after midnight. At that hour it was still pitch dark and the penultimate guard of the night was at exactly its halfway point and consequently its lowest ebb.

Buono and the young man, whose name was Rustico da Torcello, spent the evening before the removal at their rooms at an inn in the centre of Alexandria. Food and drink had been sent up to them but, for once, they had eaten cautiously and, in spite of Rustico's protests, drunk hardly at all.

As the time shortened, Rustico became more excited, pacing the room, unable to keep still; while Buono sat

motionless at the table, staring morosely into the flame
of a candle. Neither of them talked.

Then, soon after two o'clock, they looked at each other
for the first time for more than an hour and Buono nodded
almost imperceptibly. They collected the little they were
going to need which had to be carried, hidden about them,
and left.

As on previous nights they made for the red light quarter
which was still active, but turned off in another direction
before they got there. Now the streets were deserted and
the dangerous part of their mission had begun.

It was as well they had followed the route several
times by day for it was now pitch dark with no more
than an occasional diamond gleam of star in the narrow
strip of black sky between the roof-tops which seemed to
be straining towards each other overhead.

Before they got to the derelict building they changed
course once again according to their prearranged plan, for
they wanted the guard to have no warning of their approach.
They had to make a long deviation which finally took them
out into a melancholy copse behind the building. They were
near the city walls beside Lake Mareotis and, though it had
been still and hot in the centre, a light wind blew in here
from the lake making the tree-tops above them whisper like
souls in limbo. This was an unforeseen piece of good fortune
as it would cover up the sound of their approach.

Again the two men looked at each other and again Buono
made a slight movement of his head. Rustico grinned in the
darkness. Then as softly as a fall of snow they moved up to
the rear wall of the building.

It was said in Venice that not even a cat could climb like
Rustico and, on one famous occasion a few years earlier,
the doge and fifty guests dining in a second floor chamber
had been surprised to see a figure suddenly appear outside
the large window from what they knew to be a sheer drop
to the ground below and then swarm up out of sight with
the agility of a spider towards the dizzy roof. That was the

first time Rustico, who had done it for a bet, had drawn the attention of the authorities onto himself.

And now his skill was to be put to the service of the state. Like an amphibious creature moving from land into water, Rustico appeared not even to slow down as his motion changed from horizontal to vertical, and it seemed not so much that he reached out for the various footholds and projections as that they drifted to him across the suddenly liquefied stonework. Buono might have waited until Rustico's work was done, but at this stage even seconds might be vital. As he went up Buono started to feel his way round to the front of the building, clinging to the wall.

Although he was a heavily built man he could move in complete silence, but even he couldn't prevent something snapping gently under his foot. Instantly he petrified, a statue set in the wall. If the guard came to investigate with his lamp there was a good chance that Buono might get him first, but not such a good chance that he would do so in time to prevent the alarm being raised at the nearby guard command. And that would mean certain death for them both and – what was far more important for the Venetian Republic – the failure of their mission.

He waited for five century-long seconds and then, when no sound of movement had come from the front of the building, started to move forward again. He reached the corner and paused, his back pressed against the stonework. Now only about twelve yards from the guard, he would have to wait until his partner's work was done.

Above him Rustico was swarming silently over the roof, its principal features being supplied to him more by memory from his earlier, daytime observations than by sight. But these observations had necessarily been made from a distance and they couldn't tell him if there were any loose tiles or other potential sources of noise. Danger loomed over him in the dark and he grinned at it as one would at an old sparring companion.

And as though the smile had momentarily tricked danger

into conceding Rustico a point, he succeeded in reaching the edge of the roof without mishap. But he well knew as he got there that all the odds were on danger's side in the next few seconds. He looked down and could just make out the form of the guard and the lethal shape of his scimitar which, if Rustico's leap were not silent and totally accurate, would soon be ploughing through his guts.

Below him, about twelve yards away to his left, Buono would be waiting, but powerless to save the situation if Rustico lost in his duel with danger. When they had made their first survey of the building, they had at once realised that a ground approach to the guard would be hopeless. From his position in front of the heavy wooden door buckled with iron there were about a dozen yards either way to the corners of the building, the nearest points of unseen approach, and in the light from his lamp they could never have covered those twelve yards without his seeing them in time to raise the alarm. The only way was from above.

But it had to be made perfectly.

Slowly Rustico drew himself upright from a crouching position. For an instant he hovered, and then he jumped. But as he did so his foot dislodged a piece of stone and Rustico, as he toppled downwards, saw the guard's moonlike face lifting up towards him and the scimitar lashing to the ready.

Almost simultaneously he crashed into the guard's shoulders making him stumble and fall. He felt iced lightning cut into his left arm and knew it was the scimitar. At the same time he saw the man's mouth open to call out and couldn't understand why only silence came out. And then he realised that almost unknown to him his right hand had been at work with the dagger and that warm blood was pumping and spurting into his face.

'Dead?' Buono had arrived unnoticed and was standing over them.

Rustico looked and nodded.

'Quick!'

Rustico got off the body and the two men, after looking round quickly to see nobody was about, went to the heavy door, the opening of which was Buono's job. He worked swiftly and silently except for almost inaudible little grunts which betrayed the strain of it.

Five minutes and the door opened with a creak which made them both tauten. Then taking the guard's lantern they went inside. Shadows leapt at them like a pack of wolves and massive stone pillars reared up as though to smash their brains out. To Rustico, who was the more fanciful of the two, it seemed as though they had broken into the underworld.

But already Buono was running forward. Travellers' reports over the years had enabled the authorities in Venice to piece together and pass on to the two agents a remarkably accurate description of what they were looking for, exactly where to find it and how to get at it.

At the other end of the building was an apparently solid rectangular block of stone, waist high and about eight feet in length. But round the other side of it, they had been told, was a low iron grille inside which, in a jewel-encrusted casket, was the object of their mission. Breaking through the grille would have been impossible to anybody without Buono's skill and training as well as the tools which had been specially made for him in Venice. Again he set to work with the same little grunts of strain.

Time poured agonisingly away like a haemorrhage and it seemed as though at any moment the guard's body would be discovered and his comrades would be storming into the building to hack the two Venetian agents to pieces. But the silence persisted, interrupted only by Buono's little grunts and the sound of his instruments working on the grille.

Finally these sounds were climaxed by a slow grinding as the grille at last gave way. Precisely, as he did everything, Buono placed it on the floor before reaching inside.

Neither of them was prepared for the splendour of the casket. Its precious stones gleamed in many-coloured regality in the lamplight; arguably it was worth more than the entire Venetian treasury.

'Pity we can't take this as well,' said Rustico. But they both knew it was out of the question. Any attempt to take the bulky casket might seriously jeopardise their chances of getting its incomparably more valuable contents safely back to Venice.

Opening the casket took Buono less than a minute and, when it was open, in spite of their essentially pragmatical natures and the appalling danger of their position, they couldn't help looking at the contents with something like awe. Then Buono scooped them carefully into a little silk bag they had brought for the purpose. Only when this was done did they see that there was something else in the casket.

'What is it?' said Rustico.

'Let's get out,' said Buono impatiently.

'Wait a moment – I want to see— ' Rustico took it out of the casket and saw that underneath it was a sort of plaque with some writing engraved on it.

'Come on!' said Buono with urgency.

Rustico held the lantern over the plaque and saw that the writing was Greek, in which he was fluent. He read through it and whistled softly. 'We'll take this, too,' he said. 'It'll be something for our pains.'

Sister Margherita Teresa had a streaming cold which was hardly surprising. She was a native of Sardinia and when she had first taken her vows she had been sent to a convent in Sicily where the climate was, if anything, even warmer than on her native island. She had stayed there for three years and then, with all the abruptness which characterises these things in the world of a religious, she was told that she would be leaving the next morning for the convent of their order in Venice.

As she had been trained to do she had received the news with downcast eyes and no sign of surprise.

'*Si, madre,*' she said.

But she was still too young to have disciplined her
mind which was set in a complete whirl by the news.
Venice. It immediately made her think of a little gondola
with coloured lights and a golden cabin which played 'O,
sole mio' when you wound it up. This gondola had been
bought by Aunt Ermengilda when she had gone to Venice
with the parish outing and, standing on the sideboard with
its Sunday evening tinkle, it had always represented Venice
for the little girl who was to become Sister Margherita
Teresa.

But the images evoked in her mind by the gondola had
little bearing on the Venetian reality. Perhaps if she had
come in spring or summer it might have been different,
but it was already late autumn when she arrived and the
fogs had started so that the dampest city in the world was
wrapped in yet another layer of damp. The calles were
muffled corridors of mystery, the waterbuses hooted like
aquatic phantoms and the buildings, as though in tardy
reaction against all the staring they had been subjected
to during the summer, wrapped themselves modestly in
misty swathes.

To make matters worse the convent was housed in one
of the dampest buildings in the city, a large house near the
Accademia which seemed to be on the verge of drowning in
the canal by which it stood. Accustomed to the climate of
Sardinia and Sicily, Sister Margherita Teresa caught a cold
two days after her arrival and had not got rid of it since.

She now sat in the porter's cubby-hole, to which she had
been assigned, huddling by the electric fire installed for her
by the Mother Superior, saying her rosary and watching the
fog which seemed to be clamouring for admission at a high
window above her head.

Unexpectedly the street doorbell rang and, as she
pressed the button to open it, she wondered who it
could be; it was normally a dead period of the morning – too early for the shifting population of the poor

who came in around midday for bowls of soup with bread.

Through the glass panel in front of her she saw the door open and then, with a drift of fog, a man came into the hall. She at once recognised that he was what her mother would have called 'a fine figure of a man'. Moreover, he was obviously southern, a fellow countryman in a strange land. For both these reasons, she realised, she would have to be particularly strict in her behaviour.

'*Buon giorno,*' she said, not looking at him.

'*Buon giorno,*' he replied. The tone of his voice, she noticed, was warm, but with a thread of something counter in it. Irony? The whole effect he had on her, indeed, was disconcerting, causing her mind to stray towards paths she thought she had made it forget altogether.

'Can I help you?' she asked in as official a voice as she could manage.

'I'd like to speak to the Mother Superior,' he said. 'Or rather,' he corrected himself, 'the Mother Superior would like to speak to me. She's expecting me.'

'Who shall I say it is?'

'Questura.'

If his arrival had caused an upheaval within her, the announcement of his provenance caused another almost as great. Nuns have a grapevine all of their own. They do not consciously set it up or willingly use it, but it operates in spite of them; it is entirely wordless and an outsider would be at a loss to see how it could possibly work; it is the product of close proximity. From this grapevine Sister Margherita Teresa had learned that something alarming had happened in the convent that morning. What it was she had no idea, but she knew that the atmosphere was profoundly wrong. And now the arrival of a man from the police seemed to confirm the most alarming possibilities.

Nothing of what she was thinking, however, showed on Sister Margherita Teresa's face which remained professionally blank.

'Please follow me,' she said.

Her mind still a turmoil from the nearness of this man and her speculations about the cause of his visit, she led him out of the hall and along the stone corridor to the Superior's office where she knocked a timid, nun-like knock.

'*Avanti!*' came the authoritative, peremptory voice of a woman who sounded like a female general.

Sister Margherita Teresa opened the door. 'A gentleman from the Questura,' she said.

'Show him in.'

As she was closing the door, Sister Margherita Teresa just had time to hear the policeman introduce himself.

'Peroni,' he said, 'Achille Peroni.'

Fortunately the contents of the casket were sufficiently meagre in bulk to be concealed under their cloaks. More worrying at the moment was the wound in Rustico's arm. It was deep and had bled profusely. Once they had got safely away from the area immediately surrounding the derelict building, Buono had bandaged it as best he could, but Rustico was dangerously weak and it seemed touch and go whether he could reach the harbour.

They kept as close as possible to the walls on the western side of the city where the streets were still almost deserted. Disaster almost struck when they ran into a patrol of Muslim police. Two foreigners at that hour, wrapped in unseasonable cloaks and one of them covered with blood and scarcely able to stagger could not have failed to arouse suspicion. And if the theft and the dead guard had not been discovered by now, they surely would be before long. Fortunately the two men managed to disappear into the darkness of a stone arcade before the patrol had spotted them.

Then, when it was safely past, they resumed the painful drag towards the harbour.

Dawn was just fingering the sky when they finally got

there, with Buono more than half carrying Rustico. The Venetian ship, the *Santa Maria*, straining at her hawsers by the quayside, was the most wonderful sight they had ever seen, by far outstripping one of the official seven wonders of the world, the four hundred foot high Pharos lighthouse which stood on its island in the mouth of the harbour.

People were about now, and they looked curiously at the blood-smeared, deathly pale young foreigner being shouldered by his companion through the docks.

'If they stop us now . . . ' muttered Buono.

But the captain of the ship had seen the two Venetian agents and sent down a group of men to escort them on board. He was aware that they were on some kind of mission for the Republic, and even though he had no idea of the nature of the mission, he felt it could be no bad thing to enjoy the favours of two men employed by such very highly placed members of the state.

The sailors took over Rustico and carried him up the gangplank.

'Are you ready to sail?' asked Buono.

'Never readier.'

'Then cast anchor immediately.'

He and Rustico with their precious loot were conducted down to their cabin where a doctor was sent for to dress Rustico's wound. While he did so, his patient gulped wine and Buono covertly examined what they had removed from the casket in the derelict building.

The ship cast anchor, the sails puffed royally in the wind and the prow turned slowly towards the Pharos lighthouse, the Mediterranean and Venice. It seemed as though the mission had been safely brought to its conclusion, with nothing left between them and a triumphant home-coming with wealth and honour from a grateful state which, as a result of their mission, was now set to become the most powerful city state in the world.

And then they realised that the ship was inexplicably turning back towards the quay and slackening speed. Buono and Rustico looked at each other in anxious surmise and, at that moment, the captain, white with anxiety, burst into the cabin.

'The port authorities!' he said. 'They've ordered us back – they're boarding now! I couldn't disobey them or they'd have sunk the vessel.'

Again Buono and Rustico looked at each other. What had happened was all too obvious. The dead guard and the removal had been discovered and now they were going to search the ship. They could hardly fail to find the contents of the casket and then, even if they got away from Alexandria alive, that would mean ignominy and probably death, for the Serenissima Republic was none too scrupulous about assessing responsibility when it was thwarted of something it wanted as badly as this.

The captain was aware that something of vital importance was at stake and stood ready to give any help he could. Buono looked wildly about for a safe hiding place and found none.

Rustico looked into his cup of wine, and in its dark red depths he saw the answer. He looked up and told the captain what to do.

Mother Elisabetta was a remarkable woman. She had degrees in ancient languages, psychiatry, philosophy and musicology; she was an accomplished organist, could speak half a dozen modern languages and had written what many people considered to be the definitive biography of St Catherine of Siena. She ran her convent like a ship and grew an encyclopaedic variety of herbs in its garden.

She had faults, too, and she knew it. She could be overbearing, was more Germanic than Italian in her insistence on discipline and her tongue was cruelly cutting if she forgot (which she rarely did) to control it.

Also she couldn't tolerate men. This was no mere physical aversion and it was not countered by any morbid attachment to her own sex. She mentally excluded her Redeemer and one or two other figures from this otherwise all-embracing contempt which was both emotional and intellectual. She just found that women were wiser, kinder, more intelligent and reliable than men.

She would have preferred it if the Questura had sent a policewoman, but as she understood they were in the minority (no wonder crime was both rampant and undetected!) she resigned herself to making do with a man. She would also have preferred it if they had sent a northerner, for southerners were another of her pet antipathies.

None of this showed on her face as she stood up and gave her hand to the policeman who had just introduced himself as Achille Peroni.

'Please sit down,' she said.

'How much of St Catherine's subsequent activities would you say were influenced by the fact that she came from such an exceptionally abundant brood of children?' was the policeman's surprising response.

Within her mathematically fitted wimple Mother Elisabetta shook her head slightly and blinked as though she had seen something impossible. A man, a policeman, a southerner, asking such a remarkably perceptive question as that?

'The question,' she said, 'is both deft and profound. As a matter of fact, I am coming more and more to the belief that not enough attention has been devoted to St Catherine's brothers and sisters. Their influence upon her . . .'

As she talked she got deeper and deeper into the subject which enthralled her above all others, and the southern policeman led her on with the most searching questions. She began to feel that one more name would have to be added to the extremely short list of males who met with her approval.

'However,' she concluded as it slowly dawned on her that she had forgotten all about the truly appalling motive for his visit to her, 'you mustn't let me waste your very

valuable time with my poor ramblings, however fascinating
their subject might be. Much though I should prefer to
discuss Siena's greatest daughter, I fear that a graver and
more urgent affair demands our attention.'

'Yes, of course.' Peroni's attitude put her in mind of an
attentive and polite young friar awaiting instructions from
his superiors.

'Something,' she said, 'has disappeared from the convent
chapel and, reluctant though I am to draw the conclusion,
I am afraid its disappearance can only be explained on a
hypothesis of theft.'

Without even a pretence of deference for the Venetians
and with their scimitars ready for instant use, an officer
and three men pushed into the cabin where Rustico, Buono
and the captain were waiting.

'Who are these men?' the officer asked the captain,
eyeing Buono and Rustico with open suspicion.

'Two Venetian merchants,' said the captain.

'And where were you during the night?' the officer
went on, turning directly to the two merchants.

'On board,' said Buono.

'Have you any witnesses of that?'

'Certainly,' said the captain. 'The gentlemen dined with
me and we sat up throughout the night playing cards.'

'Hum.' The Muslim officer didn't sound convinced.
'What's this wound?' he snapped, suddenly pouncing on
Rustico.

'A mock duel,' said Rustico, 'with one of the ship's
officers. We do it to keep in training.'

'I can fetch the officer in question to bear it out,'
said the captain with the smooth mendacity of a true
Venetian.

The Muslim stood for a second in hostile uncertainty,
then nodded curtly to his three men. 'Search the cabin,'
he ordered.

As they started to take it to pieces, he stood in

the middle, his eyes prying speculatively about him for possible hiding places.

'What's in that?' he said, pointing suddenly at a large wooden chest standing by the window.

'Look for yourself,' said Rustico, 'it's open.'

Going to it the Muslim lifted the lid and stood for about half a second in perplexity, then he smelled the contents of the chest before slamming the lid shut in disgust. 'Filthy infidels!' he said.

'In Venice it's a great delicacy, I assure you,' said Rustico.

The search went on for another half hour in the cabin and then was conducted throughout the ship for the rest of the morning. Only by mid afternoon did the Muslim officer admit defeat, withdraw his men and give the captain permission to sail.

Buono and Rustico waited until they were safely out in the Mediterranean to take out from the belly of the carcass of salted pork the headless remains of St Mark, the proto-evangelist.

Along with the other object which they had been covering.

'Perhaps you won't mind, Commissario,' said Mother Elisabetta, 'if I tell you a story.'

'I like stories,' said Peroni, and you could almost have sworn that his Pucci tie and English-looking suit had been transmuted into a friar's habit.

'In 829 two Venetian merchants, by name Rustico and Buono Tribuno, removed the headless body of St Mark from its place of rest in Alexandria and successfully hiding it from the Muslim authorities in a carcass of pork – which, as you know, they abhor as unclean – they brought it back to Venice. This was probably the greatest single coup in the entire history of the Republic, however doubtful it might be morally. There has always been a profound devotion for St Mark in Venice of which he is said to be the spiritual founder.'

'I never knew that,' said Peroni.

'Oh yes. One day, when he was helping to spread the gospel throughout the world, he was blown by a storm onto an island in the lagoon where he fell asleep to be awoken by an angel who said to him, *"Pax tibi Marce evangelista meus* – Peace be with you Mark, my evangelist."* And this angel then foretold to him the future foundation of Venice. So you see the Venetians have good cause to have a special cult for him. But they had no relics of him and so, following the logic of the time, they couldn't adopt him as their official patron and had to make do with the somewhat hazy St Theodore who stands with his even hazier crocodile on one of the two columns in the piazzetta to this day. But now thanks to Rustico and Buono Tribuno they had, not a mere finger or toe, but his entire mortal remains (all traces of the decapitated head were lost). This gave an unprecedented boost to the morale of the Venetians. In fact, you can date the Republic's spectacular rise to power to that period. And in case you might think the importance of this relic is exaggerated, it is worth remembering that as recently as 1967 Kirillos VII, the patriarch of the Orthodox Coptic Church, appealed to Pope Paul VI for the return of it to Alexandria.

'The relic itself,' she went on, 'was placed in the basilica of St Mark's and there it is to this day. All that, however, is merely to give you the necessary background. One day in 1885 a certain Angelina Tribuno presented herself here as a postulant. When she was admitted to the novitiate she had a curious story to tell. She said that she was the last surviving member of an ancient Venetian family.'

'Descended from *the* Buono Tribuno?' said Peroni.

Mother Elisabetta didn't usually like being interrupted, but the things which irritated her in the vast majority of men had the contrary effect of meeting her approval coming from one of her select list of favourites. So now she nodded benevolently. 'Exactly,' she said. 'And her ancestor and Rustico, Angelina said, found something else at the same time as they found the body of St Mark. I don't know,' she went on, apparently going off at a tangent, 'if you read the bible?'

'Not as much as I should do,' said Peroni diplomatically.

'Well, in the fourteenth chapter of the Gospel of St Mark there are two very curious verses. The scene is in the garden of Gethsemane and Judas has just brought the temple guard to arrest Jesus. All his followers have abandoned him and escaped. All except one. "And there followed him a certain young man having a linen cloth" – or sindon in the Greek – "cast about his naked body; and the young men laid hold of him: And he left the linen cloth, and fled from them naked." This young man is mentioned in none of the other gospels and it is an ancient tradition that he is none other than the evangelist himself – *pace* Chrysostom and Ambrose who opted for John the apostle. And if Angelina Tribuno's story is correct, Chrysostom and Ambrose are wrong and tradition is right, for she asserted that her ancestor and his companion found this sindon together with the remains of St Mark. There was some sort of plaque in the casket containing them which said that the cloth had been kept by the soldier who had stripped it off St Mark. Subsequently this soldier was converted to Christianity and met St Mark again with whom he became very friendly. But – one presumes with the evangelist's approval – he retained the sindon which, in a sense, had brought about his conversion. Only when he heard of St Mark's martyrdom in Alexandria did he feel that it should be reunited with its proper owner, and so he had it buried with the body. And there it lay for over eight hundred years until it was discovered by Rustico and Buono.'

'A remarkable story,' said Peroni.

'It has not yet reached its conclusion. When the two men reached Venice they told the authorities nothing of their second discovery. After all, they must have reasoned logically enough, they had been commissioned to get the body; anything they happened to find with it was their perquisite. And a relic such as that would have been considered a very considerable acquisition in those days.'

'But how did they decide which of them should have it?' said Peroni. 'You can't share a linen cloth.'

'Exactly. It is believed that Rustico died mysteriously very soon after their return from Alexandria, so the natural assumption is that they, too, found the problem of sharing an awkward one and that Buono killed Rustico or had him killed in order to have the full possession of the sindon. Certainly, Angelina said, it had been retained in her family ever since and down the centuries it had always been kept a closely guarded secret for fear that the Venetian authorities would demand it. But by the eighteen-eighties the family was about to become extinct, with its one remaining member taking the veil. So Angelina asked if the sindon could come into the convent with her, the Superior agreed and it has been kept in our chapel ever since.'

'But wasn't there a big fuss made about it at the time?'

'Not really. You see, what is there to guarantee its genuineness? After all, we're dealing with a family legend dating back over a thousand years, and the day of relics has largely passed.'

'And it is this cloth, I take it, which has been stolen?'

'That is so.'

'When did you discover it was missing?'

'This morning, shortly after ten o'clock. I went to examine its condition.'

'Is it on display?'

'Not directly. It was kept in a reliquary, and that was on display.'

'Was it locked?'

'Yes, but the key was kept behind the reliquary. I'm afraid that years of perhaps subconscious scepticism about the genuineness of this sindon made us careless. We took it very much for granted and it never occurred to anybody that it might be stolen.'

'When did you last see it?'

'Last year at about this time.'

'So it could have been stolen any time in the last twelve months?'

'Exactly.'

'Who had access to the chapel?'

'I'm afraid I'm not going to be very helpful there either, Commissario. Everybody had access to the chapel – it's open to the public.'

'But would an ordinary member of the public coming into the chapel know that this relic was there?'

'Most probably not.'

'Is there anything written in the chapel saying what it is?'

'No.'

'So in other words it had the anonymity of the vast majority of relics in churches everywhere – bits of bone, hair, clothing and so on. For most people going into the chapel it would be as though it didn't exist.'

'That is so.'

The thought lay heavy between them that, in this case, the theft could only be the work of a relatively small number of people, most if not all of them professed religious. And both Peroni and Mother Elisabetta knew that the other was aware of it, but neither of them alluded to it.

'Perhaps,' said Peroni, 'you would show me the chapel?'

'Terrorists of the right and the left are tearing the country apart, the crime rate is escalating to unprecedented figures, the age at which drug-taking begins has been lowered to the first classes of junior school and the illegal export of currency is draining away the country's life blood. And with all this going on, we are expected to spend our time looking for a piece of cloth. That is Italy for you!'

Dott. Amabile, the police chief of Venice, was a native of Friuli and he possessed the imperturbability of people from that region, but from some ancestor who fought with Garibaldi, he had inherited a virulent strain of anti-clericalism which occasioned the present display of wrath. Peroni had never seen Amabile so unlike his usual calm, headmasterly self. The cloud from his pipe that usually drifted indolently about his head was replaced by vicious little puffs of smoke like bullets.

'And,' went on Amabile, his wrath apparently stoking its own fires, 'we can't go and tell her what to do with her wretched piece of cloth as we would with any other ordinary member of the public who asked us to embark on such a futile enterprise. Oh, no! Because if we do she'll be straight on to the Cardinal Patriarch and the Cardinal Patriarch will be on to the Mayor and the head of the region and heaven knows who else and they'll be on to me – even the Communists – as though I'd refused to rescue a child drowning in the Grand Canal! Nuns! How long,' he went on, calming down a little, 'are you going to take to clear the ridiculous business up?'

'If the field of investigation is to cover the entire past year,' said Peroni, 'and take in everybody who went into that chapel, there'll be no end to it.' Amabile shuddered. 'But if we narrow the field down,' Peroni continued, 'to include only the people who could reasonably be expected to know about the relic and have some motive for wishing to remove it—'

'Superstitious rubbish!'

' —then I think we might clear it up fairly quickly.'

'But what possible motive could anybody have for stealing such a useless article?'

'People used to think that relics could heal diseases.'

'Are you seriously telling me, Dottore, that in this latter end of the twentieth century when man has walked on the moon, when practically every organ in the human body can be transplanted, there are still people who believe such nonsense?'

'I believe so, Dottore,' said Peroni whose Neapolitan soul was awash with the most outrageous superstitions and who, beneath his Pucci tie, wore a medal of St Januarius, the patron saint of Naples whose blood still miraculously liquefies on specific dates in the cathedral of Naples.

'Hum!' Dott. Amabile looked like a headmaster who had been told that voodooism was being practised in his school. 'And how do you propose going about it?'

'I've got a list from the Mother Superior of all the people who knew of the existence of the cloth and would have had the opportunity of taking it away – that's to say two women who come in from outside to help with the cleaning, a nun from Sardinia who's been given leave to visit her sick mother, a nun from Vicenza going to the funeral of her little sister who died of hepatitis in Vicenza, a nun in a clinic with a nervous breakdown and another nun— '

'That's quite enough nuns for me, Dottore,' interrupted Amabile. 'It sounds as though you take a perverse delight in listing them.'

As a matter of fact, nuns were one of Peroni's special interests. Half hidden within their habits and disciplined to complete reserve, each one nevertheless had her own character and Peroni always found it a challenge to find traces of that character.

'Get on with it as quickly as you can,' said Amabile, 'and please get the whole thing cleared up without involving me.'

'*Sí*, Dottore,' said Peroni.

Peroni organised enquiries concerning the cleaning women, the nun in Sardinia and the nun in the clinic but kept the third nun in Vicenza for himself. He didn't hope to make any startling discoveries there, but he did hope to get away from the fog for a while. He worried excessively about his health and fog terrified him.

He went to Piazzale Roma by police launch, huddling in the warmth of the cabin and looking out at the meteorological cotton wool swirling over the waters of the Grand Canal. At the Piazzale he covered his mouth with a handkerchief and ran to the huge garage where he kept his new Lancia for such trips as he was able to make inland.

With the heating on at the maximum he drove over the causeway to Mestre and onto the Serenissima motorway. Less than half an hour later he was in Vicenza, but unfortunately the fog was there, too, thicker if anything than it had been in Venice. It transformed the gracious Palladian architecture, making the arches and the loggias and the columns seem part of a shifting, nightmare landscape which shaped itself as you went.

He managed to park at the end of the narrow street where the nun's family lived which meant a short walk in the fog. To fortify himself for this he went into a bar and ordered a grappa. His normal drink was Chivas Regal whisky, but he was a believer in the therapeutic value of grappa, and as he walked quickly down the street he could almost feel the burning spirit combat the icy fog.

The number he was making for was a low, two-storey house of the late eighteenth century with a dullish green front and bars before the ground floor windows. There was a single bell with a long since illegible name beneath it. Peroni pressed the bell and waited, hoping they would let him in quickly out of the lethal fog.

But they seemed in no hurry to answer the door. He looked at his watch – not yet two o'clock. A minute went by while Peroni covered his mouth and nose with his handkerchief. Maybe they were all out, though it seemed unlikely with a funeral at five. He rang the bell again and decided that if there were no answer this time he would retreat to the bar at the end of the road and treat himself with more grappa, but just as he was on the point of doing so he heard the door being opened.

The person who opened it was, undoubtedly, Sister Beatrice. She was young, still in her early twenties with a pretty, slightly spotty face and large dark brown eyes behind metal-rimmed spectacles. But it was not so much her appearance that struck Peroni as her manner. She looked as though she were sleep-walking and, at the same time, dreaming of something indescribably awesome.

'Sister Beatrice?' said Peroni, but she seemed not to hear him. 'Sister Beatrice?' he tried again and this time got through. She moved her head a little uncertainly as though there was some doubt about whether she were Sister Beatrice. '*Sì*,' she said eventually. '*Sì.*'

'I'm from the Questura in Venice,' said Peroni.

He had expected some reaction from this. When you said you were from the police, people, however innocent, usually look at the very least curious. But Sister Beatrice's expression was unchanged; she was still totally caught up in her mysterious dream.

'Come in,' she said after a moment and, turning, proceeded him across the musty, dark hallway. As he followed her Peroni suddenly thought that the interview might be awkward to handle; you can hardly let a nun know that you even suspect the possibility of her removing a relic from the convent chapel. He began to shape suitably diplomatic questions.

She opened a door at the other end of the hall and stood aside to let him go in. There were a number of people in the room; the usual family gathering that you expect at a funeral, but Peroni was surprised to notice that everybody had expressions similar to that of Sister Beatrice; they all looked bewitched and seemed unaware of Peroni's entrance.

In the centre of the room on a table was a small white coffin with its lid beside it, and its pull on Peroni's eyes seemed to be ineluctable.

And then he saw that the coffin was empty.

He looked, wildly questioning, at Sister Beatrice and she met his gaze with the same awed look as before. There was a curious silence in the room, too, he noticed, the sort of silence that swarms with a jostling crowd of unspoken thoughts. Suddenly this silence was broken by a voice.

'Mamma, can I have another cup of chocolate, please?'

The voice was that of a child of about five whom Peroni

hadn't noticed before as she was almost entirely hidden by a group of relatives.

He looked back, still questioningly, at Sister Beatrice and after a second she spoke for the first time since they had come into the room.

'My little sister, Luisa,' she said as though that explained everything.

'But,' said Peroni, lost, 'I thought she was dead.'

'She was,' said Sister Beatrice. 'Half an hour ago she was.'

The Evidence I Shall Give

H. R. F. Keating

Sergeant Moos was a dashed bore. Inspector Ghote thought he was actually the most boring person he had ever known, a one hundred and one per cent burden and bugbear. The trouble was the man could talk about just one thing only. His job, his kaam. Fingerprints.

Certainly there was no-one to touch him in entire Bombay Crime Branch as an expert. For that reason, though he was past the statutory age of retirement, he had somehow stayed on in his little cabin, its filing cabinets crammed with the prints of every miscreant who had ever come to police notice. He was, in fact, one famous fellow. It should have been a great honour even to know him. Except he was altogether unable to speak of anything else than his whorls, his loops and his arches.

So, although from time to time Ghote felt obliged to allow himself to be caught by Moos, who seemed to know by some sort of telepathy if he had gone across for something to eat or was on the point of leaving for home, mostly he went to a good deal of trouble to keep out of his way. He had heard Moos's stories and accounts too often, each and every one of them.

'Ghote bhai, was I ever telling you one trick your clever badmash is sometimes trying? You know what it is such a fellow is attempting? He is presenting his fingers to be printed in wrong order only. Yes, yes, one devilish cunning move. He is thinking that when the said card is coming before me and I am seeing twinned loops and tented arches on third finger of right hand when on my records I have such on fourth finger I would be altogether deceived.'

At that point in this story – each time it was told – a glow of simple pleasure would come into the big, soft, brown eyes in Moos's round moon-like face and the cigarette that seemed to dangle permanently from his thickly loose lips would for a moment burn with a brighter light.

'But what a badmash like that is not at all counting on,' Moos would continue, filling in every possible corner of the picture, 'is that I am having a tip-top memory for any shape or form of fingerprint. Yes, tip-top though I am saying it. So every time I am catching out such fellows. Never once failing.'

'Shabash, Sergeant, shabash,' Ghote would dutifully offer congratulation.

But congratulations never brought to a halt the steady dribble of fingerprint fact and fingerprint theory, the be-all and end-all of Sergeant Moos's existence. He had no other interests. He was not married, and all he did when at last he left his cabin after a day's work was to get something to eat and then retire to his quarter where – Ghote had heard this at least a hundred times – he was collecting information to write the really definitive Indian book on – well, fingerprints.

So, when at the end of his own long day Ghote might be heading for home, thinking only of his Protima with his food waiting or ready if he was particularly tired to press his feet, and Moos would appear suddenly at his elbow with 'Inspector, what luck I am spotting you,' his first reaction would be to put up some excuse. Any excuse.

'Oh, hello, Moos bhai. Just off to . . . Well, I am in one devil of a hurry, you know.'

But then, more often than he could have wished, that excuse would fall away into nothingness. The look of pleading in Moos's big brown eyes would be too sad to ignore.

'But perhaps I can spare some minutes only.'

Then, over a cold drink at Moos's expense – he was punctilious about paying for his pleasure – there would come once again the story about how such-and-such a history-sheeter had failed to beat Moos's fabulous memory by presenting his fingers to an inexperienced print taker in the wrong order. Or perhaps it would be some other piece of oft-repeated information.

'Did I ever tell, Inspector – not many people are knowing this – it is between the third and fourth what they are calling foetal month that the fingerprints are formed on the unborn child. And those prints thereafter are remaining for the whole of the said person's life unchanged? Those unique prints. Did you know that?'

And Moos would lean back from the little round table with the two fizzing glasses of Thums Up or Limca on it and a look of sun-effulgent pleasure at the beauty of that fact would spread all over his round face. The wet-tipped cigarette between his lips would perk up till it was pointing straight out in front of him, jauntily.

How then could Ghote say, 'Yes, Sergeant, you have told me this already'? But after each such session he would say to himself that he was now entitled to adopt any evasive tactics that came to hand to prevent himself being caught again. For at least two weeks.

So it was with a feeling of entirely justified fury that late one afternoon he looked up from his desk to see Moos come bursting in. Only two days before had he not listened patiently for nearly three-quarters of an hour while he had been told – as if it wasn't something he had known since he had been a probationary sub-inspector at Nasik Police Training School – that a workable method of classifying fingerprints had first been developed in India in 1897 by Mr

Edward Henry, later Sir Edward, Commissioner of Police at Scotland Yard, and that his trusted assistant, Sub-Inspector Azizul Haque, had earned the title Rai Bahadur and an award of Rupees 5,000?

'Oh, Ghote, you are here?'

'Yes. Why would I not be in my seat? Unless I was out on a case. As I have been till one hour past, and my report not yet finished.'

But the pointed remark went for nothing. Moos simply slouched forward, pulled away one of the chairs in front of the desk and slumped down on to it.

On his innocent typewriter Ghote took out the rage he felt at this blatant disregard of the unacknowledged agreement that he should be badgered by Moos only when he was not actually at work. He seized the wretched machine and dumped it on the floor beside his narrow desk with a crash that risked yet another key becoming appallingly stuck.

But then, as he looked across at Moos, something in the fellow's wide round face drained all his anger away. He did not look at all well. He looked, in fact, grey with illness, or with perhaps the effect of some catastrophic news. And, for surely the first time ever in his recollection of him, he was not mangling a cigarette between his lips.

'What is it you are wanting, bhai?' he asked then, fearing what he might hear in reply.

But to his surprise Moos answered with his usual request.

'I was wondering – if – if you have some minutes only to spare, Inspector, can we go for a cold drink?'

For a moment Ghote contemplated, in the face of this, saying straight out that they did have an arrangement, however much it had never been spoken of, that Moos would not get more than one chat per fortnight. But the grey look on the fellow's face was still there, undiminished. So, although this happened to be the first evening for a week that he was going to be able to get home at a decent hour, he yielded.

He received another surprise then. Moos, although scrupulous about standing treat, invariably took him to an Irani restaurant some way from Headquarters where the prices were moderate. Now unexpectedly he proposed a complete break with tradition.

'It is good of you to find some time, Inspector,' he said. 'I am well knowing you must be wanting to get back to your wife and child. But – but – well, shall we go to Badshah Juice Bar? You were once stating you were very much enjoying their Ganga Jamuna.'

It was true that the mixture of fresh lemon and orange juice, called in comparison with the confluence of the two holiest of India's rivers a Ganga Jamuna, was something, served deliciously chilled, that Ghote particularly delighted in on the rare occasions he felt he could allow himself to sample the air-conditioned luxury of the Badshah, just over the way from Headquarters. But it was extraordinary that, since there could be no fingerprint link to that indulgence of his, Moos should ever have remembered it.

And why was Moos offering to take him to such a posh place at all?

Evidently he was not going to find the answer in a hurry. Once having secured himself the promise of an audience, Moos lapsed into heavy silence. Ghote rapidly cleared the papers from his desk, acknowledging to himself that he had had little intention of finishing his report that day, called to the office peon that he was leaving and made his way, with Moos a looming stone-like presence at his side, out and across the jostling, horn-hooting streams of traffic to the Badshah Juice Bar.

When at last he was seated in front of a tall condensation-pearled glass of Ganga Jamuna, and Moos, opposite, had a simple mosambi juice, which despite the fact that he was still not smoking it looked as if he had little intention of touching, he ventured to put a question.

'Well, Sergeant, what is it you are wanting to chat?'

But Moos did not answer.

Ghote shot him a glance in the cool dimness of the bar's upstairs room. Certainly, he did not look at all well.

'Bhai, are you ill itself? Is it serious?'

Thoughts of cancer – all those cigarettes – of leprosy even flashed into Ghote's mind.

'No, no,' Moos replied, however. 'I am hundred per cent fit, Inspector. You are knowing I have never had one day of sick leave in all my years of service?'

'Yes, yes. I remember you saying it. But – but, all the same, you look as if you are not keeping well, bhai.'

'Well?'

Moos sounded as if this was the first he had ever heard of any suggestion that he might be ill. But, if he was not so, what could be wrong with him? And this silence? He was hardly reluctant normally to talk, to talk and to talk, whenever he had secured a captive audience. So why was he saying nothing now?

Ghote took a sip of his Ganga Jamuna. It was, as ever, delicious. But somehow he could not quite savour it to the full.

He looked across at Moos.

'Inspector,' the old fellow said at last, seeming to drag the word syllable by syllable, letter almost by letter, from deep inside himself. 'Inspector, there is something I have to tell.'

'Yes? But that is what we have come here for, isn't it? For you to chat.'

Moos picked up his glass of mosambi juice, looked at it and put it down again.

'Inspector,' he asked, lowering his voice almost to a murmur. 'Inspector, you are knowing the Phalnikar case?'

'But yes, Sergeant. Of course. Up in court tomorrow, no? Plenty of kudos for Crime Branch there. Who would ever have thought we would be able to lay hands on the culprit when they were first finding His Honour's body in that flat that day? And your evidence will be the clincher, bhai. No getting past fingerprints.'

Sergeant Moos was famous, too, for his demeanour in the witness-box. No Defence pleader, however wily his tactics, however hectoring, had ever been known to shake Moos's simple certainties.

But, instead of the slow smile of satisfaction Ghote had hoped to call up on Moos's face by that tribute to the part he would play next day in bringing a murderer to justice, he replied only with a heaving groan.

'Moos? Moos bhai, what is it? What has happened?'

'It – it – it is this.'

But there followed only another groan. From the depths.

'Yes, bhai? What it is?'

'Inspector, I have found – I have found something.'

'Found something? What? Surely not that you have mis-identified that print from the Phalnikar flat? You were telling a fortnight ago how good it was.'

'No, no. It is not that.'

'But then what is it, bhai? It is to do with the Phalnikar case? It cannot be anything too bad if it does not affect the evidence you would be giving.'

'Inspector, it is worse. Worse. Altogether worse.'

'No? What? Tell me, bhai. Tell me.'

'Inspector . . . '

Moos's voice had sunk yet lower. A mere sloshy whisper.

'Inspector, it is this. I have found – I have found one print that is altogether identical with the one belonging to the culprit in the Phalnikar case.'

'Identical?' Ghote repeated, struggling with bafflement. 'But – but that cannot be, bhai. So often you are telling. I was learning it at PTS even. No fingerprints are identical.'

Wearily, with bowed-under weariness, Moos wagged his head in negative.

'No, Ghote, that is not what I have ever said. It is not what you were truly taught at Training School either. What I have always stated is that chances of two prints being one and the same have been calculated from the number of variable factors to be found on each finger, ridge endings, islands, lakes, spurs, crossovers and bifurcations, as coming out at one in one hundred thousand crores. It is because of this that it is always accepted that prints constitute infallible evidence.'

Figures slowly surfaced in Ghote's mind. 1:10,000,000, 000, 000. It was an incredibly small chance.

He looked at Moos across the narrow marble table.

'And you are telling that this fantastic chance has actually happened?' he asked. 'That you have seen a print that is cent per cent the same as the Phalnikar murderer's?'

'Yes.'

It was a whisper of a whisper.

'You are sure?'

The question was ridiculous, he knew. Moos, when it was anything at all to do with fingerprints, was always doubly, trebly cast-iron sure.

'Yes, bhai. I am sure.'

The voice came as a series of small dull hammer-strokes.

After a moment Moos gave another of his beaten and battered groans.

'You are knowing, Inspector,' he went on ploddingly after a moment, 'that in different countries they have different standards of comparison for prints. It is something I must have told one lakh times. We are having different standards in the different states of India even. In Karnataka it is twelve points that must agree before identity is accepted. In the UP it is six only. While in France it is as many as seventeen. And in UK it is sixteen.'

'Yes, yes.'

It was true, as Moos had said, that he had produced these figures and others like them time and again in their chats. But never, till now, had he admitted by so much as a hint that the substance of their conversations had often been repeated and repeated.

'Well, Inspector, in these two prints I am telling you about I have checked, point for point, more than twenty-five

agreeing. It was just only this morning that I was going over
my evidence for court tomorrow – I am liking to have everything clear in my head, you know – and, suddenly, looking
at the Phalnikar culprit's print, something became triggered
off in my mind. A similarity, a most close similarity. I
thought for a few moments only, and then I was able to go
straight to the file in question. It was that of one Ram
Prasad, just only one conviction for HB.'

'One housebreaking conviction only, and you were
remembering that print? Moos bhai, you are altogether
a wonder.'

But the flattery did nothing for old Moos. He sat there
at the table, his face still as grey as if he was working up
to a dose of high fever. His expression, that of a man who
has just learnt he is going to be hanged or shot.

'But,' Ghote said eventually, 'this is going to cast doubt
upon all fingerprint evidences in each and every court, no?
I mean, I can hear Defence pleaders one and all referring
to this discovery which you are making and stating that
someone other than the accused must have committed the
crime.'

'Yes, yes. But it is worse, much worse. I have been
sitting all day since I was checking and double-checking
what I had found, and I have been thinking. It is not just
only our cases, Inspector. It is worldwide also.'

'Worldwide?' Ghote thought. 'Yes,' he said. 'Yes, you
are right. It would be worldwide. As soon as the news
is getting out, everywhere in the world where a case is
depending on fingerprint evidence your discovery will be
brought in. You will be more famous, Moos bhai, than
Rajiv Gandhi himself.'

But Moos was as stolidly unimpressed by this as ever he
was in the witness-box by the bullying tactics of a Defence
pleader.

'Soon there would be no more cases depending on
fingerprint evidence,' he said. 'Before the year is out,

I tell you, the fingerprint departments of every police force in the world will be closed down. All the science that has been accumulated since year 1897 is destined to be doomed. All the energies and efforts of nearly one hundred years will be like dew on the grass before the scorch of the sun itself.'

Now it was Ghote's turn to sit in silence. Moos, too, his terrible secret told, was again deprived of speech. His glass of mosambi juice remained untouched in front of him. Ghote's Ganga Jamuna seemed equally now to be a mere token allowing him to sit in the dark cool privacy of the almost empty upstairs room of the Badshah Bar. To sit and think.

Everything Moos had said was true. That single discovery of his, made thanks only to his phenomenal memory for every detail of his day-in, day-out study, was going to put paid for ever to a whole highly important branch of the science of criminal identification. Yes, the name of Moos would be heard on the lips of lawyers from the furthermost west of America to the easternmost parts of Japan. Of Moos, destroyer of Sir Edward Henry, of Sub-Inspector Azizul Haque, of all the scientists and police technicians who had ever worked to create the vast system of fingerprinting.

And then at last his slow-circling thoughts arrived at a conclusion.

He looked up.

'Moos bhai,' he said. 'There is one thing only for you to do. You must forget what you have seen. You must put back into the files that fingerprint of Ram Prasad and forget that you were ever even suspecting that it was identically the same as that one of the Phalnikar culprit's.'

'No, Ghote bhai. Do not think I have not asked myself one lakh times if I should do that. If it was not my bounden duty even. But do it I cannot. It is there. I have seen it. I cannot persuade myself that I have not.'

'But, bhai, you must. You must. You know what would

be the terrible consequences if you do not. You have
yourself said it. Criminals by the thousand, by the lakh,
by the crore, will escape justice if what you have found
ever becomes— '

An appalling thought flashed into his mind.

'Moos bhai,' he said with frenzied intentness, 'have
you already told any other person except myself?'

'No, no, Ghote bhai. You know you are the only man
in entire Crime Branch who will ever listen to me.'

Ghote registered that, for the second time, Moos had
admitted the inadmissible. So it was certain that only the
two of them, Moos and himself, knew what had been discovered. Himself. He, too, now knew the world-shattering
secret.

He sat in silence again, examining his conscience. What
did he feel was his course in answer to the dilemma that
now faced him and Moos equally?

Before long he found that his mind was made up. There
must be some occasions in life when to lie, or at least to
blot out the truth, was the one and only right thing to do.
And this, beyond doubt, was one such occasion.

'Moos bhai,' he said with renewed earnestness, 'what
you have found out must go no further. Not one inch.
Ever.'

'But, Ghote, have you thought? I have been thinking
and thinking all day, remember. It is not all so simple. I
cannot, I cannot, forget what I have seen with my own two
eyes. I have seen it. And you, you will not be able to forget
either. Because I will show you the evidence. I must. That
much I am owing you. And, once you have seen, you will
have always before you the temptation to speak.'

'No,' Ghote jerked out in absolute denial. 'No, no, no.'

'Yes, my friend, you will. I have thought whether I
would have this temptation, and I know that it would
come to me. Perhaps on my death-bed only I will suddenly
crave for that worldwide fame you have spoken of. Or when
I am giving my bi-annual lecture at Nasik PTS, that lecture

which Commissioner sahib himself was insisting I must give, perhaps then, even as I am explaining about odds of one hundred thousand crores to one, I would suddenly succumb to this temptation. Or what if I am one day getting drunk?'

'But, Moos bhai, you are never getting drunk.'

'Yes, yes. It is true I have never touched any kinds of wines. I have not dared. But in my remaining life who can say that I will not, and then . . . '

'But, no. No, that will not happen. It must not. It will not for me, I am promising. I will never fall to the temptation to speak of this. Never. I have decided. Already my mind is made up. Moos, old friend, I am going to forget we have ever met today.'

'Ghote bhai, you would not be able.'

'Yes. Yes, I shall. It is possible to forget as well as to remember. By one effort of will. From this moment on I am putting out of my mind each and every word that you have said. And I am telling you to do the same. Forget. Forget. Make yourself to forget.'

'No.'

'Yes. It can be done. It can. If you are willing. Go back to your cabin now. Take that card with the prints of Ram Prasad on it, and – yes, burn the same. Take out your lighter or your match-box, and then, better than putting the record of a two-per-paisa criminal back into the files, burn it. Just only burn it.'

'But, Ghote, tomorrow itself I am to give evidence. In the High Court. And when I am asked by the State pleader, as they are always asking as a matter of routine only, whether the fingerprint put in as evidence is that of the accused and the accused only, what am I to say?'

Ghote braced himself.

'You are going to say,' he ordered Moos with all the authority he could bring to bear, 'that the print put in as evidence is that of the accused. You know that this is so. Say it.'

'But, listen, the Phalnikar culprit committed his atrocity in the course of housebreaking, you remember that. And Ram Prasad, whose fingerprint is utterly the same as the one I myself was finding at the scene of the crime, has one conviction for HB itself.'

'Nevertheless,' Ghote answered, leaning forward and directing his full gaze into Moos's big round face, 'you are not going to remember that chance discovery you were making when tomorrow you are in the witness-box. You are not.'

'Ghote, I am. I will. I cannot help myself. Ghote bhai, fingerprints have been my whole life. Without my belief in the truth of them, where would I be? Ghote, on the matter of fingerprints I cannot lie.'

'But, Moos bhai, think. If tomorrow in court you come out with this, then from that moment on the whole of your beloved science of fingerprinting will begin to crumble into dust. Into dust of dust.'

'I know, Ghote, old friend, I know. But what to do? What to do?'

'Forget, bhai. I have said. Forget, forget, forget. Tell yourself that you have dreamt the whole damn thing. Tell yourself you were for two-three moments mad. One way or another, forget.'

'Well, I have wondered that: whether I had gone mad. But that record-sheet, that fingerprint, it is there, Ghote. It is there.'

Moos picked up the untouched glass of mosambi juice and banged it so emphatically on the surface of the table that a dollop of the pale lime slopped out over his hand. He failed to notice it.

'Listen,' he said, 'you must see that card also. Come now. Come and see with your own eyes.'

Ghote wriggled on his bench.

'But what use would that be?' he said, the thought of how long he had been delaying in going home suddenly blooming in his mind. 'I am not at all a fingerprint expert.

I could not tell whether you are right or wrong, bhai.'

'No, please to come. Please. I want one more pair of eyes to see what I have seen.'

'No. No, sorry, bhai,' Ghote said, sweat springing up between his thighs despite the air-conditioned coolness all around. 'I must really be going home. Already I am behind schedule one half-hour. But I will come. First thing in the morning I will come to your cabin. I am promising.'

He drained in one long swallow all the rest of his big glass of Ganga Jamuna. It had lost its chill, and tasted only of sour sharpness.

'But, listen, bhai,' he said, looking across at Moos with all the seriousness he could command. 'Think about what I have been saying, yes? Just only forget what you saw. Burn that record card. Or at least put it back into the files. Or, better still, do what they are doing in Government offices with inconvenient letters. Mis-file same. And then forget. Forget it all.'

But Moos's big round face remained sullenly lugubrious.

'It has happened,' he said dully. 'It has happened, and I cannot forget it. I will remember all my life. In court also tomorrow I will not be able to forget.'

But he pushed himself to his feet, and Ghote knew with a wash of inner relief that he himself was free now to go home, to cast off if he could the image of Moos's woebegone face.

'Well, tomorrow we would see,' he said. 'Go back to your quarter now and get a good night's sleep. In the morning it would all look very much of rosier.'

'Yes, I will go. No. No, I will take one more look at those prints. One final-final check. Yes, I must. I must. Goodnight, bhai. And thank you for listening to me.'

Moos had never before offered a word of thanks for all the long hours Ghote had spent hearing his talk of radial loops, ulnar loops, twinned loops and lateral pocket loops or whatever aspect of his obsession happened to come into his mind at any one time. And Ghote now was sharply conscious of the change. For an instant he wondered whether he ought after all to go back to Headquarters and let Moos show him the wretched, damnable record card, little though probably he would be able to make of it. But the thought of Protima waiting for him, or, more to the point, the thought of a wrathful Protima waiting deterred him.

'Goodnight then, bhai,' he said. 'See you first thing in the morning.'

In a way, however, Ghote saw Moos much sooner than first thing next morning. He saw him in his head through most of that night. He had been unable, indeed, to rid himself of the thought of Moos and his terrible discovery from the moment he had left him. He had been thoroughly poor company for Protima all the evening, till eventually she had said that if she was not going to get one word out of him she might as well go early to bed as she had done every night of the week.

And when, after sitting for half an hour trying to push from his mind every looming remembrance of Moos and his fearful horn-sharp dilemma and not succeeding, he went to bed himself, he found, tired though he had felt, bone-tired suddenly, that he still could not chase away the sight of Moos's round face, for once without a dangling wet-tipped cigarette at its centre, and the look of battered hopelessness in his eyes.

Wryly he thought of the advice he had offered with such conviction. To forget. To blot it all out. He had said to Moos he was going to do that himself, and here he was completely unable so much as to begin.

Was Moos really right in the discovery? Had he actually point by point seen incontrovertible evidence that the two fingerprints from the hands of different men were exactly and absolutely the same? Could he, despite his years-long reputation, have been mistaken?

Had he – this was a new, sudden thought – had he somehow desired to make his discovery, appalling though it had seemed to him? Had he in his innermost self wanted to make it? That chance of two prints being identical, however mathematically unlikely, might well be something that obscurely would haunt someone as obsessed with fingerprints as Moos. So had he, perhaps driven by that obsession to the point of madness, gone so far as actually to invent what he had most dreaded? It was possible. Possible.

Now, violently, he wished he had after all gone to see those two record cards. He would not have been able to make any expert comparison, but he might have been able to see enough to decide there was a prima-facie case. Or not. He might even with a single glance have realised that the prints on the two cards were in no way like each other, and then sadly have had to escort a mad Moos to the pagalkhana.

Then, lying there in the dark and biting his lower lip in vexation, he had told himself that this was the merest wishful thinking. Of course Moos, star witness in hundreds of cases involving fingerprints, never successfully challenged, never found wrong, was bound to be right in what he had seen with his own eyes. Yes, the whole huge edifice of fingerprinting was on the point of coming tumbling down. Tomorrow in the Bombay High Court when Sergeant Moos was called to give evidence a whole new era in criminology would begin. A black era.

At last sleep spread over him.

A sleep plagued with dreams. He saw Moos sitting opposite him in the Badshah Juice Bar and showing him all his fingers and thumbs, each one of them with the same pattern clear to be seen. Whirling, twirling question-marks. He saw Moos in the High Court witness box, standing on his head. He saw the Judges themselves shrinking and shrinking away into nothingness. He saw his own fingers, and there were no tips to them at all.

He woke early, was as bad-tempered as he had been the evening before, pushed aside the beautifully crisp puris Protima had cooked for his breakfast, stamped out well before his accustomed time and rode his motor-scooter down to Headquarters with unaccustomed recklessness.

He had thought, on arriving, that he might even be too early for Moos. But it seemed not. There was a light on in his cabin, the lines of it bright above and below the door.

Strange, he thought.

But perhaps Moos was taking one more look at that fearful evidence and had given himself the very strongest possible light to check on each and every one of those inescapable points of correspondence.

He turned the knob and opened the door.

The moment he stepped into the little crowded room, where the fan in the ceiling was whirring grindingly, he realised he was seeing something which at the back of his mind he had been expecting all along, for all that he had pushed the thought down.

Old Moos was slumped across his examination bench in a limp heap. Beside him was a small blue-glass bottle with squared-off ridged sides, its stopper out. Ghote, at that moment, was unable to recall the name of the liquid it had contained, though only a month earlier Moos had shown him the bottle and told him at length for what abstruse purpose he used minute quantities of its contents. 'I have to keep always under lock and key itself,' he had said. 'It is a Number One dangerous poison.'

On the table almost directly in front of the cabin's door there was a large, stiff brown envelope. On it, in staring block capitals, was his own name.

He took a step forward and picked it up. But for a moment he found himself totally incapable of opening it.

What if inside there were, as surely there were bound to be, two fingerprint record cards, each bearing a different name, each with one absolutely identical print? Had the burden, which Moos had found too much for him, been transferred to his own shoulders? Was he going to be left with the evidence, incontrovertible evidence, that there could be two totally identical fingerprints? And if he was, would he now be able to do what he had with such

easy-come assurance said to Moos he would be able to do?
To forget that he had ever known of their existence?

Yet, just possibly, one single glance at the cards might
be enough to tell him that poor Moos had been driven by
his obsession into the mere delusions of insanity.

With sweaty, trembling, useless fingers he tore away the
top of the envelope, turned it upside-down and tipped its
contents on to the table in front of him.

A small pile of grey ashes.

Faro and the Bogus Inspector

Alanna Knight

One of the most baffling problems Detective Inspector Jeremy Faro ever faced had nothing to do with crime, but quite a lot to do with buying presents for his mother and two small daughters. Birthdays were difficult enough for a widower, but Christmas presents were worse, especially when Rose, aged eight, took one look at the familiar oblong cardboard box and cried out reproachfully: 'Oh Papa, *not* another doll.' Had his normal powers of deduction been functioning Inspector Faro might have found the vital clue in her younger sister Emily's letter, that she 'liked the dolly's frocks, but *not* very much.'

Birthdays, however, were inevitable but by the seventies the fashion set by Her Majesty and the late Prince Consort had been eagerly followed and the Christmas craze had spread to Edinburgh. Now a middle class, once content with the annual Hogmanay debauch, demanded turkey, plum pudding, a tree in the window and the unsteady march of Christmas cards across the mantelpiece. In mainly candlelit rooms this had the city's fire engines on constant alert.

Nor were fires the only hazard in the homes of the well-to-do. A rash of Yuletide parties and conviviality, with a regrettable slackening of the tough moral fibre of

Calvinism, was regarded as a positive enticement to sneak thieves. As a consequence this quite unnecessary season of peace and goodwill was greeted with less than enthusiasm by Edinburgh City Police.

Advertisements like that of Jenners in Princes Street, offering customers a chance to inspect valuable seasonal items, had been viewed by the criminal element as an open invitation to more splendid opportunities of breaking and entering in a spate of daring robberies.

Faro's young step-son Dr Vincent Laurie returned his sister's letter across the breakfast table.

'Now what do you think of that? I imagined that all little girls liked dolls.'

'They do indeed, Step-father, but not *every* Christmas and birthday. Ever since our Mama died—' he added sadly. 'Don't you see?'

Faro tried but failed. 'You wouldn't . . . ?'

'No, I certainly wouldn't, Step-father, the very idea. I find it hard enough getting suitable presents for my own list.'

Vince could be notoriously unsympathetic sometimes but seeing his step-father's anguished expression, he said: 'What about a piece of jewellery then? Small girls like lockets and bangles.' And warming to the idea. 'And a brooch for Step-grandma—'

'You really think so . . . '

'I do indeed. And what's more there's a splendid new jeweller's shop opened in South Clerk Street, just a step away. Foreign chap. Did an excellent repair on my old pocket watch – a wizard with clocks, I understand – highly recommended – '

'In the circumstances – would you . . . ?'

'No, I wouldn't,' said Vince crossly. 'The experience will do you good.'

As the last date for posting parcels to Orkney grew nearer, so did Inspector Faro's temper grow shorter and his scowls greater. Finally, with all the anticipatory joy of a man presenting himself for the extraction of a particularly sensitive tooth, he stared glumly into the jeweller's window, feeling utterly helpless faced with such a bewildering choice.

If only he enjoyed shopping. He had relied on his dear Lizzie to keep his wardrobe up to standard. His indifference to sartorial elegance was well known at the Central Office. As long as garments were comfortable and covered him in modest decency, he did not care a fig for fashion. The reflection of his greatcoat in the window glass jolted him a little, but closing his eyes, he took a deep breath and entered the shop, where a loud bell noisily indicated his presence.

He needed only a few moments to scrutinise his surroundings as he waited for the jeweller to appear. The shop was small, dark and depressing, a complete contrast to the brilliant sunshine of an afternoon already nestling into a rosy sunset, sharp with frost.

A closer look at the owner, who entered through the curtain and bowed gravely, told a delighted Faro that he might have modelled Mr Dickens's Fagin but for those gentle eyes and that dignified bearing.

Indicating a tray of brooches he found Mr Jacob most helpful. Was the recipient a young lady?

Faro shook his head. 'No, my mother.' He was both delighted and relieved when Mr Jacob after careful deliberation pointed to the very one he had in mind. 'Yes, indeed. I will take it.'

'Is there anything else, sir?'

When Faro asked to see lockets, the jeweller beamed.

'For your lady wife, sir.'

'Actually for my two small daughters. I am a widower.'

Mr Jacob sighed. 'I also. I have a daughter to look after me.'

Choosing two identical gold lockets, Faro asked: 'I'm curious to know what brought you to Edinburgh. Have you been here long?'

'A year only.' There was a slight hesitation. 'You

asked what brought me here, sir, and I will be frank
with you. Persecution – yes, persecution. We have been
dogged by utmost misfortunes, and we are still wanderers.
But Edinburgh gave us hope for a home. Here it seemed
that our race was tolerated and even encouraged to settle,
to live and to die in peace.'

So Mr Jacob had been lured by the fact that sixty
years ago, in the early years of the century, the first Jewish
cemetery in Scotland had been opened in Edinburgh, only
a stone's throw from his shop.

A sign of tolerance generous but sadly misleading,
thought Faro. To the ordinary Edinburgh citizen, a minority
racial group was something to be jeered at, despised, and
any success in business by honest dealings and the sweat
of their brows, treated with the darkest suspicion.

Mr Jacob was fitting the gifts into velvet boxes. When
Faro said they were to go through by post, a sturdy brown
envelope was produced.

'If you would write on the address, sir, I will give
you a card to enclose with a message.'

'That is most thoughtful of you, Mr Jacob.'

The jeweller studied the name and address carefully.
'Faro – you are the Inspector – Inspector Faro?'

'I am,' said Faro, surprised and flattered to find himself
famous.

'You must forgive me, sir, I did not recognise you again.'

'*Again?*'

'Yes, sir. I have the ring ready for you— '

'The ring – *what* ring?'

It was the jeweller's turn to look astonished. 'The
valuable brooch you left.' And unlocking a drawer behind
the counter Mr Jacob produced an emerald and diamond
ring. Even Faro, who was no connoisseur of precious gems,
would have hazarded a rough guess that it was worth at least
ten times his annual salary with Edinburgh City Police. He
also knew he had never set eyes on it before.

Mr Jacob mistook his expression as one of disapproval

and said anxiously: 'I hope it is correct, sir. I tried to follow your instructions exactly.'

'*My* instructions?'

'Yes, sir. I was to change the order of the diamonds and make the original brooch into a ring setting suitable for a lady to wear.' He hesitated, frowning. 'There is some mistake?'

With a shake of his head, Faro said: 'There is indeed. This piece of jewellery is not mine.'

'But you are Inspector Faro? Yes?' Mr Jacob consulted his ledger. 'The brooch was handed in two days ago by Inspector Faro.'

Now examining the ring thoughtfully, Faro said slowly, 'I didn't by any chance tell you how I had come by it, did I?'

Mr Jacob's bafflement now equalled Faro's own. 'Come by it? What is that? I do not understand.'

'Did your customer tell you that he had inherited the brooch?'

'It was my daughter you spoke to.'

Ah, and that explains the case of mistaken identity, thought Faro, as Mr Jacob darted behind the screen to reappear with a gazelle-eyed beauty. Nadia was very young, so nervous as to be almost inarticulate in her forest creature manner, but in a few years, Faro guessed, there would be few to rival her exotic looks.

And Faro smiled to himself remembering a Bible picture from his childhood. If her father could have modelled a benign Fagin then Nadia might well have been the lass setting the baby Moses adrift among the reeds.

Her father's admonishing tones in their own language made her wild-eyed and tearful. She would have disappeared behind the curtain but for his restraining hand. Urging her towards the Inspector, Mr Jacob's voice was stern indeed. At last with downcast head, she began an unintelligible explanation.

'In English, daughter,' thundered Mr Jacob.

She raised her eyes slowly to Faro. 'He came in and asked for my father. I told him he was not here. He did not want to leave the brooch but he was in a great hurry.'

'How did you know that?'

'He went often to the door and looked up and down the street as if expecting my father to come.'

Your father – or the people who were chasing him, thought Faro grimly, having now deduced the reason for the bogus Inspector's anxiety and the urgent necessity of having the brooch transformed into a ring.

'He saw someone in the street,' said Nadia. 'He seemed frightened and thrust the brooch into my hand. My father was to have it ready for him today without fail.'

'Today – you are sure?'

Nadia looked at her father. 'That is what he said.'

'He? He? Be polite, daughter, that is no way to address the Inspector. Her English – I apologise,' Mr Jacob shrugged.

'Let her explain in her own time,' said Faro gently.

In reply, Nadia touched her father's sleeve, whispered and then turning to Faro, Mr Jacob said, 'She tells me that she thinks you are not the same man.'

'Ah,' said Faro. 'Now we are getting somewhere. Your exact words, Mr Jacob, if I recall them correctly were that you didn't recognise me *again*. Your daughter's information confirms that I have never set foot in your shop before this afternoon.'

'But – but – sir, it was the day you arrested the holy man, the one who was trying to steal from my shop— '

'A moment, if you please. A holy man stealing from you, and I was arresting him? Sir, you must be dreaming.'

'If it was a dream, then it was a costly one. I lost much money.'

'I presume you have reported this theft to the police.'

Father and daughter exchanged anxious looks and shook their heads.

'No? Then I think you had better tell me exactly what happened.'

'You were in a policeman's uniform that first time.'
Mr Jacob shrugged. 'It makes a man look different.'

'Describe this uniform, if you please.'

What Mr Jacob described was that worn by police
constables. Detective inspectors, however, were allowed the
privilege of plain clothes, if they wished. The experience of
twenty years had led Faro to appreciate the advantages of
anonymity in his line of enquiries, where an approach by
an officer of the law was a hindrance rather than a help.
Innocent as well as guilty were apt to become very silent
when faced with an intimidating uniform.

'I think you had better tell me exactly what happened
that day – right from the beginning,' Faro repeated.

At his stern expression, Mr Jacob sighed. 'If you
will come inside. Nadia will look after the shop while
we talk.'

In the living quarters behind the curtain domesticity
was provided by a curtained bed in the wall for the
father and a tiny room no larger than a cupboard for
his daughter. From every corner stuffed animals glared at
them yellow-eyed and fierce. A tray of dismembered clocks
and watches ticked furiously as if in constant anxiety at
the close proximity of soldering iron and Bunsen burner.
Inviting Faro to a seat by the fire, the jeweller began
his strange story.

'A few days ago a customer, a holy man – of your
faith – wished to buy a diamond ring for his wife—'

'Ah, you must mean a minister,' interrupted Faro and
when Mr Jacob looked even more confused, he added, 'We
call them "reverends".'

'Oh. This reverend selected a ring priced at forty pounds
and offered to pay with a hundred-pound banknote.'

Fraud. That was Faro's immediate thought, considering the few hundred-pound banknotes printed and in
circulation. Only a foreigner would be taken in by such
audacity.

'I see that you too are doubtful, sir,' said Mr Jacob,

'as I was. And so was this reverend. He said: "As I am a complete stranger you must be wondering if this note is real. I noticed a bank just across the road. Would you care to ask the cashier to verify that this is a genuine banknote?" '

'Ah,' said Faro. 'How very convenient. You go across the road and leave him in the shop. When you return – my dear fellow. This is a very old trick.'

'I am not stupid, Inspector, and when I suggested that my daughter go instead, the reverend was not in the least dismayed. I was watching him intently and he was most complimentary about her. He talked – much as you have done, sir – curious about my reasons for coming to Scotland. Nadia was back swiftly. The bank cashier and the manager himself had assured her that the banknote was indeed genuine. I put the diamond ring into a box and from the safe in the kitchen, I gave the reverend his sixty pounds change.'

Mr Jacob paused and shook his head. 'He seemed such a kindly man, but just as he was leaving the shop, you entered – I mean, the policeman – who seized him and said: "I am a police inspector and I have to tell you that this man is a thief, well known to us. He has already been three times in prison." '

Faro was puzzled. A trickster like the minister who had been jailed three times, yet he had never heard of him.

Mr Jacob continued: 'I am an honest man, Inspector, and I had to protest that this time no fraud was involved for the bank had examined the hundred-pound note and said that it was genuine. You – er, this Inspector, then asked to see it. "As I suspected, like many other shopkeepers and bank cashiers, you have been tricked by a brilliant forgery. This is a master craftsman and I am arresting him. I shall have to take the fake banknote, which will be required as evidence later."

'When he brought out the handcuffs, the reverend said: "They will not be necessary, Inspector. You have my word as a gentleman that I will come with you quietly." But the Inspector just laughed at him.'

Mr Jacob sighed. 'I felt sorry for the reverend. He seemed like a real gentleman who had fallen on hard times and who knows what sorrows and misfortunes had driven him to a life of crime.'

Faro was curious about the man's identity. 'Can you describe him?'

'Garbed all in black, he was. Tall, pale-skinned, light-eyed . . . ' Mr Jacob ended with an embarrassed shrug for the description fitted Faro too and the latter suppressed a smile. Did all Gentiles look alike to the jeweller?

'He began to plead,' Mr Jacob continued, ' "There are hiring carriages outside. I will pay for one, Inspector. Allow me this last indulgence." It was a wild day, snowing, so the Inspector gave in.'

'And you were sent for a carriage and you watched the Inspector hand his prisoner in and drive away. Is that so?'

Mr Jacob looked puzzled. 'You smile, sir? I expect you know what happened next,' he added glumly.

'You came back into the shop and realised that your sixty pounds change had not been returned to you and that your fake minister had also carried off the diamond ring.'

The jeweller nodded dismally. 'I realised there had been a mistake and so when I closed the shop I went to the police station. But do you know, Inspector, no-one would believe a word of my story. They pretended that no inspector of theirs had brought a holy man in. When I protested that I was telling the truth they became very suspicious and asked a lot of questions and had another policeman write it all down. Where are your papers, they kept shouting. What about this shop of yours? How did you buy it? How did you pay for it?

'I was ashamed and upset, Inspector, and very afraid. Then there was a disturbance, a bad woman – from the streets – was brought in drunk and fighting. I took my chance and ran away as quick as I could.'

Faro shook his head. That would make the Central Office even more suspicious. He knew his men. They would think they were dealing with another criminal – or a madman. And they got plenty of both. People who came in with wild stories and tried to exact compensation for imagined frauds.

'After that I was afraid to go back again. I know I did wrong, but you see no-one, not even a policeman, wishes to believe that a foreigner is telling the truth. I could see it in their eyes as they listened to me – an expression I know very well,' the jeweller shrugged and spread his hands in a despairing gesture, 'like eager hungry dogs waiting for the chance to leap on their quarry.' He shuddered.

Faro protested with some soothing platitudes about the law and justice, which he knew were untrue. His words rang hollow for Mr Jacob was right and Faro was well aware of the strong anti-Semitic feelings. Even those with skins the same colour, English and Irish, speaking the same tongue, were abused. To the struggling mass of the Edinburgh poor, signs of affluence in any foreigner, however hard-won, were a subject of bitter hostility.

And now came the hardest part of all, for Faro had to tell Mr Jacob what was patently obvious.

'The police Inspector who made the arrest – well, I'm afraid he wasn't a real policeman.'

'Not real? But he was wearing a uniform.'

'I'm afraid that is no criterion of honesty – he could have stolen it.'

'What are you trying to tell me?'

'That your police Inspector and the minister were in league together, planning to steal a diamond ring and sixty pounds from you. Oh, yes, that hundred-pound banknote was genuine enough. It is a very necessary part of their trick to defraud shopkeepers who would be, as you were, immediately suspicious of such a large denomination, rarely exhibited in public and even more rarely handed across shop counters.'

As he spoke, Faro realised that Mr Jacob must have been the perfect foil for the crooks. The success of this trick depended on the ignorance of new shopkeepers. Particularly foreigners who might have their own reasons, nothing to do with fraud, but with past experiences of political persecution, which made them hesitant about involvement with the law.

Mr Jacob continued to look astonished and Faro said: 'There was no inspector, no minister. Don't you understand? Both men were thieves attempting to defraud you.'

'Ah, Inspector, there you are mistaken,' said the jeweller. 'There was no crime since the very day after I went to the police station the Inspector came back – to return the diamond ring with many apologies. It had been found on the minister when he was searched. He also returned my sixty pounds,' Mr Jacob added triumphantly. 'Now that is not the action of a thief.' He leaned across the counter. 'What I do not understand is why he gave your name?'

But Faro had already worked out that ingenious part of the imposture. The first episode with the minister and the diamond ring, the arrest of the minister by the bogus Inspector and the subsequent return of ring and sixty pounds were elaborate overtures to secure the jeweller's confidence.

As for the bogus Inspector, he was a seasoned criminal and perhaps their paths had already crossed. There was a certain grim humour in claiming to be Faro in the neighbourhood where the Inspector was a familiar sight.

Faro also saw that this was merely the beginning, carefully planned with intended results far beyond the mere remodelling of an emerald brooch into a ring. Of one thing, he was absolutely certain. The emerald brooch had been stolen. No doubt it would be revealed as one of the missing jewels from Jenners' recent robbery.

Mr Jacob had to be unwittingly drawn into the thieves'

kitchen. The most invaluable and hardest accessory to find, a skilled craftsman who would be adept at totally changing the appearance of stolen gems, and melting down gold.

Once the jeweller was committed to them, there was no escape for him. The gang would make sure of that and their threats would be most effective, especially since the Edinburgh City Police would be ready to suspect an alien. Mr Jacob's visit to the Central Office with his disastrous and wild-seeming accusations had landed him further into the net. A visit to be recalled with written-down evidence.

If Mr Jacob was to be saved and danger averted, there was only one way. The bogus Inspector must be seized when he came to reclaim the brooch. But how? Single-handed? Perhaps—

Faro looked out of the window. At three o'clock on a December afternoon, there was little light left outside.

'I think there is something we can do, Mr Jacob.'

Faro's success in his long career owed much to the element of patient waiting. He had given up hope by the time the streetlamps were lit and the smoking chimneys of Edinburgh that Robert Burns called 'Auld Reekie' added their acrid stench to the street's freezing fog.

The last customers had long since gone. Not one resembled the bogus Inspector and Mr Jacob exchanged a despairing glance with Faro. The plan had failed. Faro shook his head. Criminals, he knew, also have their intuitive moments. Perhaps the thief had already approached the shop in the dim light and, suspicions aroused, had decided that in his business, discretion was the better part of valour.

Mr Jacob went around the counter and was rolling down the door blind, about to shoot the bolt, when a rap on the outside announced a last customer. Through the kitchen curtain, Faro observed a young woman and groaned. His last hope had expired. But wait, what was she asking:

'I have come from Inspector Faro – to collect my emerald ring. I am the Inspector's sister and here is a note he asked me to give you.'

As Mr Jacob read the note frowning, Faro stepped out from the kitchen. 'Hello, my dear. I thought you were never coming. I've been expecting you for some time.'

The young woman was clearly taken aback and would have bolted had not he stood firmly between her and the door.

'But – but— '

'I have already collected the ring for you and outside I think you'll see a carriage awaits. Thank you, Mr Jacob, you have been most kind.'

'But – but— ' the woman protested.

Taking her arm Faro marched her firmly out of the shop and the police carriage that he had summoned earlier, which had been lurking discreetly round the corner, now approached rapidly. At the same time, another carriage bowled down the road. A man stared out and seeing that the woman had been taken and that several constables were erupting from all directions, he leaped down, took to his heels and ran down one of the closes.

'Bastard,' shrieked the woman after him. 'Bastard!' Her yells and screams as two uniformed constables seized her arms caused a few passers-by to blench. One elderly woman was so overcome by the display of unseemly emotions that she swooned on the spot.

As for Faro, he was already in hot pursuit of the bogus Inspector who had discovered too late that his headlong rush had carried him down a close with only one exit. The struggle was short and swift.

A not-too-clean fight, alas, but Faro's early training had included lessons in self-defence from a retired pugilist. The constables who had followed, truncheons at the ready, were not needed.

'You had better start talking, or it'll be the worse for you,' said Faro. 'I dare say your doxy has already told them all she knows.'

And one look at the woman's frightened face, the way she hissed and spat as her confederate was hustled into the police carriage, obviously convinced him that he need expect neither discretion nor mercy from that quarter.

'All right, Inspector Bloody Faro, you've won this time. . . . '

As Faro suspected, the bogus Inspector was only one link in the organised gang of jewel thieves and most of the missing gems from the haul at Jenners were recovered.

But that is another story.

A Case of Butterflies

Peter Lovesey

Before calling the police, he had found a butterfly in
the summerhouse. It had unsettled him. The wings had
been purple, a rich, velvety purple. Soaring and swooping,
it had intermittently come to rest on the wood floor. His
assumption that it was trapped had proved to be false,
because two of the windows had been wide open and it
had made no move towards the open door. He knew what
it was, a Purple Emperor, for there was one made of paper
mounted in a perspex case in his wife Ann's study. As
a staunch conservationist, Ann wouldn't have wanted to
possess a real specimen. She had told him often enough
that she preferred to see them flying free. She had always
insisted that Purple Emperors were in the oak wood that
surrounded the house. He had never spotted one until this
morning, and it seemed like a sign from her.

'You did the right thing, sir.'

'The right thing?'

'Calling us in as soon as you knew about this. It
takes courage.'

'I don't want your approval, Commander. I want my
wife back.'

'We all want that, sir.'

Sir Milroy Shenton made it plain that he didn't care

for the remark, mildly as it was put. He rotated his chair to turn his back on the two police officers and face the view along King's Reach where the City skyline rises above Waterloo Bridge. He stared at it superficially. The image of the butterfly refused to leave his mind, just as it had lingered in the summerhouse. Less than an hour ago he had called the emergency number from his house in Sussex. The police had suggested meeting in London in case the house was being observed, and he had nominated the Broad Wall Complex. He had the choice of dozens of company boardrooms across London and the Home Counties that belonged in his high-tech empire. The advantage of using Broad Wall was the proximity of the heliport.

He swung around again. 'You'll have to bear with me. I'm short of sleep. It was a night flight from New York.'

'Let's get down to basics, then. Did you bring the ransom note?'

Commander Jerry Glazier was primed for this. He headed the Special Branch team that was always on stand-by to deal with kidnapping incidents. International terrorism was so often involved in extortion that a decision had been taken to involve Special Branch from the beginning in major kidnap enquiries. Captains of industry like Shenton were obvious targets. They knew the dangers, and often employed private bodyguards. Not Shenton: such precautions would not square with his reputation in the City as a devil-may-care dealer in the stock market, known and feared for his dawn raids.

Glazier was assessing him with a professional eye, aware how vital in kidnap cases is the attitude and resolve of the 'mark'.

First impressions suggested that this was a man in his forties trying to pass for twenty-five, with a hairstyle that would once have been called short back and sides and was now trendy and expensive. A jacket of crumpled silk was hanging off his shoulders. The accent was Oxford turned cockney, a curious inversion Glazier had noted lately in the business world. Scarcely ten minutes ago he had read in *Who's Who* that Shenton's background was a rectory in Norfolk, followed by Winchester and Magdalen. He had married twice. The second wife, the lady now abducted, was Ann, the only daughter of Dr Hamilton Porter, deceased. Under *Recreations*, Shenton had entered *Exercising the wife*. It must have seemed witty when he thought of it.

Now he took a package from his pocket. 'Wrapped in a freezer bag, as your people suggested. My sweaty prints are all over it, of course. I didn't know it was going to be evidence until I'd read the bloody thing, did I?'

'It isn't just the prints.' Glazier glanced at the wording on the note. It read, 'IF YOU WANT HER BACK ALIVE GET ONE MILLION READY. INSTRUCTIONS FOLLOW.' 'There's modern technology for you,' he commented. 'They do the old thing of cutting words from the papers, but now they dispense with paste. They use a photocopier.' He turned it over to look at the envelope. 'Indistinct postmark, wouldn't you know.'

'The bastards could have sent it any time in the last six days, couldn't they?' said Shenton. 'For all I know, they may have tried to phone me. She could be dead.'

Glazier wasn't there to speculate. 'So you flew in from New York this morning, returned to your house and found this on the mat?'

'And my wife missing.'

'You've been away from the house for how long, sir?'

'I told you – six days. Ann had been away as well, but she should have been back by now.'

'Then I dare say there was a stack of mail waiting.'

'Is that relevant?'

The pattern of the interview was taking shape. Shenton was using every opportunity to assert his status as top dog.

'It may be,' Glazier commented, 'if you can remember what was above or below it in the stack.' He wasn't to be intimidated.

'I just picked everything up, flipped through what was

there and extracted the interesting mail from the junk.'

'*This* looked interesting?'

'It's got a stamp, hasn't it?'

'Fair enough. You opened it, read the note, and phoned us. Did you call anyone else?'

'Cressie.'

'Cressie?'

'Cressida Concannon, Ann's college friend. The two of them were touring.'

'Touring where, sir?'

'The Ring of Kerry.'

'*Ireland?*' Glazier glanced towards his assistant, then back at Shenton. 'That was taking a chance, wasn't it?'

'With hindsight, yes. I told Ann to use her maiden name over there.'

'Which is . . . ?'

'Porter.'

'So what have you learned from her friend?'

'Cressie's still over there, visiting her sister. She last saw Ann on Wednesday at the end of their holiday, going into Cork airport.'

'Have you called the airline to see if she was on the flight?'

Shenton shook his head. 'Tracing Cressie took the best part of half an hour. I flew straight up from Sussex after that.'

'Flew?'

'Chopper.'

'I see. Did your wife have a reservation?'

'Aer Lingus. The two-fifteen flight to Heathrow.'

Glazier nodded to his assistant, who left the room to check. 'This holiday in Ireland – when was it planned?'

'A month ago, when New York came up. She said she deserved a trip of her own.'

'So she got in touch with her friend. I shall need to know more about Miss Concannon, sir. She's an old and trusted friend, I take it?'

'Cressie? She's twenty-four carat. We've known her
for twelve years, easily.'

'Well enough to know her political views?'

'Hold on.' Shenton folded his arms in a challenging
way. 'Cressie isn't one of that lot.'

'But does she guard her tongue?'

'She's far too smart to mouth off to the micks.'

'They met at college, you say. What were they studying?'

'You think I'm going to say politics?' Shenton said as
if he were scoring points at a board meeting. 'It was bugs.
Ann and Cressie's idea of a holiday is kneeling in cowpats
communing with dung-beetles.'

'Entomology,' said Glazier.

'Sorry, I was forgetting some of the fuzz can read
without moving their lips.'

'Do you carry a picture of your wife, sir?'

'For the press, do you mean? She's been kidnapped.
She isn't a missing person.'

'For our use, Sir Milroy.'

He felt for his wallet. 'I dare say there's one I can
let you have.'

'If you're bothered about the media, sir, we intend to
keep them off your back until this is resolved. The Press
Office at the Yard will get their co-operation.'

'You mean an embargo?' He started to remove a photo
from his wallet and then pushed it back into its slot. Second
thoughts, apparently.

Glazier had glimpsed enough of the print to make out a
woman in a see-through blouse. She seemed to be dancing.
'I mean a voluntary agreement to withhold the news until
you've got your wife back. After that, of course . . . '

'If I get her back unharmed I'll speak to anyone.'

'Until that happens, you talk only to us, sir. These
people, whoever they are, will contact you again. Do you
have an answer-phone at your house?'

'Of course.'

'Have you played it back?'

'Didn't have time.' Shenton folded the wallet and returned it to his pocket. 'I don't, after all, happen to have a suitable picture of Ann on me. I'll arrange to send you one.'

'Listen to your messages as soon as you get back, sir, and let me know if there's anything.'

'What do you do in these cases – tap my phone?'

'Is that what you'd recommend?'

'Commander Glazier, don't patronise me. I called you in. I have a right to know what to expect.'

'You can expect us to do everything within our powers to find your wife, sir.'

'You don't trust me, for God's sake?'

'I didn't say that. What matters is that you put your trust in us. Do you happen to have a card with your Sussex address?'

Shenton felt for the wallet again and opened it.

Glazier said at once, 'Isn't that a picture of your wife, sir, the one you put back just now?'

'That wasn't suitable. I told you.'

'If it's the way she's dressed that bothers you, that's no problem. I need the shot of her face, that's all. May I take it?'

Shenton shook his head.

'What's the problem?' asked Glazier.

'As it happens, that isn't Ann. It's her friend Cressida.'

Between traffic signals along the Embankment, Glazier told his assistant, Inspector Tom Salt, about the photograph.

'You think he's cheating with his wife's best friend?'

'It's a fair bet.'

'Does it have any bearing on the kidnap?'

'Too soon to tell. His reactions are strange. He seems more fussed about how we intend to conduct the case than what is happening to his wife.'

'High-flyers like him operate on a different level from

you and me, sir. Life is all about flow-charts and decision-making.'

'They're not all like that. Did you get anything from the airline?'

'Everything he told us checks. There was a first class reservation in the name of Ann Porter. She wasn't aboard that Heathrow flight or any other.'

The next morning Glazier flew to Ireland for a meeting with senior officers in the *gardai*. Cork airport shimmered in the August heat. At headquarters they were served iced lemonade in preference to coffee. A full-scale enquiry was authorised.

He visited Cressida Concannon at her sister's, an estate house on the northern outskirts of Cork, and they talked outside, seated on patio chairs. She presented a picture distinctly different from the photo in Shenton's wallet; she was in a cream-coloured linen suit and brown shirt buttoned to the top. Her long brown hair was drawn back and secured with combs. Like Lady Ann, she was at least ten years younger than Shenton. She had made an itinerary of the tour around the Ring of Kerry. She handed Glazier a sheaf of hotel receipts.

He flicked through them. 'I notice you paid all of these yourself, Miss Concannon.'

'Yes. Ann said she would settle up with me later. She couldn't write cheques because she was using her maiden name.'

'Of course. Porter, isn't it? So the hotel staff addressed her as Mrs Porter?'

'Yes.'

'And was there any time in your trip when she was recognised as Lady Shenton?'

'Not to my knowledge.'

'You remember nothing suspicious, nothing that might help us to find her?'

'I've been over it many times in my mind, and I can't think of anything, I honestly can't.'

'What was her frame of mind? Did she seem concerned at any stage of the tour?'

'Not once that I recall. She seemed to relish every moment. You can ask at any of the hotels. She was full of high spirits right up to the minute we parted.'

'Which was . . . ?'

'Wednesday, about twelve-thirty. I drove her to the airport and put her down where the cars pull in. She went through the doors and that was the last I saw of her. Surely they won't harm her, will they?'

Glazier said, as if he hadn't listened to the question, 'Tell me about your relationship with Sir Milroy Shenton.'

She drew herself up. 'What do you mean?'

'You're a close friend, close enough to spend some time alone with him, I believe.'

'They are both my friends. I've known them for years.'

'But you do meet him, don't you?'

'I don't see what this has to do with it.'

'I'll tell you,' said Glazier. 'I'm just surprised that she went on holiday with you and relished every moment, as you expressed it. She's an intelligent woman. He carries your picture fairly openly in his wallet. He doesn't carry one of Lady Ann. Her behaviour strikes me as untypical, that's all.'

She said coolly, 'When you rescue her from the kidnappers, you'll be able to question her about it, won't you?'

Before leaving Ireland, Glazier had those hotels checked. Without exception the enquiries confirmed that the two women had stayed there on the dates in question. Moreover, they had given every appearance of getting on well. One hotel waiter in Killarney recalled that they had laughed the evenings away together.

Within an hour of Glazier's return to London, there was a development. Sir Milroy Shenton called on the phone. His voice was strained. 'I've heard from them. She's dead. They've killed her, the bastards, and I hold you responsible.'

'Dead? You're sure?'

'*They're* sure.'

'Tell me precisely how you heard about this.'

'They just phoned me, didn't they? Irish accent.'

'A man?'

'Yes. Said they had to abort the operation because I got in touch with the filth. That's you. They said she's at the bottom of the Irish Sea. This is going to be on your conscience for the rest of your bloody life.'

'I need to see you,' said Glazier. 'Where are you now?'

'Manchester.'

'How do they know you're up there?'

'It was in the papers. One of my companies has a shareholders' meeting. Look, I can't tell you any more than I just did.'

'You want the killers to get away with it, sir?'

'What?'

'I'll be at Midhurst. Your house.'

'Why Midhurst?'

'Get there as soon as you can, Sir Milroy.' Glazier put an end to the call and stabbed out Tom Salt's number. 'Can you lay on a chopper, Tom?'

'What's this about?' Salt shouted over the engine noise after they were airborne.

'Shenton. His wife is dead.'

'Why would they kill her? While she was alive she was worth a million.'

'My thought exactly.'

Salt wrestled with that remark as they followed the ribbon of the Thames southwards, flying over Richmond and Kingston. 'Don't you believe what Shenton told you?'

'She's dead. I believe that much.'

'No kidnap?'

'No kidnap.'

'We're talking old-fashioned murder, then.'

'That's my reading of it.'

There was a break in the conversation that brought them across the rest of Surrey before Salt shouted, 'It's got to be Cressie Concannon, hasn't it?'

'Why?'

'She wasn't satisfied with her status as the mistress, so she snuffed her rival and sent the ransom note to cover up the crime.'

Glazier shook his head. 'Cressie is in Ireland.'

'What's wrong with that? Lady Shenton was last seen in Ireland. We know she didn't make the flight home.'

'Cressie didn't send the ransom note. The postage stamp was British.'

The pilot turned his head. 'The place should be coming up any minute, sir. Those are the South Downs ahead.'

Without much difficulty they located Shenton's house, a stone-built Victorian mansion in a clearing in an oak wood. The helicopter wheeled around it once before touching down on the forecourt, churning up dust and gravel.

'We've got at least an hour before he gets here,' Glazier said.

'Is there a pub?' asked Salt, and got a look from his superior that put him off drinking for a week.

Rather less than the estimated hour had passed when the clatter of a second helicopter disturbed the sylvan peace. Glazier crossed the drive to meet it.

'No more news, I suppose?' Sir Milroy Shenton asked as he climbed out. He spoke in a more reasonable tone than he'd used on the phone. He'd had time to compose himself.

'Not yet, sir.'

'Found your way in?'

'No, we've been out here in the garden.'

'Not much of a garden. Ann and I preferred to keep it uncultivated except for the lawns.'

'She must have wanted to study the insect life in its natural habitat.'

Shenton frowned slightly, as if he'd already forgotten about his wife's field of study. 'Shall we go indoors?'

A fine curved staircase faced them as they entered. The hall was open to three floors. 'Your wife had a study, I'm sure,' said Glazier. 'I'd like to see it, please.'

'To your left – but there's nothing in there to help you,' said Shenton.

'We'll see.' Glazier entered the room and moved around the desk to the bookshelves. 'Whilst we were waiting for you I saw a couple of butterflies I'd never spotted before. I used to collect them when I was a kid, little horror, before they were protected. Did you know you had Purple Emperors here?'

Shenton twitched and swayed slightly. Then he put his hand to his face and said distractedly, 'What?'

'Purple Emperors. There were two in the summerhouse just now. The windows were open, but they had no desire to leave. They settled on the floor in the joints between the boards.' Glazier picked a book off the shelf and thumbed through the pages, finally turning them open for Shenton's inspection. 'How about that? Isn't it superb? The colour on those wings! I'd have sold my electric train-set for one of these in my collection.' He continued to study the page.

'You must have lived in the wrong area,' said Shenton, with an effort to sound reasonable.

'I wouldn't say that,' said Glazier. 'There were oaks in the park where I played. They live high up in the canopy of the wood. You never see them normally, but they are probably more common than most of us realised then.'

'This isn't exactly helping to find my wife,' said Shenton.

'You couldn't be more wrong,' said Glazier. 'How long ago did you kill her, Sir Milroy?'

Shenton tensed. He didn't respond.

'She's been dead a few weeks, hasn't she, long before your trip to New York. She didn't visit Ireland at all. That was some friend of Cressida Concannon's, using the name of Ann Porter. A free trip around the Ring of Kerry. No wonder the woman was laughing. She must have thought the joke was on you, just as the expenses were. I don't suppose she knew that the real Lady Ann was dead.'

'I don't have to listen to this slanderous rubbish,' said Shenton. He'd recovered his voice, but he was ashen.

'You'd better. I'm going to charge you presently. Miss Concannon will also be charged as an accessory. The kidnapping was a fabrication. You wrote the ransom note yourself some time ago. You posted envelopes to this address until one arrived in the condition you required – with the indistinct date-stamp. Then all you had to do was slip the ransom note inside and hand it to me when you got back from New York and alerted us to your wife's so-called abduction. How long has she been dead – four or five weeks?'

Shenton said with contempt, 'What am I supposed to have done with her?'

'Buried her – or tried to. You weren't the first murderer to discover that digging a grave isn't so easy if the ground is unhelpful. It's always a shallow grave in the newspaper reports, isn't it? But you didn't let that defeat you. You jacked up the summerhouse and wedged her under the floorboards – which I suppose was easier than digging six feet down. The butterflies led me to her.'

Shenton latched onto this at once. Turning to Tom Salt he said, 'Is he all right in the head?'

Salt gave his boss a troubled glance.

Shenton flapped his hand in derision. 'Crazy.'

'You don't believe me?' said Glazier. 'Why else would a Purple Emperor come down from the trees? Listen to this.' He started reading from the book. ' *"They remain in the tree-tops feeding on sap and honeydew unless attracted to the ground by the juices of dung or decaying flesh. They seldom visit flowers."* ' He looked up, straight into Shenton's stricken eyes. 'Not so crazy after all, is it?'

Angela Rider

Haydn Middleton

As a history student in her late teens, Eve read of a torture attributed to the Muslims of the Middle East. They would perforate a man's navel, drag out a length of his intestine, knot it to a stake, then make him walk round and round until he dropped down dead. Implausible though the torture seemed to Eve, the image of a gradually unravelling man stayed with her.

Thirty years later, on receiving a phone call from a complete stranger, she felt as if she were being tied up in preparation for just such a disembowelment herself. The caller, a girl who gave no name save that of the literary agency from which she was phoning, wanted to meet Eve. She said she had picked up an old second-hand copy of Eve's novel, *Angela Rider*, which had been out of print for twenty-five years. 'I'm so glad I've been able to trace you,' she told Eve. 'It's an absolutely marvellous book. I'd like to help you get it reissued.'

Eve shivered. She needed several moments to digest this news. Then she said, in little more than a whisper, 'I beg you to leave that book alone.'

'Well of course,' the girl replied, 'I wouldn't do anything without your consent. But please, could I come and see you? Just to talk it over.'

'I'm sorry,' said Eve. 'There's really nothing to talk about.'
But the girl wouldn't be deterred. She spent ten minutes out-
lining why she felt that the book had to be republished. Eve
listened with mounting alarm. First time around the book
had been savaged by reviewers, sold fewer than two hundred
copies, and – most painfully of all – scandalised Eve's family
and friends. The experience had affected her so badly that
she had never written another word of fiction. She had tried
to look back on *Angela* as an aberration in her emotional
development, and thanked God that few people could ever
connect her with its heroine: a thinly disguised version
of herself at twenty-four. Even her husband of twenty
years knew nothing of her brief literary career. And now, a
quarter of a century after Angela had seemed safely dead
and buried, someone wanted to resurrect her.

The girl talked on. Twice, to substantiate her claim
that *Angela* was 'years ahead of its time', she quoted
passages from the original edition – one of them a graphic
physical description of Angela as she had appeared to her
much older lover. Eve blanched – although the quality of
the writing did surprise her. But her deep embarrassment
over the book's content remained.

'I don't understand,' the girl said at last. 'It's an
erotic story certainly, but none of the sexual episodes
are gratuitous, least of all the climactic encounter. No
one could possibly doubt the book's sincerity.'

'No,' Eve murmured, clutching at her stomach. 'But I've
changed so much in the years since I wrote it. My life has
changed so much. I'm . . . I'm no longer the same person.'

'It's the book I'd like to reissue,' the girl laughed. 'Not
its author! But to be serious – what does your book actually
say? That a young woman of twenty-four shouldn't repress
her true self, that if she wishes to form an intimate relationship with a woman twice her own age, then nothing
should stop her. *You* may have changed, but your message
is as valid as ever.' She paused. '*I* certainly found it to
be so.'

Eve was torn. A latent, previously unsuspected vanity made her want to see the book back in print; it had, after all, been her sole public achievement. But she feared the repercussions if her strait-laced husband should learn, after so long, about her youthful fantasy. And it *had* been just a fantasy, all of it, including Angela's 'climactic encounter' with the older woman. Eve herself had never made love to a person of her own sex. Since marrying, she had held that as an article of faith.

'I'm no longer the same person,' she repeated. 'I don't stand by what I wrote then. The very idea of lesbianism . . . it horrifies me now.'

Eve trembled at the lie. The idea had never lost its appeal. Marriage had made no difference to the way she felt about other women. Deep down, Eve knew just what she was – but, a child of her time, she had never been bold enough to declare herself. She had chosen instead to hide behind a rabidly illiberal husband. And it would be reckless now to let him know that she had even *considered* taking Angela's path. She closed her eyes. Dizzily she staggered around this stake of her own devising, watching her insides begin to unwind; and at her back she could feel strong hands, urging her to go faster. 'No!' she cried out. 'No, it can't happen.'

'Oh, Eve,' the girl cried back. 'You can't deny this part of yourself, this *good* part. Please – won't you just let me come and see you?'

'*No!*' Eve was almost in tears. 'That book mustn't come back.' And she slammed down her phone.

But moments later, as she regained some of her composure, she began to suspect that the call had been a hoax.

In the days that followed, Eve's suspicion turned into certainty. But she couldn't imagine who might be playing so cruel a trick on her. (*Anyone* could have discovered a copy of the book in a secondhand shop and then tracked down its author.)

Neither could she face calling the literary agency and reopening the issue. Somehow the damage had already been done. Perhaps by simply having discussed Angela Rider again after so long, Eve sensed that the infernal girl was now *at large*. Furthermore she sensed that the phone call's purpose had been to make her feel just that way.

Whenever she closed her eyes, she felt as if she were still circling the stake, paying out great lengths of her entrails, screaming for the torture to stop. And each time she stumbled or fell, those unkind hands would wrench her to her feet and force her on again. There was to be no respite. This could end, Eve knew, only with her complete evisceration.

After a week her constant state of panic made her delirious. She fancied that everyone in her village knew the precise nature of her ordeal. She grew fretful in her husband's presence, expecting him at any moment to confront her with the newly fleshed skeleton in her closet. She was devastated by guilt – because of the book, because of her true sexuality, and because she had kept both secrets from him for so long. In a sense, her commitment to him had always been a deception. A betrayal. And if ever he were to find that out, he would – Eve knew – find it impossible to forgive.

But he was away from the house, driving to one of his regular golfing weekends, when, early one evening, she answered a knock at her front door.

'Eve?' asked a breathless young woman. Her face and voice seemed distantly familiar. Behind her in the curving driveway stood a small red sports car. 'I've just read your book,' she said, tapping her shoulder bag. 'It's absolutely wonderful. I think it's going to change my life.'

Eve's hand fluttered of its own accord to her stomach. 'What is this?' she gasped. 'Who are you?'

The girl laughed. 'Don't you recognise me? I'm Angela Rider.'

*

Eve slammed the door and backed down the hall into her kitchen. Then she stopped, drew herself up, and returned to the front door.

The girl was still on the doorstep, her face radiant with a smile. She wore a thin contemporary sundress, but in every detail of her eyes, her lips, her pallor, her wrists, fingers, legs and ankles, this *was* Angela Rider: a flawlessly accurate embodiment of the passage which had been read over the phone to Eve seven days before. And Eve's immediate longing for her was indistinguishable from the longing of Angela's older lover, from whose perspective that passage had been written.

'Was it you who phoned me?' she asked hoarsely.

The girl composed her face, then she shrugged. 'I'm here now,' she replied. 'May I come in?'

Eve found herself stepping aside, letting her pass, and closing the door. Whoever this girl really was, whatever she wanted, it was too late now to try to shut her out.

'What a beautiful home you have, Eve,' she said, pirouetting in the hall and dropping her bag to the polished wood-block floor. 'So spacious! So elegant!'

'Is this blackmail?' Eve asked, closing her eyes, weakening by the moment, feeling the unseen hands pushing her more roughly than ever into this last excruciating circuit of the stake. 'Tell me what you want.'

The girl crossed the floor to Eve. 'You,' she said softly.

Eve bowed her head. 'Why are you doing this?' she pleaded. 'Who are you? Why are you tormenting me?'

The girl didn't answer, but twirled away, entered the kitchen and passed through to the twilit garden.

Eve followed, and found her standing on the croquet lawn, transfixed by the view of the valley below. Eve stared at her from the arbour, stupefied in spite of herself. For the girl was quite lovely – the image of Eve's idealised version of herself at twenty-four: Angela. *Angela!* Whoever she was in reality, during these pitiless moments of pretence she *was* Angela Rider. And Eve, whose own deceptions had been laid bare for ever, found herself beginning to respond to this game – even before its rules and penalties had been made clear. Already she was aware of what she was going to have to do.

The girl turned, half her face in shadow. 'You wrote my story,' she called back to Eve, her manner far more subdued than before. 'You understood.'

Then she turned full face to Eve. 'Before I read it, I didn't understand. But now I do. I really do, and I'm so grateful to you.'

She smiled and held out a hand. 'I love you, Eve. I want you. I want to be with you. I want you to be with me.' She stopped smiling as her meaning became clear to Eve. 'Please let it happen, even if only this once. Please . . . '

Eve quaked. There could be no further circuits after this. She felt weak, almost entirely emptied out. In her delirium she could barely put one foot in front of the other. But the unseen hands continued to push her from behind.

She came before the beautiful young girl, and felt her own limp hands being taken up. She felt the touch of the girl's lips between her eyes. Eve stiffened. It was deathly silent in the garden. Eve looked back at her home: a temporary haven, the compensation for all her years of self-denial.

The girl disengaged her hands. Languidly she slipped the straps of her sundress over her shoulders and presented her small, high breasts to the older woman. She was being Angela, taking the word and making it flesh, guiding Eve toward the climactic encounter which Eve herself had scripted twenty-five years before.

Eve looked, intoxicated by her closeness and beauty. Nothing had changed. She wanted this girl too badly, this part of herself that she had failed to lay to rest. And she ached with the certainty of what she would have to do.

She closed her eyes, and heard the girl slip out of her dress. Through tears she looked again, and she saw

what she had never stopped wanting. The girl kicked off
her sandals, placed one finger for a moment on Eve's lips,
and glided past her into the house. Eve turned to watch
her disappear, then glimpsed her long legs again as she
mounted the stairs.

It's over, Eve told herself. She could not come back
from this. As if in a dream she circled her husband's home,
not noticing the second car that now stood in the driveway.
And when she arrived back at the spot from which she had
started, she knew that there was no other way. There could
be no peace unless she were to acknowledge the truest part
of herself. Drying her eyes, she returned to her kitchen. She
shut the back door and locked it. Then, glancing up at the
ceiling, Eve let herself smile.

Upstairs in the master bedroom the actress rode him harder
– mouth wide open, nostrils flaring. The colour was high in
her throat and shoulders. She was perfect. A consummate
Angela. He reared up from the bed, surging deeper inside
her. He wrested her against him and sank his face in her
breasts. Urgently she pushed his face away and hooked the
fingers of one hand into his mouth to use his lower jaw like
reins. Her hold on him tightened, loosened, tightened,
loosened. He raised his own fingers to her lips. She licked
them, then grasped him by the wrist and bit into his palm.
Eve's husband widened his eyes, swarming with the perfection of it all.

Her entire performance had been faultless: the phone call,
the compromising of Eve in the garden – and now this, so
much wilder than he had asked her for, paid her for. Impaled
up there in her abandonment, she was surpassing herself.
And it was all for him. *She* was all for him. The only way it
could ever truly be. *This* was what his deviant wife had to be
made to see.

But he couldn't wait for Eve to finish her agonising in the
kitchen and climb the stairs to find them. She had to see it
all. Roughly he grabbed the actress, drew himself free, went

to the door and motioned for her to follow him. Breathless, naked, he descended the stairs. He crossed the hall and stopped in front of the kitchen door. It was slightly ajar. She was behind that door: his sham, pornographer wife. His betrayer. He turned toward the foot of the stairs. The actress faced him, ready. He beckoned. And without looking back, he nudged the kitchen door open with his heel.

The actress approached slowly, staring beyond him, her face now drained of colour. As soon as she was close enough, he dragged her on to himself. She let out a short, high cry. *Perfect.* He made the girl cry out a second time, a third. She was full to the brim with him, weeping with him. It was more than he could ever have hoped for. Shouting aloud, he let himself go and shook out every last drop of his disgust into her. The actress still wept. He stepped back, ran one finger from her forehead right down to her crotch, then turned to his wife, smiling.

In her own fashion, Eve smiled back, suspended by her neck from the further of the two oak beams which ran the length of the room. She had used an enormous length of rope to kill herself. Yards and yards of it coiled down from the knot at her neck on to the chair which she had nudged aside.

In the evening gloom, as she swung into profile and then away, her husband had the bizarre notion that the rope was a length of intestine gushing *out* of her. But it was her face that intrigued him most in the moment before he grasped what had happened: for in death – sealed with her ghastly smile of triumph – Eve looked so much *younger* than he had ever seen her before.

Let Nothing You Dismay!

Ellis Peters

The girl in the patched jeans and the voluminous black sweater got off the bus from Comerbourne at the stop opposite the Sitting Duck at ten minutes past seven in the evening, on the twenty-third of December. It was too early then for the landlord to be doing much business in the bar, too late for any delayed shoppers or honest folk coming home from work to be about the single street of the village, and only one other passenger descended from the ancient bus, and scurried away at once into the darkness, to vanish with the crisp click of a gate-latch and in through a house door just beyond the pub. There was no one to notice the arrival of the girl in Mottisham, and by the time the bus rattled away up the valley road towards its final halt at Abbot's Bale, a mile further towards the Welsh border, she, too, had vanished into the tree-shrouded darkness of the lane that climbed the slope behind the church.

The long cleft of Middlehope climbs the valley of a border stream, dwindling as it mounts, until the river shrinks into the spring that is its source, the final village of Abbot's Bale is left behind, and nothing remains but the bare moorland and occasional marsh of the watershed between England and Wales. The local bus, family-owned and driven, turns about at Abbot's Bale after its final evening run, the driver

has a meal, a break, a gossip and a single pint at the Gun
Dog before driving back down the valley to Comerbourne,
which is home. Why go further? Over the two bleak miles
of the crest there are no houses to be served. The road
goes on, and winds its way down to civilisation again on
the other side, but for practical purposes Abbot's Bale is
the end of the road.

Even at the more congenial level of the village of
Mottisham, population is still sparse, in spite of some
new development on the lower slopes, and there was no
one abroad to see or hear the girl in the patched jeans as
she walked briskly up the winding lane, past one or two
lighted cottage windows, towards one of the older houses
on the fringe of the village. She was small and lightly built,
almost silent on the unpaved road surface, almost invisible
in her dark clothing. The night was moonless and overcast,
relatively mild for December, though there might well be
frost later, in the small hours.

She had left the few lights of the village behind, and
the stone wall of a well-treed garden began on her right
hand. Fifty yards along the wall was pierced by a modest,
square-pillared gateway, its white gate wide open on a drive
flanked by old shrubberies. The girl turned in there, and
proceeded confidently up the drive until it curved to the
left, and for the first time brought into view, clear-cut
against the sky and rearing out of the cloudy shapelessness
of old trees, the line of the roof and the square bulk of the
upper part of the house. A solid, respectable, middle-class
house, probably mid-Victorian, a silhouette cut out in black
paper against a mount just perceptibly less black. And
profoundly silent, to the point of menace.

The girl halted in the cover of the trees, and stood
a moment perfectly still, contemplating the unrelieved
darkness. Not a light in the entire bulk, outside or in.
Even the heaviest of curtains could hardly have sealed
in light totally, had there been any to conceal. Still, you
never know! The girl marched on boldly, climbed the steps

to the front door, and rang the bell. For a moment she stood listening, an ear inclined to the door, but not a sound of any kind responded from within. Appearances were confirmed, the house was empty.

She descended the steps again, and without hesitation set off by the path that rounded the corner of the house, and made for the back premises. Evidently she already knew the ground well enough to know where she could find what she wanted. The garden was old, closely treed, cover available close to the walls on every side but the front. Round at the rear there was a small, rather high window, the kind to be found in cloakroom or scullery or larder, and this one probably as old as the house, never replaced by a more modern and more secure one. Under the bushes that crowded near it the girl dumped the duffle bag from her shoulder, rummaged inside its outer pocket for a moment, and produced a long nail-file. Reaching the latch of the window was no problem. An old creeper that covered half of the rear wall had its formidable roots braced almost under the sill, and took her light weight without a quiver as she climbed nimbly to the casement and levered the file in beneath the latch. It rose obligingly easily, and she drew the window open, held by the gnarled stem of the creeper, and slid one slim leg over the sill. The rest of her small person folded itself neatly and followed, and a moment later she was standing on the tiled floor of a small room, apparently a cloakroom, listening to the silence as it settled again gradually after the small agitation of her own movements.

She was in, and she had the house to herself.

Moving with unruffled confidence, she let herself out into a dark passage, and felt her way along it with fingertips brushing the walls, past a kitchen door and towards the front of the house. By this time her eyes were becoming sufficiently accustomed to the darkness to distinguish faintly the broad sweep of the banister rail of the staircase in the wide Victorian hall, and feeling her way along the wall parallel to it she found the light switch, and was hesitating with her finger on it when the first slight, disturbing sound came to her ears, and she froze where she stood, listening intently.

A car's engine, quiet and distant as yet, but not so distant as to be on the main road, on the other side of the house from the narrow lane by which she had come. It was coming gradually nearer, cutting through from that road by the short piece that would bring it round to the lane, and to the gate. Her acute ear caught the check and change in the note as it turned into the drive, and the sudden cautious crescendo as it rounded the curve. No doubt about it, someone was at this moment driving up to the front door— No, correction! – *past* the front door, and on round to the right, deep into the cover of the trees. Wheeling, backing and turning now. Ready for a quick departure?

The girl took her finger hastily from the lightswitch instead of pressing it, swooped round the ornate newel-post, and went scrambling up the stairs, hands spread to feel her way, and into the first bedroom on that side of the house. The large window showed as a shape of comparative pallor, the curtains undrawn, and prolonged acquaintance with the night had given her a fair measure of vision by this time. Peering down into the open between the house and its encircling trees, she could distinguish movement and form even when the car lights were switched off. Not a car, though, a van, middle-sized, elderly, backed unobtrusively into cover before it halted. And a minute later, after profound, listening silence, the cab doors opened quietly, and two figures slid out and crossed like shifting shadows to the window immediately below the one where she crouched in hiding.

One of them spoke, but it was only a wordless murmur. But when the second figure stepped back briefly to look up at the face of the house she saw that he carried something under his arm, and the something had the unmistakable shape of a gun. Shotguns they were carrying, these days, and this was the precise outline of a man with a shotgun, used to it, and probably all too ready to use it at the drop of a hat. A flicker of light reflected briefly from under the wall. They had a torch, and were using it to locate the fastenings of the window. A minute later she heard the sharp, tinkling fall of glass. They were in the house with her.

She took a moment to consider both the room she was in, and the alarming possibilities. They had brought a van, that meant larger plunder, pieces of furniture, antiques, silver. But not a very large van, not the kind to accommodate half the contents of the house. They were after chosen pieces. Probably they knew already what they wanted, collectors' pieces, whatever they had customers for, or could most profitably find customers for. Professionals specialised, handling only what they knew best. And here she was in a bedroom filled with good furniture, and she had better not stay there, if she could find a less likely place to provide desirable loot. And meantime . . .

She crossed the room to the dressing-table, detected by the ghostly gleam of mirrors. Where they found the light to reflect as they did she had no time to consider. She found what she was searching for in the second drawer, a roll of soft Indian leather as thick as her wrist, tied with brocaded ribbons. Without staying to untie it and confirm what was within, she could feel the shapes of bracelet and brooch and necklace through the silky folds. With luck they wouldn't even look for this, if clocks and china were what they fancied, but she meant at all costs to retain it if she could. She stuffed it down the neck of her sweater, made for the door, and opened it cautiously to listen for what was happening below.

They had not ventured to put on a light, but seemed to know, even by the beam of a torch, carefully shaded, exactly where to find what they wanted. There were voices now, subdued but audible, one gravelly, laconic and professionally calm, one sharp and edgy, and distinctly disquieting in its suggestion of hair-trigger nervousness.

'Take this an' all, eh?' He was close under the stairs, handling glass by the sound of it, but still with the gun under his arm. The gravelly voice swore at him, but still low and placidly.

'No, leave it! Come on with this clock 'ere, and look sharp.'

The edgy one came, as ordered, but still mutinous. 'What you turning it up for? That's good stuff.'

'Good stuff, but no buyer. Stick to what I know. Safer.'

And there went the clock aforesaid, out through the open window, to be stowed away in the van. They were working fast and methodically. The two of them, now, were carrying a piece of furniture between them, very carefully. Some sort of cabinet. They were in and out of other rooms, there was no moment when she had any chance to steal down the stairs in their absence, and get back to the rear of the house, and the open cloakroom window. She would have to sit it out, somewhere as safe as possible, and hope for them to go. How if they decided to come and continue their hunt upstairs?

The girl retreated warily along the dark landing, feeling her way against the wall. Down below her the shaded torch beam focused on the foot of the stairs.

'What's up there?' demanded the nervous voice, uneasy about time passing.

'His coins. Worth a packet sold in one go.'

'Dead risky!' hazarded the doubter, but he was already on the stairs.

'Got it all set up, safe as houses. They're going west.'

The girl felt behind her, softly opened the rearmost bedroom door, let herself in with feverish haste, and closed it behind her. Flattened against the wall behind the door, she heard them enter the bedroom she had quitted. There were a few minutes of silence, and then the sound of wood splintering, and a murmur of satisfaction. They had got what they had come for. Collectors sometimes allow their pride and joy to be viewed and recorded, whether in professional journals or regional television news programmes, and expert thieves digest and remember every detail. But now surely they would leave, and she could make her own departure once they were clear of the house.

They were out on the landing again with their loot, they must be nearly as eager to leave as she was to hear them go.

'What else they got up here, then?' wondered the edgy voice, turning towards where she hid, instead of away. 'Might as well take a look.'

'We got what we know we can deal with,' said his mentor sharply. 'Doesn't pay to take risks out of your depth. Come on, let's get out of here.'

A hand grasped the outer knob of the door. The girl gripped its fellow on her side with both hands and all her strength, and struggled to prevent it from turning. It seemed that his touch had been no more than tentative, and for a moment she managed to hold it fast. But that was her undoing, for at once he said, with rising interest: 'Locked! Let's have a go, then!' and she heard him lay his shotgun aside, leaning it against the jamb of the door to have both hands free. The next moment the knob turned, jerking her hands away, his shoulder thudded heavily against the wood, and the door flew open so violently that he shot half across the room, and let out a yell, suddenly thrown off-balance. The door, flung back hard against the girl's body, rebounded again with a dull sound that should have covered the gasp the blow fetched out of her, but did not quite cover it. The professional of these two had acute hearing. In his business he needed it.

'Hi up! What's here?' He was inside with them in an instant, the shotgun braced under his right arm, the torch in his left, sweeping the room. He kicked the door shut, and spread both feet firmly to bring the barrel of the gun to bear on the intruder. There was one instant when the girl gave herself up for lost, and as instantly recovered when the alarm point passed and nothing happened. All over in about half a second. Thank God it was the professional, not the lout, who held the gun, and his nerves were considerably stouter than his colleague's, and his wits quicker. The beam of the torch swept the girl from head to foot, and the most dangerous moment was past. Not that she could reckon on that as the end of danger, but at least it hadn't wiped her out on sight.

'Well, well!' said the expert, slowly lowering the barrel of the gun, but holding her pinned in the ray of the torch. 'Look what we've found!'

His mate was certainly looking, dumbstruck and plainly in a state of panic which would have been her death if he had been holding the gun. 'My Gawd!' he babbled, still breathless and splayed against the wall. 'How come she's here? You said they was gone for hours. What we goin' to do with 'er now? She 'as to go, or we're goners. What you waitin' for? We *got* to . . . '

'Shut up!' said the elder shortly. And to the girl, standing mute and still and very wary in the beam of the torch: 'Who the hell are you?'

She had a vague view of them both now, at least their bulk and shape, even glimpses of features in the diffused light. The older man was stocky and square and shaggy, in what seemed to be overalls and a donkey jacket, middle-aged and composed, even respectable-looking, like an honest transport driver working late, a good appearance for a professional burglar. The other one was young, large, unshaven and lumpish, with a general bearing between a cringe and a swagger. Hard to account for why so competent a pro should tolerate so perilous and probably unreliable an aide. Perhaps they were father and son, and there wasn't much choice, or perhaps the lout had his own peculiar skills, like breaking open doors, or battering people to death if they got in the way. Anyhow, there they were, and she was stuck with them.

'Well, I'm not the missus here,' she said, venturing close to sounding tart, 'that's for sure. Nor the parlourmaid, neither.'

'No, you for sure ain't,' allowed the interrogator. 'So what are you doing here?'

'Same as you, if I'd had the chance,' she said resignedly. 'If you hadn't come butting in I'd have been off a long time ago. You're one of a kind yourself, it seems, you should know another when you see one. What else you think I'd be doing here?'

'You reckon?' He was not impressed, but he was willing to think about it. 'You got a name?'

'Not one you'd want to know, no more than I want to know yours. What's the use of names, anyway, wouldn't mean nothing to you. I told you what you asked me.'

'What you wasting time for?' demanded the younger man feverishly, and laid a hand on the stock of the gun, but his companion held on to it and elbowed him off. 'Get rid of her and let's get out of here. What else can we do with her now? She's nothing but trouble, whoever she is.'

'Shut up!' repeated his elder, and kept his eyes unwaveringly upon the girl. 'Two of a kind, are we?' he repeated thoughtfully. 'How'd you get in here, then? Go on, show me!'

'Through a back window, round by the kitchen. Go on, have a look for yourself. I left it open, ready to get out again quick. Bent me nail-file, levering up the latch. Go on, see for yourself if you don't believe me. I left my duffle bag under the bushes, outside there. Go on, send him to have a look! I'm not telling you lies. Why should I? I got nothing against you. I know nothing, I seen nothing, and sure as hell I'm saying nothing.'

The elder man hesitated for a long minute, and then abruptly jerked head and gun in the direction of the stairs. 'Come on down, and go softly on the way, I'll be right behind. I dunno yet. Go on round the back, Stan, and

see. How big is this window, then? I never spotted none
we could use.'

'I got through it, didn't I? Show you, if you like.' She
was feeling her way down stair by stair ahead of him, only
too conscious of the shotgun close behind, and devoutly
grateful that it was not in the younger man's hands. '*He's*
too big to get through, though. Pays to be a little person,
on these capers.'

'You done many?' He was sceptical but open-minded.

'None round here before. Never strike twice in the
same place. Like lightning!' she said, testing the water
a little deeper.

'Come from round here?'

'Not me! I came in from Brum, tonight. Came up here
by the bus, and I aim to go back by the bus. He comes
back down the valley about half past nine.'

The young man Stan, however suspicious and uneasy,
had done as his chief instructed, and made off ahead across
the hall, out through the window they had forced, and round
to the rear of the house. She felt somewhat reassured in his
absence, however brief it might be. This one at least was
a professional, and elderly, and professionals who have
survived to reach middle age have normally done so by
avoiding unnecessary complications like murder.

'How long were you in here ahead of us?' he asked
suddenly. They had reached the foot of the stairs, and
could hear Stan's steps faintly crisping the gravel outside.

'About a couple of minutes. Frightened me to death
when I heard you driving in. I thought the folks were
coming home too soon.'

'Get what you come for?'

'Bits and pieces,' she said, after a momentary hesitation.
Whatever she said would be a gamble.

'Down the neck of your jumper?' And when she was
silent: 'What's your preference, then?'

'You got what *you* come for,' she said, reluctant and
aggrieved. 'You wouldn't grudge me a ring or two, would

you? I don't trespass on your patch, you might as well leave me mine. What you got to lose? We're both bound to keep our mouths shut, we're in the same boat. I never been inside, and don't intend to go, but you could shop me just as easy as I could you.'

Stan was coming back, sliding in through the open window to dump her duffle bag in front of his leader. 'It was there, sure enough, slung under the bushes. The window, an' all. That's how she got in. So what? You can't trust women.'

'Why not?' she said indignantly. 'We *are* in the same boat. I can't grass on you or anybody without putting my own head on the chopping-block. I broke in, as well as you.'

'It takes some thinking about,' said the elder, 'except we don't have time. Sooner we're out of here, the better.'

'Then that's it,' she agreed firmly. 'So let's get going. And you can give me a lift out to the main road, where the bus stops. Wherever you're heading, you've got to go that far to get started.'

'I say make sure,' insisted Stan. 'If her mouth was shut for good we'd know where we were.'

'Yes, up the creek without a paddle,' said his leader with decision. 'What, with a body to get rid of? I'm driving nowhere with that in the van. Leave it here? It wouldn't be silence you'd be making sure of. If you're ambitious to be a lifer, I'm not. Come on, let's get the van away while we're safe. Pick up your bag, kid, and hop in the cab. Might as well drop you off. Sooner you was in Brum than hanging around these parts.'

In the cab of the van she was glad to see that Stan did not mind taking the wheel. That was a relief. He couldn't very well commit murder while he was driving, and she had the elder man in between.

The first few house lights of the village came into view. At the crossroads she would get down and walk away, still in one piece, still with the soft roll of leather and its contents snugly tucked away inside her sweater.

'Where will you be slipping a catch next?' the man beside her asked, as civilly and normally as if they had just picked up a young hitch-hiker out of the kindness of their hearts, and felt it only courteous to take an interest in her prospects.

'A hundred miles away, for preference,' said the girl. 'I'm going to enjoy my Christmas first. Never work at Christmas. This'll do, drop me off here.'

It was under the light, just opposite the Sitting Duck. She dropped her bag out first, and jumped down after it, lifted a hand in ambiguous acknowledgement, and stood a moment to watch which way the van turned into the main valley road. Uphill, towards the border and the watershed. That made sense, small chance of being intercepted on that road on most winter nights.

The van, hitherto just a shape in the dark, took on form as it drew away along the road. The rear numberplate was muddy, but perfectly legible.

The girl watched it for only a few seconds. Then she crossed the road and went into the Sitting Duck.

The bus which would presently set off on its last trip of the evening, down the valley and back to Comerbourne, was parked at this hour just aside from the minute open space which was the centre of the village of Abbot's Bale, leaving the green free for an assembled crowd surprisingly large for so apparently modest a community. At this hour of the evening most of the shepherds and hands from all the surrounding farms would in any case have been congregated here in the Gun Dog, but on this evening they had brought wives and families with them, for the church choir was carol-singing for charity on the green, and there was warmth, welcome and the harvest of a dozen farm kitchens to be found in the church hall, on sale at nominal prices for the same good cause that was stretching the lungs of all the local choirboys, and filling the night air with a silver mist of frosty breath. The driver of the bus was sitting in a corner settle in the bar over a pie, along with Sergeant Moon, who was the law in Middlehope, rather than merely representing it, and without whom no function could be a complete success. The driver, a conscientious man, was making his single pint last as long as possible. Or if, for once, he had exceeded it, no one was counting. Sergeant Moon was on his second when the landlord called him to the telephone.

He came back in a few moments to haul the driver out with him into the night, and shortly thereafter the driver was seen to climb into his bus and move it several yards lower down the valley road, clear of the full-throated assembly presently delivering 'The Farewell of the Shepherds' to the listening night, and there to stow it face-forward up the considerable slope of the hedge-bank, and abandon it, tail looming over the empty road. At the same time Sergeant Moon was seen to emerge from the yard of the Gun Dog with a red and white traffic cone in either hand, and place them judiciously in the fairway, a few yards below the point where the bus's rear loomed out of the hedge. A third such cone, brought out to join the first pair, completed a sufficient barrier on this narrow road.

The next thing that happened was that a word in the ear of the Reverend Stephen and his choirmaster unaccountably shifted the singers to a position in the middle of the road, instead of neatly grouped on the triangle of green, and effectively blocked the way to all traffic. Their horn lantern, reared on a long pole, stood out like a battle standard in the midst.

They were in the middle of 'Good King Wenceslas', with the leading bass cast as the king, and the star treble as the page, when the sound of a motor climbing the slope was heard, and Sergeant Moon, hands benevolently clasped behind his back, and legs braced apart, took his stand in the middle of the road, and turned about at the last moment to confront the battered van with a large hand and a benign smile, as it baulked, hooted, and stopped. His pace as he approached it and leaned to the window was leisured, and his smile amiable.

'A happy Christmas to you, too, sir, I'm sure! Sorry to hold you up, but you see how it is. This is for the Salvation Army. They'll be finished pretty soon now, I'm sure you won't mind waiting.'

'Well, we need to get on, officer,' said the elderly man in the passenger seat. 'Got a long way to go yet. You sure they won't be long? You couldn't clear a way through for us?'

The tension within the cab, which had smelled strongly of panic as soon as the window was rolled down, seemed to ease very slightly at the seasonal greeting. The barrier seemed to have nothing to do with anything more menacing than some village choir collecting for charity. Sergeant Moon radiated placid reassurance.

'They can't keep the kids out too late. They'll soon wind it up now. The bus has to leave on time, some of 'em will be travelling down the valley a piece. Soon be on your way now.'

The Sergeant had already located the shotgun, laid along the seat behind the driver and his passenger, and covered from sight with a rug, but the shape of the stock showed through. It would not be simple to produce and level it quickly from that position. All the same, the driver was getting distinctly more jumpy with every second, drumming his fingers on the wheel and twitching his shoulders ominously. The older one was tough enough to sit it out, but he was getting worried about his mate's liability to blow up at any moment. The Sergeant was glad to observe the three or four solid villagers emerge from the yard of the inn and amble innocently into position a few yards down the road. If anyone abandoned ship and ran, it would be in that direction, since there

must be some fifty or more people deployed in the road
ahead.

'God rest you merry, gentlemen,
Let nothing you dismay . . . '

sang the choir imperturbably, embattled round their lantern
banner.

The bus driver had climbed into his cab, and was
watching with vague, detached interest. The man at the
wheel of the van stared ahead, and had begun to sweat
and blink, and curse wordlessly, his lips contorting. The
older man kicked at him sidewise, and precipitated what
he was trying to avoid.

It all happened in a second. The young man loosed the
wheel, uttered a howling oath, shoved his mate sideways,
and grabbed for the shotgun. At the same instant Sergeant
Moon waved a hand, and the service bus, brakes released,
rolled ponderously but rapidly down the slope of grass, and
careered backwards directly towards the front of the van.

A shriller yell followed the first, cutting through the carol
with a note of utter hysteria. The shotgun, hurled aside as
suddenly as it had been seized, and still somewhat tangled
in the rug, went off with a tremendous bang, fortunately
spattering nothing more vulnerable than the roof of the
van, as Stan fought his gears and tried to back off in a
hurry, and failing, stalled his engine, flung open his door,
and hurtled out and down the road, to be engulfed in the
arms of a six-foot shepherd from one of the hill farms, ably
supported by the cellarman from the Gun Dog.

'God rest you merry' was never finished. The choir
broke ranks with a view halloo, and piled into the affray
with enthusiasm, in case the van should yet serve to
extricate its remaining occupant, by some feat of trick
driving. But the professional knew when he was beaten,
and had sense enough not to aggravate matters when they
were past mending. The bus had braked to a halt at least a
foot short of his right front wing, but still he sat motionless

in his place, staring bitterly before him into the unexpected revelry, and cursing with monotonous, resigned fluency under his breath.

Sergeant Moon reached in unresisted, and appropriated the shotgun. Large, interested locals leaned on either door, grinning. The Sergeant moved round to the back of the van, and opened the rear doors.

'Well, well!' he said, gratified. 'Aladdin's cave! Won't the Harrisons be pleased when Father Christmas comes!'

The girl in black silk evening trousers and bat-winged, sequinned top sat, cross-legged, in front of the fire she had kindled in the living room before her uncle and aunt had returned from their dinner party, and recounted the events of the evening for them with relish as she roasted chestnuts. It was no bad start to a Christmas vacation to be able to take her elders' breath away, first with shock and dismay, then with relief and admiration.

'So you see, it's all right, you'll get everything back safely. I did rescue your jewellery, I was determined they shouldn't have that, but all the rest will be back soon. Sergeant Moon has been on the phone already. I knew he'd manage everything, somehow, and I did warn him they had a gun. But isn't it lucky for you that I decided to come down a day early, after all? I did ring you, but you were out already. And anyhow, I knew how I could get in. Now who was it said I'd never make it as an actress?'

'But, for God's sake, girl,' protested her uncle, not yet recovered from multiple shock, 'you might have got yourself killed.'

'Well, that's what I was trying to avoid! I was there, and they found me, I didn't have much choice. When you're cornered, no use coming apart at the seams. You have to use what you've got – same as Sergeant Moon had to do. And I *had* broken in, and I suppose I *did* look every inch the part. Anyhow, they believed it. Finally!' she added, somewhat more sombrely. 'I admit there *were* moments . . . '

'But you're taking it all so coolly,' her aunt wondered faintly. 'Weren't you even afraid?'

'Terrified!' said the girl complacently, and fielded a chestnut which had shot out upon the rug. 'But I tell you what – as soon as my folks get back from Canada I'm going to put it to them they should let me switch to drama school. I always said that was my natural home.'

Et In Arcadia Ego

Julian Symons

Gerald was brought up in Arcadia, which was no doubt a problem. But he had more difficulties than that.

Arcadia was the name given by the builder to an estate of what were called in the brochure individually designed houses for top class executives, combining the peace and grace of country living with all the nearby facilities of a market town, plus an hourly train service to London. The development, of no more than thirty houses, was snapped up before they were built, but their popularity prompted a second eager entrepreneur to acquire several adjacent acres on which was built in due course Greater Arcadia. The original Arcadians thus found themselves part of a much bigger complex, and one less socially desirable than they had envisaged. The original Arcadia had been a couple of miles out of town, but its much larger offshoot plus the shops and petrol stations set up to serve it meant that the town merged almost indistinguishably into Arcadian country. But there were still green fields and country walks around, and it was said that nobody had ever sold a house in the Arcadias at anything but a handsome profit.

Arcadia, then, was still more or less Arcadian. Until the Soft Shoe Rapist came.

Mr Burke worked in London in a ministry, something

to do with what was called social development, and he had risen in the gradual, almost inevitable Civil Service way to become quite important. Very important? No, not that, a secondary figure who as he sometimes said was subject to the demands of his lord and master, the Minister. He had left a comfortable London suburb and come to Arcadia at the urging of his wife Pearl, who had aspirations to a more gracious way of life. And Pearl did find Arcadian life more gracious, although it worried her that so many of the other Arcadians (not Greater Arcadians, an inferior breed) had swimming pools and Jacuzzis that the Burkes could not afford. She was trying to persuade her husband that a Jacuzzi, at least, was an essential adjunct to Arcadian living when she ran her car into a tree and died instantly. Gerald, three years old at the time, was in the car with her, and insisted when the police arrived that his mother was asleep.

Up to that time Mr Burke had hardly been aware of Gerald's existence. He saw the child only for a couple of minutes in the morning before taking the London train, and by the time he returned in the evening Gerald was being put to bed. Pearl's death, however, made him uncomfortably aware that he was responsible for this rather large three-year-old child. A few months of life with a housekeeper worried about what she called Gerald's persistent naughtiness, which she tried to cure by smacking him frequently on the head, arms and legs with a ruler, convinced him that this wouldn't do. He married Emerald, exchanging, as he said in one of his few but often-repeated jokes, one jewel for another.

Emerald was a secretary in the Ministry, and already had a son of Gerald's age named Gavin, the outcome of an affair that had ended even before Gavin was born. She was looking for security rather than romance or social status, and rightly thought that in Mr Burke she had found it. When she first visited Arcadia she held out her arms to Gerald, who backed away. Later on the same day the boys quarrelled when playing a game together and Gerald, who was much the larger, got astride Gavin and began to bang his head on the floor. Emerald said Gerald seemed rather uncontrolled, and Mr Burke said she would soon lick him into shape. Then he spoke to his son. 'Gerald, this is your new mother. Come and kiss her.' At that Gerald ran out of the room.

Emerald did not lick Gerald into shape, had no desire to lick anybody into shape. She was a simple, easygoing woman whose voice retained traces of her East End origins. She thought she had made a lucky marriage, enjoyed life in Arcadia, and hardly noticed the whispers among those Mr Burke regarded as his friends that he had certainly taken a step or two down in the social scale with his second marriage. Emerald knew the importance of keeping her man happy, and the not unrelated problem of keeping her figure. She looked after Gavin, the second star round which her life revolved, and would have looked after Gerald and helped him with homework as she did Gavin, but Gerald wouldn't let her. Once she had, unfortunately, suggested a wrong answer to a question about history, and when he came home the next afternoon he tore up his exercise book and threw it at her. After that she gave up. 'When he wants help he'll ask for it,' she said to her husband, and Mr Burke nodded agreement.

As the years went by it became obvious, or should have been obvious, that Gerald needed help from somebody. The difference between his abilities and those of Gavin became more marked with every year. They both went to the primary school in town and then to the state-aided grammar, and Gavin at once showed his aptitude and eagernesss for learning, while Gerald was never better than sluggish, regarded by some teachers as backward, by others as deliberately lazy. Gavin won prizes for best essay, most original drawing, biggest contribution to class harmony. Gerald won no prizes at all, and was consistently near the bottom of every class.

The differences extended to their appearance. Gavin was small, neat and tidy, Gerald an outsize boy, six foot tall at thirteen and bulky with it. His clothes always seemed too small for him, buttons somehow became torn off his jackets, his shoes were sometimes unlaced, his lank hair all over the place. The only area in which Gerald might have excelled was sport. His reactions were too slow for him to get into the cricket or football teams, but he was anchor man in the tug-of-war competition and won the heavyweight boxing, although in the following year he refused to go in for it. 'What do I want to hit him for, he's done nothing to me,' he said to the sports master, who was tickled enough to tell Mr Burke.

Gerald's father was not tickled at all. He set out to give his son some friendly advice about the need for competition in life, but found him so unresponsive that, most unusually for him, he began to shout. 'You're ready to let everybody walk all over you, is that it, is that what you mean to do in life?'

Gerald shuffled his size twelve shoes. 'Don't know.'

'Don't know, you *ought* to know, you've got to stand up for yourself, not let people walk all over you. Otherwise you'll end up as a crossing sweeper.' Afterwards he spoke to Emerald. 'I don't want to be hard on the boy. Has he got any school-friends?' She shook her head. 'No friends, doesn't work at school, sits up in his room reading comics or wearing those earphones and listening to pop music. It's not natural, he's got no interest in anything. I tell you, Gavin's more like my son than my own flesh and blood is.'

Emerald laughed. 'You're so impatient, it's not like you. You just see, I think he's a late developer, he'll do something that surprises you one day.'

There was no sign of Gerald doing anything surprising at the end of his schooldays. Gavin got a scholarship to Oxford. Gerald did get a job, indeed several jobs, but kept none of them for long. He was an assistant in a record shop, served behind the counter in the local fast food restaurant, worked on a lathe in a shoe factory, did odd jobs in a timber yard, and was a rider for a messenger service. He puttered in and out of town on a scooter wearing a mauve woollen hat to which he became much attached. He had no girl-friends, and went on reading the comics that most of the boys he knew at school had given up at the age of fourteen. Emerald was indulgent as ever, but Gerald's jobs and his appearance fulfilled all Mr Burke's worst fears. He could hardly bear to look at the boy.

The thing that infuriated him more than anything else was that Gerald seemed quite unaware of the ludicrous figure he cut among the neat lawns, gleaming Volvos, Vauxhalls and sports Escorts, and the designer jeans of his young contemporaries in Arcadia. When Gavin came home and brought friends with him the appearance of Gerald, shambling and awkward, dressed in baggy and not very clean trousers, sitting on a sofa reading comics in which heroes endowed with miraculous powers got the better of villains armed with germ bombs and remote control devices that could trigger off the destruction of cities, was almost more than Mr Burke could bear. Something, he said, must be done. Supposing he was set up in the town with a small flat of his own, how would that do? Perhaps Gavin could speak to him?

So Gavin spoke but, as he had warned his mother and step-father in advance, without effect. 'He really didn't seem to understand what I was talking about,' he reported. 'He says this is his home, he doesn't want to leave it. I think he'd be lost in a place of his own, he wouldn't look after himself. He says if you don't want him to read comics downstairs he'll keep them in his room.'

'What about your friends, what do they say?'

'Don't get me wrong when I say they think he's a joke. But they don't mind him, nor do I.' Gavin hesitated. 'I think you should accept him as a sort of force of nature.'

Emerald's eyes filled with tears, and she said they mustn't send Gerald away, it would be too cruel.

So Gerald stayed. He was now six foot five and very broad, with enormous hands. Shoes had to be specially made to fit him.

Then came the Soft Shoe Rapist.

He appeared in Greater Arcadia, visiting three houses within a month. He was evidently adept at climbing drainpipes and getting on to roofs, his means of access being through windows left marginally or wide open on the upper floors of houses. He wore a mask, was clothed in black, and threatened his victims either with a revolver or a large curved knife. All the attacks were made late at night. His first two victims were young women with small children whose husbands were away, something that suggested knowledge of the people in the houses, or careful study of their habits. The third victim was in Arcadia itself, a middle-aged woman who slept in another room from her husband. He woke, however, entered his wife's bedroom, and was stabbed twice in the ensuing fight. He was rushed to hospital, and for a week was on the critical list, but recovered.

Because the rapist operated in the dark descriptions were necessarily vague, but the victims agreed that he was big, with powerful hands. He spoke in a soft hissing voice, and moved soundlessly. A footprint of a light-weight hi-tec shoe was found at the bottom of one drainpipe he had climbed, and the press christened him the Soft Shoe Rapist.

A Guardian Committee was set up to organise the protection of Arcadia. Its chairman was a local car dealer named Frampton, and one of the members was the owner of the timber yard where Gerald had worked, whose name was Tilsley Williams. It was Williams who came round to the Burkes' house and suggested that Gerald should join the committee. Gerald was out, and he saw Mr Burke who stared at him when Williams made the request.

'There's nobody from this part of the estate has joined the committee,' Williams said. Mr Burke did not care for

Arcadia to be lumped in with the much inferior houses of Greater Arcadia as 'the estate', but he did not comment. 'And he's a good strong lad, Gerald. And willing, or was when he worked for us, we were sorry to lose him.' At this Mr Burke winced. The very idea of his son working in a timber yard, and of this bristly-moustached little tradesman talking about him familiarly, was odious. 'Course we'd like it if you'd join us yourself, but I don't suppose you can spare the time.' The sarcasm in Williams's voice was kept just within the limits of politeness. 'Trouble is, we're all chiefs and no Indians, if you take my meaning. Jerry'd be useful helping around, delivering rotas and such. That's if he felt inclined.'

Mr Burke said distantly that he would speak to his son when he came in, and let Mr Williams know the result. He talked to Emerald, who was all in favour of the idea, and then Gerald, who listened to him carefully, then said, 'He's a bad man, isn't he?'

'What, the— ' Mr Burke could not bring himself to use the ghastly media term. 'Yes, very bad.'

'He ought to be stopped.'

'Of course, but— ' He checked himself again. 'Some people would think catching this sort of man is best left to the police.'

'They haven't caught him. The good men have to join together to catch the bad ones.'

'I don't think they expect you to catch him. From what I can make out they want you as a kind of messenger boy.'

'I don't mind about that.' Gerald smiled. He had a sweetly innocent smile, or so Emerald said. Mr Burke simply felt he would like to knock some sense into the boy's head.

So Gerald became a member of the Guardian Committee, which operated enthusiastically for the next few weeks. Frampton had lapel badges printed for committee members saying 'Guardian', and Gerald wore his all the time on his jacket or pullover. A roster was organised by

which Guardians in couples took turns keeping watch in
Arcadia and Greater Arcadia throughout the night. All of
them were men, something commented on unfavourably,
but as Mr Peabody the assistant bank manager pointed
out, men were better able to cope with somebody ready to
use a knife than a woman. Gerald took his turn at watching,
carried messages on his scooter, and seemed not to notice
the jokes, some good natured and others less so, based on
the fact that he was the only resident of the original Arcadia
to join the committee.

'Think they're too good for us, I daresay,' Mr Frampton
said. 'Don't want to join the *hoi polloi*.' He smiled as he said
it, indicating how absurd it was to think a man like himself
who drove a Roller (even though the firm's, not his own)
could ever be classed among the *hoi polloi*.

The police viewed the Guardians' activities with tolerant amusement. Some hundreds of men convicted of
various sexual misdemeanours had been turned up by their
computer, and they were slowly eliminating them, but if the
residents wanted to form this kind of vigilante committee –
well, it could do no harm, and kept them occupied. But after
several weeks, as there were no more attacks, and the nights
grew colder, and there was a whole week when it rained
every night, the Guardians' ardour faded. There had been
some rather similar attacks twenty miles away, and it was
agreed that the Guardians could be disbanded. 'We scared
him off,' Mr Frampton said. 'He knew if he tried it again
he'd get more than he bargained for.'

So, with mutual thanks and self-congratulation, the
Guardians ceased to exist. But Gerald continued to walk
round the executive houses of Arcadia with their wide
pavements and large lawns, then round Greater Arcadia
where the pavements were narrower, the lawns smaller and
the houses much less individual, all of them having been
built to one of four designs. He wore his woollen cap and
the Guardian badge, and carried his father's cane, which
had a large brass loaded top, in the shape of the dog-faced

Egyptian god Anubis. Mr Burke had been amused by his son's insistence on acting as solitary watchman, and gave him the stick.

'It belonged to my father, and his father too. Give anybody a tap with the business end of it, and he'll know all about it.' He smacked the dog's head on to a cushion, and made a dent. Gerald nodded.

It was on a dark night in early November that Gerald caught the Soft Shoe Rapist.

His evening walk took a little less than an hour. He was halfway through Greater Arcadia when he heard the sounds of a window being thrown open, and a woman's cry. The lighting throughout the Arcadias was discreet, and it was a few moments before Gerald made out the house from which the cry had come, and then sensed rather than saw a figure moving down the drainpipe. He opened the house gate, ran across the lawn, and reached the figure just after it touched the ground. With a sweeping blow the figure knocked dog-faced Anubis out of his hand, but Gerald managed to catch hold of a leg, and the two bodies writhed together on the grass. A light showed in one of the houses and glinted on steel. Gerald groped for the knife. It disappeared, then he felt something push at his side, saw the knife raised again, now dark with blood. He felt no pain but the sight of blood made him angry; he put two great hands round the figure's neck and squeezed. There was another push at him, and another, then the figure was beneath him and his hands still round its neck, but the strength seemed to drain from them and they loosened. The figure lay beneath him, a gurgling sound coming from the throat. Then there were lights, lights everywhere, and voices. After that, nothing.

He woke in hospital several hours later, and learned that he had been stabbed three times, once within a few inches of the heart. He had caught the Soft Shoe Rapist, who was escaping after another rape in which the victim had ignored his threat that if she did not remain silent he would come back and kill her. The rapist was a member of the Guardian Committee, Mr Peabody the assistant bank manager. He was not on the police computer.

Gerald recovered to find himself a national hero. The headlines ranged from ONE MAN GUARDS ARCADIA to UNARMED JERRY FACES KILLER RAPIST, with half a dozen variations in between. He gave several interviews from his hospital bed, and proved to be a natural headline maker. 'Jerry says it's Goodies versus Baddies', one paper said. Another headed its story, 'The Simple Faith of the Man in the Woolly Hat', and a third, ' "I Just Did What I Had To," Hero Says'. The punning possibilities of his name were not ignored. 'Jerry Is No Berk' said Britain's best-selling tabloid, at the top of a story which began, 'Jerry Burke may look a bit of a berk in his woollen hat, but when it comes to defending law and order he's a tiger.'

After he came out of hospital Gerald was stopped in the street by people who shook his hand, and said it was young men like him, ready to go in there and take a chance, who were making Britain great again. He declined invitations to speak to local schools, Rotary Clubs and Chambers of Commerce, but appeared for three minutes on local TV, where in answer to a question about what he felt when tackling a man with a knife, he said, 'I didn't feel anything, I just did it, I knew he was a bad man and had to be stopped.' The messenger firm that employed him found he was in such demand that they doubled his wages.

To say Mr Burke was astonished by Gerald's sudden fame would be an understatement. Charles Cloudesley, a retired merchant banker who lived only three or four minutes' walk away, embarrassed him by saying he had a hero for a son, and even his lord and master noticed one of the press stories, and said he was to be congratulated on having such a fine young man for his son. He felt like asking his lord and master if it was a matter for congratulation to have a son who was content to be an overgrown messenger boy, and read nothing but comics. He was irritated by Emerald, who said Gavin and his friends had been very impressed, and that she had always said he would be proud of Gerald if he gave the boy time.

The person who seemed least affected was Gerald himself. He went on reading comics and listening to pop records, and continued making his round of the two Arcadias at night, taking with him the loaded stick, which in reference to the dog-headed god who topped it, he called the dog. 'I'm taking the dog for a walk,' he would say, looking at his father and step-mother to see if they laughed.

The dog was of service when, at the end of November, Gerald was patrolling (which was how he thought of it) Greater Arcadia, and saw a girl trying to get out of a car, and being stopped from doing so by a man inside. He was thirty yards away when he saw the car door open and the girl get out, then heard her scream as she was pulled back again. When he reached the car a struggle was taking place inside. He pulled open the door. The driver had his hands round the girl's throat, she was shrieking something and clawing at his face. When the door opened they both looked round.

They seemed astonished when Gerald shouted, 'Leave her alone.' The girl shrieked something at him, got out and pushed past. The man also got out of the car and came round towards her. Gerald barred the way. The man let out a volleyful of obscenities and hit Gerald on the jaw. Gerald brought the dog into action and gave the man a tremendous crack on the shin. The man collapsed to the ground. The girl jumped on to Gerald's back and pulled his hair, knocking off his woollen hat. He staggered, trying to shake her off, and inadvertently struck the car's side window with the dog. The tinkle of glass brought people out of nearby houses.

The encounter remained unreported in the press, perhaps fortunately. The couple proved to be man and wife, the man threatened to sue Gerald for assault, Gerald pointed out that he had struck the first blow. The matter ended with Gerald paying for the broken car window. He did not mention the incident to his father or to Emerald, but it became known, and he was transformed from a hero into something like a figure of fun. People at work asked if he had broken up any more happy families lately. Nevertheless, he continued to patrol Arcadia.

In December the weather became colder, the roads were icy, a little snow fell. Decorations appeared in windows, fairy lights on Christmas trees, circlets of holly round front doors. Gavin came home, bringing with him a girl student who seemed to view Gerald with the curiosity appropriate to a creature of another species. Both of them were bursting with high spirits and their gaiety infected Mr Burke, so that one night he joined with Emerald in a sentimental sing-song, with Gavin playing the piano. Gerald had no voice, and when he joined in the girl almost collapsed with laughter. At the office he was no longer in demand as a despatch rider, his fame seemed altogether forgotten.

In late December it began to snow in earnest, thick flakes that settled on the ground, and provided a carpet that silenced footsteps and made driving dangerous. A week before Christmas Gerald went out on what proved his last patrol. His faithful dog went with him.

He was still in Arcadia, the original Arcadia of big houses and discreetly dim street lighting, when he saw the man. Under the mantle of snow the individual outlines of houses were not easily distinguishable but Gerald was almost sure that it was the Cloudesley house from which the man emerged. The place itself was in darkness, and the man who came, not out of the front door but round the side of the house, was carrying a large bag over his shoulder. He made his way quickly yet stealthily to the gate, and hurried down the road.

Gerald quickened his own pace to catch up with the man, although this was not easy. There was nobody about, for they were in the midst of a really heavy snowfall. Snow blew into Gerald's face, blurring his vision, snow was wet on his mouth, and his wellingtons were more suited for trudging than hurrying. But still he gained ground, was near enough to call out. 'Stop,' he shouted, 'stop.' The man turned for a moment, long enough for Gerald to see that he appeared to have no proper face. Then he pulled a hood over his head and went on, more quickly than before. Gerald started to run.

He felt an exultant certainty that he had found a thief, a baddie, for if he was a goodie why did he not stop when hailed? Perhaps, with the baddie caught, that moment of fame would return.

He caught the man at the point where Arcadia ended and Greater Arcadia began, put a hand on his shoulder, swung him round. To his horror the stranger revealed, not a face but a hideous mask. He put down the bag he carried, fumbled inside it. Before his hand could come out holding a knife or revolver, dog-headed Anubis struck. Raised high and then swung down like a mallet, he hit the stranger once, twice, three times. The man fell to his knees. The hood had fallen aside and the wig beneath it was askew, revealing a bald pate. He had been not only a thief, but one in disguise! Anger filled Gerald, anger and a wonderful awareness of his own rightness as he rained blows on that wickedly dishonest bald head until dog-headed Anubis was wet and dripping and the man lay still on the snow, his coat rucked up to show the red clothes beneath, his bag fallen open and a couple of the toys in it spilled out. The Santa Claus mask had slipped off too, revealing the face of old Mr Cloudesley.

The Inspector who took Gerald's statement had a sense of humour, and prided himself on being a bit of a wag.

'And you really thought he was – what did you call it? – a baddie.'

'Yes, I thought he was a baddie.'

'My my. And it was just old Mr Cloudesley taking along a bag of presents to the Greater Arcadian Jumbo Christmas Gift Gala. He was going to be Santa Claus, you know.'

'I know it now, yes.'

'But you never recognised him?'

'It was the snow.' The Inspector's geniality was somehow more frightening than the long faces his father and Emerald had pulled when they came to see him. 'He should have stopped when I asked him.'

'And when he opened his bag to show you the toys for the kiddies, you thought— '

'He was going for his gun. Or his knife.' But Gerald only whispered the words.

Well, the Inspector thought, they say there's one born every minute, but they don't all go round thinking they're Wyatt Earp. Aloud he said, 'You know, you're going to be famous.' The young man's head was raised when he said that, the eyes sparkled for a moment, then dulled as the Inspector went on: 'You'll go down in history as the man who killed Santa Claus.'

Two's Company

Michael Underwood

From the moment that Howard decided to murder his
wife, he began being nicer to her. Decisions like that can
often cause a complete change of outlook. Uncertainty is
always demoralising and a determination to end it raises
the spirits.

It was not that Howard had ever, during their twenty
years of marriage, physically ill-treated Yvonne. If anything,
it was the other way. Once she had thrown a book at him (a
solid historical romance of over four hundred pages) and on
another occasion she had hurled a jar of skin cleanser at his
head. Neither time had she hit her target.

Howard was now forty-nine and Yvonne fifty-one, and
Stanley her brother was forty-six. It's necessary to mention
Stanley as he played a prominent role in their lives and it
was through him that Howard had come to meet his future
wife.

Howard and Stanley had been members of the same
small suburban tennis club and one Saturday afternoon as
they came off court Stanley mentioned that his mother and
sister were coming along for tea and he would like Howard
to meet them.

Howard's first impression had not been particularly
favourable. Mother, daughter and son seemed curiously

wrapped up in each other's conversation so that Howard felt left out. Not that this greatly bothered him and he decided to get back on court as soon as possible.

'I hope you're going to play on a court where we can watch you, Mr Shankland,' Mrs King said as he excused himself. 'Stanley says you're very good.'

'I wish that were true,' Howard said in a deprecating tone. 'Playing one afternoon a week is not the best recipe for improving one's game. But I enjoy it and I suppose that's the important thing.' He was aware that Yvonne had been observing him closely during this brief conversation.

When he returned to court for a mixed doubles, he couldn't fail to notice that Yvonne continued to watch him. There was something mildly disconcerting about her cool, appraising stare.

At the end of the afternoon as he emerged from a shower, Stanley came up and said, 'My mother wonders if you'd care to come and have supper with us one evening?'

'I'd like to,' Howard replied, somewhat taken aback by the unexpectedness of the invitation.

Several weeks were to pass, however, before it was translated into reality.

Since his mother's death the previous winter, Howard had lived on his own, his father having died several years earlier. He was the only child of elderly parents and had a safe job in the local Council offices where he was already regarded, at the age of twenty-eight, as a confirmed bachelor. He gave the appearance of being set in his ways and of having little interest in the opposite sex. In fact this aspect of his life was as well regulated as the rest of it. On the second Friday of each month, he would go straight from the office to a dowdy flat behind Leicester Square where a motherly blonde named Nadine would minister to his needs.

Supper with the Kings proved to be a more enjoyable meal than tea at the club had been, though there were times when he still felt out of things, as mother, son and daughter chatted about people and events of which he had

no knowledge. The meal, however, was excellent; cooked
and served by Yvonne.

'That was delicious,' he said appreciatively, as he mopped
up the last few drops of gravy on his plate. 'Very different
from the lamb stew you get in our staff canteen.'

Yvonne gave him one of her cool, thoughtful looks.
'I'm glad you enjoyed it.'

'Wait till you taste her lemon meringue pie,' her mother
said.

Stanley nodded. 'My sister's the best cook I know,'
he said.

'Well you needn't think I'm going to cook for you the
rest of my days,' she remarked with an affectionate laugh.

A few weeks later the tennis season finished (Howard
didn't play in the winter) and then around the middle
of October, he saw a notice of Mrs King's death in the
local paper. Being a punctilious person he went out and
bought an appropriate bereavement card, but then wasn't
sure whether to send it to Stanley whom he knew better or
to Yvonne who was the older. In the event he wrote, 'Dear
Yvonne and Stanley . . . '

Ten days later he received a note from Yvonne thanking
him for his condolences and adding that she and her brother
hoped he would come to supper again soon.

Thereafter he became a regular visitor to their house
and early in the new year, almost to his own surprise,
he proposed marriage. One should add that he had had
more than usual to drink on the evening in question and
his monthly visit to Soho was in the offing so that his mind
tended to be aswirl with sexual fantasies. Yvonne accepted
his proposal in a matter-of-fact way and three months later
they had a quiet, register office wedding. Stanley gave his
sister away and a couple of neighbours acted as witnesses.

That had all been twenty years ago. . . .

Twenty years had given him more than enough time to
reflect on the pros and cons of marriage. As far as marriage

to Yvonne was concerned, the pros had long since vanished. Admittedly she was still a splendid cook when it suited her, as when her brother was coming for a meal which was an all too frequent occurrence.

Howard had soon realised that he had not only married Yvonne, but Stanley as well, though he had put his foot down firmly when she had suggested about a year after their wedding that Stanley should come and live with them.

'We could convert the top floor into a self-contained flat,' she had said.

'I don't think that would be at all a good idea,' he had replied. ·

'What's the objection?'

'It would be like having one's mother-in-law living with one,' he had retorted.

'I always thought you and Stanley got on well.'

'We do and I'd like to keep it that way.'

Somewhat to his surprise, Yvonne had not pursued the subject and Stanley had bought a flat about a mile from where they lived, which was handy for dropping in on them.

Howard supposed he must be grateful that his brother-in-law was a sales representative, which meant that a large part of his working week was spent on the road and away from home. But that didn't prevent them all going on holiday together each year.

At first, Howard had resented the number of times that the people they met seemed to assume that Stanley and Yvonne were the married couple and that he was the third party. It was a humiliating situation, though they always pretended to treat it as something of a joke. But Stanley and Yvonne so clearly relished each other's company that the assumption was hardly surprising.

When Stanley was away from home, he would call his sister most evenings and they would talk endlessly on the telephone. And if, for some reason, he failed to call her, she would leave messages on his answering machine to greet him on his return, which Howard found ludicrous.

Fortunately, there were no children of the marriage; indeed, Yvonne had never shown more than a tepid interest in sex, which had left Howard to continue his visits to Soho. If Yvonne had any inkling of these, she never revealed it and the point was reached where Howard wouldn't have cared if she had found out.

When eventually he decided to kill her, he couldn't think why it had taken him so long to reach the decision. He supposed it was largely due to apathy. Though his life had become no more than an existence, it wasn't wholly insupportable.

So why, after twenty years, had he reached a decision which, to put it mildly, was going to change all their lives? It was a question he was to ponder, not out of self-doubt but out of interest in the workings of his own mind. In the event he decided it was a seed which must have been germinating in his subconscious for years before breaking surface.

The day on which it presented itself as a decision in his conscious mind was no different from any other. Howard had just finished shaving one side of his face and was about to start on his upper lip when, bingo, the decision appeared as clearly as if it were printed on the bathroom mirror. When a short time later he went downstairs to breakfast, he was in an unusually cheerful frame of mind.

'Stanley's been on the phone,' Yvonne said as he sat down. 'He's coming home a day earlier than he expected and I've asked him round to supper this evening.'

'Fine,' Howard said with a smile. His mind had been so filled with thoughts of doing away with his wife that he hadn't even heard the phone ring.

'I'd been planning to make a steak and kidney pie,' Yvonne went on, 'but I think I'll get some liver. Stanley likes nicely grilled liver more than anything and I've not given it him for weeks.' She paused. 'You don't mind, do you? I know it's not one of your favourite things, but you can eat it, can't you?'

'Yes, particularly the way you cook it.'

'Well, that's settled. And I'll make a damson pie and get some cream.'

'Anything I can do to help?' he enquired, almost eagerly.

'You could bring back a bottle of wine.'

'Of course. I'll get two.'

Yvonne frowned. 'One'll be enough. We're not celebrating anything particular.'

That's all you know, he thought cheerfully to himself.

The evening was an unqualified success and Howard had seldom been more affable, when given the chance.

'You're a lucky fellow, Howard,' Stanley remarked at the end of the meal, adding that his sister knew better than anyone that the way to a man's heart was via his stomach.

'You don't have to tell me that after twenty years of marriage to her,' Howard replied with a contented smile.

'I'll go and make some coffee,' Yvonne said, after a thoughtful pause.

As he lay in bed that night, Howard felt tired but exhilarated. His mind was in far too much of a whirl for sleep to come easily. He and Yvonne had been occupying separate beds for the past twelve years, but he could tell from her breathing that she was already asleep. That suited him as he wanted to give his mind to the details of her murder and if she had been awake, he'd have had a creepy feeling she was reading his thoughts.

He had decided that her death must look like an accident. He had once read that murders that appeared to be accidents were the most difficult to prove. So it followed that Yvonne should have an accident. Perhaps in the kitchen where she spent most of her time. Electrocution as a result of a faulty connection? But there his inspiration ran out. Moreover his knowledge of electricity was so elementary that he would never be able to tamper with one of the fittings and subsequently return it to normal. Indeed, it was usually Yvonne who changed plugs and replaced fuses.

He next gave thought to the possibility of drowning her when she was taking a bath, though that, too, carried its risks. Yvonne was quite strong and would be likely to struggle and he could envisage most of the water ending up on the floor. Moreover, she had always disliked his entering the bathroom when she was there.

He felt himself getting sleepy as he turned his mind to the possibility of an accident with the car. But what sort of an accident would encompass her death and leave him unscathed? Suddenly out of nowhere he remembered Gorsing Wood where they used to go for picnics when first married. His heart gave a small joyful leap as he turned on his side and fell asleep.

It was a sunny morning about two weeks later that he said to Yvonne over breakfast, 'I'm not working this afternoon; why don't we go for a picnic?'

'A picnic?' she said in surprise. 'Where?'

'I was thinking of Gorsing Wood. It's been years since we've visited the area and we used to have lovely picnics there.'

'All right,' she said after a moment's contemplation. 'At least it'll make a change. What time do you want to go?'

'I'll be home around two. Any time after that.'

'Three o'clock will be quite early enough,' she said firmly. 'And there's one other thing, who'll carry the picnic basket?'

He gave a good-humoured laugh. 'Me, of course.'

'That's all right then. I seem to remember that you were never very keen on doing so and more often than not we ended up eating just inside the wood where every known insect used to breed.'

'I promise I'll carry it right to the top of Gorsing Hill where there's that marvellous view.'

'Let's hope it's still there.'

It is, he was about to say, then bit his tongue. A few days earlier he had been on a reconnaissance and found to his delight that the area was virtually unchanged. There was still the escarpment with the pond below and the path that ran along the rim. One couldn't think of a better scene for a tragic accident.

The path in question was about eighteen inches wide. On one side was a steep slope of tufted grass which fell away for about eight feet to the top of the chalk face which, in turn, was sheer to the water below. As with many quarries, the water was still and deep. All he would need to ensure was that Yvonne was propelled down the initial slope with sufficient momentum to take her over the edge. Thereafter she couldn't possibly survive. He had already selected the spot where he would suddenly turn and give her the push which would despatch her on her way to the next world.

The sun was still shining when they set out about three o'clock and Howard kept up a flow of bright conversation as they drove to Gorsing Wood.

'It should be perfect there today,' he enthused. 'It'll be like old times.'

'Stanley would have enjoyed coming if he'd been home,' Yvonne remarked.

'Next time we'll make it a Saturday or Sunday and he can join us,' Howard said without a qualm.

It had been no accident that he had chosen a day when he knew his brother-in-law would be away. Stanley was in Ireland on business until the end of the week. That put him well out of reach even though he had phoned his sister the previous evening.

Howard parked the car on the grass verge at the edge of Gorsing Wood and they got out.

'We'll probably have the place to ourselves,' he observed cheerfully.

A few minutes later they were on the path that made a gentle ascent through the trees.

'All right?' he asked, turning to Yvonne who was a few

steps behind him. She nodded. Ten minutes later he said, 'Almost there. There's just that stretch round the top of the quarry and then a final hundred yards.'

'You seem to remember it as if it were yesterday,' Yvonne remarked as she paused for breath.

'Want a hand?' Howard enquired solicitously.

'No, I can manage.'

Soon they reached the point where the path began its course round the rim of the quarry.

'Are you sure it's safe?' Yvonne asked doubtfully, as they paused once more for breath.

'No problems,' he replied. 'Give me your hand.'

She shook her head. 'I'm better on my own.'

He shrugged. Not for long you won't be, he thought.

About halfway along the path he paused so that Yvonne could close up on him. Her expression told him that she was concentrating everything on keeping a firm foothold. Even though the path was generally safe, there were a few places where it had crumbled at the edges.

Abruptly he swung the picnic basket in a wide arc and caught her a heavy clout on her left side. She let out a sharp cry and stumbled forward clutching at his arm. The next thing they were both slithering down the steep grassy slope towards the edge of the escarpment. He grunted with exertion as he tried to break her grip on his sleeve. The picnic basket bounced ahead of them and disappeared over the edge.

The next moment he and Yvonne followed it.

It was an hour and a half later that two men returning along the top of the quarry from a pigeon shoot heard faint cries for help. They moved cautiously to the edge of the escarpment and looked over. About twenty feet below they saw Howard clutching a tree which was growing out of the side of the chalk face. He was balanced precariously astride the trunk.

'Hold on, mate. We'll get help,' one of the men shouted.

It was a further forty minutes, however, before Howard was slowly and laboriously hauled to safety. As soon as he realised he was no longer in danger, he passed out.

'My wife,' he murmured when he regained consciousness. 'We slipped and fell. . . . '

It was much later in the day that Yvonne's body was recovered from the water. A pathologist was to confirm that she had died from drowning and that marks on her body were consistent with a fall from the top of the escarpment.

'I reckon you're lucky to be alive, sir,' a police sergeant remarked to Howard as he waited to be driven home.

Nobody was more keenly aware of this than Howard himself. On the other hand, during the hour since his rescue he had come to realise how events had turned out even better than he could have planned. Nobody could possibly doubt the authenticity of the accident, which had rid him of Yvonne and left him alive. He knew he would have to face police questioning about what exactly had happened, but that no longer worried him.

Fate's original snarl had turned into an approving smile.

He half-expected Stanley to phone from Ireland that evening, but when he didn't Howard decided to leave a message on his answering machine. He couldn't help smiling as he dialled Stanley's number and waited to hear his brother-in-law's recorded voice informing him that he was not at home, but please leave a message after the pips.

'It's Howard, Stanley,' he said in a suitably grave tone. 'I'm afraid I have terrible news about Yvonne. She's been involved in a tragic accident and is dead. Please call me as soon as you get home. I'm too upset to say any more at this moment.' He replaced the receiver, hoping his tone had reflected the grief he should be feeling, but wasn't.

As someone recently bereaved, he didn't think it would be appropriate to go to work the next day, but time hung on his hands as he mooched about the house waiting for something to happen. The police had told him they would get in touch about the inquest which the local coroner would be bound to hold.

It was early evening, however, before anything further happened. He was looking out of the sitting-room window when a car pulled up and three people got out. Two men in suits and a young woman in a red and white dress.

'Mr Shankland?' the older man said when Howard opened the front door. 'I'm Detective Inspector Scobie and these are my colleagues, Detective Sergeant Young and Woman Detective Constable Noakes. We'd like to have a word with you if it's convenient.'

'Certainly,' Howard said with an obliging smile. 'Please come in. I'm still trying to come to terms with what's happened. It hasn't really sunk in.' He led the way into the sitting room. 'What can I do to help?' he said when they were all seated.

'I'll come to the point straight away,' Scobie said briskly. 'It's been suggested to us, Mr Shankland, that you murdered your wife.'

Howard felt the blood drain from his face and his skin became clammy. He shook his head in bemusement as he sought for words which wouldn't come.

Scobie now went on, 'Mr King, your brother-in-law, tells us that when he arrived home earlier today and played back calls recorded on his answering machine, there was one from your wife.' He reached into his pocket and pulled out a slip of paper. 'Best if I read you her exact words,' he said as he cleared his throat. 'The message she left him was as follows . . . ' Howard could only stare at him with a totally mesmerised expression while he waited in numbed disbelief at what was happening. Scobie cleared his throat again as he began to read. ' "I feel Howard is up to something, Stan. Should anything untoward happen to me, I think you should consider informing the police." ' Scobie removed the spectacles he had put on to read from the piece of paper. 'Well, Mr Shankland?'

Howard let out an anguished groan. A groan that was as eloquent as any written confession.

... Who Needs Enemies?

John Wainwright

It began about three months ago. . . .

Give or take a few days, that's *about* when it began, even though, at the time, I wasn't aware of the fact. Chris was having tummy trouble and he'd made an appointment and, as always, he'd fixed himself to be last in the surgery list in order that we might have a chat after the check-up. I diagnosed colic and it didn't seem to please him too well.

'Colic? I thought *horses* had colic?'

'Bile, old son. A little too much for the system to handle without temporary assistance.'

I was writing out the prescription when he said, 'Poison.'

'No, it's not poisonous. It's just . . . '

'No, I mean *poison*.' He was tucking the tail of his shirt back into the waistband of his trousers as he spoke. 'Assuming you wanted to do somebody in, what poison would *you* use?'

'I wouldn't,' I smiled. 'The Hippocratic Oath and all that. Anyway, why not the old-fashioned blunt instrument?'

'It wouldn't do.' He'd buttoned his shirt and was straightening his tie. 'It would be out of character. The chap I'm describing isn't a physical type. Very studious. Very cunning.'

'Something of a coward?'

'Could be.' He shrugged his jacket more firmly onto his shoulders and returned to the chair alongside the desk. As he took the prescription, folded it and slipped it into his wallet, he added, 'I was toying with the idea of strychnine, but I'm damned if I can figure out a way of getting hold of the stuff.'

'It's around,' I assured him. 'It's been around since the beginning of the nineteenth century. Palmer used it. So did Vaquier. It's rather a popular poison . . . so I'm told. Very painful, but very final.'

'True.' He nodded, solemnly. 'But, how can an ordinary, run-of-the-mill chap *get* the stuff without giving the game away?'

'You mean signing a Poison Register?'

'That *would* be stupid.'

'Make him a pest control officer,' I suggested. 'They seem to handle the stuff like so much granulated sugar.'

'He couldn't be *that*.' He was very serious. 'Whoever heard of an academic pest control officer?'

We'd known each other for twenty years. We'd met at high school, then gone on to university. We'd spent most of our spare time together. He'd had a leaning towards the arts, whereas I was more at home with the scientific side of things. We'd both been moderately successful and, having worked like crazy for our respective degrees, we'd taken a couple of months off and, in a mild sort of way, roared and whored our path through the wine-producing districts of France.

Thereafter (for me) the flog through medical school, a stint as a hospital dogsbody, a spell of locum work and, finally, I'd joined three other older General Practitioners in my present four-medic set-up.

Chris had gone literary. He'd concentrated on English Lit., taken to schoolmastering and ended up as Deputy Head at the local Comprehensive.

At times we seemed to have been linked to each other

with invisible parachute elastic. Each time we'd moved away to further our respective careers, the next step had brought us within easy reach of each other. And now – and for a few years – he was my patient.

We were both members of that loosely knit clique of professionals to be found in every small town: the bank managers, the accountants, the solicitors . . . the guys who are reputed to be slightly more 'educated' than the average hewer of wood and carrier of water. It was all crap, of course. It was merely a convenient you-scratch-my-back-and-I'll-scratch-yours set-up. Chris knew it – I knew it – but we played along, if only for the regular get-togethers, the good nosh, the convivial surroundings and to pass around the latest gossip and *risqué* jokes.

Meanwhile, Chris had found a personal niche for himself. He'd discovered he could write detective stories. I doubt if he could have made a living at it. I doubt if he even wanted to. I think he looked upon it as a paying hobby. He trotted them out at about one every two or three years. Light reading. Escapism. The sort of Agatha-Christie-maybe-the-butler-*did*-do-it brand of puzzle. Chandler would have laughed his socks off at some of the denouements, but what matter? Chris never pretended to be a Chandler.

He also married.

Not that I have anything against the married state, you understand. Merely that Mabel wasn't the sort of mate for a guy like Chris. She'd been some sort of secretary and, whereas Chris was one of those old-tweed-jacket-corduroy-trousers types, Mabel was a slim and leggy female with never a cracked finger-nail and never a hair out of place. She was the sort of filly about whom lewd remarks were made, behind Chris's back, at the Round Table get-togethers. Indeed, on more than one occasion I had to warn a fellow-member that there *was* a limit . . . and that *he* had just over-stepped it.

Me? I damn near broke the bank by buying an Aston

Martin. She was a beaut of a car and, having provided myself with the wheels, I took up rallying. Chris, too. I discovered that he could read a map as easily as he could read a book. He also had one of those crossword-puzzle brains. Flogging away at his whodunits, I suppose. To him, the clues were kiss-easy. We were quite a team. We won trophies. Local and regional.

We also became very close. Closer than we'd been since we were kids.

Out there, on a night rally, miles from anywhere. Just the two of us, with Chris reading the map via the dim light of the dashboard lamp. The car taking the bends like the thoroughbred she was and the great headlights slicing a way ahead. It was best in winter – in the small hours – with the fleece-lined coats snugging us away from the frost-cold slipstream and the car's heating system pushing gentle warmth up from around our feet.

Such moments make for the sharing of confidences.

'I don't go much on amateur dramatics . . . do you?'

We had a five mile stretch of Forestry Commission land ahead of us and, apart from not wishing to slaughter nocturnal wildlife, all I had to do was steer.

'Not my cup of tea,' I murmured.

'Mabel's going in for it,' he said, flatly.

'Oh!'

'I wouldn't give a damn if it was Priestley – Rattigan – even Shaw. But the bloody producer seems besotted by the Tennessee Williams muck. *The Night of the Iguana. Cat on a Hot Tin Roof.* A load of sexy drivel.'

'I'm no judge,' I fenced.

'Foul language and just about everything short of open fornication up there on the stage.'

'Maybe it's just a walk-on part,' I soothed.

'Not likely.' It was a low, outraged mutter. 'She's got a bit of a retentive memory . . . so it seems. Rarely fluffs a line. Does all the right things at the right time. A "natural" for the lead in all these steamy melodramas.'

'Chris, old son, she's play-acting.' My chuckle was meant to calm his agitation. 'It's a hobby, that's all. We do rallying. She does amateur dramatics. It's a *hobby* . . . that's all.'

'Let's hope so.' He sniffed, gave a wry grin and added, 'I still wish she'd gone in for knitting.'

Poor old Chris. I felt for him. Mabel earned quite a name for herself, both on stage and off. I spent a few bob and went to see her in Osborne's *Look Back in Anger* and she didn't just act. She *lived* the part . . . and enjoyed herself!

I'd seen amateur theatrics before and, in the main, I'd found them a pain in the rump. Dopes who deliberately moved to stage-centre, delivered their lines directly to the audience, then stepped aside to allow a fellow-dope to spout the dialogue. But, not this time. This time the applause was not merely a polite acknowledgement of a fair-to-moderate effort. This time it was for a magnificent portrayal of a middle-class tart. I didn't join in the applause because maybe it *wasn't* acting. Maybe she was allowing her true self to surface.

One thing for sure. She was giving Chris hell.

Another near-midnight exchange, on another rally.

'I hear things. Things I'm not supposed to hear.'

'Forget it, Chris. Some people are born trouble-makers.'

'I – y'know – I go into a pub, see a group of the chaps and join them. And, what they were talking about before I arrived, they *stop* talking about. They change the subject.'

'You could be imagining things, old chap.'

'You'd tell me, wouldn't you?' There was heartbreak in his voice. 'I mean . . . *you'd* tell me.'

'Chris. For Christ's sake, *do* something if you feel so strongly about it.'

'What?'

'Confront her. Tell her what you suspect. Give her a straight warning . . . either she stops being a tease, or she moves out.'

'Is she a tease? Is *that* what you're telling me?'

'I'm telling you what *you* think. How the hell do *I* know?'

'You're hinting.'

'No. Be damned for a tale. You're thinking on the twist, Chris. She's *your* wife, and you're driving yourself crazy about something . . . maybe *nothing*. Maybe you're working too hard. Maybe you need a holiday. Both of you. Maybe *anything* . . . but don't just whine about it. *Do* something. Get together. Seek advice. Talk it out.' I blew out my cheeks. 'Go out and get monumentally pissed, then go home and give her the works. Anything. But, for your own sake, do *something*.'

A couple of weeks after that little exchange he made the appointment, complained of tummy trouble and I diagnosed colic.

'Vitamin E.' The Detective Inspector sounded almost bored. He'd heard it all before – seen it all before – if he lived to be a thousand, he'd never again be shocked or even surprised. He added, 'E for energy . . . that's what they tell me.'

'As a rough guide,' I agreed.

'She figured she needed a top-up with energy, now and again.'

It wasn't a question. It was, at most, a statement of fact and, at least, a considered opinion. I let it ride.

I'd been asked to call at the police station in order to 'assist with enquiries'. I hadn't even known she was dead, much less murdered. The Inspector had told me that, in the same dreary, couldn't-care-less tone.

'The husband found her when he arrived home.'

'Chris?'

'Been to some sort of writers' convention, in London. A three-day job. Found her when he arrived home. Stiff as a board, on the kitchen floor.'

'Good God!'

'These things.' He used a forefinger to push the bottle

a fraction of an inch nearer, across the Interview Room table. 'The usual thing. Vitamin E capsules . . . but they aren't anymore. They've all been doctored. Refilled with strychnine. We think she took a couple.'

I said, 'Good God!' again.

'Nasty stuff, strychnine. Not a nice way to go.'

'You mean Chris . . . '

'Oh, no. Not the husband. It's a new bottle . . . see? We've checked with the manufacturers. Just two missing. That tallies with the pathologist's estimate. That and the estimated time of death. Couldn't be the husband. He was two hundred miles away. Witnesses galore.'

'In that case, why ask *me* to . . . '

'You mentioned strychnine.'

'Eh?'

'As a possible poison. That's what the husband tells us. Strychnine.' He pronounced the second syllable slowly and as if he was mouthing the last of the single figures. 'You seemed very taken with it . . . so the husband says.'

'Taken? With strychnine?'

'So the husband tells us,' he repeated.

'You mean – you mean . . . ' I gaped at the man.

'I mean nothing, Doctor. Not yet.'

'Not *yet*!'

'Somebody,' he said, wearily, 'shoved strychnine down her throat. Somebody conned her into believing she was swallowing vitamin E when, in fact, she was swallowing strychnine.'

'That doesn't mean . . . '

'And *you*, Doctor – we have to say these things, I'm afraid – *you* mentioned that particular poison to the husband fairly recently.'

'In passing. A remark. No more than that.'

'Strychnine, eh?' One eyebrow lifted itself a fraction of an inch. 'A passing remark? I would certainly hate to get into serious conversation with you, Doctor.'

'If . . . ' I swallowed, then, in as firm a voice as I could muster, said, 'If you're suggesting that *I* poisoned . . . '

'You knew her.'

'She was Chris's wife. Of *course* I knew her.'

'Well?'

'As Chris's wife.'

'No . . . I mean *how* well?'

'More innuendoes?' I sneered.

'It's a straight question, Doctor,' he droned. 'How well did you know her? Well enough to sleep with her, for example?'

'That's a foul suggestion.'

'Aye.'. The impression was that he was stifling a yawn. 'One of the drawbacks of this job. You end up with a dirty mind . . . but, it *has* been known.'

'What?'

'Single men jumping into bed with married women.'

'It's also been known for doctors to commit murder,' I snapped.

'Poisoners,' he agreed, amiably. 'Even strychnine.' He linked the fingers of his hands behind his neck and tilted his head backwards. It was a stretching motion, as if easing tired muscles after a wearying drive. 'Y'see,' he said, 'there wasn't a break-in. Which means whoever spiked the capsules had access. And, it was a new bottle. Bought on the Friday afternoon . . . when hubby had left for London. Not hubby, therefore somebody she knew. A friend. Somebody she invited into the house. Somebody with a key.' He took a deep breath and sighed. 'We've done our basics, Doctor. There are no surprises left in the bran barrel.'

'It would need time.' I found myself gradually becoming interested – even fascinated – by the problem. 'If *all* the capsules were doctored.'

'They were.'

'And, somebody with access to strychnine.'

'Pest control officers,' he murmured, gently. 'They handle it like granulated sugar.'

'A quote from Chris,' I said, sourly.

'Of course . . . but, she wasn't on friendly terms with any pest control officers. She *was* on friendly terms with *you.*'

'As her doctor.'

'As *a* doctor . . . and as a good friend of her husband.'

'Are you trying to fix me, Inspector?' I asked the question quite calmly. I suddenly *was* quite calm. The situation had moved from the stage where anger and indignation was a response. It was bordering upon the realms of nightmare and the choice was either panic or controlled calm. I chose the latter. I said, 'You need a murderer. Is my name already in the frame?'

'It's among the probables,' he admitted. He unlinked his fingers, tilted his head forward, shoved his hands into the pockets of his trousers and slouched farther down in the chair. He droned, 'The hubby took off for London – for the convention thing – at three fifteen, Friday. Thirty minutes later – thirty-*five* minutes, if we want to split hairs – wifey trotted along to the local chemist and bought a new bottle of capsules. Fifteen minutes, and she was back home. An hour later – again, hair-splitting, at seven minutes past five – a car arrived. A very flash car. The boy-friend's car.' His eyelids drooped and, for a moment, it looked as if he was about to fall asleep. He seemed to rouse himself with a distinct effort, then said, 'Forty-three minutes later, wifey and her boy-friend left the house, climbed into the car and drove off. Destination, a quiet little hotel on the west coast.' He looked across the table at me, and drawled, 'I'll repeat my question, Doctor. Did you know her well enough to sleep with her?'

'Your timings are remarkably accurate,' I observed.

'I don't go for 'em.' He resumed his dormouse posture. 'The good ones are on a retainer from insurance companies – multi-national organisations – people like that. Most of the others spend their time key-hole squinting. I don't like 'em. Not a "Sam Spade" – not a "Phil Marlowe" – among the lot of 'em. But, they have good eyesight, they own accurate watches and they make careful notes.'

I attended the funeral. Why not? What Mabel and I had had was on a strictly carnal level. More than that, I'd known Chris far longer than I'd known *her*. And, despite the nasty suspicions of the police, I *hadn't* poisoned her.

I was not one of the 'official' mourners. Indeed, other than Chris, I knew none. Presumably they were members of her family gathered together for the occasion. Nevertheless, I watched from a discreet distance as, indeed, did a duo of heavily built gentlemen who, while not wearing standard unbelted macs, had 'detective' stamped plainly across their respective personalities.

As the mourners trooped around the open grave one of the detectives strolled across and joined me.

'It's true, then,' he said, pleasantly.

'What?'

'The one about the murderer returning to the scene of the crime.'

'You're the expert in these things,' I smiled.

'Just that touch more proof.' His tone remained amiable. 'They're like the Windmill Theatre . . . they never close.'

'Sorry. I don't follow.'

'Murder files,' he explained. 'It will remain open until the day we see *your* coffin being lowered.'

'The assumption being that *I'm* the man you're after?'

'Who else?'

'Who else?' I echoed his question. 'Your Inspector, too, seems to have reached a firm conclusion. Erroneous . . . but, very firm.'

'That's what they all say,' he chuckled. 'The prisons are overcrowded with people we've dumped there by "mistake".'

'You're not infallible,' I reminded him, gently.

'Agreed.' He nodded in mock solemnity. 'We sometimes

allow guilty men to get away with things . . . as, by now,
you must know.'

And yet, I had friends in the police force. Perhaps 'satisfied acquaintances' might be a better way of putting it.
The Detective Sergeant's daughter had been taken ill very
suddenly. Very ill, very suddenly and in the small hours.
I'd been on call, my snap diagnosis had been correct and
my prescribed treatment had worked what seemed like a
minor miracle. That had been more than a year ago, but
the DS still had enough gratitude left to do me a favour.

'Just the name,' I insisted.

'As long as you don't ask me to remove the copy
of his report from the file.'

'No. Just his name, and where he operates from.'

This small, but important, exchange had resulted in
me meeting a vaguely scruffy individual, with gob-stopper
eyes peering at me from behind pebble-lensed spectacles.
His pinched nose and thin, bloodless lips did nothing to
enhance his appearance and the hint of an adenoidal whine
in his tone was proof that, unlike the 'private eyes' of fiction,
he was not anxious to become too involved in an undetected
murder.

'I wish to make use of your services,' I explained.

'Very unusual.' He sucked his bloodless lips. 'Very
unethical, really.'

'Unethical?' I tried to keep the sarcasm from my voice.

'He was my client, y'see. I owe him a duty of confidentiality.'

'He paid you to snoop,' I said.

'No . . . I wouldn't say *that*.'

'I would.'

'I – er – I suppose it depends on what . . . '

'Now, *I'm* prepared to pay you to snoop. No, not
even that. Just to ask a few questions.'

'It's – y'know – this confidentiality thing.'

'He bought you . . . did he? For the rest of *your* life –

for the rest of *his* life – he owns you? You can't put your
services on the market without his permission?'

'No! It's not that at all.' He sounded quite shocked.

'I wish to employ you.'

'Yes. I know that, but . . . '

'You advertise – in the yellow pages – you offer to
undertake enquiries.'

'Of course, but . . . '

'That's all I want. One day – no more than two days –
of your time. The answers to a few pertinent questions.
And, if it will ease what you're pleased to call your "conscience", I don't mind if you hand a copy of your final report
to the man whose confidence you seem to hold so dear.
Indeed, I *insist* that you provide him with a copy.'

It ended where it began. In the surgery, with Chris
making an appointment and arranging to be last on
the list. We were, it seemed, still buddies. No ill-will. No
animosity. Merely a woman whom he'd married and I'd
bedded, who'd paid for her folly via strychnine. A small
matter of murder coupled with an attempt to dump the
killing in an innocent lap.

Nothing that a few quiet words couldn't mend.

He settled in the chair alongside the desk, crossed
his legs, smiled a little self-consciously then said, 'I don't
blame you, you know.'

'Blame me?'

'For having an affair with Mabel.'

'Oh . . . *that*?'

'She was a beautiful woman.'

'Moderately good-looking,' I conceded.

'I married her. I was in love with her. I can't, in
all honesty, blame anybody else for . . . '

'I wasn't in love with her,' I interrupted.

'Oh!'

'Slap and tickle, old boy. No more than that. And
I was one of quite a few.'

He said, 'Oh!' again, and looked quite crestfallen.

'I had no reason for murdering her,' I reminded him. 'You *had*.'

'I – er – I understand the police have questioned you.'

'They have,' I agreed. 'Thanks to the snooper you paid to keep an eye on your erring spouse.'

'I was suspicious,' he muttered. 'Jealous.'

'With cause.'

'I'd no idea it was going to be *you*.'

Very deliberately, I said, 'I don't think you gave much of a damn *who* it was. You conned me into suggesting an easily obtained poison then, quite deliberately, gave her a clear field.'

'The private detective – the one you call a snooper – let me have a copy of the report you asked for.'

'Good. I asked him to do that.'

'I – I'm sorry – but I don't see the point.'

'Of what?'

'Of getting him to ask questions.'

'Chris, old boy, come in out of the rain.' I think my smile held little humour and even less friendship. 'All those corny detective stories you concoct. Life isn't *like* that.'

'I don't see what . . . '

'Bear with me,' I cut in. 'Forget fiction for a few moments. Listen to a few facts, for a change. Facts about a motor car, for example. A Ford Granada. *Your* Ford Granada. Not an Aston Martin, perhaps – not as "obvious" as an Aston Martin – but still one hell of a car. A car capable of reducing a two-hundred-mile jaunt to little more than a spin round the houses.

'Three fifteen one Friday afternoon and, in a Ford Granada, the Great Northern Hotel at King's Cross becomes the spot at which you can enjoy late-afternoon tea and scones. Given the right driver, of course. And, you *are* the right driver. Our mutual rallying experience has seen to that. Facts . . . right?'

'I was at a writers' convention.'

'Of course you were, old chap. A gaggle of scribblers, all telling each other how it's done. But, where's the car? Where is this Granada? Not in the hotel car park. To all intents and purposes, the Great Northern doesn't *have* a car park. The tiny patch of tarmac it *does* have is full by mid-afternoon. But, that's OK. You prefer to park somewhere in one of the side streets. Again . . . less "obvious".

'Early evening, you have a phone call. From the west coast, up here. From your tame snooper. A "progress report". Mabel is out of the way. The guy she's with drives an Aston Martin. He's booked the two of them in as man and wife, at a nice little hotel.'

'I've already said. I apportion no blame. Mabel was . . . '

'Mabel was a mug. *You're* a mug. You counted on *me* being a mug. Mug enough to sit back and let things happen. That phone call *was* made. Snoopy-Pants includes it in his report. His report to *me*.

'Meanwhile you have dinner with your buddies. A drink at the bar. Then, suddenly, it's "Migraine Time". That's what you tell them. Migraine. Brought on by driving all that way. Something that had been worrying you for the last few days. That the drive might bring on an attack. That you're a "Migraine Sufferer" . . . that's the spiel you feed to your fellow-conventionists. That gives you a neat excuse for retiring early. You also hope it gives you an alibi.

'After that, it's out of the hotel by another door, pick up the car, belt north, doctor the capsules, belt back to London and be ready to meet up with the other crimesters over breakfast.'

I leaned back and waited. I was hitting dead centre and it showed in his expression.

He cleared his throat before breathing, 'You can't prove that.'

'I can prove you've never had migraine in your life. I'm your medic . . . remember? Migraine doesn't work that way. I can prove you can go without a night's sleep and, instead, drive at speed around lanes a damn sight narrower and more twisting than motorways. *And*, that you're still button bright next morning. Come off it, Chris. I'm your long-time buddy. I *know* you, old son. I know you better than you know yourself. Do as much wool-pulling as you like, with other people. Not with *me*. Don't even *try* it, with me.'

There was another prolonged silence, then he sighed and asked, 'Where do we go from here?'

'Nowhere.' I chuckled. 'Just as long as Mabel's murder stays unsolved. She asked for it. I'm prepared to accept that as a good enough reason.'

'She asked for it,' he agreed.

'Fine. Let's hope it stays unsolved . . . for everybody's sake.'

I'd called him a mug. He was all that, and more. As I pulled the partly open desk drawer out and pressed the 'Off' switch of the cassette recorder I contemplated what he'd say when he knew. When he realised how *big* a mug he was. When the Detective Inspector played the tape back to him and asked for explanations.

We'd been friends a long, long time. Too long. I needed a new buddy – a new navigator for the rallies . . . because (although he didn't yet know it) Chris was going to spend the next few years inside a prison cell.

Freeze Everybody

David Williams

The little doctor dismounted at the end of the long gravelled driveway and wiped his forehead. It had been a hot ride from the village. He leaned his bicycle against the outside wall of the substantial, covered porch, and carefully removed his jacket from the wicker basket attached to the handlebars. When he had just as carefully unfolded and donned the jacket, he removed the oblong medical case from the same receptacle. Instinctively he glanced up at the main bedroom window in the east wing of the big Victorian house. This was to the right of the front door, under a heavy pointed gable. Then he ascended the two wide marble steps and rang the bell. It was a rather timid ring, but then he was a rather timid man.

He was glad that it was the maid, Bridget O'Mara, who opened the door.

'Would you be caring to bring your bike inside the porch, Doctor Slansky?' she asked, stuffing a bunched handkerchief into the pocket of her plain black dress.

She was a sturdy, full-bodied woman, with dark eyes, a possibly sensuous mouth, and good legs, but she was still no beauty. Her skin was rough, the features coarse, and the short wiry hair unkempt and already flecked with grey. Bridget had been in service in this Norfolk house for twenty-two of her thirty-eight years, and though she had never lost the brogue, it was more than a decade since ever she had thought of Limerick as home, or spinsterhood as anything other than a permanent status.

'The bike should be all right there. Yes. Thank you. Thank you,' Rudolf Slansky repeated, bobbing his close-cropped head, over-grateful as always and now with an added nervous concern. He could tell Bridget had been crying and he was unsure whether it was proper for him to enquire why.

'Shall I go straight up?' he asked, after deciding that the tears were none of his business – regretfully so, because he was naturally compassionate and because he was drawn to rough country women.

'If you please, Madam wants to see you in the drawing room, Doctor.' There was a little choking noise at the end of the words which suggested the tears were still, as it were, available on tap.

Bridget closed the door, and without further comment or attempt at pleasantry, led the way through the stone-vaulted hall to the drawing room.

The doctor's worn, leather-soled shoes tapped out his progress on the shining, coloured tiles in a way that reduced him to tiptoeing out of inane but acute embarrassment. It was a house that filled him with insensible awe every time he entered it – and this was the fourth visit in the ten days he had been in temporary charge of the medical practice in the village. In the diminished number of practices where he usually got locum work there were few Gothic mansions and none with living-in maids.

'No car today, Doctor Slansky?' Mrs Chalfont questioned when he entered the room, establishing that she had watched part of his slow and demeaning approach to the house from where she was sitting near the open French windows. She regularly pronounced his name as 'Shlansky', which was wrong, but he would not have dared tell her so. It didn't matter, except her invention seemed to be in some

way a product of disdain, like the no more than patronising
smile that regularly passed as her initial greeting.

Maud Chalfont was a widow of nearly sixty, which made
her several years older than the doctor, though indubitably
better preserved than he. She was slim and erect, with a
striking countenance, and a presence and voice that spelt
breeding and authority. Her tinted hair seemed always
recently arranged. Her clothes were good, though styled
to suit the owner, not the current fashion. Today she was
wearing a pale blue silk dress, the half sleeves and three-
quarter length skirt advantaging both her firm forearms and
the well turned ankles gracefully crossed above high-heeled
court shoes. A double row of pearls at her neck matched the
bracelet on her right wrist.

For Slansky to come before Mrs Chalfont was like
having an audienccce with the Queen, not that he had
ever had an audience with the Queen. He imagined the
drawing room at Buckingham Palace would be very similar
to this one though – elegant, tidy, crammed with antique
furniture, priceless pictures, and with carpet so thick that
it put extra effort into walking.

'The car I was to use has broken down again. I'm
thinking it's not a very good car,' he said in a strained voice,
unable either to prevent both cheeks twitching nervously,
or a reversion to the halting constructions of his refugee
days fifteen years before this. 'It's a not very new car, of
course,' he added apologetically, eyes blinking too often in
the moon-shaped face.

'Foreign,' Mrs Chalfont snapped back imperiously.

Slansky felt that the deprecating of the vehicle's origins
might easily have been intended to cover his as well. 'It's
a Ford. I think it was made— '

'No matter,' the other interrupted. 'Doctor Riggle should
have left you better provided. Since you don't have a car
of your own.' But the last words implied that the lack of
a powered conveyance was still due to Slansky's wilful
carelessness. 'Sit down, please.' She indicated an armchair

somewhat smaller and definitely lower than the one she was occupying.

'Thank you. Thank you.' He nodded his way to the chair, then sat on the edge of the seat cushion, very gently, hoping not to squash it too much, and with his elbows tight to his sides. He kept the bag upright on his lap, as if it were there for use as a means of defence. His sweating hands clasped the handle.

'How much longer will Doctor Riggle be away?' asked Mrs Chalfont.

'Two weeks yet. Two weeks and three days.'

'Good.'

Out of natural humility, the doctor couldn't imagine why she should think it was that. 'I hope Mr Gripp is making progress,' he offered.

'We'll talk about my brother later. Where do you go after this?'

'After this? Back to the village. I have the surgery to take at— '

'I don't mean this afternoon,' she broke in impatiently. 'I mean when Doctor Riggle gets back. Have you another temporary position to go to?'

He swallowed awkwardly. 'Perhaps I will have. Nothing is arranged yet. Then it will be the middle of September. You understand there is not so much need for locums then. Not after the school holidays. But the medical agency— '

'How many weeks have you worked this year, Doctor Slansky?' came as a demand not as a polite enquiry.

He hesitated. 'Quite a lot, I think.' Nervously his left hand moved to cover the frayed right cuff of his shirt now revealed as buttonless, and as conspicuous as a flag of surrender – a soiled one at that.

'I wonder if you're being quite accurate? You were engaged at very short notice by Doctor Riggle. When the doctor who usually stands in for him had to cancel. So you were available at no notice in the middle of the school holidays, when there is very great demand for locums. Good ones, that is. But evidently no-one had demanded you, Doctor Slansky? You are Czech?'

'Yes . . . That is . . . No . . . I'm naturalised British now. Since fourteen years.' The change of subject had thrown him. He leaned forward earnestly, over the case. 'Also I requalified. Since I am coming here from Prague. After the Russian invasion, you understand?'

'And your family?'

'Family? My mother and father are dead now. A long time. I have a brother. In Czechoslovakia still.' He loosened his collar. The button on that came off too as he touched it.

'You're not married?'

He shook his head, wondering if a nearly total lack of buttons had suggested the question. 'It was never possible.'

'And do you have a home anywhere?'

His cheeks twitched again. 'Not at the moment.'

'Why did you leave the permanent practice you were in? In the Midlands, wasn't it?'

He could feel the cold sweat running down his reddening face and neck. The eyes first registered denial, then dulled with resignation before he spoke. 'That was five years ago. I was assistant doctor only in the practice.' He fumbled for his handkerchief. 'I wasn't needed any more.'

'After eight years?' She fixed him with a merciless gaze. 'Surely it was because you were struck off the medical register? I have made enquiries.'

He looked down, wiping his face. 'Not struck off so much as . . . as suspended. I was reinstated after two years.' His head came up again slowly. 'It was not for something immoral. Nothing like that. A wrong diagnosis only.'

'But a fatal one? A patient died, I believe.'

'A very old patient, yes. It was better I took the blame. The other doctor, the senior partner . . . ' But he left the sentence unfinished. There was no point in trying to explain to people. It was too complicated. Too undignified.

'And you haven't had a permanent post since that time?'

'No.' He straightened, then gave a little sigh. 'Mrs Chalfont, why are you asking me all this? If you think I'm not a good enough doctor for your brother, I won't come again.'

'On the contrary, Doctor Slansky, I think you're an excellent doctor. So much so, I have an important proposition to put to you.'

'To me?' He looked about as if there might be someone else she was addressing.

'I hope you will agree to become my brother's personal physician, giving your attention entirely to him.'

'Entirely? Just to him?' His mouth dropped. 'But I don't think such an arrangement would be possible. I am only staying at Doctor Riggle's house until— ' He was stopped by the dismissive wave of an elegant hand.

'Of course, you'll need to live here. Rent free. There's an unoccupied flat above the garage. It's furnished, and very comfortable. A main meal will be provided.'

'I see.' His face was still showing perplexity, but the glimmerings too of something like hope. 'You're very kind, but since I have no money— ' He shook his head, confused and embarrassed. 'What I mean is— '

'Your salary will be twenty-five thousand pounds a year, paid monthly in advance. But I shall require you to sign a contract letter stipulating you will stay for seven years. At the end of that time there will be a hundred thousand pound bonus in addition to your salary. You will be sixty-five then. An appropriate time to retire, perhaps? You would be wise to make pension arrangements out of your income meantime, but that, of course, is up to you.'

'Yes,' said the doctor making a breathy noise in his throat that was really a strangled shout for joy.

'You will be entitled to four separate weeks' holiday a year. But you must never be absent for more than a week at a time. Never.'

'Never,' he repeated with spirit, and as though longer holidays should properly be regarded as sinful.

'You will keep daily written reports on my brother's condition. Noting the times of day you see him, his temperature, his blood pressure at appropriate intervals, the medication you prescribe. So that there's a record.'

'Of course.'

'Good.' Mrs Chalfont gave a gracious nod. 'So do I take it you accept the post, and the conditions?'

'I have to accept so soon?'

'Is there any need for delay on your part?'

He hesitated for a brief moment, then shrugged. 'No, not at all. So, yes, I accept. Thank you.' Then his face clouded. 'Only . . . '

'Only what, Doctor?'

'Your brother, Mr Gripp, he's had two strokes. Not so serious as they could have been. Except all strokes are serious. And he's already sixty-six, I think. It's not certain that to have a doctor here all the time will stop him having another stroke. Perhaps one that will be most serious.'

'If you're concerned about keeping my brother alive, you needn't be.' She turned to ring the silver handbell on the table beside her. 'You see, he's dead already. Oh yes, he went very peacefully. Another stroke. When he was asleep. At about this time yesterday. His body is in the deep freeze. I had it put there immediately.'

'More tea, Doctor,' Mrs Chalfont asked some minutes later, holding her hand out for his cup. 'So we have to maintain the pretence that my brother Edwin is alive for the next seven years. If his death were reported now, sixty per cent of the estate would go in taxes. I consider that's nothing less than confiscation, but it's the law.'

Still dazed by events, Doctor Slansky passed over his cup. 'It would be such a lot of money? For the taxes?' he asked, tentatively.

'Several million pounds. Despite the fact that my brother

had recently transferred most of his wealth to my two sons and their children. Regrettably, it was necessary for him to live for seven years for his gifts to be free of Inheritance Tax. You'll know enough about Inheritance Tax to understand?' But her expression made it clear she hardly expected him to know more than the minimum – but enough to appreciate the special hardships of the very rich.

'I think so. And it wasn't possible to make the gifts earlier?'

Her mouth tightened. 'It was not until after his wife Rachel died, a year ago, that my brother was free to see reason. I mean in relation to making a just and equitable disposition of his great wealth.'

'That would have been after his first stroke?'

'Yes. It was when I came to live here. To look after him.' She handed him back his cup. 'Rachel always disliked me, and the feeling was mutual. For some reason she resented me my scholarly husband, though she was aware that as a lecturer at a provincial university his income was quite inadequate. I fear Edwin was no intellectual. He made his fortune at a fairly early age. In property development.' She pronounced the last phrase as though it rated about level with prostitution and drug trafficking. 'Our father was a general in the army. A fine soldier, but not wealthy, you understand?' It was plain, however, that the General must have had other qualities, no doubt to do with moral not monetary values. 'My sister-in-law was also jealous of our children. She and Edwin were childless. She was a good deal younger than he was, and her death was unexpected. In a car accident. Until then, Edwin had left everything to her. He had naturally expected to die first.'

'She would not have had to pay this Inheritance Tax?' the doctor asked.

'No. It isn't levied on widows. Only on their estates after death. If she had survived, Rachel would have left nothing to me or to my children. It was providential that Edwin survived her. Except he didn't do so for long enough.'

Slansky nodded, but he looked troubled. 'Seven years is a long time to . . . to pretend, Mrs Chalfont.'

'But not if things have been planned properly. I had anticipated my brother's death might occur too early, though not nearly so early as it has. He seemed to be recovering well enough from the first stroke, but not from the second, as you know. However, I was prepared for the loss. Emotionally and in practical terms.'

'In practical terms,' he echoed involuntarily: it was difficult to picture Mrs Chalfont being emotional in any circumstances.

'I am quite satisfied the body will store satisfactorily where it is.'

'In a deep freezer?'

'A large one. Acquired for the purpose some time ago. It's in the basement. Locked. When the time comes, we shall need to remove the body and allow it to defrost. I have concluded that no ordinary undertaker is going to suspect what has happened. Provided we are careful. Do you agree?'

The doctor nodded slowly. 'Not an undertaker, no. But if there is an autopsy— '

'There will be no autopsy, Doctor. Why should there be? An autopsy is required only if someone dies who hasn't been seen by his doctor for two weeks. Or if the circumstances are unusual or suspicious. Otherwise the attending doctor is perfectly entitled to issue a death certificate. If you were reporting my brother's death today, would you have any doubts about the cause?'

Slansky stared at the little pile of cake crumbs he had made on the plate he was holding. 'No. None. When I saw him two days ago he was not so good. He had made very little recovery since his last cerebro-vascular accident. Another could have happened soon. Or a coronary thrombosis. His death also.'

'Exactly. So you would have issued the certificate. I would have taken it to the Registrar. The funeral would have taken place later this week. Everything would have been normal. What difference is there that we delay the whole matter by seven years?'

'None really, I suppose.' In truth, the question had made him a good deal more comfortable about the plan. 'Except no-one can see him in that time?'

'People will accept that you see him. That I shall see him. That Bridget will see him. It will appear we shall all be seeing him daily. No-one else has been near him since he came back from hospital six weeks ago. No-one except Doctor Riggle, before he went on holiday and you took over. It's unlikely anyone else would have seen him. Ever. No matter how long he had survived. He has certainly been in no state to receive visitors, nor shown any signs that he ever would again. Isn't that true?'

'I'm afraid so. It's not likely he would have improved much. A little perhaps.'

'Quite. It's why his passing has been a blessing for him. But that's no reason why his heirs should suffer.' Mrs Chalfont nodded decisively. 'You know there are no servants besides Bridget? Not any more. Except for Moffat the gardener, and he doesn't live in. He's in the kitchen from time to time, that's all. Naturally, he's to know nothing of the arrangement.'

'And your sons, Mrs Chalfont? Your two sons?'

'They and their families live far from here. They have never been in the habit of visiting my brother. There's less reason than ever that they should begin now. I shall, of course, visit them from time to time.'

'Will you tell your sons about the . . . the . . . ?'

'The subterfuge? Certainly not. That will be neither appropriate nor necessary.'

'Doctor Riggle— '

'Is no problem,' she interrupted. 'Edwin never really cared for him, and Riggle never relished coming here. It's too out of the way. Too isolated. I shall simply explain that Edwin has taken a great liking to you, so much so that we've decided to retain your services full time.'

'So could I ask, Mrs Chalfont, what would you have done if I hadn't been here?' It had taken some courage for him to put the question.

'I was in the process of finding a doctor similarly placed to yourself. Someone ready to accept the position of personal physician to my brother while he was still alive,' she replied.

'And to carry on, like you've asked me, if he died too soon?'

'Yes. Obviously there would have been a risk. It was imperative I chose the right man. As it happens, I was using the same medical agency as you. I didn't expect Edwin to die so soon, of course, which is why I was overtaken by events. So your presence and your . . . your suitability were both fortuitous.'

Slansky nodded thoughtfully. 'And your maid also knows everything.'

'Bridget was devoted to my brother. It was she who took him to . . . to where he is now. She showed such reverence.' Mrs Chalfont looked out onto the terrace, her eyes indicating stoic forbearance if not actual grief. 'Naturally, like you, Bridget will benefit immediately and in the long term from the arrangement.'

'Naturally,' he repeated, putting his plate on the side table with his cup. 'It is breaking the law, of course.'

'Yes. We shall both be doing that, Doctor. If we are discovered, I imagine the consequences for you would be worse than for me. However, I see no possibility of that happening. Even so, it is why I shall need your signed acknowledgement of the terms we have agreed. Just so that we know exactly where we stand.' She paused to be sure that the consequences of her words, like the meaningful look, had registered properly. 'Of course, the rewards for a successful conclusion are ample compensation, don't you agree?'

'Yes, Mrs Chalfont.' He swallowed, steeling himself not to contemplate going back on anything. 'I think I should examine the body now.'

'Quite right. Bridget will show you.' She rang the bell again.

And so began the period of nearly seven years through which three people successfully maintained the apparent survival of Edwin Gripp.

Doctor Slansky gradually settled for a standard of living he had never remotely enjoyed in the whole of his previous and disjointed career. The flat was as comfortable as Mrs Chalfont had claimed. Bridget brought him lunch each day on a tray, and did his laundry, cleaning, and shopping. He indulged his taste for literature and music, building a substantial library of mostly scholarly paperbacks, and tape recordings of classical orchestral works. He had needed to buy a good radio and tape player, but the price had been relatively minor. It was not until the second year that he abandoned bicycling as his normal mothod of transportation. That was when he acquired the small, reliable second-hand car. Even so, it was some time before he could bring himself easily to accept that he could afford modest luxuries.

The doctor grew not to miss his active professional life. In his way, he had been dedicated to medicine. Yet, since his suspension and reinstatement, the opportunities for work had diminished almost into infinity. If it had not been for Mrs Chalfont's offer he could well have been forced to find another kind of employment, and at his age that might not have been easy. However, he was assiduous in maintaining his fictitious patient's medical records, to the point where they came to be a useful, perhaps even a necessary sublimation. The completeness of the notes was matched by the inventiveness that went into their compiling. In course of time, they built up into a meticulous case study in the care and rehabilitation of a stroke victim.

Mrs Chalfont was duly impressed, but in the distant manner to which she had reverted soon after the arrangement had been agreed.

Like a priest repairing to church to say the daily offices, Slansky twice a day visited Edwin's empty bedroom, each time being sure to appear at the window so that Moffat the gardener, or the postman, the milkman, the garbage collector or those others who regularly came to the house might note his presence in the sickroom.

Bridget regularly took meals up to Edwin's room – trays of genuine food which she stayed there to consume herself, on the pretence that the patient needed help with his eating. In fact this was the way she took most of her own meals, while watching the television set installed at the bedside.

It was this last habit as much as anything else that brought Slansky and Bridget closer together.

The doctor was not gregarious by nature, but after a while the intellectual content of his new life began to pall as his main source of fulfilment. Quite simply, he felt a loneliness, and more, the renewal of a primeval sense of incompleteness that had pervaded his old impecunious existence, but which his present affluence made unnecessary. Naturally, the constrictions of his life were hardly conducive to the making of new friends, and in any case he was basically shy. Mrs Chalfont provided no companionship, indeed she tended to treat him rather as she would an upper servant. After she was satisfied that he was going to further her seven-year purpose in a much better than adequate manner, she tended to absent herself from the house more and more, making visits to family and friends. Sometimes she was away for quite long periods.

So there was only Bridget.

At the start, the doctor took to dropping into the kitchen for coffee mid-morning, though that sometimes involved suffering the company of garrulous old Moffat, who did the same, and who was no stimulus to anything. Bridget was usually too busy to linger when she brought the lunch tray, which was why Slansky finally elected to take his lunch with her in Edwin's room. He thus became a fairly frequent viewer of early afternoon television, just as, in course of time, Bridget became an awed listener to taped Mozart and Beethoven: this was after she took to accepting the doctor's regular invitations to wine and light suppers in his flat.

Proximity between members of the opposite sex serves to reveal hidden attractions and to obscure blemishes, the more so with a couple left in isolation. The Irish woman's rough exterior and untutored mind soon ceased to register in the doctor's perception of her. Increasingly he came to see her as someone altogether companionable, and, as time went by, physically desirable as well.

For her part, Bridget came to revere the little refugee doctor, to hang on his every accented word, to marvel at his knowledge, education and culture, and most of all to be overwhelmed at the attention he was paying her.

Even so, the period during which friendship ripened into courtship was a very long one: it was nearly six years before Slansky proposed marriage. But neither party was practised in wooing or being wooed, and both came from backgrounds where protracted courtships had been the rule rather than the exception. Nor was time ever a conscious consideration. What developed into an always chaste romance came to provide the central theme in their lives – something to savour and not to condense, for patience had been a way of life to both since childhood. In truth also, the two had reached ages where the more intimate physical aspects of the affair needed to be approached with some trepidation – on her part out of a modesty born of total innocence, and on his because of an illogical, persistent, and spectral presentiment that when put to the test his sexual capacities might prove less than adequate.

So it was that, even during the year following the formal engagement, Slansky still took no liberties with his future bride.

The wedding finally took place in the middle of the last year of Slansky's contract with Mrs Chalfont. The ceremony was at a register office with only Moffat and his wife present as witnesses.

Mrs Chalfont approved the union, believing that the stronger the dependence between her two conspirators, the more they would be obliged to keep faith with her and each other to the end – the end that was in any case very near.

The honeymoon was spent in Scarborough, and lasted a week. This was the longest time the doctor was permitted to be away, and the only time he and Bridget had ever been absent from the house at the same time. This was a concession on Mrs Chalfont's part since it meant she had to stay at home for the whole week. One of the three had to be there always for fear of fire, or burglary, or some other hazard that could result in outsiders learning that Edwin was no longer alive or even reasonably unwell.

The couple returned with their love strengthened by lusty passion. The doctor's misgivings about his likely performance in bed had been dispelled on the first night, a result more than a little due to an unexpected and enduring influence beyond his own control.

For when it came to the point, Bridget's own demure inhibitions had quite evaporated – dispersed by the triumph of a formidable, natural instinct. Once she had savoured the ecstasy of the sexual act, her appetite for more of the same had become insatiable: despite her inexperience, the woman had proved to be a veritable Aphrodite. It was as though love-making came more easily to this robust Irish housemaid than bed-making ever had – and with many more variations.

The couple had scarcely left their Scarborough hotel room except for meals. In her enthusiasm, Bridget would even have done without the food for most of the time, except that after a little while Slansky clearly needed to increase his calorie intake to maintain his strength.

Nor did Bridget's joy in uninhibited and frequent sexual concourse diminish one bit on their return. There was no more television viewing after lunch in Edwin's room, not when there were livelier things to do in Edwin's empty bed. And the light suppers, in the flat the couple now shared, were consumed in the bedroom not the living room – still often with wine, and a musical accompaniment, though Bridget had developed a strong preference for the noisier climactic pieces.

It never occurred to this simple woman that so much draining of his manhood might be doing her husband a mischief. Nor could the now sixty-four-year-old Slansky bring himself to impugn that very manhood by denying his wife her consuming pleasure, or even to explain why moderation might be indicated.

In truth, of course, Slansky enjoyed their physical relationship just as much as his wife did, which is why he took a daringly fatalistic view of what it might be doing to him.

'That pain in your chest is mild angina all right,' said Dr Riggle in his surgery, after examining Slansky thoroughly six months after the marriage. He had agreed to keep the result of the consultation confidential. Slansky had told Bridget that he had needed advice about a backache. 'Probably not serious yet, but you should see a cardiologist all the same. Meantime, you want to take it easier. That new wife of yours is too demanding perhaps?' Riggle added, but half in jest. No-one except Slansky credited uncomely Bridget with a boundless sexual appetite.

Slansky promised to do what the other doctor advised, though he wasn't quite as good as his word. He decided to delay seeing the heart specialist, and simply to take the pills prescribed, while conserving his energy as best he could. He determined to eat carefully, avoiding animal fats, dosing himself with extra vitamins, and sneaking as much sleep as possible when Bridget was busy at her duties in the main house.

Mrs Chalfont had noticed no change in the doctor, but she never paid much attention to his appearance. And she was bringing her own grand design to fruition just a few days after he had been to see Riggle, so there were much more important considerations than Slansky's health to engage her.

'I telephoned the undertaker, Doctor,' she announced on the day appointed for Edwin's second 'death': it was a Sunday. 'As I expected, there was no-one there. Only an answering machine. I'll call again first thing tomorrow. So you can date the death certificate for today or tomorrow. Whichever is most credible.'

'Today is best, I think. If you want the funeral to be on Thursday.'

'Very well. You'd better give me the certificate straight away. And you can ring Doctor Riggle tonight. About the extra certificate he has to sign. For the cremation.' She had the order of events set firmly in her mind – as might have been expected of a general's daughter.

Seven years and six months had passed since Edwin Gripp had formally given away his money to his sister's family. Mrs Chalfont had regarded the extra half year as a necessary touch, to avoid arousing suspicion at the Inland Revenue.

It was mid-January, and snowing hard – the kind of conditions that prompted people to be concerned more with their own comforts than with the over-zealous execution of official duties. Mrs Chalfont had thought of such things – which included the undertakers being closed on Sundays: that had given her a full day in hand, in case anything had gone wrong.

Slansky and Bridget had removed the body from the deep freezer the night before. It had been left to thaw out slowly in the cellar. Then they had dried it, carried it upstairs and put it to bed.

Everything seemed to be going exactly as planned. That was until a panicked-voiced Mrs Chalfont summoned

Slansky, over the house telephone in the flat, at three o'clock the next morning.

'I think he's gone too soft. Much too soft,' she clamoured when they were both standing at the bedside. It was quite exceptional for her to show such nervousness. Unable to sleep, she had gone in a few minutes earlier to check on the condition of her brother's corpse. 'I mean he looks as if he might . . . well, flatten out altogether. Like . . . like heated wax. Is it because it's been so long?'

Edwin's face was wan and sunken, but there was every reason for that: he was dead, and Slansky knew the time of his dying had no relevance. 'He's quite normal, Mrs Chalfont. I mean for someone who's . . . He's quite normal.' The doctor had hesitated over stating the obvious, finding words sleepily, and breathing hard. There was a pain in his chest. He had raced to the house half dressed, then hurried up the stairs – and he had been exhausted before Mrs Chalfont had woken him: Bridget was extra demanding at weekends.

'Should we open the windows? To stop him getting too warm?' asked Mrs Chalfont, still on edge.

'If you like. He won't alter now. But it won't do any harm.' Slansky moved across the room. He had to wrestle with the catch of the heavy casement before he got it to budge. He shivered as the icy wind blew in on him.

'That's all right, then, Doctor. I'm sorry I disturbed you. I'll see you in the morning.'

Except it was not all right. Little Dr Slansky died suddenly a few moments later, on the way back to the flat – in the driveway, in the freezing snow, of a massive heart attack.

It was Bridget who found him, and demented Bridget who then had to be coaxed into saving seven years' work from going to waste on the very last day.

'A doubly sad event, Mrs Chalfont,' said the grey-haired, venerable Dr Riggle. 'Two deaths in such a short time. Your brother a week ago today. Doctor Slansky this morning.

Bridget is bearing up well, as you are.' He shook his head.

It was midday on the following Sunday. The two were seated in Mrs Chalfont's drawing room.

'It was good of you to come so promptly, and with the roads still in such terrible condition. Thank you too for attending my brother's funeral on Thursday, Doctor.'

'I was glad to pay my respects. There were not many left hereabouts who knew him well.' He paused. 'I understand now why Doctor Slansky wasn't there.'

'He was quite unwell. Throughout the week. He insisted it was only a chill,' she put in solemnly. 'Of course, we had no idea he was seriously ill.'

'Hm. After I'd examined him, I'm afraid he made me swear I'd tell no-one what was wrong with him.'

'He really shouldn't have ventured out this morning. Neither Bridget nor I knew he was going, of course. We were both here in the house. He should never have gone to the postbox. Not on foot.'

'That's right, I'm afraid. This east wind can play the very devil with angina sufferers.'

'He didn't go out at all in the week. But he wouldn't stay in bed. In case he was needed. In case there were any other formalities to complete. Over my brother's death. There weren't, I gather.' She chilled at the thought of what fresh subterfuges she'd have had to invent if there had been.

As a last resort she had been going to say Slansky had been called to Prague urgently. It simply wouldn't have done to have admitted his death so close to that of her brother. It could so easily have produced enquiries, which, worst of all, could have resulted in someone ordering an autopsy on Edwin. As things now stood, a decent interval had elapsed between the two events.

Altogether, though, it had been the worst week of Mrs Chalfont's life. 'Thank you for signing the second certificate approving Edwin's cremation, by the way,' she said.

'Ah yes, there have to be two doctors for that,' Riggle replied. 'In this case it was only a formality, as Doctor

Slansky suggested when he phoned me last Sunday night.
The authorities need to be sure there's nothing fishy, you
see? Before a cremation.' He cleared his throat. 'I didn't
think it necessary to come out here. I just took a quick
glance at the body. In the drawer at the undertakers. On
Tuesday. I didn't need to . . . to fiddle about with it in any
way. I thought you'd like to know that. Relatives usually do.'

'Thank you.' She had been right in calculating it would
have been an insufferably long way for aging Dr Riggle to
have come to the house in the snow for a formality. If he
had seen the body here instead of in a refrigerated drawer
at the undertakers he might have been prompted to look
more closely – even to 'fiddle'.

She had taken an extra risk by insisting on a cremation –
because there would be nothing to exhume for examination
afterwards.

'Indeed, it was a great credit to Doctor Slansky that
your brother survived as long as he did. Great credit.
Better physician than I took him for, as a matter of
fact,' Riggle continued in a patronising tone. 'Those case
notes are almost good enough for publication in a medical
journal. I told Bridget as much just now. And I gathered
from her— '

'That I am arranging to have them published privately?'
she interrupted. 'Yes. The idea seemed to please her.' In
fact, it had proved to be Mrs Chalfont's *coup de main*. 'I
was deeply grateful to Doctor Slansky. It was a very great
comfort to me to have Edwin for all those years more. His
mind was quite active, you understand? To the end.'

'Yes, the case notes show it.'

Mrs Chalfont rearranged the folds of the black lace
dress she had chosen for the occasion of the doctor's
visit. 'By the way, will there need to be an autopsy on
Doctor Slansky?'

'Oh no. I examined him only last week.'

'I wondered about that.' It was a gross understatement:
she had counted on it – on the rule about two weeks.

'I told him he had angina. His dying of a heart attack today is no surprise. Classic end from classic symptoms. I've given Bridget the death certificate already.' He sighed. 'Poor simple creature. Heart-broken, of course. She'll be all right, I assume? Financially, I mean.'

'Quite all right, yes. I can vouch for that.' Except the simple creature was refusing to accept the money due to her dead husband. It was true she was heart-broken, certain that Slansky's death had been divine retribution, because they hadn't been married in a Catholic church. She was sure that meant she had lived in sin like a wanton, wicked woman for all those months, glorifying in the weaknesses of the flesh.

Mrs Chalfont had at first found this attitude superstitious and difficult to credit, particularly since Bridget had stopped going to mass years before. On the other hand, in a curious way it seemed actually to help with Bridget's stoic acceptance of events. And if she hadn't felt so guilty she would probably not have been ready to accept there was atonement in helping Mrs Chalfont's deserving children and grandchildren. But it had been the offer to publish the case book as a memorial to Dr Slansky that had finally tipped the balance.

'Well, I must be going.' The doctor rose from the armchair, then gazed for a moment through the window at the snow-decked landscape beyond. 'I don't believe Slansky could have suffered at all. But, you know, with his body lying there in these nearly Arctic conditions for anything up to three hours,' he paused and gave a shrug. 'You wouldn't believe, it was as though he'd been in a deep freezer for a week.'

'Oh, I can *well* believe it,' said Mrs Chalfont earnestly.

The Luck of the Draw

Margaret Yorke

She'd been looking forward to it for weeks, ever since the letter arrived.

She'd bought the two raffle tickets, one for herself and one for Micky, from a woman who came to the door when she was staying with him. Ten pence each, they'd been, and now she'd won the first prize, a cruise to the Mediterranean. The ticket and other documents would follow, said the letter, and she must be in possession of a passport. No special inoculations or vaccinations were necessary, and cheques could be cashed on board.

She'd rung Micky at once to see if he'd also won a prize, but he hadn't. He couldn't have gone, anyway, he said; business was too demanding. Micky was her nephew who ran a used car business outside Glasgow and lived in a small grey bungalow overlooking the Clyde. His wife had departed some years ago, taking the children, and this saddened Carmen for they were the only family she ever saw. Micky's father, her elder brother, was dead, and her own sons had left long ago, one for Australia and the other for Singapore. She never heard from either, which was hard to accept after all she had done to bring them up alone. Things hadn't been easy for widows then, not like it was for single mothers today when the best way to get your own place was to become pregnant and be housed by the council.

Micky didn't seem to have any regrets. He was out a lot and had a series of women friends, some of whom Carmen had met. He took her out to dinner at least once during her annual visit, and last time they'd had lunch one Sunday at a grand granite hotel where he seemed to know most of the other clients. Carmen managed to make them laugh at the jokes she told; she'd always been the life and soul of the party.

'What a character,' she'd hear them say, and would smile. She liked attention.

It seemed that Micky was used to the high life, but for Carmen such occasions were treats to remember when she went back to the council flat in Southampton where she had lived for years.

She liked the sea. She'd spent all her life near it, so going on a cruise was certain to be a success, and it was free! She planned her wardrobe with care, for there would be smart dinners, all that: it would be like old times when she used to dress up to go to the palais.

That was where she met Tom, in a Paul Jones. They didn't have such things these days; you grabbed whoever you fancied to dance with but then didn't touch them at all which seemed to Carmen a funny way of going about things. Tom wasn't her first, by any means, though he never knew that, but he was different because he wanted to marry her and in those days to be married was very important. It conferred status, meant you wouldn't have been passed over if all the men got killed like they did last time, leaving so many girls on the shelf. Tom was so smart in his bell-bottoms and square rig. He was thin and fair, with blue eyes, and he was twenty-two when his ship was torpedoed on convoy duty in the Mediterranean.

Billy was born two weeks after she heard that he was dead.

Things were tough then. Carmen was still living with her mother, and she soon got a factory job, working shifts, so that one of them was always there with the baby. When Billy was two she met Jock, who was Stuart's father. They couldn't get married because he had a wife in Aberdeen, or so he said.

That was the beginning of the black days. Her mother was killed, not by a bomb but by slipping on an icy road and being run over by a bus whose driver had no chance to stop. After that it was a struggle to keep the boys, but she'd done it, working nights in a club, and she'd always done a bit on the side. She'd been choosy, though, and over the years some of the men became regulars, real pals, bringing her presents from their trips and being fatherly to the boys before they were packed off to bed when it was time for business. She'd been soft enough to get really fond of one of them, Stavros, who called whenever his ship was in port. She'd woven a dream about him, imagining herself wafted to one of those Greek islands he'd told her about, where the sun always shone and the sea was blue and olives hung heavy on ancient trees.

He was married, of course. He showed her snaps of his wife and his sons, first two, then a third, then four. He was generous to her, though, and for nearly ten years looked nowhere else for the comforts of shore. She missed him when he stopped coming, and for a while worked as a maid in a hotel, living in. The boys had left home by then and Carmen saw no point in keeping a place on just for herself. But after she entertained one man friend too many in the hotel she lost her job. For some years she rented a room and found what work she could: bar-maiding, selling sweets in a cinema, helping out at a newsagent's, picking up employment here and there, and also men.

Carmen's real name was Doris Watkins, but she became Carmen when she started in the clubs. It suited her dark looks and she said that she came from Brazil and was the illegitimate daughter of a diplomat, though the truth was that her father had been a travelling salesman who had left her mother when Doris was five. Doris had adored him and she wept for him for years. It was only after her mother's death that she discovered he had had several wives and had been sent to prison for bigamy. Since then, she had told her invented story so often that she had begun to believe it.

It was difficult, these days, to find company but occasionally, even now, there was someone she met in a pub who came home with her. Mostly, though, she had to be satisfied with having an occasional drink bought for her. She went to bingo because there were prizes, but too many of the players were women; she did like a man or two about the place. She'd enjoy telling her fellow bingo players about the cruise when she returned; some of them were quite spiteful in their remarks – jealous, of course, because she so often won – but now they'd really have something to gripe about.

Carmen had never before been further south than the Isle of Wight, but she admitted to no fears as she set off with a new suitcase, larger than the one she used for her trips to Scotland. She went by taxi to the station to catch her train for the port of embarkation and several neighbours watched her go. She waved triumphantly, then inserted her stout body into the comfortable seat. She used taxis when she returned from the pub a bit the worse for wear, but otherwise, except during her visits to Micky, she never went in a car.

This was the life!

'Of course I've travelled a lot,' she told the driver, practising what she would say on board. Carmen's method of compensating for her own inadequacies was to attack. She asked a man on the platform to lift her case into the train for her, and another to take it down when she reached her destination, and both instantly obeyed. A second taxi swept her to the dock and there a friendly man bore her luggage away as she joined a short queue at passport control, handing over her new passport. A smiling young woman directed her to a bus which took her out to the ship and Carmen stepped confidently up the gangway. She'd been aboard ships before, though usually clandestinely.

Her cabin was on a lower deck. It was very small, with two bunks and a tiny cubicle containing a shower and lavatory. There was no porthole. That was a pity; she would have liked to look at the sea. Carmen felt a cool breeze on her head: the air conditioning. She picked the further bunk and began spreading her clothes about; there was plenty of room.

Then she set off to explore.

The ship seemed vast. She went along corridors and up and down companionways and eventually found an enormous lounge where tea was being served. Carmen would have liked a slug of something in hers, but there seemed no chance of that so she slurped it down as it was, and secured three slices of iced sponge cake, looking about at the other passengers who seemed to be mainly elderly couples. There was head after head of grey hair. Carmen's was rinsed jet black, and her eyebrows were dyed. She'd never given up on her appearance.

When she went back to her cabin to change for dinner she received a shock, for her belongings had been moved to make space for others: an alien toothbrush was slotted into the bathroom holder and a sparse array of clothes shared the hanging space. The things that Carmen had left draped over the second bunk had been gathered together and deposited neatly on the one where her nightdress already lay.

Was she to share?

Such a thought had never occurred to Carmen. She picked up the telephone and asked for the purser whose assistant, to whom she made known this fact, replied that yes, indeed, she was sharing with Mrs Ford and no other arrangement was possible.

Carmen shrugged. She was a sound sleeper; it would not worry her.

She had a shower, put on her black satin pants and gold lamé top – you must start as you mean to go on and she intended to create an impression straight off – and was

sitting on her bunk buckling her high-heeled sandals when
Frances Ford came in, blinked at the moist atmosphere for
the cabin was full of steam, and smiled anxiously at Carmen.

'I do hope you didn't mind my moving some of your
things,' she said in a soft, nervous voice. She was a tall, thin
woman with stringy brown hair and Carmen later learned
that she came from Rye and was a widow with no children.
She had a black poodle called Hetty whom it had been a
wrench to deposit in kennels.

'I didn't reckon to be sharing,' Carmen told her bluntly.

'But it's so expensive having a cabin to oneself,' said
Frances. 'Of course, if you've paid for that, there must be
some mistake.'

'I didn't,' said Carmen. 'I won the trip in a raffle
and I just thought it meant a single cabin. Not to worry
– Frances, was it, you said?'

'That's right.' Frances wrinkled her nose at the damp
air. 'How thoughtful of you to get changed early so that
we weren't both wanting the bathroom at once,' she said. 'I
wonder if the air conditioning will cope with this steam?'

'Give it an hour or two and it will,' said Carmen,
now busy applying petunia lipstick to her mouth.

'Are you having first sitting dinner?' asked Frances.

'Yes.' Carmen pouted, blotted her lips and gave them
another wipe with the shiny lipstick.

'Ah – I'm second. That will make things easier, won't
it?' Frances peered at her companion through the opaque
air.

'If you say so,' said Carmen and picked up her handbag.
'I'll see you, then,' and she swung out of the cabin leaving
Frances in possession. She was ready for a nip, and there
would be company in the bar, if she could find one. There
were at least three on board, according to the plan of the
ship she'd received with her ticket.

Sipping a double gin, Carmen stoked up on dutch
courage to face the ordeal of dinner where she would
be among strangers. Looking around, she noticed that

everyone else was plainly attired, though most were tidy, the men wearing ties, the women in skirts and blouses or simple dresses. She'd expected to see dinner suits and long gowns. Ten minutes before the meal was due to start she moved towards the restaurant and found a queue had already formed leading down the stairs.

'Greedy lot,' muttered Carmen under her breath, and heard a woman remark that some people were overdressed as it was not customary to change on the first night at sea.

'Stuff you.' Carmen tossed her head, scarcely shifting the crisp cap of her new perm. You could carry anything off if you had the nerve, and how was she to know that? Far worse if she'd just worn her old jersey slacks and sweater and everyone else had been in satin.

She was shown to a round table for eight where her companions were two couples whom she at once labelled as stuffed shirts, one pair from Ealing and the other from Tunbridge Wells; a lone man with a hearing aid; and two elderly widows who were sisters and lived in Bath. They all hid their faces behind the long menus handed to them by a waiter and Carmen, studying her copy, was at a loss. How could you choose? It was all written in French. However, it seemed to be for information only, for without consulting anyone, the meal was served. When a plate of soup was placed before her, Carmen began to behave as she always did when insecure, by complaining that it was too cold. She found the pasta which followed it too sticky, and the beef too rare. Used to small, snacky meals, she soon felt full and messed her plate about, pushing the vegetables around with her knife and fork and grumbling. One of the widows raised a pained brow during these displays and exchanged a sad glance with her sister. You found all sorts on cruises: they knew that, having travelled in other ships before this one. The deaf man bought two bottles of claret for the table, and one of the other men, thanking him, declared that it would be his turn tomorrow. Carmen accepted her share; no one would expect her, a widow, to stand treat.

Their table waiter, a Greek, who wore his name, Giorgio, on a badge pinned to the lapel of his green monkey jacket, bore no resemblance to Stavros but Carmen had remembered a little of the language and the pale, thickset, tired man, who had finished clearing ship of the last lot of passengers only hours before the embarkation of the present company, was moved. He forgave her crude complaints and wished her *Kalynikta* when everyone left the restaurant.

Carmen laid a hand on his arm and, as one of the sisters later commented, positively leered at him.

'*Agapo*,' she stated. '*Agapo* all Greeks.'

Giorgio patted her hand.

'*Oraia*,' he replied, and she took it to mean that he thought she was beautiful for that was what Stavros had told her many years ago.

Some of the passengers went on deck to watch the lights of shore fade away as the SS *Aphrodite* put to sea but Carmen went to the lounge where bingo was on the programme.

She enjoyed herself, though she won nothing. A friendly couple at her table bought her a drink. She had dipped heavily into her savings for the trip, buying not only the suitcase but a purple kaftan on which she'd stitched several packets of sequins, her lamé blouse and satin pants, a purple taffeta skirt and a low-necked velvet top, and she had very little spare cash. Moving about, attaching herself to different people, should make it possible for her to accept drinks from others most nights, she decided. The second couple at her table bought another round before the cabaret and Carmen made sure that hers was a double. People were generous, she'd always found, if you were lively company and hadn't let yourself go to pieces.

The lounge filled up when the second sitting of diners arrived in time for the show. Carmen, in a good seat, enjoyed it all, especially the comics, and stayed on to watch the dancing. Maybe someone would ask her to dance.

But nobody did.

Afterwards there was supper in an upper lounge. Carmen felt quite hungry by this time and was able to put away a hearty snack. When she teetered on her high heels back to the cabin, Frances was asleep, neat under the duvet, her face to the wall.

She woke up as Carmen clattered round, bumping into the furniture, tittering drunkenly, making noises in the tiny bathroom, and sighed, drawing the covers tight round her ears. Quiet came at last, broken only by Carmen's light snores. Frances inserted earplugs; she never travelled without them.

In the morning she had gone to breakfast by the time Carmen woke up, and that was the pattern of the days that followed. Breakfast was a serve-yourself affair and quite a scramble, with a splendid buffet laid out to tempt the greedy. After that, it was up on deck and into a deck-chair to pass the morning until coffee and biscuits were served.

Carmen took her crochet with her to a chair on the main deck. She crocheted beautifully and was making a shawl which later she would sell. It was a skill she had learned in hospital after Billy was born; a girl in the next bed had taught her. There was a boutique owner who would buy anything she made and it was something to do in winter, watching television.

People kept themselves to themselves, Carmen found. No one seemed to want to talk. Passengers were reading or sleeping. A brisk man in a pork pie hat walked round the deck. Ping-pong was played by some energetic younger people and deck-quoits was available, as she learned when she tried to start a conversation with a woman sitting next to her.

Her neighbour had an appointment to play on an upper deck and left after a minimal exchange.

Luncheon could be taken either in the restaurant or from a buffet on deck. Carmen decided not to face the prim people from her table again until she must, at dinner, and went to the buffet where she loaded two plates with every morsel that took her fancy. After that, she went below for a nap.

Frances, immersed in the latest Catherine Cookson, saw her go and resigned herself to snoozing on deck, well tucked up in the blanket she had had the foresight to bring from the cabin. It was cold in the fresh westerly wind but soon it should get warmer as they proceeded southwards.

That night the Captain's welcome aboard party was held and Carmen, in her purple skirt and low top, was photographed shaking the hand of the handsome dark-haired man with the neat beard. She'd have to buy a print of that as a souvenir.

She managed to lower quite a few free drinks during the party.

At dinner, she and Giorgio exchanged witticisms in Greek. Giorgio assumed she knew more of the language than was the case, and he wanted to please her. Many women passengers required all sorts of services from the stewards or crew, and, used to reading signals that were seldom subtle, Giorgio took to resting his hand heavily on Carmen's shoulder as he took away her plate, hiding his weary revulsion at the messed-up food she always left. She flirted with him, archly, in the manner that had been effective when she was young but now disgusted her table companions.

The two sisters asked to be moved to another table but were told it was not possible. The deaf man, one of nature's victims, found himself sitting next to Carmen every night, but the place on her other side always remained vacant for the last comer. Sometimes one of the sisters was her neighbour, and whoever drew her made no effort so that she sat in an island of neglect as they spoke across her.

People soon discovered that Frances was Carmen's cabin-mate, and her restrained accounts of washing hung from every corner of the cabin, half-eaten oranges left

about, steamy use of the shower, snoring and other anti-
social practices earned her sympathy from her own table
companions and anyone else who heard her soft comments,
which were never forceful enough to be complaints.

'You run risks, sharing with someone you don't know,'
was the general opinion, and those other passengers who
had chanced the same thing counted their blessings if they
had been luckier.

Carmen came to bed later and later – or rather, earlier
and earlier in the small hours.

Frances mentioned this, ashore in Lisbon, to the Major
and his wife from Surrey at whose table she sat.

'I wonder where she goes?' she said. 'Is the bar open
all night?'

'Hardly,' opined the Major's wife.

'She's got very little money,' Frances said. 'She won
the cruise in a raffle.'

'Bully for her,' said the Major, the man who, in his pork
pie hat, walked a mile on deck every day. 'Probably running
a line on the side,' he added, and earned a reproving frown
from his wife.

'What, at her age?' Frances was shocked. 'She must
be nearly seventy.'

'It's never too late for some,' was the Major's sage reply.

Carmen went on none of the organised shore excursions.
She had been sent vouchers for several with her ticket, but
she had discovered that she could surrender them and
receive a refund. This helped finance her gambling in the
casino where once or twice she won small sums, and her
bingo, and the drinks she was forced to buy for herself.

At Agadir she walked round the town until her arthritic
joints ached. Recognising some people from the ship,
including the Major and his wife, she followed behind
them and entered a carpet factory where they all sat on
rolled-up rugs and were given mint tea while a handsome
young man in robes and a fez described how the carpets
were made. Afterwards, they were encouraged to buy not

only rugs but handbags and leather coats. Carmen tried on several jackets, causing a good deal of commotion while she searched for her size and demanded different colours, but as she could not afford to buy anything, she left empty-handed. The Major and his wife took a taxi back to the ship, leaving her standing on the pavement.

It was the deaf man from her table who took pity on Carmen. He was escorting the widowed sisters, and they saw her limping along towards the harbour.

'She'll never make it,' he murmured. 'We must stop for her.'

'You're a nice man,' said the elder sister, truthfully, but he did not hear her as he alighted from the cab to rescue Carmen. He put her in the front seat beside the driver and she was noisily grateful.

On her wrist she wore a gold bracelet which the sisters had not noticed before. Had she bought it, or had she managed to steal it when no one was looking? They could believe anything of Carmen.

Approaching Gibraltar, the cruise two-thirds over and the voyage homewards about to begin, Carmen stared at the steep grey rock and thought how forbidding it looked. Tom had been there during the war, and so a tear came to her eye as the ship berthed.

She'd mentioned him to no one. No one had wanted to know her history, though she'd told plenty of people whom she found herself sitting next to on deck while she crocheted about her diplomat father and her sons in important overseas posts. It was strange how restless people were: no one stayed sitting next to her long, moving off on some mission without a word of apology.

She saw the deaf man and the sisters going down the gangway and went ashore after them, tagging along, aiming to scrounge a lift into town in their taxi. They were doing a tour of the island which did not interest her. Who wanted to gaze at Barbary apes? The passengers themselves were apes enough.

She knew there were pubs in the town and she wanted to visit one, for she was homesick for what was familiar.

'Drop me off in the main street,' she instructed, and was soon pushing her way along the crowded pavement.

Inside a pub, which could have been one in any town in England, she had several gins and began to feel better, though she couldn't get the thought of Tom quite out of her mind, which was silly. He'd been dead more than forty-five years, after all. Maybe food was what she needed. If she returned to the ship there would be lunch provided; ashore, she would have to pay.

She began the trudge back to the harbour and met Frances coming out of Marks and Spencer's, carrying one of their green bags.

'You can go to Marks at home,' she remarked. 'Why bother here?'

'I needed a nightie and a few other things,' said Frances. 'There's so little space in the cabin, I can't get my washing dry.'

'Shall we share a cab back to the ship?' Carmen suggested airily, not rising to this taunt. She'd been lucky to run into someone she knew; it was a fair walk back to the quayside.

Frances accepted the inevitable, and was not surprised when Carmen sprang out of the cab with remarkable speed, leaving her to pay the driver.

'Ta,' Carmen said, heading up the gangplank. 'That was ever so kind.' A nice thank-you went a long way in life.

Africa lay to the south as they sailed through the Straits of Gibraltar, land visible only a few miles distant on either side. The Germans had strung nets under the water across this narrow space to trap submarines during the war, the Major told his table companions, and Frances listened as he went on to talk about his days as a Desert Rat. Earlier at her table, Carmen had staged diversions while the others discussed their day ashore. She dropped a roll on the floor, asked for more butter, put the skeleton of her trout on the side plate of her neighbour, the deaf man. In only a few days now they would be steaming up the Channel, bidding one another farewell, exchanging addresses and promises to keep in touch that would remain unfulfilled. Carmen dreaded her return to solitude.

The weather grew colder every day. Thick jerseys and trousers replaced sundresses and shorts, and red sunburned skin was shrouded. Passengers with peeling faces paced the deck while oily fumes from the funnel streamed out like a pennant behind the ship as she sailed northwards with no land in sight. Funny how you missed it after a day or so, thought Carmen. Once they saw whales, spouting; another time, a school of porpoises followed the ship. An occasional cargo vessel would be left astern as the captain hurried on, anxious to beat bad weather heading in from the west before he made landfall and held his farewell parties.

Carmen knew the drill now. You could go to both and have two lots of free drinks, slipping into the lounge by a side door to dodge the reception line the second time.

On the last evening, the deaf man bought three bottles of wine to celebrate the end of the cruise and Carmen remarked that he'd been too quick for her when it should have been her treat.

'You can say that again,' said the elder widow, and her sister nodded in agreement. They'd insisted on standing their turns.

The lights dimmed and the waiters bore in trays of flaming Baked Alaska. Carmen received a generous helping from Giorgio, whose manner towards her had become aloof and correct since the deaf man, not expecting much response from her, had begun talking to her at dinner. When she spoke, he had difficulty in hearing what she said, so he adopted the tactic which he found worked well in any social circumstance: he did the talking. He spoke to her of his golf club and his grandchildren, his garden and his Vauxhall car, of his past career as a tax inspector and of the china he mended as a hobby. Carmen let his words wash over her as she tried to picture him before age and deafness took their toll. Maybe she'd have fancied him then, but now his neck was wrinkled and his cheeks were gaunt. His thin old hands had brown spots on their backs but were steady as he poured the wine.

He bade her good night very formally after the final cabaret, to which he escorted her, not wanting her to sit alone on the last night. He felt pity for her, out of her depth in every way as she was and, like a child, craving attention. He had seen her smile and had realised that she had once been a very pretty girl. Together, now, they watched the lively young dancers who by day ran the library and the bingo, and the comedian who supervised trap shooting on deck.

'It's been lovely,' Carmen said. 'A real treat to remember in the winter.'

'Yes,' said the deaf man, who was returning to his lonely retirement bungalow in Essex.

Overnight, the ship berthed, and in the morning the crew dashed ashore as soon as the baggage had been unloaded. In groups, the passengers disembarked to claim their luggage.

Carmen had bought only her duty-free allowance of spirits and cigarettes – she didn't smoke but she could sell those at a profit – and the gold bracelet, her one souvenir. She went through the green channel and was asked to stop.

The Major and his wife, passing blamelessly by, saw Carmen's possessions disposed about the table, her shabby underwear displayed, her lamé blouse and her shiny kaftan, and, among them, little mounds of the sealed butter and jam cartons put out for breakfast. She had secreted dozens of them, and packs of cracker biscuits, too, even cheese, anything that could be hoarded for the weeks ahead.

There was another packet: a small one wrapped in brown paper which, undone, proved to contain a thick plastic bag filled with white powder. Carmen stared at it. Where had that come from? It looked like sugar.

Protesting loudly, not understanding, she was led away by two customs officers.

Frances went through the red channel and declared her purchase of a small oriental carpet. No one looked inside her jacket, where some much bigger packs of cocaine were stitched into the lining. It had been simple to plant the decoy in Carmen's suitcase, where, in the baggage hall, a trained dog had sniffed it out, just as she had planned when Micky, whom she'd got to know when he began handling stolen cars for her brother, had mentioned his aunt. It had been easy to set the old woman up, go to his place when he was at work and sell Carmen the raffle tickets. She'd worn a wig and tinted glasses, and a wool cap pulled low over her forehead, an adequate disguise.

She'd collected the stuff from her contact in Gib, exchanging carrier bags in Marks and Spencer's without a word passing between them. The cost of Carmen's cruise ticket scarcely dented the huge profit she would make when she passed it on, and after all, what was a year or two in gaol to Carmen? She'd have her travels to remember.

And it might have been missed altogether: it was just the luck of the draw.

Biographical Notes on the Contributors

Robert Barnard has spent most of his adulthood behind a desk, either marking student essays or writing detective novels, but since he has mostly done this abroad (first in Australia, then in Norway) people often comment on his adventurous life. He has now moved back to the United Kingdom, lives in Leeds, and still spends much of his life behind a desk.

Simon Brett has written thirteen novels featuring the actor detective Charles Paris, two featuring the elderly widow sleuth Mrs Pargeter, and two non-series crime novels. He is also responsible for the radio and television series *After Henry*, as well as various humorous books and anthologies. He was Chairman of the Crime Writers' Association in 1986–87.

Colin Dexter graduated from Cambridge in 1953, and spent his years wholly in education until his retirement in 1988: first in teaching Greek and Latin; then moving to Oxford in 1966 to work for the University Examination Board, where he fought in vain against the cradle-to-coffin philosophy of the GCSE. Opening the batting for England, and crossing swords with Mrs T. in parliamentary debate, remain unfulfilled ambitions (two more lost causes for Oxford). He began writing detective fiction comparatively late in life, the first Inspector Morse book appearing in 1975.

David Fletcher was the pseudonym of Dulan Barber (1940–88) who wrote and edited over thirty books. A full-time writer with an extensive range, he avoided literary shenanigans and drew nourishment from his record collection, his garden, and a nightly reading of back numbers of *Opera* magazine. He was probably Maria Callas's truest fan.

Antonia Fraser has read crime novels avidly since youth, and in 1977 wrote the first one of her own, *Quiet as a Nun*. Five more full-length mysteries featuring Jemima Shore, Investigator, have followed, the latest being *Your Royal Hostage* (1987). The first crime short story she attempted (*Death of an Old Dog*) was directly inspired by an invitation to appear in *Winter's Crimes 10*; she had a volume of short stories, *Jemima Shore's First Case*, published in 1986.

Jonathan Gash is a doctor (medicine, not science) who has worked in Germany, Hong Kong and the Middle East, but is now going straight, as it were, in the Faculty of Medicine, University of London. Loves all evidence of fraud, as proving the existence of normality and order in most walks of life, and with the assistance of many helpers has made a lifelong study of the subject. Subjects: forensic pathology and infectious diseases in 'real life'; antiques, greed and deceit in the 'unreal'. He is still unsure which is which.

Paula Gosling was born in America, but has lived in England since 1964. She is the author of eight crime novels, and past Chairman of the Crime Writers' Association. She says: 'I started my career in fiction by writing advertising copy, and then turned to crime. The urge to get people into trouble on the page is a puzzling addiction, but as it is the *only* thing in my life that isn't fattening, I intend to carry on. No matter what anyone says.'

Nigel Gray was born in Ireland, but spent most of his life in England – a country in which he never felt at home. He has recently deserted the sinking ship and become an Australian. In 1988 he was awarded an MA in Creative Writing by the University of East Anglia – which proved to be of no use whatsoever. He continues to create remarkable fictions for adults and children for little reward.

James Hamilton-Paterson prefers to remain incognito.

Tim Heald does occasionally write obituaries in real life for a national newspaper, and has indeed tempted fate by writing his own, for which he has successfully insisted on being paid on delivery rather than publication. He has also written a series of crime novels featuring a Board of Trade investigator called Simon Bognor and his more impressive wife Monica. He thinks his books are pretty funny and is easily upset when critics don't see the jokes.

Timothy Holme was born in 1928 and began his working life in the theatre. After seven years of acting he switched to journalism and during this time he spent a holiday in Italy where he met and married his Italian teacher, Bianca. After publishing several biographies he turned to crime writing and created the popular Inspector Peroni who made his début in *The Neapolitan Streak*. He died in 1987.

H. R. F. Keating has been writing novels and short stories about Inspector Ghote since *The Perfect Murder* won the Gold Dagger of the Crime Writers' Association in 1964, a feat repeated in 1980 with *The Murder of the Maharajah*. He is now president of the Detection Club, following in the steps of G. K. Chesterton, Dorothy L. Sayers, Agatha Christie and Julian Symons. Somewhat fixated on fingerprints, he is contemplating some stories about fairly unlikely crimes committed in the village of Princefinger.

Alanna Knight Celtic storyteller of Scots-Irish parentage. Writing career began in 1969 as young mum with two small sons and scientist husband. Historical novelist, biographer, radio writer, lecturer in creative writing and authority on R. L. Stevenson. In 1988 turned to a literary life of crime with Inspector Faro series *Enter Second Murderer* and *Blood Line*, set in Victorian Edinburgh and published by Macmillan.

Peter Lovesey writes: 'I was handed a cheque for £1,000 at the party to celebrate the first *Winter's Crimes* in 1969; not, I'd better make clear, for a short story, but for my first novel, *Wobble to Death*, the winner of a Macmillan competition to find a new crime novelist. George Hardinge, the founder of *Winter's Crimes*, also found me. Twenty books on I'm still riding my luck, profoundly grateful for that flying start and George's far-sighted advice and encouragement.'

Haydn Middleton has written two novels, *The People in the Picture* (Black Swan) and *The Lie of the Land* (Macmillan). His story in this volume is part of a projected collection entitled *The Phoenix Farm*. He is thirty-four years old, and lives in Oxford with his wife and two children.

Ellis Peters writes: 'My ambitions while at school were: to write, to act, to sing, to dance and to paint, not necessarily in that order, though writing always came first. By the time I left school only writing was left, and I was already at it, and have been ever since. Naturally I had to begin by doing a few other curious things, like temporary duty in a Women's Labour Exchange in the Potteries over a Christmas when most of the employees were laid off for the holiday, mixing medicines in a chemist's dispensary, and teleprinting naval signals in the HQ of Western Approaches Command throughout the war. But the writing never stopped, and after the war became a full-time job. I've been doing it now for fifty-three years, and I'm not bored with it yet. As long as the readers aren't bored, either, I intend to continue.'

Julian Symons Born 1912. Waits for the sound of the dreaded word *doyen* when introduced at dinners or at parties.

Michael Underwood (a pseudonym) was called to the Bar in 1939 and, after seven years of army service, joined the Director of Public Prosecutions Department in 1946 where he remained until retirement in 1976. His first crime novel was published in 1954, since when he has written over forty, plus a number of short stories for *Winter's Crimes* volumes and other anthologies. He lives on the Sussex coast and regards writing as an essential weapon in the battle against increasing sloth and incipient senility.

John Wainwright Born 1921 at Leeds. Came to authorship late in life and, after twenty-five years, is now one of the ancient monuments of the crime-writing world. Despite seventy-two operations over Germany in the rumble seat of a Lancaster bomber, twenty years on the streets as a working copper and eighty books in which murder and mayhem are committed, he remains a mild, gentle, long-suffering Yorkshireman – at least that's his story.

David Williams Born in Wales 1926; educated Hereford Cathedral School and St John's College, Oxford, with three years in between as an RNVR officer. A successful career in advertising enabled him to switch to full-time writing in 1977. His thirteenth whodunnit, *Holy Treasure!*, appeared in 1989. Married with two children, he lives at Wentworth in Surrey. *Freeze Everybody* is his ninth published short story: the idea came during an expensive funeral.

Margaret Yorke was born in Surrey but spent her childhood in Dublin, later moving to Hampshire. She was the first woman ever to work in Christ Church Library, Oxford, where she made a catalogue of the working books. She has also worked as a bookseller. She has lived in Buckinghamshire for more than thirty years and enjoys reading, the theatre and travel.